Praise

Greenlight

'A hugely original premise and a plot that won't lie down. A great debut.'   CHRIS HAMMER

'Thought-provoking and densely plotted, *Greenlight* is compelling and timely.'   SYDNEY MORNING HERALD

'An outstanding debut – confident, compelling, with a surprise around every corner. I loved it.'   JANE HARPER

'A clever, heart-racing read.'   COURIER MAIL

'A truly magnificent story on so many different levels, [*Greenlight*] should be at the top of everyone's must-read list.'   NEW YORK JOURNAL OF BOOKS

'Such an assured, intricately plotted novel full of mind-bending twists and turns.'   CANDICE FOX

'An absolute knockout . . . you will not be sleeping until you know how this one ends – trust us.'   BETTER READING

'A gripping, densely plotted debut . . . kept me guessing until the very last page.'   MARK BRANDI

'Filled from the opening prologue with devilish twists and turns.'   ADELAIDE ADVERTISER

Either Side of Midnight

'A gripping, gritty thriller with an ingeniously shocking premise and twists and turns you'll never see coming!' LIANE MORIARTY

'A complex and hugely original page-turner. Stevenson has officially made my auto-buy-author list.' CHRISTIAN WHITE

'Stevenson writes solid Australian crime thrillers with a command of psychology and suspense and a dark comic edge. That the series extends its tendrils into satire – it neatly skewers the culture of our television industry – only adds to its appeal.' THE AGE

'The male relationships in *Either Side of Midnight* are layered in a way that transcends the crime genre. Funny, disturbing and unpredictable.' JACK HEATH

'*Either Side of Midnight*, which trips between light and dark, city and country, and twists the reader into knots, is for fans of solid Australian crime authors like Chris Hammer, Christian White and Candice Fox.' BOOKS AND PUBLISHING

'A gripping thriller.' WHO WEEKLY

Everyone In My Family Has Killed Someone

'Readers won't want to put his story down . . . This is undoubtedly a future classic.'   BIG ISSUE

'What an exceptionally fresh, smart, funny book – I've never read anything like this before.'   JANE HARPER

'Clever, unexpected, and not to be missed.'   KARIN SLAUGHTER

'Elegantly sinuous, superbly plotted, and surprise-packed . . . One of the best damn things I've read this year.'   WRITTENBYSIME

'The most original novel you will read this year . . . a funny and clever novel that pays homage to the classic British murder mystery.'
                                                        CANBERRA WEEKLY

'For something different, look no further than the very clever and entirely experimental *Everyone In My Family Has Killed Someone* . . . One of the most anticipated books of the year.'
                                                        WEEKEND AUSTRALIAN

'With a set of finely crafted characters, and a plot that is equal parts guile, humour, and ingenuity, this is a book that promises to satisfy readers from all points on the mystery writing compass.' ARTS HUB

'If you're a classic murder mystery fan looking for something fresh and original, you will absolutely love this. I did.' ANNA DOWNES

'Terrific fun.'   AUSTRALIAN BOOK REVIEW

© Monica Pronk

Benjamin Stevenson is an award-winning stand-up comedian and author. His first novel, *Greenlight*, was shortlisted for the Ned Kelly Award for Best Debut Crime Fiction, and his second novel, *Either Side of Midnight*, was shortlisted for the International Thriller Writers Award for Best Original Paperback.

Everyone In My Family Has Killed Someone, his third novel, was a huge bestseller and has been sold to over twenty territories around the world. It will soon be adapted into a major HBO TV series.

Benjamin has sold out live shows from the Melbourne International Comedy Festival all the way to the Edinburgh Festival Fringe and has appeared on ABC TV, Channel 10 and The Comedy Channel.

@stevensonexperience
The Stevenson Experience

EITHER SIDE OF MIDNIGHT

BENJAMIN STEVENSON

PENGUIN BOOKS

For James and Emily

PENGUIN BOOKS

UK | USA | Canada | Ireland | Australia
India | New Zealand | South Africa | China

Penguin Books is part of the Penguin Random House group of companies
whose addresses can be found at global.penguinrandomhouse.com

Penguin
Random House
Australia

First published by Michael Joseph in 2020
This edition published by Penguin Books in 2022

Copyright © Benjamin Stevenson 2020

The moral right of the author has been asserted.

Cover photography by photopsist/Shutterstock (broken glass)
and Boris Schmalenberger/plainpicture (Ferris wheel)
Cover design by Adam Laszczuk © Penguin Random House Australia Pty Ltd
Typeset in Sabon by Midland Typesetters, Australia

Printed and bound in Australia by Griffin Press, part of Ovato, an accredited
ISO AS/NZS 14001 Environmental Management Systems printer

A catalogue record for this
book is available from the
National Library of Australia

ISBN 978 1 76104 883 8

penguin.com.au

MIX
Paper | Supporting
responsible forestry
FSC® C018684

We at Penguin Random House Australia acknowledge that Aboriginal and Torres Strait
Islander peoples are the Traditional Custodians and the first storytellers of the lands
on which we live and work. We honour Aboriginal and Torres Strait Islander peoples'
continuous connection to Country, waters, skies and communities. We celebrate
Aboriginal and Torres Strait Islander stories, traditions and living cultures;
and we pay our respects to Elders past and present.

PART 1

WE INTERRUPT THIS BROADCAST

This stage is holy, and this is how we pray
Anonymous scrawl, backstage wall, Athenaeum Theatre, Melbourne

You are going to die in the arse
Anonymous scrawl, toilet door, The Comedy Store, Sydney

PROLOGUE

If you're going to do it, do it somewhere quiet, thought Beth Walters, watching her boss straighten his tie. I wouldn't even chance it in a restaurant. I wouldn't be able to do it in front of people. I'd do it in the parking lot.

'Do you think he'll do it? Or chicken out again?' asked a cameraman, turning away from the lens. His fingers twiddled a gadget without looking. Muscle memory. 'How tight in do you want to be?'

'Tight enough to see the blood drain from his face,' called an associate producer. 'Fifty bucks says he pikes it.'

'Keep your voice down,' snapped Beth. Mr Midnight was absorbed at his desk, but if he heard them . . .

The cameraman, Geoff, now tuned back into his view-piece, ignored her. 'I'll take you for a hundred. If he's going to ruin his life on national television, we may as well profit.'

'Ruin his life?' said the producer. 'More like end it.'

'Great modern attitude to marriage there, guys.'

'Well, ain't that something.' Geoff leaned back. His chair was mounted to the same rig as the camera so he could swivel with it, like a machine gun turret. 'You didn't strike me as the type.'

'Every girl likes a bit of romance,' Beth fired back. 'That said, a girl likes a free lunch even more. Hey Andy' – the associate producer looked up from his iPad – 'I'll take your odds. Camera Two, can we zoom out a bit? If we're framed like that in the monologue, we'll lose the top of his head.' Back to business. 'We ready on the cue?'

The autocue operator was dressed in the classic stagehand uniform – all black, cap indoors, utility belt that put Batman to shame – and didn't bother to look up from his screen. He flicked her a backhanded wave: *Shoo, I've got this.* Most people don't have the confidence to swat their boss away like an insect, but stagehands aren't most people. Beth could see from the reflection that the white text on a black background had flickered up on the screen. Good enough.

'Hey, Midnight,' she called. The host looked up at her from his notes. He insisted on having them, even though everything he said was rehearsed and cued up. He wanted to be taken seriously, he'd told her once, and shuffling papers meant the audience thought you were intelligent. Recently she'd taken to drawing a big dick and balls across them before she put them on his desk. The first time she'd almost got him, a wry smile leaking out mid-interview with a politician. Live television meant no second takes, and she was determined to crack him one day. Today, just because she was expecting him to be especially nervous, she'd added some extra spurts. She'd also written, amid the splatter: *You are going to die in the arse.* Sure, they were entertaining people at home, but she had to keep herself entertained too. She continued. 'You good?'

He shot her a smile and a nod.

He'd wuss out, all right.

'It's going to be a big show tonight, guys,' Sam 'Midnight' Midford called to the room. The last of the assistants scurried off the set. Sam straightened his back at his desk. The director cued the intro music, called for quiet on set, and handed the floor back to Sam, who rallied the troops a final time. 'Let's give it our all!'

The intro music swelled and Sam started talking. Despite a career in television, Beth was still struck by the dazzle of it. Sam Midford seemed to switch to Mr Midnight in a breath. Calm blue eyes locked forward on Camera One. Anyone would guess he had to be a bit of a wunderkind to host his own nightly television show at twenty-nine, and he delivered on that expectation. Warm. Charming. Everything about him polished and image conscious. He flashed a giant smile. His teeth were like American Republican voters: white and straight.

'Hello, and welcome to *Midnight Tonight*! I'm your host, Sam Midford – you can call me Mr Midnight – and it is a pleasure, as always, to join you in your homes. Hello . . .'

At this, Sam paused and squinted. Andy raised an eyebrow. *He's nervous*. Beth patted the air with her hand. *Settle down, no big deal*. Though she did think it was rare for Sam. It wasn't a problem yet.

Sam straightened his tie and cleared his throat. 'Hello, and welcome. I may have already said that. Just a small technical error there. But I guess I'm just so excited for tonight's show I wanted to do it twice!'

The smoothness of a veteran, the only remnant of his nerves an agitated drumming of his fingertips. Every broadcaster has a tic: clicking pens, shuffling notes. Sam just had a nervy left hand. His little finger was shorter than the others; he'd lost the top of it as a child. But this tic wouldn't cost her the bet. He fidgeted every episode. They'd had a production meeting to discuss reframing the shot, but Sam had insisted the audience see the top of the desk so they knew he had research notes. The director told Sam his fidgeting made him look like a drug addict. Sam told the director his face made him look like a fuckhead. That meeting was four hours

Beth would never get back, and the shot remained unchanged. So the finger-drumming was par for the course.

Beth raised her hand at Andy and rubbed her fingers against her thumb. *Get ready to pay up.*

'Let's look back at the week that was.' Sam spun into a quick recap of each of the week's headline stories, followed by a one-liner. This was classic television monologuing. Politicians kicked off the roasting tonight, as they could always be relied upon to take a gormless photo in a public place. These gaffes were displayed in triplicate on the plasma screens behind Sam. Canned laughter followed each zinger on the broadcast, just in case the warm-up guy, by now jumping around and flapping his arms like a bird, wasn't drawing enough from the crowd.

After the pollies came the celebrities, equally reliable for their divorce rates and loose social-media fingers. They were easy targets but more photogenic than the pollies. It also helped to have beautiful people on screen, because people channel-surfing often mistake attractiveness for interesting and dawdle on the channel change. If talking about a divorce, they always used the photo of the wife, for example. Bikinis helped. Sure, Beth was a feminist, but she knew what got ratings. The more beautiful or wealthy people they showed, the less it felt like punching down.

Speaking of, the next section was sports scandals, which Sam jovially introduced with, 'Right, let's check in with who's been drinking their own piss this week.' Behind him, a tacky 3D title – *Who's been drinking their own piss?* – whirled onto the plasmas, landing with a shake and a rockslide of cartoon debris. In this segment, Sam would run through the headlines and decide whether a sportsperson's revelry was better or worse than the guy who had been caught urinating in his own mouth. If it was decidedly worse, and Sam deemed it a 'pisser', he presented them an honorary golden trophy that had a little fountain on it. Beth had the pleasure of explaining to any international guests that, yes, the piss-drinking had actually happened, and, no, it wasn't a typical Australian pastime.

Sam was halfway through the pissers when he faltered again. This time he reached under the desk with his right hand, fidgeted for a second. Then, barely noticeable on the screen and under his foundation, Beth saw the pall on his cheeks. He was fiddling with the ring in his pocket, she realised. And he wasn't going to do it. Coward. Andy mouthed at her from across the studio, two syllables. Pursed lips, pulling back against teeth. Unmistakeable: 'Pussy'.

'Right.' Sam was talking again, but the recovery was not as smooth this time. He looked down at his script, as if it might give him the support he wasn't getting from the prompt. Beth felt a pang of guilt; he would have looked down to see her message: *You are going to die in the arse*. Just when Beth thought he was about to panic, he talked his way back into it. Only a millisecond of dead air, but in-studio it felt like a lifetime. There was a collective exhale. 'Russia. Okay. Tonight we're also going to send our special correspondent over to parliament house to find any secret Russian spies. And later in the program, I'll be having . . .'

He was cut off by a scream, someone grappling with a security guard onstage.

'I swear! I'm not Russian. I'm a New Zealander! Listen . . . Fish and chips. Sixty-six! Fish and chips!'

The actor was dragged off the stage. Once off camera he straightened up, patted the security guard on the back, and rushed off to get changed. The actor playing the security guard stayed in costume; he had another part to play later on. As simple as that, and they'd set up the running joke for the episode.

Sam had fought to increase their political content in recent months. Whenever Beth had reviewed a script with him and suggested that perhaps it would skew the demographics, alienate the younger viewers, Sam would raise his eyebrows at her. *Screw the demos.*

And so political material stayed in. Tom Dwyer at Channel 12, Sam's main competitor in the timeslot, would have baulked at paying two actors for a throwaway gag, but Sam always pushed for risk taking, and he had a penchant for theatrics.

No wonder he was going to propose to Celia on live TV.

If he proposed at all, Beth thought. An intern had started the whispers that they'd seen a ring in his dressing room, and that got them all buzzing. Beth had been sure it would be tonight. But Sam still looked pasty white. *Man up, Sam*, she willed him. *Stop fidgeting with the ring under the table and just do it already.*

He was nearing the end of his monologue now. Beth heard him crack a line about the newest *Star Wars* film and knew he was about to cut to ads and then they'd be moving to reset the stage. Rotate Sam's seat to the left, bring in a guest seat on the right. She should go to the green room and check on the next guest. Some popstar, here to plug a reality singing competition. Screw the demos, huh? Even Sam couldn't argue with the network on cross-promotion. She'd do it in the break. She wanted to see if Sam would deliver.

'Well, before I throw to a break here, I just wanted to say something.'

Beth inwardly fist pumped. Mouthed a silent 'fuck you' over to Andy. He gave her the finger. Of course Sam delivered. Those goddamn theatrics.

'Whatever he does, Geoff, keep rolling,' she said, patting the cameraman on the back. Geoff nodded. Andy's shoulders slumped with defeat. The autocue operator calmly scrolled the text along the teleprompter. The assistants knew something was up; they'd all lowered their clipboards and turned to the stage.

'Celia,' Sam said. His left hand was calm and flat on the desk now, his right lingering underneath.

Here we go, Beth thought. Her nails pressed moons in her palm. Hope it's a nice ring.

'Celia,' Sam repeated. And then his right hand came out from under the desk.

He wasn't holding a ring.

Something bigger.

Beth's brain was playing catch up. Only time for half a thought: *Is that a . . . ?*

'I love you. Forgive me. Change the channel.'

He sat stock still for five seconds, as if counting it out.

Then the host of *Midnight Tonight* put a gun in his mouth.

And pulled the trigger.

PART 2

REBOOT

'In keeping with Channel 40's policy of bringing you the latest in blood and guts and in living colour, you are going to see another first: an attempted suicide.'
Christine Chubbuck, live on air, July 14, 1974

'Get off it! Get off it! Get off it!'
Reporter Shepard Smith demanding the live footage is cut after a suspect in a police pursuit commits suicide, September 28, 2012

CHAPTER 1

When Jack Quick was told he had a visitor, he certainly didn't think it would be Sam Midford.

His surprise was partly because they barely knew each other, except for a rare brushed shoulder when Jack had worked at the same television network. But mostly because Jack had watched Sam Midford die three days ago. Everybody had.

Jack had been lying on his back on the top bunk, notepad in hand, arm outstretched to catch the sunlight from his only window, a chewed pencil running a victory lap around his teeth. The notepad was covered in numbers: added up, divided and crossed out. He'd started hunched over his desk but couldn't get the answer he wanted and decided his maths might be more productive upside-down. But mathematics is not easily coerced by will. The result was the same as when he'd calculated it that morning. Forty-eight.

His cell at Long Bay Correctional Facility wasn't exactly comfortable, but neither was it strictly spartan. He'd visited before he'd been arrested, to bribe guards and arrange phone calls with a convicted killer, so he'd half-known what was coming, but he hadn't been allowed in the cells. Now it was home.

There was a bunk bed kidnapped from a school camp, with a thin aluminium frame that creaked at the joints and threatened to fold flat every time Jack climbed the ladder. The top bunk was the only way to get natural light from the solitary window, so he climbed it anyway. The floor was concrete but large enough for pacing between the bunk and a set of cubic shelves on the opposite wall. Closest to the door was a desk, a white stool, and above that, bolted in the corner, a small television. Jack rarely watched it. Sometimes the news. Definitely not documentaries.

In the far corner there was a lidless toilet and a stainless-steel basin. Jack kept that area the cleanest. That was no surprise. If he broke, he had to vomit in calm silence. Leave no trace.

To distract himself from the numbers, Jack had been thinking about who he'd give his dinner to. He was eating fine these days – or fine enough, at least, because his illness was always knocking somewhere, in his head or his gut – but he still swapped his dinners with other inmates. The prison physician, Dr Kensington, who used the term *bulimia* and Jack was certain had never treated an eating disorder before, demanded that he get high-calorie meals, custom-made. Nothing isolates an inmate more than tucking into a burger and chips when everyone else is eating macaroni and cheese.

Jack had, for personal safety, quickly adopted a bartering system. He didn't need friends, but the deep-fryer was hot enough to forge a few alliances. He wasn't doing it to get rid of the food, he told himself as he over-chewed whatever he'd traded for, it was a social necessity. Still, whenever Kensington caught on, which he did every couple of weeks, Jack would have to eat alone in his cell. 'Some punishment,' other inmates moaned, 'tucked away eating ice cream.' Jack agreed. Stocked up on chocolate bars and cans of Coke. Such strange torture. If you want to be well fed in prison, try having an eating disorder.

Jack's thoughts were interrupted when someone knocked twice

and paused. Jack knew the beat was procedure, so inmates could move back from the door. Based on Jack's spindly physique and general threat level, he could only assume the policy was arbitrary.

The guard who entered was young, strawberry blond and wearing a uniform several sizes too big. Even if Jack hadn't known Lee McCormack, the uniform alone would peg him as a new recruit, recycled from one of the more hirsute seniors.

'Looks good on you,' said Jack, sitting up.

'Man, I wish they'd deliver mine already. I feel like a medium chips in a large pack.' McCormack hen-pecked his shirt's shoulders, lifted them so they engulfed his frame, and let them flop back down. 'Whoops.' He stopped himself. 'Is that offensive?'

'You're allowed to talk about food around me.'

'I did this extra training for in-clus-iv-ity.' He sounded it out, and Jack could almost see the bouncing karaoke ball skim across his forehead as he built the word. 'Know you're not supposed to, like, ask someone "where are you from" these days. But, man, you're not fat. I don't get it. I ain't never seen a bloke spew before that ain't had gastro or a skinful.'

'If it helps you to think of it like gastro, it's like gastro. Except you don't get it in Bali,' Jack said, because Kensington had encouraged him to articulate his illness more often. He still didn't call it the medical term. Couldn't wrap his tongue around the burr of that first 'B', recoiled at the way it spat from his lips. So much had passed through those lips. But not that word. Because to people like McCormack, he had no claim to it. They'd never seen a *bloke* spew before. 'What do you need?'

'Sam Midford's here to see you.'

'Wait? Who?' Jack hopped off the bunk. Icy concrete seared his bare feet.

'Midford.' The guard shrugged. The shoulders of his too-large shirt barely moved. 'Said you might know him better by Mr Midnight.'

'You don't watch the news much, do you?'

'He famous or something?'

'Was.'

'You want to see him or what?'

Jack looked out the window; it flared orange. 'Sure. What's the time?'

'Five o'clock,' McCormack answered without looking at his watch.

Another one down. Jack walked to the opposite wall, rubbed out one of the chalk tally marks queued across the flaking blue paint. Forty-eight left now. As expected.

'Most people count time served.' McCormack gestured at the line of markings. 'You're the only person I've ever met who counts down the days left in *business hours*.'

'Have to measure it somehow.'

'You got your days wrong, anyways. You've got heaps less than that left.'

'Means I'll be surprised when it comes early.' Jack turned to his shelves, lifted a black garbage bag from one of them and untwirled the lazy knot at the top. 'Now. Visitor after hours. Requires payment, I think.' He upended the bag on the desk. 'Which one do you want?'

McCormack thought for a second, and then picked up a Snickers from the motley collection of chocolate bars. He made to put it in his pocket, but Jack gave a small cough and held out a flat palm. McCormack's mouth formed a ring of understanding. He unwrapped the chocolate, then handed the packaging back to Jack, who put it in the bin. Doctor's orders. Kensington would check the bin, pat Jack on his battle-axe shoulder-blades and tell him he was making progress. And he was. But Jack still enjoyed this small rebellion. He had always been good at breaking the rules. That's why he was here.

McCormack, munching on his Snickers, led Jack out of his cell and down rows of closed doors. Long Bay had three levels; the cells ringed a vacant, floor-to-ceiling central column, with metal stairways crisscrossing at the end of each level. Early in Jack's sentence he'd been woken by two sounds: a loud yelp and the whip-like *crack* of something slapping concrete. The guards had made everyone stay in their cells through the morning. Chores were skipped. When they were let out, a wide broom leaned against the far wall, stiff bristles soap-sudded. The floor was already scrubbed, although that was supposed to be an inmate's job. No one mentioned when the headcount was one under.

'Reckon one of the guards pushed him?' Jack had overheard someone say over dinner. The cafeteria had been chatty that night. Their repetitious existence starved them of events worthy of conversation, so some might say the dead man had made a worthy sacrifice, if only because he'd given them something to talk about.

'Nah. I heard he managed to jam the lock,' said another. 'Got himself out.'

'Jumped,' a gravel-dusted voice chipped in. Jack knew that one. Ivan Fraye. Ivan spoke in single words because he'd been shot in the throat resisting arrest and it hurt to say more. The documentary producer inside Jack tickled, as it did sometimes, if only to retreat to a fantasy of his old life. Ivan's punctured rasp and word economy would sound great on a podcast.

'I didn't say he jumped,' said the other guy. 'Sometimes the world pushes you.' Semi-meaningless, pop psychology aphorisms ran riot in prisons: the original Instagram.

'Pussy,' rasped Ivan.

Jack had poked at his traded meal and thought of his brother.

Now Jack subconsciously walked on the inside of McCormack, away from the railing, still thinking about the sound a fallen body makes. He didn't like heights. His brother, Liam, falling. Gone in a cloud of dust. Jack shook the memory. On the top level, before they descended the stairs, the flooring changed from polished concrete to corrugated iron, hastily laid over some ancient gap in the floor. Above was a thick wooden beam. Non-structural. A new floor and a strong mount left little mystery. They used to hang them here.

Capital punishment was well past its use-by date, but the prison kept it like that as a reminder. It always made Jack's stomach roll. How many men had hung here? How many ghosts haunted these walls?

Ghosts like Sam Midford.

Jack refocused. What the hell would Sam want with him? He quickened his steps. He figured it was bad manners to keep a dead man waiting.

Sam Midford not only wasn't dead, he was grinning.

'Jack Quick!' Sam stood and extended his hand, his voice like a drum, deep and booming. Like many people Jack had met in television, he had a large frame. It wouldn't be fair to describe him as exclusively tall or fat, but he filled a room. He had presence, that was certain, in the way that celebrity often struggled to distinguish between charisma and volume. Jack pegged him as thirty, if that, which made his charisma all the more remarkable. Jack gingerly shook his hand. It didn't feel quite real, like this was a man in costume. His eyes darted around the walls. Hidden cameras? Some stupid reality TV stitch-up?

They sat down in two white plastic chairs on either side of a gleaming steel table, which had an eye-bolt drilled into the surface. In a rarity, this furniture was not bolted down (Jack assumed this was because it was hard to bash a skull in with a garden chair). Jack held his wrists out while McCormack threaded a pair of handcuffs through the bolt, and then slid the cuffs on loose. His breath was sickly with chocolate as he leaned over Jack to secure them. Jack could shake them off if he wanted; it was for show. Like the pause after knocking on the cell door. That's what prisons were all about, anyway: the illusion of safety, so people could say to their kids, 'We've rounded up all the bad people in one spot.' So society could pretend evil only existed in this one protected place. And that we could catch, control it.

'Sporting some cold hands there, mate,' said the recently deceased sitting across from him.

'Bad circulation.' Jack's hands were a roadmap to his illness. Icy from malnutrition. Scars on the backs of his knuckles from jamming his fingers down his throat: skin broken and re-healed, split under teeth. And how thin his fingers were. Could pick locks. 'Not as cold as yours should be.'

'Right. Of course.' Sam drummed the table.

'Well?'

'You've probably guessed, but I'm not Sam Midford.' He let out a small laugh. Nerves. 'Look. Sam shot himself in the head three days ago. You know that. I just figured lots of people try to visit you, with crimes and murders and shit, *and* I heard you were a bit of a curmudgeon. But I thought if Mr Midnight came to see you, that might get your attention.'

'You had it. Now you don't. Who are you?'

'I'm Sam's twin brother. And I want you to solve his murder.'

CHAPTER 2

Not-Sam peered expectantly at Jack, as if he'd leap to his feet, whisk an overcoat and a fedora from thin air, and swing into detective mode. The sad clink of Jack's cuffs against the table broke the fantasy. Jack opened his mouth to say something, but Not-Sam started shaking his head.

'I know what you're going to say. Don't say it. Everybody's said it.'

'It must be . . .'

'It is. And you're sorry for my loss. And I'm holding up okay. And I never could have seen it coming. And you never could have expected me to. And' – he tilted his head back, top teeth perched on bottom lip, there's only one word that gets loaded in the chamber like that – '*fuck* all that.' Not-Sam threaded his fingers, lowered his head and exhaled. 'I'm not asking for sympathy, I'm asking for help.'

'If we're skipping the platitudes . . .' Jack said.

'Please.'

'Your brother wasn't murdered. He killed himself. I know you don't want me to say it, but I *am* sorry. And there's no crime here. I saw it.'

Since his sentencing Jack had avoided most factual crime shows, but he didn't mind watching *Midnight Tonight*. It was light entertainment masquerading as news: human interest stories laced with gentle political ribbing. Harmless stuff.

Until the host had told his girlfriend to change the channel.

'So did I.' Not-Sam nodded slowly.

Jack felt a pang of pity. He remembered half-watching in bed, his pulse in his neck as he sat up, gawking at the frozen screen. He was trying to decipher if he'd seen what he thought he had, but the body's innate sense for tragedy – the dip in his stomach, that cold fluid across his chest – worked faster than cognisance.

Live TV usually factored in a seven-second dump, and someone in the studio had hit it just in time. Jack's screen was frozen with Sam's death mask, the pistol a blur of grey motion in his right hand: recoil, Jack knew, shattering teeth. His mouth was still clamped in the picture, but his cheeks were puffed out, rippled. His eyes had been scrunched shut, and the freeze-frame had caught the moment his left eye flew open. One more millisecond and it would have shown the top of his head dissolving. They'd caught the feed just before the blood. There were leaked videos of the rest popping up on YouTube, other sites, culled as fast as they were uploaded, but not so hard to find. Jack didn't bother. That one-eyed squint was enough.

The image had held on the screen for almost twenty seconds, and then it all cut to static. Slowly, the static was overwhelmed by the sounds of the prison moving: people banging on doors; yelling. The violence invigorating. Cell by cell the news travelled from those who had seen it. An almost gleeful gossip.

But sitting across from the brother, Jack now recalled Mr Midnight's final words. 'I love you. Forgive me. Change the channel.' He imagined Sam's family – his parents, his partner, his child (Jack had read with horror in the news that Mr Midnight had a young daughter) – watching him on television. Maybe as they always did. Maybe his kid got a pushed-back bedtime sometimes when Daddy was on television. God. Had they all been watching? He imagined Sam's partner, screaming, rushing for the telephone, trying to cover their daughter's eyes. How old was the daughter? Jack didn't know. Old enough to understand? Sam's parents, looking at the frozen screen and grumbling that they didn't understand the new digital television anyway. His father standing – Jack's mind added a groan with the effort – and smacking the top of the television. Oblivious until much later. Jack imagined Sam's brother, the weight on his chest, the *is-this-real* onset of horror that Jack himself had felt, multiplied. Before he could even blink twice and process what Sam had just pulled out from under the desk. Before he could question whether this was a skit or a prank. Then a bang.

Thinking of them made it so much more real. A constellation of Sam's life bound together by signals soaring through the air. Jack, too, in prison, and so many others, brought into this strange familial bond with the man sitting across from him. A spiderweb of radio signals. They'd shared a death.

Jack felt like he understood a tiny piece of Sam's brother then. How do you deal with seeing that? You build yourself a fantasy and try to find someone to blame. You try to make sense of it, any way you can. That's why he was here, asking Jack to solve a murder that didn't exist.

'You're not telling me anything I haven't already heard,' Not-Sam said. He was quite relaxed in the face of Jack's obvious doubt. 'I heard you like the tough cases.'

'What I don't like is talking to a dead man. What's your name?'

'Harry,' he relented, squinting back at Jack. Squeeze one eye a little tighter, Jack thought, and you'll look like your brother's death mask. 'Harry Midford. And you're Jack Quick. You solved that murder up at that vineyard a while back. The cops wouldn't touch that either. It's no surprise, but they're not treating Sam's death as suspicious.' Harry shrugged. 'Seemed up your alley.'

'I don't have an alley,' Jack said, hoping to shut down further discussion of the murder that had been the subject of his last television documentary, and that had sent him to prison for impeding the concurrent police investigation – the fact that he'd solved it, kind of, be damned. 'And I'm getting pretty sick of people knowing who I am.'

'If you didn't want people to know your name, you probably shouldn't have got yourself caught interfering in a quadruple homicide. Not that I'm criticising.' He cracked a laugh in surrender. 'That's why I'm here.'

'It was two homicides,' Jack said bluntly. 'The other deaths were self-defence. I'm not in here for murder.'

'I know,' Harry said. 'I read up on you. You're here for perverting the course of justice. Obstructing a murder investigation. Evidence tampering. Two years. But I hear you're a gold-star pupil. You're getting out soon.'

He said it as a fact, not a question, and it irked Jack that he was still in the press. Seventeen months into a two-year sentence. They'd told Jack it was good behaviour, but he suspected they needed the bed. Besides, he was more expensive and less dangerous than a regular inmate, so he was the perfect person to function on the outside. Because prisons only spent money to stop people hurting someone else. Outside, Jack would only hurt himself. Bargain.

'I figure you might need a fresh start. A new show,' Harry said. 'Take this on and you can record it, sell it. All the rights are yours. I don't want any money.'

Jack tsked. 'And here I thought you'd done your research. I don't make documentaries anymore.'

'You don't make the bullshit ones.' Harry leaned forward and lowered his voice, as if the interview room was full of people, 'but you still like the hunt for a good story. I listened to a few of your podcasts from in here. They're good. Simple.'

Jack averted his eyes. After the colossal mistakes that had ruined his television career and sent him here, he had waved away the glorified production and television spectacle of high-profile crimes and had launched a simple podcast that focused on inmates' stories. Despite the rigorous supervision process, the demonetisation and the direction of the warden not to *interview anyone vile*, Jack felt it had been an enjoyable and important step forward, like going back to where he started; just a microphone and a free platform to publish it online. Jack tried his best to be impartial, his voice barely present except for an occasional 'Tell me more on that' or 'And how did that make you feel?' But Harry had sensed something deeper. That if Jack wasn't making these stories, what was he even worth?

Harry continued. 'But you still like the mystery. You still like being the one who gets to find, to tell, the truth. You can't walk away from that.' Harry placed a hand on his front, below his ribs. 'You and me, my brother, we're all entertainers. And there's a *need*. Whether it's under lights or with a microphone. Tugs you like a string in your navel. You'll want to tell *this* story, I know it.'

Jack wondered what Harry had walked away from that he could understand this feeling. Jack wasn't a man who walked away from an unanswered question. Wasn't that why he'd started making programs – podcasts, then moving into television – in the first place? Before he'd been corrupted, and layered on lie after lie in a hunt for ratings. But even then, he'd gone back out to the Hunter Valley wineries with the aim of setting things right. With the aim of finding out the truth. And he still felt it in that hollow beneath his ribs, just like this faux-dead man said he did. Did he miss it? Goddamn right he did.

But there was no mystery here. Just shattered teeth wrapped around cold metal. Static on a prison television.

'Everything you've said is wrong,' Jack lied. And then, because he wanted to hurt him: 'Your brother pulled the trigger. I'm not going to pretend to investigate a murder just because you can't accept that.'

'I'm not wrong about everything.' Harry straightened up, smiled again with his bright-white TV-ready smile. Just a little bit dimmer than his brother's? 'You *are* a bit of a curmudgeon.' It was almost like discussing his brother's death was secondary to working the room, making an impression; Harry's energy would swing to jovial whenever he felt the conversation was tracking too seriously. He was trying to impress him, Jack thought. 'I shouldn't have editorialised. Maybe murder is too strong a word. I was trying to get your attention. But there was a crime, even if I don't know which one it is yet. Coercion? At the very least blackmail. Surely.' Harry reached into his jacket and pulled out an envelope. He placed it on the table and slid it into the centre. 'You'll still be interested. Promise.'

'Hire a PI.' Jack left the envelope untouched. 'They'll be more useful.'

'You used to work there. You knew him.'

'Just a little.'

'A little is enough. You know the station, how these shows work. You can talk to people, get inside, check things out.'

'A lot of people have asked me to solve their crimes for them. I've said no to every one of them.'

Harry shot a look down, raised his eyebrows at the envelope.

'Is that money, then?' Jack relented. His bluff dropped, ever so slightly, his voice rising in pitch. He had forty-eight tally marks on his wall, after all.

'Fuck no.' Harry laughed, then stood. 'Though *Midnight Tonight* was one of the most popular nightly TV programs for a reason. Money's no problem. You tell me what you want when you change your mind.'

'If I change my mind.'

'Sure. Whatever.'

'The envelope?' Jack persisted, now more curious.

'Oh.' Harry picked it up and ripped it in half. It fluttered, empty, to the table. 'Nothing.' He laughed again.

Jack couldn't get a hold on the man, simultaneously exuberant and devastated. Grief slid through the blood differently, but this man was almost manic. Must be hard, wearing a dead man's face.

'Wanted to see what you'd think was in there. I thought you might want fame. But you want money. Great, that's easy. In any case, I thought it'd make me look serious.' A beat. Jack's expression didn't change. 'Jesus, lighten up.'

He reached into his pocket again and this time grabbed a pen, with which he jotted a number on one half of the envelope.

'I won't call.'

Harry paused mid-four and raised his head. Despite his shambolic and unpredictable nature, Jack realised he was sharp. He'd set up and caught Jack's slip on the mention of the money. He had confidence now.

'You want the envelope to have a big fat cheque in it? Fifty thousand dollars. There. And what you find, you keep. Make a show.' He put a hand up. 'I know, I know. You don't do that anymore. But handy to have in the back pocket all the same. You allowed to keep this in here?' He held up the phone number. Jack nodded. 'Call me when you're out.'

'I still don't un—'

'Yeah, well, me neither. You got a brother?'

Jack assumed that Harry already knew he did. Already knew everything about him, that Liam was at his father's house, tied up in tubes, nothing to do but wait for Jack to come home.

'They found stuff on his laptop. The one at work. I don't know how much. I don't know what. I haven't seen it but they told me – as if that'd help. Your brother killed himself but, hey, he's a paedo, so, like, chalk that one up as a win. They reckon that's why he did it.' Harry walked to the door, turned away from Jack and for the first time dropped his shoulders, leaned a tired flat hand on the door. Some reality behind his gregarious facade. 'I know my brother. I know that's not him. I also know that's what they all say, and that no one knows a sicko till you trap 'em. But no, not him. Not Sam.'

Then he knocked on the door. Jack heard McCormack's keys clink as he worked the lock.

'I won't call,' said Jack quietly. Not looking at him, staring down at his murky reflection in the tabletop's aluminium sheen. He heard the door open.

'I'm not asking you to buy the whole story,' Harry said. 'I'm asking you to believe *one small thing*. That Sam wasn't what they're calling him. From there it's logical. If the photos were planted, they're there to cover something up.' That booming voice, calm and even, goaded Jack into looking up. Harry's eyes were scanning him; Jack couldn't tell for what. Compliance? Cowardice? Could he tell Jack was trying to divide fifty thousand dollars by three hundred and fifty-seven? Harry prompted, 'You say my brother shot himself in the head?'

Jack nodded.

'A million witnesses saw him pull the trigger?'

Jack nodded again.

'He did. But if someone put the stuff on his laptop, maybe they can put a gun in his hand. And that's why you'll call.'

'I googled it,' McCormack said, as he walked Jack back to his cell, iPhone in his hand. 'His head just *fucken disappears*.'

He thrust the phone at Jack, but Jack swivelled his gaze away. He didn't want to see it. The prison was busier now, prisoners out of cells and moving towards the cafeteria. There was dawdling, leg-stretching, a lack of urgency in this parade. Inmates were dotted across the three levels of walkways.

'I don't think you should be showing me that,' Jack said.

'Shit, man.' McCormack frowned. 'We did suicide trigger warnings on our training. Is this one? Didn't realise you'd thought about it.'

The implication, which slid so casually from the guard's mouth without a glimmer of awareness, surprised Jack. Doctors had asked him this before, but he'd figured out pretty quickly to answer as close to 'Never' as the paperwork would allow. Otherwise they took things away from you. Shoelaces. Belts. 'I never thought of killing myself with toenail clippers,' one of Jack's hospital friends had said, years ago, 'until they took them away, and now in my head I keep conjuring this absurd massacre.' Then in a week they gave you another form. *How do you feel now?* And, apart from having longer nails, nothing else had changed, but you told them you were better so you got your stuff back. Jack was wary of this bureaucratic cycle and had never answered the question honestly – he'd always ticked the right box, put the chocolate wrapper face-up in the bin – but something about the off-handedness of Lee's comment gave him pause.

Had he thought about it? Maybe. At his worst. Head down, tongue fizzing, nose dog-wet from toilet water. *Fuck*, he almost said, *hasn't everybody?*

'Nah,' he said instead. 'Not me. Tell me something.'

'Sure.'

'That inclusivity training you did – what score did you get? Or was it a pass–fail kind of thing?'

'Don't know,' said McCormack. 'Had to leave after half the day.'

Jack allowed himself a smile; McCormack's cluelessness was almost endearing. He was glad for it. After the conversation with Harry he felt over-exerted, feeling his grief by proxy (because Sam's brother was still too deep in the denial phase), the agony of the money in front of him, and that itch: that something was wrong with Sam Midford's death. And that Jack probably wanted to know what it was.

He felt tired. Hungry. Had he eaten today? That wasn't good. He was more likely to binge. Balance was important, Jack knew, because his illness was too deceitful to be conquered by mere avoidance. Too little, too much. A sickness at each end of the spectrum waiting to ambush him. He stood in the middle of a circle of sneering ancient soldiers, ready to ricochet him from illness to illness if he slipped too far to either side. And that dead-centre equilibrium was hard to maintain. When he was emotional, when he was tired, when he was lying, the soldiers stamped their feet and clashed their rectangular shields together. Took a step forward.

'Fuck!' McCormack interrupted his thoughts with a yell. He was poking at his phone. 'I used the staff wifi for the video. Fuck!' He hurried off, leaving Jack to follow the stragglers to the cafeteria.

Jack sighed. He reached into his pocket and pulled out an object with a glowing orange screen, two directional microphones protruding from the top like a small claw. He'd lied to Harry: of course Jack's interest had been piqued when a dead man came to speak to him. He'd had to take his audio recorder. An ear for a story doesn't fade. It was strange to feel so known.

He heard a hand grenade of a cough from above him. Looked up.

Ivan Fraye sat on the level-one catwalk, green-tracksuit-clad legs swinging over the lip. He had a wry smile. Jack could see the scar tissue, glossy on his neck. He'd been listening to their conversation, had heard McCormack ask about suicide. Had heard Jack say to McCormack: *not me*.

Ivan licked his lips, as he always did before he spoke. Choosing his perfect word that was worth the pain. And when it came, the word ripped apart in his throat, fired in a shrapnel blast: 'Bullshit.'

CHAPTER 3

They only sent one reporter. And a junior one at that.

Twelve days earlier (his wall tally had got down to thirty-six before a guard had thrown a bucket of water at it and scrubbed the chalk to zero), Jack had been annoyed when Harry told him he was still in the press. But now there was a strange strike of disappointment, a slice off his pride. Last time Jack had been in the carpark of Long Bay for a prisoner release, it had been bustling to the point of riot. Even though Jack was glad to be left alone, it still felt like no one had shown up to his birthday party. And alongside that feeling, a rumble of caution: if he wasn't in the papers, just how much research had the Midford twin done on him?

It was midday, March, the sun plump in a clear sky, though just for show: it preened rather than warmed. A sea breeze kicked the chill into him. Jack's illness made him susceptible to the cold. He was wearing a collared button-up shirt, sleeves rolled to the elbows, runners, and jeans that cut slightly into his waist. He'd yanked them on with some delight at the fit this morning. His belt lay curled in a plastic bag, which also included his phone, wallet and keys, unneeded. The carpark was sparsely dotted with cars. A VW Golf flashed its lights from the far end. Jack headed towards it.

Jack hadn't slept well. Long Bay wasn't known for farewells, but Kensington had given him a weigh-in and smugly organised a cake the night before. Jack suspected he might be chalked up at conferences as one of the doctor's great success stories. *I let him eat cake.* Jack spent all night trying to hold it down. Prison was a breeding ground for irony.

Some prisoners had said, 'See you later.' Others had patted him on the back. Some were genuine, others merely filling the air out of obligation while lining up for a slice. That morning Ivan had given him a salute, two fingers on his forehead, but didn't spare him any words.

Now, walking across the carpark wasn't the revelatory experience Jack had quietly been anticipating. The air wasn't any fresher. The world no larger. He didn't feel any freer.

The lone journalist had parked closer than the Golf and, unhurried, strolled up to Jack. No cameraman and an unkempt beard marked him as off-screen talent. He had a small lined notepad and a pen. Jack often liked to consider people by how he'd cast them. In this guy's case, Jack would have written on a casting brief: *early twenties; wears t-shirts to meetings; struggles to hail a cab or push through to order a drink at a crowded bar; not the love interest's best friend, but the best friend's best friend.*

'Jack?' the journalist said. Didn't offer a hand or name.

Jack kept walking. The seam of his jeans gave a slight and satisfying chafe.

'You've just served a year and a half?'

'About that,' Jack said, figuring there was no point denying the public record.

'What's the first thing you're going to do with your freedom?'

In the face of such hard-hitting journalism, Jack saw no point in not answering. 'What everyone does: breathe the air, see my family, talk to an intern in a carpark who'll misspell my name in tomorrow's paper. Been looking forward to that the most,' he said.

'Cool,' said the reporter, but he didn't write anything down. 'You know Sam Midford?'

'I keep to myself.'

'Sure. But Sam Midford. You used to work with him. You know him?'

'I know *of* him. Who are you with?'

'With?'

'You're not TV. Which paper?'

'It's not important. You talk to Sam much?'

'Good morning. Hello. That kind of thing. Not for years, been busy.' Jack stopped, turned. In the wind he heard the grunt of the Golf starting up. 'Are you police?'

'Sure.'

'Sure, as in, you are police?'

'Sure. I'm police. You know he shot himself, right?'

'Impersonating a police officer is a crime.'

'Just a citizen, then.' The bloke shrugged, flicking the notebook shut and ending the masquerade. The ghost of a chuckle haunted Jack's chest: not even here for the 'birthday boy'. 'His brother came to see you?'

'Harry hired you too, huh?' said Jack. 'So you're on the payroll at a firm that's happy to take his money to dig around, even though you know he's barking. Look, I told him what I'll tell you. I didn't know Sam. At all.'

'Did he seem weird? Like, his mental state?' This guy didn't take a hint.

'I just told you—' Jack was about to explain again that he hadn't seen Mr Midnight in years when he noticed the man's pen, up to here just a prop, was now poised to the paper. That movement, meaning something was important enough for this guy to write down, twigged something in Jack's mind: *insurance*. Might be the network's. Might be the family's. Either way, while Jack was happy to entertain a journo or even a cop (he'd resolved to play nice with police from now on), he did not want to get caught up further in the Midford business. Though he had a feeling he was already in it.

'His mental state?' Jack said. 'Last time I saw him was on the telly, and he was busy painting the wall behind him. Work backwards.' The Golf rolled up beside them. Gravel cracked. The guy was still tapping his pen. Jack put his hand on the car's door and smiled: 'I hope I've assisted your investigation, *officer*.'

He opened the door and got in, shutting the door quickly before he could be interrogated further.

'Who was that?' Jack's father asked, putting the car in neutral.

'Insurance, I think,' Jack said. 'About someone else. I couldn't help him.'

Jack looked at his father. Peter was the only person who'd visited Jack in prison, and he'd visited often, but his appearance still surprised Jack. The red polo shirt with an embroidered yellow logo, a recent look that would take some getting used to. As would Peter's noticeable ageing. Not from ill health, he'd just reached a certain point where the physicality of life was becoming much more obvious. Like a drag race, the most noticeable changes are at the start and the end: acceleration and deceleration. Peter's parachute was out. He wore glasses now. The lines in his face had deepened, drought-struck. He had a short, scruffy grey beard to compensate for the lost battle on top. As if his crown had just thought, fuck it, and rotated.

Even a couple of weeks was enough for noticeable changes. In prison everyone was in stasis. They wore the same green tracksuits. Ate the same food. Got the same amount of sunlight for the same sickly pall, the same haircuts. Everyone still looked different – skin colour, tattoos, heights, muscles – but there was a blurring of identity. And eventually you began to believe that the whole world might be like that. And then Jack's dad would visit, and he'd be a little bit shorter, a little more brittle, than the time before. And he'd look so *sharp* in contrast to the homogenised population Jack had become so used to. It was like watching a movie with a reel missing. His father ageing in blinks, black spots in between, the differences so clear. Now there are glasses. Now there's a yellow tooth. Now there's an old man. It kept catching Jack off guard.

Peter scanned the carpark. Seemed surprised by the lack of media. 'I thought it'd be busier,' he said.

'I didn't kill enough people.'

Peter gave him a small smile. Paused. His hand hovered over the vibrating gearstick, unsure of whether to put the car in drive or whether the occasion called for something more. Jack and his father loved one another in a classic Australian fashion, unspoken and unacted. Jack could feel the tension: did they hug now? That's why men like cars. You don't have to hug anybody. The handbrake's in the way.

Peter settled for giving Jack a squeeze on the shoulder. It lingered just a little bit too long. Checking the weight on him. Out of prison: still watched.

'Had enough of this place?' Peter said, letting go, having satisfied both his fatherly and medical obligations. He put the car in gear.

Jack nodded. 'Let's go home.'

CHAPTER 4

In the forty-minute drive from Long Bay, Jack started to feel his newfound freedom. The vibrations of the seat under his legs. The blast of air through the window, cracked a finger's width. The cold of glass on his cheek. The rattle of a road-side jackhammer. There wasn't much different with the world itself – he hadn't been in prison long enough for that – but there was something almost overwhelming about it. For the last year and a half everything he'd handled was made out of the same cold polished aluminium, concrete or plastic; every sound – the slamming of a door, the hum of the cafeteria – rotated on a schedule; every view repeated, the rooms duplicated through the prison; even the temperature stayed within the same chilly range. His senses had atrophied. So he sat quietly while his father drove, his body catching up with the bombardment of unexpected minutiae.

There were some notable differences. The pedestrian bridge over one of the major roads had been finished. Then they'd started building something else a kilometre further up, because God forbid a road in Sydney was ever finished. The pet shop on a busy corner had morphed into a yoga studio. His phone had been two models out of date when he'd gone inside, and now it didn't even look like it was from the same decade as the ones on the billboards. His still had a number after the model, while the new ones were tagged with Roman numerals. When your technology is so out of date the *Romans* are ahead of you, it might be time to get a new phone, Jack mused. Bus stops showed different superheroes in front of the same explosions. And, of course, the biggest difference of all: there was a woman waiting for them at his father's house.

Her name was Madeline. She was twenty years younger than his father. And she cost three hundred and fifty-seven dollars a day.

Even though it wasn't in her job description, Madeline made Peter and Jack tea. It was strange to have a female presence in the house. After their mother's death, Peter had raised the two boys on his own. The main difference, Jack noticed, was that more curtains were open. The light splayed between rooms, unrestrained through doorways, because, just like in Jack's old home, all of the doors had been removed from their hinges. That was an old treatment recommendation back when Jack would lock himself in a room to throw up in a wastebasket. He couldn't be trusted, first with any lock, and then with any privacy whatsoever. So the doors had to go.

Peter had put his doors back up when Jack had improved, but Jack kept his own stacked in a pile in his garage. Peter must have decided to remove the doors again as some form of homecoming. Although the 'I'm watching you' tone of the shoulder squeeze in the car lingered in the act, Jack appreciated it. He'd been behind enough doors lately.

The three of them sat around the kitchen table, nursing their mugs. Jack could tell Madeline didn't feel it was her place to say anything, but neither did she have the discretion to leave. Peter was rotating the mug in his hands, scraping the table.

'I might go see him,' said Jack, standing. No one said anything. Peter looked into his tea. *Scrape.*

Jack walked up the stairs into Liam's room. He paused outside the door. His breathing was shallow, nervous. He'd seen his brother on Skype over the last few months, but he'd only got glimmers of his condition. He felt a wave of exhaustion. Those soldiers in his brain stomped and slammed their shields into the ground. Orange dust rose. He shook them off, opened the door.

Liam was lying on his back, the bed flat. The curtains in this room weren't open. He was a shadow on the bed, a dark mass on white sheets. The smell was of talcum powder mixed with sweat: nothing foul, just a room that's pretending to be clean when it isn't. A teenage boy covering for a shower with deodorant. Jack wondered if the smell was really that strong or if he was just feeling overpowered again. The soft sounds of the heart rate monitor and the respirator laid a baseline. *Beep. Beep. Wheeze.*

Jack flicked on the light. There was his brother, amid a spider's web of tubing. Neither asleep nor awake, chest rising up and down in a calm mechanical fashion. *Beep. Beep. Wheeze.*

Liam had fallen from a rock formation when he was fourteen years old. Jack had been only twelve, but he'd been mucking around with his brother at the time. They weren't supposed to play there. Jack remembered very specific details. Liam's arms pinwheeling the air. The plume of orange dust. The jagged shape his body made. The way they strapped him to a bright-red stretcher with canvas straps, as if securing a fridge. The helicopter beating stinging debris into his eyes. The stretcher skimming the treetops. The firey's hand on Jack's back. How dry Jack's mouth had been when he'd lied and told them Liam had gone up alone.

The helicopter had got Liam to a hospital in time to save his life, but the lack of oxygen to his brain had caused serious damage. Peter explained it to Jack as a coma. The doctors called it a vegetative state. After three months, they upgraded him to a 'persistent vegetative state'. After another year, they promoted him to 'permanent'. The career ladder of the comatose is the most bureaucratic of the illnesses. Performance reviews are based purely on time served. Sit in your chair long enough and you get a gold watch and a new title. Permanent Vegetative State is basically tenure, with no long-service leave.

Just like seeing his dad age, it was strange watching Liam grow. And grow he did, as his body morphed from teenager to adult with the slowest of progress, but none of the wear of someone who'd *lived*. No scars or spots or burns or wrinkles. The human body ages by breaking and healing. It was almost as if Liam was in a test tube, and while his bones changed to man, the soul (and the soft, pale face) remained the teenage boy who'd been hurt and had never woken up. Jack and his father would cut hair, clip fingernails and shave beards, because they, too, were preserving something.

Liam needed all the basic things – nutrition, hydration and respiration – but didn't need complex physical care, so they'd been able to set him up at home. Later, the money Jack had made on his Curtis Wade documentary, in which he'd trawled through a cold case murder in a vineyard in the hope of exonerating a killer, had made it easier. He'd bought nicer equipment: a state-of-the-art breathing apparatus, a new bed that moved electronically. Jack surveyed the machines. The wheezing machine, a rubber accordion pumping up and down. The tube at Liam's hip to gurgle down thick brown nutrient-rich paste (in one of his many lessons from the last two years, Jack had at last realised his problematic relationship with food may have started with watching his brother transparently digest his meals; it made it feel like nothing more than tasteless sludge in Jack's own mouth). The IV in Liam's arm gave fluids. There was no alchemy to it. No magic. The human body is a shell: put enough basic functions into it and the chest moves and the heart beats. Liam, forced into life, had been stable for twenty years.

Then, six months ago, he'd got pneumonia.

The decline had been sharp. Jack could see now that Liam's weight had severely dropped. His bones were prominent and, lying flat, the skin, dragged by gravity, pooled at his joints, as if he were partially melting. Jack sat in the armchair by the bed and held Liam's hand. His fingers were thinner than Jack's, colder too. Quite a feat.

'Hey, mate,' Jack said. 'I'm back.'

Since the pneumonia, they'd pumped him full of all kinds of things and got him back to equilibrium. But the body, the shell, was wearing out. The care requirements – the observation and the medicine – had increased. Blood clots in his legs. Bedsores and skin infections ran riot. Liam's eyes had been taped shut to prevent corneal ulcers; two tabs of clear plastic held them closed. Jack had had a nightmare in prison that Liam might wake, try to open them, and be too weak to conquer the tape.

And, somewhere along the line, someone had mentioned withdrawing treatment.

Jack had learned a lot of official terms in his years in and out of hospitals. They liked to tick boxes, name things. Jack didn't use the dreaded 'b' word for his own illness. He and his father had compressed the plethora of buzzwords into simply 'a problem with food'. There were lots of terms the specialists had for Liam, but Jack thought about it in the same language. Liam had a problem with food. Liam had a problem with breathing. Liam had a problem with living. Stick the machines in him, and he had a problem with dying too.

Withdrawing treatment was a new term though. Euthanasia was illegal in New South Wales, but this was the opposite. All they would do was stop providing the mechanical functions, and the body would naturally die. It had been *recommended*. As if it were a film the doctor had quite enjoyed.

Were it on the taxpayer's dime, Liam would have almost certainly had his treatment withdrawn. People didn't wake up from PVS. Every single documented case of a recovery had been attributed to an initial misdiagnosis. In the public system, he'd be a liability.

Liam had a problem with financially viable recovery potential.

But because Liam was in home care, and because the patient's wishes were unclear (as if any gloomy fourteen-year-old had the foresight to provide their parents with a Do Not Resuscitate), it was ultimately their decision. Jack and Peter had gently talked about whether it was time, but both of them wanted to hang on for just a bit longer. They'd researched it, and it seemed that as long as they didn't rely on anything government-run they would be fine. However, if the public system felt burdened, the Supreme Court had the capacity to intervene, and almost surely would, on the doctor's recommendation.

Enter Madeline. A private nurse. Paid for out of Jack's own pocket. The problem was, Jack's pockets were getting thin. He'd been sued by the television network, by the family of the winery murder victims, both of which had settled (Jack had just signed whatever had been put in front of him, his stomach churning), not to mention the costs of his own legal team. Much of his income from his show was considered profiteering from the crime he'd committed, so his earnings had been confiscated. To say he had been wealthy when he went to prison would be understating it – he'd been at the helm of one of the most successful television shows in decades. But now he was close to broke. He'd sold his home. Luckily, he had been able to save his father's. But after that they had nothing left. In television, you're only as good as your last episode. Just ask Mr Midnight.

Madeline was expensive. She worked from two to five. Every day at five o'clock, when she finished, Jack would rub another tally mark off his cell wall.

They were doing all they could. Jack, not needing it, had sold his car. His heart had splintered when he'd gotten out of the prison and seen Peter in that uniform. A red polo with an embroidered yellow logo for LiquorMania, the bottle shop where he'd been putting in part-time shifts. Jack had spent most of his spare time trying to squeeze living costs and expenses into different calculations, his notepad scrawled with hope but no answers. Just to get one more day. One more tally mark.

When he left the prison, he'd been down to thirty-six tally marks. Thirty-six days of care left. Just shy of thirteen thousand dollars. And when that ran out . . .

On a three-way call, one doctor had explained it as exceedingly simple. Liam wasn't conscious, so he wouldn't notice the change. They would just remove the respirator, and the body would naturally settle into death.

'He won't feel a thing,' the doctor had assured them.

'Yeah,' replied Jack, 'but I will.'

CHAPTER 5

'I wanted you to see him,' Peter said. He was standing in the door-way, leaning against the frame. No door. He was still wearing his bottle-shop uniform.

'Thanks, Dad.'

'Madeline thinks—'

'I know what she thinks. Same as all the others.'

'Well. They're professionals.'

'Are you serious? We're doing this now?'

Peter rubbed the back of his neck. 'I wanted you to see him,' he repeated. 'Wanted to wait until you got out.'

'Wait? For what? This is quite an ambush.'

'Just to talk about it. I'm not saying I've decided either way. But it's worth thinking about more, now you're home. We won't do any-thing unless we do it together.'

'Dad, it's fine.'

'I don't know how much longer—'

'Thirty-six days.' Jack heard the front door close downstairs. He looked at his watch. 'Thirty-five.'

Peter didn't seem to know what to say to that. Now that Jack had said it, five weeks didn't seem very long at all. The respirator wheezed.

'I have to work tonight.' Peter settled on something factual, non-contentious. 'You'll be okay?'

Jack looked at his father, now dressed up to serve teenagers pre-mix cans. He realised Peter must be pulling a double shift. Morning shift, a few hours off, and now close. Jack imagined his father asking his pimple-faced boss if he could have a few hours off. *I need to pick my son up from prison.* Jesus. He was supposed to be retired. Two sons, both imprisoned: one in body, one in bars. And Peter, on the edge of it all, persistently and permanently, weathering the disappointments, trying to hold their family together.

'I got a job.' The words shot out of him before he'd even thought about it.

Peter raised an eyebrow.

'Pays well,' Jack said. He restrained himself from adding 'It's above board' because he felt it would acknowledge that he didn't believe his father trusted him. And because he wasn't sure if it was. He settled on 'We'll be fine.'

Jack could tell Peter had neither the time nor the inclination to challenge him further. 'All right,' he said. 'We'll have to talk about it sometime.'

'Sometime. Not until we have to. And not in front of him.'

'He can't hear us.'

'I'm not an idiot,' Jack said. He traced a line with his thumb on the back of Liam's hand. He knew the touch would go unfelt. In the bed Liam lay silent, calm and thoughtless. Did he dream? 'But I can't stop imagining if he could. Doctors don't know everything about the brain. And maybe he's lying there listening to us. And he can't talk and he can't scream and his eyes are taped shut. He's banging on the walls of his cage.' Jack locked eyes with his father. 'And we're standing here talking about when we're going to kill him.'

Peter turned from the door to go. Then he had second thoughts, and gave Jack a gentle shrug. 'I might sound callous, but I've been with him every day. You've been away for—'

'Don't use that.'

'It's not like I *want* to talk about this.'

'Then don't.'

'It's natural. It's not killing.'

That was doctors' language. Peter had been indoctrinated. It almost felt like a betrayal.

'Letting someone die . . .' Jack bristled. 'Isn't it the same thing?'

Peter made a non-committal *hmmm*, looked at his watch, and left. Jack listened to the creak of the stairs, tried to track his father through the house by sound (it was difficult without doors closing), to make sure he wasn't coming back. The click of the front door settled it. Jack already had his phone in his hand, had thumbed the number in. He didn't know why he wanted to wait until he was alone, but it felt appropriate, given the almost conspiratorial circumstances.

'We'll be okay,' he said to Liam. To himself.

He pressed dial as he squeezed his brother's hand just that little bit tighter. Liam was a good confidant. He kept secrets.

'Knew it,' said a deep voice on the other end of the call.

'I've got a no-gloating policy,' Jack said.

'I'll try. But, shit, with that attitude, how'd you make it in TV?'

Jack ignored the barb. 'I've decided to help you.'

The phone was silent.

'Did you hear me? I said I'll help.'

'Sure. Yeah. I heard. You said no gloating.'

Jack imagined the shine of his teeth, the sly wink, through the phone. Harry was still playing to the back of the room. Jack wondered if he had an off switch. Probably not. TV guys with ego tend not to. If this guy dropped the act, there might not be anything at all behind the curtain. A magic trick laid bare and boring.

'Right. I want to be clear on something. I don't believe you. I'm not an investigator. I'm not even a journalist. I make docos. Made. I barely even do that anymore. I don't even believe that you have a case, but you're offering me money to look into it and – you've already got this figured, I'm sure – I need the cash to take care of my brother. I just wanted to be honest. It's a new thing I'm trying. I'm not doing this because I want to, or because the death intrigues me. Definitely not because I like you. I'm doing this because I want your money. Just so you know what you're buying.'

'I hear you. I prefer cards on the table. Work for hire is fine by me.'

'I have terms.'

'Expected nothing less.'

'You said fifty thousand. I want seventy.'

'Deal.' No hesitation.

'And . . .' Jack racked his brains to think of more to ask for. He wanted to appear assertive, in control. Harry had answered so quickly he needed to up his demands to make himself sound more serious. What do people normally ask for in situations like this? 'I want half in advance, and the other half when we're out of leads. I'm not going to cut corners, but if the only answer we find is one you're not happy with, you still gotta pay up if I tie it in a bow for you. For the record, that includes the conclusion that this is a suicide. Which we both know it clearly is. And it includes not finding anything at all.'

'Deal.'

'And you pay costs.' That sounded good. Did he have costs? He'd have to find some.

'Deal.'

'Right then. Meet me at Channel 14 tomorrow at nine. I should be able to talk us in, and we can start looking around. You got a pen?'

'I know the address.'

'It's for my bank details.'

Harry chuckled, which made the audio fizz. There was a sound of rummaging, then he was back. 'You don't fuck around.'

'I told you what I'm here for.' Jack gave the numbers.

'Sure thing, mate. Takes a day to clear. Should land tomorrow.'

Jack felt uneasy. Had he really just made thirty-five thousand dollars in one phone call? He turned it over in his head: he knew Sam was a popular television entertainer, but where was Harry's money coming from? Sam's will was the obvious answer. But that could have been split any number of ways. He had a daughter. A partner. Jack remembered the chilling tone of Sam telling her to change the channel. He wondered what he was getting himself into. He looked over at Liam. Recalled his father standing in the doorway. *It's not killing.* Steeled himself. *Not until we have to.*

'I just want to know one more thing,' Jack said. 'You keep saying I'm right for this. I don't get it. I solved a murder that was four years old and created a new victim.' And that was only what was in the press; Harry couldn't know the whole truth. No one did – only the killer and the dead. 'I crossed lines, lied and went against the police, and got a whole heap of violence and trouble for the effort. I won't again. I don't have some magic touch. I'm not some crime-solving genius. I stumbled through it. I used to work at the same station, sure, but I didn't know your brother that well, if at all. I'm not even sure they'll let me in. There are heaps of journalists there who would be a better fit. I'm happy for you to piss your money away if you want, but I've got to ask, why me?'

'You know, before we met, I was wondering the same thing.' If it was possible to audibly shrug, Harry would have just done it. His tone flattened. He clicked his tongue. 'It's not really to do with your podcasts. It's not really even to do with the network. I needed someone who'll believe something weird. You've got the head for it.

You can follow a story in a way that others don't. Why? Because you're hoping it goes somewhere wild. Somewhere *entertaining*. You've got an eye for narrative over truth, so that means nothing is off the table. I need a mind like that to solve a problem like mine. But I'd sussed that much before I came to see you.'

'What sold you?'

'Those scars on your knuckles. Figured you'd be good in a fight.'

Jack looked at his hand, resting in Liam's. Harry thought he'd been in punch-ups in prison. He was wrong. Torn by teeth and re-healed.

'Mate, I'm always fighting. Nine a.m.'

He hung up.

CHAPTER 6

Nine o'clock was late enough that *The Breakfasters*, Channel 14's flagship morning program, was finishing. For broadcast the hosts sat with their backs to a concave window looking out on the street, around which crowds could gather and wave incessantly. Viewers at home could see them through the glass. Actual adults braved a biting Sydney morning to stare at the back of someone's famous-but-not-that-famous head. Actual adults made cardboard signs. Shit, thought Jack, sitting on a low concrete wall and watching them disperse, assumedly to spend the day phoning radio stations. These people can breed.

The sun was up in a clear sky but battling with a crisp breeze. Neither heat nor chill was winning. Jack was in jeans and a plain blue t-shirt (he'd deliberately chosen something not prison-green). He'd brought a light jumper but was too hot with it on, too cold with it off. He settled for off, drumming his hands on his thighs to fight the chill.

Just as Jack was chalking up tardiness as a character flaw with some satisfaction, Harry had materialised, punctual to the second.

Harry was, as before, clean cut and commanding in presence. He wore a brown leather jacket. Strode with purpose. He could have walked right on set for *The Breakfasters* and looked perfectly at home. Jack resented Harry's TV sheen, rubbing his unshaven jaw in quiet inadequacy. He had slept too well in his own bed and, after making a conscious effort to eat two slices of toast, one even buttered, had chosen to skip a shave to get there on time. He figured seventy thousand dollars bought a little bit of professionalism. Jack had no qualms taking Harry's money, but he wasn't going to swindle him. Although the money hadn't cleared yet. Jack had checked.

'Morning,' Jack said, standing. They shook hands because they felt like they should. This was business, after all.

Jack looked over to the station. It was an older building, seven storeys tall, with thick stone abutments between floors. The ground floor had more showbiz pizzazz with floor-to-ceiling glass. Neatly trimmed hedges lined the walkway at hip height. Jack's stomach gurgled with unease. It felt strange to be back at the place that had both built him up and cut him down. He was glad he'd had breakfast. His internal soldiers were unalarmed but wary, shields laid down nearby.

'Let's go,' Jack said.

Harry skimmed his hand across the hedge tops as they walked. He didn't seem particularly interested in where they were, but Jack reminded himself not to take Harry's casual nature as ambivalence. He'd played Jack with the empty envelope – he was sharper than he let on. Jack reckoned he was waiting to see what Jack would do. Get his money's worth. The doors slid open.

The foyer was chilled by the combination of glass and tile. There was a reception counter, and then a series of plastic barriers that swung in when you scanned a pass. The ground floor was the news floor, felt-walled cubicles in a grid. The network liked to show off their productivity, just like the windows into the street for the breakfast show, and putting the news floor in public view of the foyer kept up appearances: *Look how busy we are.* Jack could hear the hive murmuring through the foyer, see people jogging back and forth. People walk quickly on news floors. Good cardio. In this studio, the speed at which people moved decreased the higher up the building you were. First floor was marketing, still hurried. Second floor was sales, similarly urgent but they walked less and talked more. You could take a breather on Third with the editors (unless there was a deadline), and keep decelerating all the way up to the leisurely board rooms.

In front of the entry gates were tall, rectangular arches. Metal detectors. Jack made a note; Sam hadn't got his gun in through the front door. Jack didn't recognise the man at the reception desk. He walked over. 'I'm Jack Quick. I used to work here.'

The guy looked unimpressed and waited for Jack to continue. His stance wasn't quite rudeness, but it was designed to assert disinterest. He probably thought Jack was a sign-holding window-watcher. 'I used to work here' didn't hold much sway. The speed gradient carried right through from the news floor to terminal velocity in the foyer. The fastest you'll walk in television is when you're leaving it, Jack knew.

'The two of us are here to see Gareth Bowman.' Jack gestured at Harry, who was inspecting a pot plant.

The receptionist started a rebuttal, along the lines of how people just can't come in and demand to see the CEO, when Harry noticed he was being talked about and started walking over. Mid-spiel, the receptionist stopped. Pointed at Harry. 'You look familiar,' he said.

'Don't I just,' Harry boomed, arriving next to Jack. He stooped to the counter, melted both arms across it and smiled. 'Blew my damn head off two weeks ago. Never felt better! Now, let's see about this Bowman fella.'

Two minutes later, in the lift on the way up to meet Gareth Bowman, Jack felt very small indeed.

Gareth insisted they meet in the boardroom, on the sixth floor and with a view of Sydney Harbour. The water was choppy, tufts of white foam cresting the blue surface. The boardroom table was hulking, red oak, and had sixteen places. Jack and Harry marooned themselves in two on the far end, curling around a corner. Harry grew impatient quickly and stood. Gripped the back of a chair and rocked it.

'What's the plan?' he asked.

'Talk to Gareth.'

'Any more detail?'

'Sure. Wait for Gareth to show up. Then talk to Gareth.'

Harry pursed his lips, nodded. Jack wondered if he was, for the first time, seeing a real emotion: Harry was annoyed.

Jack didn't really have a plan, but he figured if he bought into Harry's 'one thing', then at the very least they needed access to the 'crime scene' (for what? Blackmail? Corporate espionage? Certainly not murder). That was the studio, including the staff, and ideally Sam's laptop. The problem was that Jack was not only an ex-employee, but now a former jailbird. They needed the CEO to get them in. But seeing as it had been Harry who'd talked their way in, Jack figured it was in his interest to try to make it seem like it was *his* influence that carried weight. The less Harry knew, the more valuable Jack was. He planned to keep it that way.

Jack looked around. A muted TV on the back wall played the pitch-package for the new ratings season line-up on a loop. All different shows of all different genres. The imagery was erratic. A slap. Tears rolling down cheeks. A gun. A hospital bed. A car down a dirt road. Someone saying something serious that you didn't need lip-reading skills to be able to guess was some derivative of 'this isn't over yet'. A plate of food. Someone lifting a trophy above their head. The gun again, this time close up and firing. People running outside what looked like a movie theatre on fire. A now-dead man smiling behind a desk. A rose on a silver platter. A woman walking out of a pool in a bikini. Because under the TV sheen, people always *walked* out of pools, Jack mused, instead of scrambling out the side on their bellies. Logos and titles slid in diagonally. There'd be a pumping summer hit behind it all, Jack knew. Something with the word 'happy' or 'love' in the chorus so everyone could pretend that sitting in front of the screen is living life to the fullest. That's how you make Must See Television: everything thrown into a blender of colour and fury. Pour ingredients into the mix and hope it's exciting. TV was no different from Liam: pump enough into it, pretend it's alive.

Gareth Bowman strolled in. Strolling was a sixth-floor luxury. He was holding a KeepCup of coffee. Lean. Played squash. That was all Jack really needed to sum up the CEO of Channel 14. If it was a casting brief he'd scrawl *keepcup, plays squash* on it and let the casting director fill in the blanks of some rich, fit, middle-aged bloke who cares about the environment to the extent of saving fifty cents a cup on coffee and plays a land sport with goggles on.

'Jack,' Gareth said in greeting, setting his coffee down. Then he nodded at Harry, 'Good to see you again.' *Again?* Jack looked at Harry, who was clearly displeased with the reunion. Gareth walked over and placed a hand on his shoulder. 'Of course, we would have both hoped for different circumstances. Must be so hard. Especially today.'

Harry shrugged off the hand and sat down. Gareth slid his coffee to the seat across from Jack, but with an intervening chair between him and Harry. As if setting up that he was interviewing them, and not the other way around.

'What's today?' whispered Jack.

'Sam's birthday,' said Harry quietly.

'Oh.' That seemed a strange thing for Harry not to have mentioned. 'Happy birthday, I suppose.'

'It's not my birthday.'

'What?' Jack didn't hide his confusion very well.

'It's Sam's. We're born on different days. Christ. *Midnight* Twins ring a bell? Aren't I paying you to investigate something?' Harry hissed.

Gareth cleared his throat, a bunny-hop of a noise that implied they were wasting his time. 'I can guess why you're here, Harry,' he said. 'Jack, you're a little bit more of a mystery.'

Jack fished his recorder from his pocket. If this turned into anything useful he'd need something better than the handheld. Directional mics. Wind muffs. But this was mainly to show Harry he was taking it seriously; Jack had no intention of using the recordings. It would do for now. Just like Harry's empty envelope, or any good interview. You played the person across from you, not the cards in your hand.

He turned it on and the screen glowed orange. He felt a little bit of his old self rattle inside him. 'Here's a clue,' he said.

'Last time we did this, Jack,' Gareth eyed the recorder, 'you cost me a lot of money.'

'Don't pretend you didn't make it back covering my trial. And then some. I saw the ads. A TV show inside a TV show. What a concept.'

'And you threw someone off a building.'

'They fell,' Jack said.

'I don't want to be recorded.'

'How am I supposed to make a show if I don't record you?'

'Your new show's not about me.'

'Isn't it?'

Gareth looked between Jack and Harry. It clicked. He took a sip of coffee, extended a finger and tapped it twice on the table in front of the recorder. Then he leaned back and took another sip. Waited. He was wearing a grey suit, no tie. Top two buttons undone. The type of corporate outfit that said *hey, I'm a fun guy, I work in TV*. Provided you ignored the two-thousand-dollar jacket. Jack took the hint and pocketed the device.

Gareth put his coffee down. 'I liked your show, Jack. Good ratings. So I'll give you a few more minutes. But Sam Midford has made the last two weeks of my life very' – he touched his mouth with a fingertip – 'complicated.'

'Complicated is interesting.'

'And you do complicated very well. Investors . . .' He knotted his hands, shrugged. Jack was out of touch with interviewing. Gareth had control here. His body language was closed off, disengaged. Leaned back from the table, arms folded. He wasn't under any pressure. 'Not so much.'

'I think it's a ripe story.'

'Sure. Maybe it is. Guy kills himself on live television, and on my station too. Everyone who wants my footage has my watermark splayed across it. That's great. You know what our highest rating show this year was?'

Jack shook his head. It couldn't be Sam's final episode. That would be watched again and again online, but it had been over in a dramatic flash. Word couldn't have built enough to grow the ratings during the episode itself. 'The late news bulletin?' Jack guessed. 'After his death?'

'Wrong.' Gareth smiled. 'One week later, in Sam's usual spot, we had half an hour dark. A tribute of nothing but a black screen. A minute's silence but longer, and televised.'

'Smart move,' Jack complimented. Hoping that maybe buttering him up was a better strategy than sparring.

Gareth seemed unimpressed by the attempt. 'I know,' he said smugly, disinterested in Jack's praise but taking it all the same.

'You just had nothing to program over it,' Harry contributed. 'Cleverness has nothing to do with it. A repeat of *Midnight Tonight* would have been insensitive. Choosing the episode would have been a nightmare. You don't want some inadvertent line, a monologue joke that was off-colour, or any action or sideways glance to be seen in a new light. You've pulled all his episodes from your streaming platform too, so you're aware of that. And not to mention the scrutiny that somebody had done this in your studio. Your work environment, your security. Everyone's watching. But you didn't want it to seem like you didn't care for him, or that you were in the process of putting up these shields, so you couldn't cover the slot with a movie or something quick and commercial. So a blank screen it was.'

'Nice,' Gareth said. He was now focused on Harry and ignoring Jack completely. Still under no pressure. Jack watched Harry talking about television with interest. There was skill there. Experience. These men knew each other, Jack reminded himself. 'You missed one. We could have done a tribute concert.'

'You're too cheap for that,' rebutted Harry.

Gareth laughed. 'Right you are. So what? Twenty-three minutes of a black screen. With ads, of course. Still put it in the guide, so two million people tuned in, convinced it was some kind of prank and Sam was going to suddenly appear. Reincarnated. Or that it might be the secret start to some exposé or documentary. We were prepared to add in a slide-show of pics if people turned off, but Twitter exploded. People wanted to watch, *just in case*. And once they're in, you make them chase their losses – because if they turn it off and something *does* happen, who's the one that wasted that invested time? Give 'em nothing, make 'em wait for something. It's why cricket works.' He shook his head, indulging in the memory.

'Close as I'll get to a Moon Landing.' He paused. 'This was, obviously, before people learned about who he really was.'

'And who, exactly,' said Jack, trying to steer the conversation back, 'was the real Sam?'

'He's your new show idea, is he? Listen, I'm on Team Quick.' A placating palm in the air. 'I am. Short of a newsreader killing themselves next week, your triumphant return would be publicity domination. But I've got bad news. This isn't it. This is a story that every network has told by now. Multiple times. Me included.'

'Sam was—'

'Sam was a man with a guilty conscience. He had child pornography on his laptop and a gun in his mouth. There's a one-hour special in that. Not a series.' Gareth checked his watch. That was a grim sign.

Jack tried to remind himself of his former self. A producer who could talk his way into any office, home or even police station. A man for whom words were weapons. 'I think the contents of his laptop were planted,' Jack said. *Believe one thing.*

'Planted?' Gareth raised his eyebrows. But it was mocking, exaggerated. Jack hadn't had the impact he'd hoped for. The bonanza of podcasts and television shows, like his original Curtis Wade documentary, had gifted planted evidence with a boy-who-cried-wolf quality. The default position of any criminal, these days, was *conspiracy*. It had to be, in television, for anyone to watch. Sam Midford's pornography had to be discounted, construed as artificial, because otherwise he was a criminal, not a victim. And if you have a criminal, you don't have any empathy. And without empathy, you don't have any viewers. If Jack was filming this, that would be step number one: make Sam a victim. Otherwise he was just a bad guy who did a bad thing. Only difference was, he did it in public. The line between 'he will be missed' and 'good riddance' was a thin one.

'That's your favourite word, Jack,' Gareth continued. 'Planted. You've got the greenest thumbs out of any journalist I know.'

'I'm not a journalist.'

'You're not. And you don't work here anymore. And Sam Midford's suicide is my concern, not yours.' Gareth stood.

Jack looked at Harry, uncharacteristically quiet. Fuck him. Jack had been honest, said he couldn't guarantee he'd be useful. It was Harry's decision to pay him seventy grand, not his. He never believed the laptop was tampered with. He never believed it was anything but suicide. But the deposit money hadn't yet come through, Jack hadn't signed anything legally binding, and there was much Harry hadn't told him – not least that he and Gareth Bowman already knew each other. Jack started to wonder: if he walked out of here without at least a starting point, would Harry renege? These thoughts swirled together like the highlight reel on the wall behind him, each jostling for space. He was failing here. He could feel the blood in his ears. It wasn't about the seventy grand. It was about the one hundred and ninety-six days. He breathed in through his nose and all he could hear was a raspy mechanical wheeze. Liam's machine.

He wasn't making a TV show. But he was making something. For an audience of one: Harry Midford. It didn't matter what he believed. This wasn't a documentary, this was a drama. He had to play a part for his payday. The producer in him rose up, blood in his neck and bile in his throat. How easily he slipped into his old skin. He'd spent a career creating killers. He could create victims too, if he wanted. He knew how to grab attention. He thought about the word Harry had used to distract him in prison.

'Murder,' he said.

'What?' Gareth scoffed.

'It wasn't a suicide. It was a murder,' Jack repeated, more confident now. Louder. He could see Gareth deciding whether or not to laugh in his face. Jack continued. 'We have compelling evidence that the pornography on Sam's work laptop was planted to draw the attention away from his death.' They didn't. Jack didn't even know what was on there or how much they had found. 'That Sam was under duress from a third party at the time of his death.' He wasn't, but to create a victim, you had to create a killer, and Jack thought 'third party' sounded particularly ominous. 'He didn't own a gun. One must have been supplied to him.' That was a guess, but a reasonable one under Australian gun laws. 'And Sam loved his partner. Why would he do this in front of her? Unless he felt like he had to?' Jack could see Gareth processing the information, but the key was to keep his assertions short and in a flurry, a verbal assault of such pace that no single point could be focused on, where enough convincing half-truths somehow wound up feeling whole. Jack didn't need to fill Gareth with proof, he just needed to make it feel like he could. The lies slid out his mouth. Throat oiled. Practised. 'Someone did this to him. He would have felt like he didn't have a choice.'

Gareth gripped and massaged the leather on the back of his chair. Jack knew if he responded with a statement it meant he'd bought most of it. If he responded with a question, Jack still had a long way to go.

'What is your compelling evidence?' Gareth asked.

Damn.

Harry drew a breath, opened his mouth. Jack put a hand on his shoulder, as if to say, *I've got this*. Harry swallowed his words.

'Well, I can't tell you that, can I?' said Jack. 'Otherwise I can't sell it to Channel 12.'

'Wait. I thought—'

'Gareth, I produced one of the highest rating television shows you've ever seen. I've been in jail for a year and a half, sitting on my arse. I'm not going to sit in this boardroom any longer than I have to.' Now it was Jack's turn to stand up. Harry, not on-script, missed the cue. He sat there, gormless. 'I hope you enjoy explaining at the AGM how a murder was committed in your very own station, and not only did you *not notice*, but another channel got there first. Thank you for your time.' Then, curtly: 'Harry.'

Harry caught up and rolled his chair back.

There was a long pause. The leather of the chairback squeaked under Gareth's thumbs. 'I don't have a crew,' he said eventually. A statement.

Got him. Now Jack was doing *Gareth* a favour. Meeting him in the middle. All Jack's old tricks were coming into play.

Gareth continued, 'Production's onsite with our dating competition.'

'Luckily, we don't need one,' Jack said. 'We're still working on discovery. The two of us will do just fine. In fact, I don't need anything formal from you right now. Once we break the format, we can talk production.'

'And your evidence?'

Jack ignored this. 'I need all the footage from the day of the shooting. Of *Midnight Tonight* and your security cameras. And I want to be able to go where I want and talk to who I want. After we've done a bit of groundwork, I'll send you the bible.' A series bible was a document that laid out all the episodes, plotlines and character arcs, as well as information on the look and feel of the program. By pretending he had it, Jack was reinforcing he was in a position to pitch to other networks. 'You'll be the first to see it.'

'It's exclusive?'

'It's exclusive.' Jack reached his hand over the boardroom table, which took a fair lean. It was an easy thing to promise, exclusivity of a program that wouldn't exist. Everything in television is an easy promise.

'Get your thingy out,' said Gareth. 'You can record this bit.'

Jack took out his recorder, placed it on the table. Pressed record.

Gareth stooped over the table to be closer to the mic. Spoke vertically. 'I've got first-look at the documentary you plan to make on the death . . .' Gareth paused. 'The *murder*, of Sam Midford.' Gareth straightened, and grabbed Jack's hand at last. 'Agreed?'

'Agreed.'

'Harry Midford is also in the room as witness.' Their hands stayed connected.

'Sure,' said Harry.

'Right. You can turn it off.' They separated. Gareth pointed at the device. 'I want a copy of that. I'm serious. Channel 12 has given away the winner of our last three singing competitions, *and* this year's *Top Cook*. It's like they're determined to take us down. You thought you got sued last time? If Tom Dwyer sees this before I do, I will hunt you.'

'You're jealous of Dwyer's ratings pull?' Jack wheeled his chair back to sit again, in invitation to continue. Gareth didn't mimic him.

'Fuck no. Dwyer couldn't pull the skin off a burn victim. No more questions now. Follow me,' Gareth said, and started moving. Jack pocketed his recorder and followed. Knowing when to quit was one of his newer skills. Harry tactfully waited until Jack had walked in front of him, placing a gap between him and Gareth, before falling in behind them. Gareth led them out of the boardroom, back to the elevator, talking over his shoulder as he went. 'Midnight's show was in Stage Three. We haven't packed it up yet. Weren't really sure what to do with it. Plus, it looked good as set dressing for news crosses. No one else had that. You know your way around, right?'

They were at the elevators now. Glass walled, looking out into the central space that was ringed by each floor. Just like the prison, mused Jack. But making TV has more cigarettes.

Jack looked over the railing. Right-angled cubicle walls made the ground floor look like a maze. It was calmer up here, on the corporate floors. Editing suites, including Jack's old office, were in the middle. Sound stages were on the bottom, ringed around the news floor. Jack knew where Stage Three was. He nodded. Gareth pressed the down button.

'I'll send Beth Walters down to meet you. She's Sam's executive producer. Well, she was.' He held the door open with a forearm. Jack and Harry stepped inside and Jack deliberately waited. Harry pressed the button for One. Gareth kept talking. 'Beth will get key-cards set up for you.' He paused a second, arm still barring the lift, and looked between the two of them. 'I'm not sure how to put this in corporate wording for you, Jack.'

'Plain's fine.'

'Don't fuck me, okay?' He removed his arm. Pointed. 'And send me that recording.'

CHAPTER 7

'Mate.' Harry slapped a thick hand on Jack's shoulder, back to his shiny-grinned boisterousness. '*Compelling evidence.* Jesus. Even I believed we had something.' Then he rattled his fists up and down, as if running on the spot, an energetic tic. 'This is *fun*!' The elevator was not big enough for Harry's exuberance. Jack rested the back of his head on the glass. He was tired. Harry was still talking. 'Bowman swallowed it, but, shit, he really doesn't trust you.'

'I just spent a year and a half in prison for lying,' said Jack. 'You shouldn't either.'

Jack hadn't been prepared enough to come back here. The whole building was triggering. The epileptic rotation of adverts. The rustle of the ground floor. Any of the bathrooms where, sometimes, at ten in the morning, Jack on his knees and a man snorting a line off the basin would lock eyes conspiratorially. *I won't tell if you don't.* He let the cool glass of the elevator chill the nape of his neck. The corners of his mouth tickled with saliva. Anticipation. Spear at his throat.

He'd lied, but he'd also been lied to. Gareth was only interested when Jack had raised the potential of another station's scrutiny.

Channel 14 would have received plenty of that already, but only while the death of Mr Midnight was still a tragedy. Gareth was probably thankful that Sam's laptop had turned up what it did, because the eye of judgement would have shifted, the attention less worthy. In case it shifted back, Gareth wanted control of Jack's story. Which meant he was keen to guide the story *away* from something else. But Jack had expected nothing less from Gareth, who had a company to protect. He had been prepared to spar with the CEO.

It was Harry Midford who surprised him.

The problem was that he and Harry hadn't had a proper interview in the prison. Jack had taken everything he'd been told at face value because Harry held the promise of writing Jack's cheque. They'd had one half-hour meeting behind bars, a brief phone call, and then this morning. He had only been home eighteen hours; he hadn't had time to do background. He didn't know Harry at all.

But Gareth did. Sure, maybe they'd met at a premiere or an afterparty, but that didn't seem right. Harry knew him well enough to be intimidated. He'd been doing this flashy showman bit for Jack but dropped it with Gareth. That was more than casual. In the boardroom, Harry had talked intelligently and fluidly about the behind-the-scenes issues with *Midnight Tonight*. And, when they'd stepped into the elevator, Jack had waited for Harry to press the button for the first floor. How had he known how to get to Stage Three? Jack figured most people would guess that sound stages were on the ground floor. They're big, they have high ceilings for lights and no one wants to lug equipment upstairs. But Stage Three was opposite the elevator, so if they went to ground they'd have to weave through the news desks. It was faster to get out on the first floor and walk around on that level, before going down the stairs. Gareth had asked Jack if he knew where *he* was going. Harry shouldn't have had the foggiest. Let alone a shortcut.

They got off the elevator. Harry took a moment to lean on the banister and look down at the news floor.

'You used to work here,' Jack said, propping his elbows on the railing too.

Harry turned to him. Jack saw his cheek twitch, that gleam of a smile taking an extra second in revealing itself. Like framing a shot to catch a flash of violence but keep a PG rating intact. Draw the knife as the curtains close. Something cracked in Harry's brow, furrowed, and his teeth retreated. Jack could see he had to make a conscious effort to push the cowards forward. Then he was smiling like Jack had never said anything. Jack doubled down and took out his recorder, flashed it like a tough guy showing off the butt of a pistol, sitting on his hip behind a pulled-back jacket. The same power in this device, Jack was remembering. Words were once his weapons.

'I'm assuming on *Midnight Tonight*,' said Jack. 'You don't anymore. Which means something happened.'

'Which means bad blood. Sure.' Harry finished Jack's thought process for him. He turned back to look out over the space. Muttered, 'Fair guess.'

'You're paying me to pretend this is a murder,' Jack said, not bothering to dress it up. 'I'll play. But it doesn't work when both of us are acting.'

'Bowman's a prick,' Harry said, straightening and walking towards the stairs. Jack fell into step beside him. 'If that's what you're after.'

'Grudges make good motive.'

'It's TV. Everyone's got one. Throw a dart.'

'Say I hit Gareth.'

'I'd shake your hand.' Harry put his mask up again, then he sighed. 'Fine.' He breathed it like a petulant child. All that was missing was the foot-stamping. 'Sam and I met him in Montreal. He said he thought we'd be great on TV, gave us the show, which went to pilot. It was a big deal – we were only twenty-four. That was when it was *The Midnight Show*.'

'*The Midnight Show*?'

'Back when we were the Midnight Twins. Five years ago. Keep up.' Jack had no idea what Harry was talking about, but now he'd got him talking he didn't want to cut him off. 'The pilot went well,' Harry continued. 'The network was frothing. And then Bowman takes Sammy into his office, tells him I'm dead weight. Tells him they'll only go to series if Sam goes it alone.'

'He dropped you?'

'I quit.'

'Sounds like you were pushed and told to say you jumped,' Jack said. 'They forced you out.'

'You can put it like that if you want, but it wasn't Sam's fault. It wasn't fair on him to make that decision, so I made it for him.'

They reached a huge industrial door, floor to ceiling with hydraulic pistons crisscrossing the frame, like the door of an airport hangar. It slid from left to right, and was currently open half a metre. Dark inside. A lightbox on the wall next to the opening – ON AIR – was grey. Off.

They walked into the gap single file. It was pitch black, the light soaked up by the black floors, walls and ceiling all designed to keep the stage lights focused. The thin panel of light from the doorway didn't stretch far. Jack could sense the size of the space, his body intuiting the cavernous room. He edged in after Harry. Neither of them knew where the light switch was. He could sense a hulking mass to his right. The audience seating, he assumed. Several hundred chairs on a portable rake. He looked to the floor, hoping for some luminescent tape, laid down in guidance. Nothing. The studio lights had probably been off for days, nothing to charge the tape's glow. He followed the soft shuffle of Harry's similarly slow, exploratory steps, and wondered, for a glimmer of a second, if this was a man he needed to be afraid of.

'What about the money?' Jack said.

'I told you it'll clear.'

Harry was further ahead than Jack had guessed. He raised his voice. 'I meant that Gareth made Sam rich. Left you out. Greed's just as good as a grudge for motive.'

'It's TV,' Harry echoed. 'Every motive plays. Sex. Money. Greed. Power. Drugs. Revenge.' He listed them off like the swirling buzzwords on the promo upstairs. They might have even been the same ones. He was right, too. Focusing on such motives wouldn't narrow down suspects – not in this business. 'Half the people here would kill to sit in that chair. Your dartboard's getting pretty clogged.'

'He still made Sam a star. And a fortune.'

'I created the format, so I still get two per cent. And Sam made me a consultant. Though of course Bowman didn't want me near the thing so it was more honorary than actual work, but that was a bit more in the pocket. He looked after me. Money's not a problem.'

It hasn't come into my account yet, Jack thought. 'You work?' he asked.

'I told you, I have residuals.'

'You walked away on good terms?'

'Sure.'

In the dark, Jack was more tuned in to *how* Harry was talking, not just what he was saying. The same way listeners could zero in on a specific moment on a podcast. Everything's significant under scrutiny. A cough becomes a confession.

If he were producing this conversation, Jack would have split the audio, jacked up the volume of the bass in the cough and pulled back from the speaking voice, increased the ambient noise to add clutter, and suddenly it would seem like nerves. Jack used to use all those tricks. If he'd been editing Harry, he would have left a larger pause between their words to signify that Harry was deflecting, but in person Jack had realised Harry's tic. The way his voice almost physically shrugged when they'd talked yesterday on the phone. Harry answered questions he didn't want to answer quickly, casually, and in the affirmative. As if hearing what you wanted to hear would get you off his back. *Sure* from Harry Midford meant *if that's what you want.*

'Bullshit,' Jack said. 'Your brother would have had more power the longer the show went on. Season by season. These shows work like that. You're the star first. Then you're the executive producer. Then you're running your own production company and controlling the thing top to bottom. He could have brought you back if he wanted.'

'We had a falling out,' Harry said.

'Over?'

'Me leaving.'

'That was five years ago.'

'Yeah. Okay. We had a falling out five years ago. Over the show. You record that?' Short answers. Deflection. His footsteps stopped. Jack stopped too, in case he crashed into him. 'Jesus. You ask questions and restate the answers. No wonder you get good sound bites. It's like talking on a hamster wheel.'

'You paid for this,' Jack reminded him. They stood, faceless, apart in the dark.

'It was normal, brotherly stuff. Okay? Nothing to want him dead over.'

'What was he like, leading up to his death? Did you notice anything?'

'We didn't really talk.'

'Didn't really?'

'Didn't at all. Okay? Where are you going?' Harry had heard Jack start to move again.

'Because of your falling out?'

'Sure.' There it was again. *Sure.*

'That was five years ago.'

'Yeah.' Harry was moving too. There was a clunk as he hit something. Swore.

'You haven't talked for five years and yet you know your brother well enough to know he wouldn't kill himself?'

Harry took a long time to think on his reply.

Jack, who had made his way to the green glow of the exit sign and used its residual light to track a light switch on the far wall, stayed with his finger on the switch but kept the lights out. Let Harry stew.

Normally, an interview like this would be challenging. That was why prison interviews were so hard to get truth from, because they were always over the phone. On the flip-side, they made great TV. It's easy to make an inmate a victim – innocent, framed – when all you're doing is playing their crackly voice over a still image. It's easy to make a cop look dirty when you can zoom in on them sweating, pulling at their collar. Characterisation is in the framing. Keep anyone the audience is supposed to like away from the focus of the shot. Because people don't look natural on screen, they look uncomfortable – pallid or flushed without stage make-up, sweating under lights, squinting as they're not used to the glare. And uncomfortable looks guilty. If you want a victim shot – a tear-laden, splotchy-cheeked, snot-dribbled testimony – the line between insincere and emotive is all down to how natural they look on camera. Even the grieving widows have to be pretty enough to be ugly.

Jack should have been wary talking to Harry in this environment. Words wear disguises in the dark. There's a reason it's when we tell secrets. Late at night, under covers. A reason that's the first time most people say 'I love you'. If someone tells you they love you in daylight, believe them.

But that was any normal person. Harry, who worked so hard to keep anything genuine from his expressions, resting behind a wall of chemically whitened teeth and sparkling eyes, was the opposite. To get him to be honest, Jack had to take his face away. Harry talked a lot. In the dark, he was finally saying something.

'Yeah,' Harry said eventually. 'Even with five years between drinks, I think I know him. That's why I hired you.'

'Is it?'

'Even if there is no *who*, I was hoping you could help me find out *why*.'

'But you think Gareth planted the pornography. Or at least you want to blame him for something.' Harry was quiet, which Jack took as agreement. 'So let me ask you this – is that really why you hired me? Do you want me to clear your brother's name, or are you trying to get revenge on Gareth for cutting you loose?'

'Mate,' Harry gave a soft chuckle, 'ever heard of multi-tasking?'

Before Jack could respond, his thoughts were interrupted by a series of sequential clunks, like doors slamming in a corridor. One by one, rows of rectangular lights shuddered to life above. And Jack got his first look at the graveyard of both *Midnight Tonight* and Mr Midnight himself.

CHAPTER 8

The studio lighting was clinical, and it exposed both the size and barrenness of the sound stage. Normally a rig of reds and blues in the roof, and tripod stalks with warm yellow spots, would fill in the tones. But the spotlights had been packed away, and the rigging bar lay on the floor, wires travelling up into the ceiling, the lights stripped from it and repurposed somewhere else. Because the walls, floor and ceiling were painted black, the stark white light from the remaining fluorescent bars above bounced straight off the surfaces, leaving the whole room in too sharp a focus. Jack could see every shoe scuff on the painted floor, every seam where the stage was inelegantly bolted together: everything that was so perfectly glossed over on a broadcast. Studio shows are supposed to look fun, a panning shot of a packed audience cheering to the smiling host, but pull back and all you have is a few dozen people crammed into cold raked seating, with some sweaty part-time comedian roped into 'Audience Warm Up' as his promised big break, standing just off camera and attempting to gee-up applause as the anchor stuffs his monologue up for the third time. This was the real version. The version where the audience is tired of wheeling out praise for someone who can't get their lines right. The version where the smiling host has a bullet in his head.

Jack blinked away the harsh light, which seemed to be sharpening with time, and looked around. Harry was somewhere behind a curtain or a set dressing; Jack assumed he'd wandered off to look for a light switch. The space was huge, and it looked more like a trucking garage than a TV studio. That the space had been ransacked for its technical equipment made it feel even emptier. White tape marked the floor, crosses and right-angles in a crime-scene-chalk mimicry of what used to be in the room. There, the lights. There, the cameras. There, the teleprompter.

Jack had guessed correctly about the audience seats: they'd been on his right as he walked in and were flipped up, bolted into rows on a rake. There was more white tape creating boxed rectangular paths, showing where to walk without tripping on cords. Everything in a TV studio is taped out, set down, has its place.

As if she too had a mark on the floor to get to, a woman strode in (not at newsroom speed, but still a stride), flipped a seat and dropped into it. Beth Walters, Jack assumed. What had Gareth said her role was? A producer? She had a satchel over one shoulder, a tablet poking out the top. A black knee-length skirt, and a matching jacket over a plain white t-shirt. She crossed one leg over the other and started tapping at her phone, the soft click of her fingernails filling the silent studio. 'You're not going to find anything in the dark,' she said without looking up. 'I'm here to show you around.' She didn't move.

'Some tour,' Jack said.

'You want the tour?' She gave up on her phone and made a series of sweeping gestures with her typing hand, flicking it limp-wristed around the room as if skipping stones. She punctuated each movement with a description as she worked in a circle: 'Stage door. Stage. Curtains. Rigging. Backstage. Follow-spot. Green room. Audience.

Dead guy.' Her finger lingered in the middle of a rounded desk that dominated the set. Its front was translucent plastic and in its centre had a three-dimensional squiggle – which Jack assumed lit up in neon when filming – of the name *Midnight Tonight*. She swatted a hand as if shooing him, and then returned to her phone. 'Knock yourself out.'

'She's not here to show us around,' said Harry flatly, emerging around the side of the set and walking towards her. His gaze was steady. Sizing her up. 'She's here to keep an eye on us.'

'*Ding ding*,' she said. Then she looked up to find the owner of the new voice, clocked Harry, and said, 'Oh. Happy birthday.'

'It's not my birthday.'

'Shit. Never could tell you guys apart.'

'Most people struggle.'

'Tell you what though, due to recent events . . .' She paused. 'I think it's getting easier.'

At that, Harry quickened the last few steps between them. Beth stood in response. Just as Jack started mentally practising his witness statement, Harry spread his arms and embraced her, unleashing a bark of a laugh.

'Beth,' he said, pulling away, big hands gripping each of her shoulders. She wasn't small, but he still engulfed her. As if her coat was hanging on nothing but a wire hanger, rather than bones and flesh, and he was shaking the creases out. It occurred to Jack that Harry held her the way people held him. By the shoulders, at arm's length: dwarfed. Head cocked. Examining. But Harry's eyes were different. When people measured up Jack they were searching for flaws. Harry was just taking this woman in. 'Lost none of that black humour, I see. Been a while.'

'You deserve it. Took all this for you to come and see me.'

'I'll run out of siblings if we go get coffee.'

'So that's why you never tried to sleep with me?'

'Millions would die.'

She wrinkled her nose. 'You should be an acclaimed comedian now, you've got the trauma. Dead brother. Powerful.'

'That was a sperm joke.'

'I got it. I just expected better.' She turned to Jack, spoke to Harry. 'Speaking of wet patches, who's your mate?'

Jack didn't miss the aggression in her question. A third-person mate is no one's mate. 'This is my mate' means 'Meet a friend of mine'. 'Who's your mate?' means 'Who the fuck is this guy?'

Jack slid a hand between their reunion, pried them apart. 'Jack Quick.'

'I know *who* you are.' Beth rolled her eyes at Harry. 'I just couldn't be bothered saying, "Why are you here with the guy who parlays dead bodies for ratings, and what the hell has he convinced you to get into?"'

Jack reminded himself that she would know all of the fall-out from the vineyard documentary. HR would have had to brief everyone at the station in the way large companies respond to public crises. Banks, insurance companies, television: *right, we've been busted, so keep doing what you're doing, but now we're training you how not to tell anyone.* His past was a case study in what not to do. He had to assume he had no secrets from any of the staff here.

'Other way round,' Jack said.

'It was my idea,' Harry interjected. 'Jack's helping me.'

'Jack? *Helping*?'

'Sure.' Jack shrugged in backup. 'I don't believe a lick of it but he pays well.'

Beth furrowed her brow at Harry. 'How much are you paying him? He's taking you for a ride.'

'He's not,' said Harry.

'I am,' Jack cut in. 'I've told him.'

Beth considered this. 'Honesty a new fit for you, Mr Quick?'

'Chafes occasionally,' Jack said.

Harry, tired of people talking around him and not at him, clomped off towards the *Midnight Tonight* desk. Jack swapped a conspiratorial *I don't know why I'm here either* glance with Beth that seemed to be returned in mutual camaraderie. Even though on the surface they were here for material reasons – money, boss's orders – both of them knew they were here to entertain Harry's whims. And there'd be a point where someone had to sit him down and say that enough was enough, and that his brother was gone, and maybe he was the person his hard-drive said he was. But that was perhaps Harry's best trick: neither of them knew him well enough to intervene. By surrounding himself with acquaintances, he ensured no one cared enough to stop him trudging through any fantasy he wanted instead of dealing with his grief. An actual friend might step in. Jack blinked back to the night before, squared off against his father in Liam's bedroom, where he'd had the conviction to object. Here his loyalty was bought more out of laziness than anything else.

Jack, accepting his role as follower, trailed Harry onto the set. Beth lagged behind them. The stage itself was semicircular, like the hosting desk, arcing out towards the audience, raised a step off the floor and a good three metres away from the first row of seats. The surface was a shimmering black gloss. There were two chairs behind the desk, in the middle and on the right. Jack knew that was because Sam would sit in the middle for pieces to camera, and then shuffle to the left to interview guests on the right. That corresponded with three white Xs on the floor at even intervals around the stage. A camera for each perspective: host in host position, host as interviewer, and guest. Depending on the budget, there might have been a fourth, back further, for audience pans, or they could have used one of the main three that wasn't active at the time.

Behind the desk was ornamental cubic fake-wood panelling, crisscrossed like a bookcase that had been in a car accident.

Further right, a door was cut into the backdrop, and a set of stairs descended to the stage. Behind the scenes to get to these stairs was a simple stepladder, and every guest had to walk out and wave as if the whole thing was linked to a green room. Jack could picture the entrance: jangly music, the host saying 'please welcome a very good friend of mine' (which they always do even when they've never met), and polite applause. Harry disappeared up the steps into the backstage area. Also mounted to the set were two large flat-screen televisions. There should have been three, in symmetry with each chair position. The middle one was missing.

Jack peered under the table. There was residue under the desk. He pressed a finger to it. Sticky. He stood up.

Beth was standing on the other side of the desk, watching him pick his way through the set. 'Duct tape,' she said, before Jack could ask. 'He made a makeshift holster under the desk. We removed it.'

'What did it look like?'

'Silver tape. Looped over itself, pretty sturdy. Pretty far back too. No one would have had cause to look for it while we set up.'

Jack sat in the central chair and tried to imagine himself in Sam Midford's place. Spotlights on, sweat on his neck, stage make-up on his forehead like a tight wetsuit with an oiled lining. He looked at where the central camera would have been. Reached under and tapped his hand until he felt the stickiness, where the gun would have been waiting for Sam. It was far back, stretched his shoulder. Well hidden. 'I saw the metal detectors on the way in,' he said.

'We figured the same thing. He didn't walk on set with the gun in his pocket.'

Jack agreed. 'So he put it here in advance. The front desk, that's twenty-four hours?'

'Of course.'

'Any other way into the studio?'

Beth pointed to the large roller door that served as a side wall if closed. 'If we open this. It's not for casual entry, though – more for bumping in sets, if we need to back a truck in, smoko.'

'Done that recently?'

'Smoko?' She rolled her eyes. 'Nah. Would you believe every single tech's reformed since you went to prison?'

'Backed a truck in.'

'Maybe. I don't have a log. I'll see if I can find someone who knows.'

Jack locked his hands on the desk and rolled the chair back and forth, trying to put himself in Mr Midnight's shoes. 'Did he seem nervous to you?'

'Yeah, a bit. Me and the crew thought he was going to pop the question to his girlfriend. They've been at it a while. Got a kid.'

'What made you think that?'

'An intern saw a ring in his dressing room. Or so she said. Confidentiality and interns rarely go hand in hand here. And once the rumour started flying, well, it made sense.'

'How so?'

'You met him, right? He was a bit of a show-off.'

'No shit,' called Harry from behind the stage, his voice echoing through the studio like the ghost of his brother.

'You don't have to yell. You can hear us, we can hear you,' Beth said.

'What are you looking for?' Jack asked.

'Murder weapon.' Harry's voice bounced off the walls again.

'And on the day,' Jack said, returning his attention to Beth, 'he looked particularly agitated?'

'Not quite. More like what you said before. Nervous.'

'And why specifically?'

'I'd have to watch the footage.'

'I can watch that myself. I'm interested in your recollection. Stand where you were standing. Maybe it'll help.'

Beth hopped off the stage and stood beside the camera marks nearest to the entryway. 'Here.' She paused. 'I think. I don't remember exactly. But this usually lets me get backstage without walking in front of the audience.'

'So tell me how you get from nervousness to an imminent proposal?'

'He looked pale.' Beth was studying Jack hard, putting Sam in his place and slowly remembering the details that may have slipped away from her in the chaos after the gunshot. 'And he kept fidgeting. Yes.' A flash in her eyes. 'He had one hand under the desk. I thought it was the ring in his pocket.'

'And where is that ring?'

'Police didn't find one on him.' Beth shrugged. 'And we didn't find one when we packed up his dressing room. Must have never had one.'

'And if he didn't have a ring – that means when his hand was under the desk . . .'

'He was fiddling with the gun in the holster, and that's what was making him nervous.'

'That's what I was thinking too,' Jack said, delicate with his wording to make them sound like a team. Another old trick, textbook. It was working, too. Beth was warming to him, talking more.

'I brought the footage you asked for.' Beth patted her satchel. She came back to the stage, grabbed the guest's chair and rolled it around closer to Jack. She pulled out a tablet, placed it on the desk, and sat down. They both hunched over the screen. She and Sam had probably held pre-show meetings in almost exactly the same position. Jack shook the thought.

'Just the last episode though,' she added, somewhat apologetically. 'Gareth told me you wanted the security cameras, but . . .'

Jack raised his eyebrows, which said enough.

'I know, I know.' Beth sighed. 'We were filming some event television and security was paramount. It sounds stupid, but it was one of our soaps, a major death, so we couldn't risk it leaking. Spoilers are big business these days.'

Jack knew this was true. In prison one of the weaker inmates had stopped a beating from the most vicious of prison gangs by threatening them with *Game of Thrones* spoilers. 'Gareth told me you've had problems with Channel 12. In the ratings.'

'Pricks,' Beth affirmed.

'So your solution was to turn all the security cameras off?'

She nodded. 'And then we forgot to turn them back on. We only noticed when the police asked for the footage after Sam's . . .' She clearly didn't want to say 'suicide', and instead left it lingering.

'Jesus.' Jack leaned in, whispering, 'We're trying to make this *not* look like a conspiracy.'

'What's a conspiracy?' said Harry, stomping down the on-set stairs. A very good friend of mine, Jack thought – Harry Midford!

'There's no security camera footage,' Jack said, as matter-of-factly as he could.

Jack wasn't sure if he expected Harry to be disappointed or annoyed, but he definitely wasn't prepared for him to be excited. Harry enthusiastically slapped a meaty hand on Jack's bony shoulder, encasing it. 'Fuck. Yes.' He punctuated each word, giving Jack a rattle per beat as he did so. 'This is great.'

'Coincidence,' Beth said.

Harry mouthed the word *conspiracy* back at her.

'We'll settle for the episode footage.' Jack nodded down at the tablet. 'You right to watch this, Harry?'

'Seen it before.' He shrugged.

'Are you sure?' Beth said. 'We dumped the broadcast on our seven-second delay.'

'So?'

'There is' – she hesitated – 'slightly more footage on the live feed.'

'I told you. I'm fine.' Then he reached over the top of both of them and hit Play.

CHAPTER 9

The episode started with a wide pan, the camera swinging from the audience to the stage, underscored by a smattering of applause and a musical sting. It was quick, hard to see every face in the crowd as it spun. They seemed older, mostly silver haired. No one grabbed Jack's attention. A woman in a green cardigan sneezed. Beth was standing almost where she'd guessed she'd been, by the camera on the left, wearing a headset and all in black. The camera finished its pivot and settled on Mr Midnight, who was acting flattered with some *thank you, thank you* gestures. He was wearing a crisp white shirt with cufflinks, a thin unpatterned tie, and a tailored blue pin-stripe jacket. Jack noticed that the missing third plasma screen was mounted behind him; otherwise the set – though lit up – was the same as it was now. Then the applause faded, the camera zoomed tight for Sam to spread his arms, lock his eyeline, and say, 'Hello, and welcome to *Midnight Tonight*!'

It felt strange to be sitting in this man's chair, watching his final moments from only two weeks ago. Jack imagined the scene with the lights on, audience packed in, the hum of activity. He tried to see it through Sam's eyes. A man about to do the unthinkable in front of not only the world, but his partner and possibly his child. Yet, on tape, Sam didn't seem nervous at all. He seemed calm, professional. He suffered a small stutter as he repeated a word in the intro to the monologue, but he glossed over it with skill. *I may have already said that. Just a small technical error there.* A small squint at the tele-prompter to correct himself, the only sign of nerves the tapping of his left hand, and then back into the rat-a-tat jokes of the opening.

The crowd laughed as directed. Even if the writing wasn't great, each joke had the cadence of comedy – an upward inflection on the end of a bit, a surprise reveal – and in a room like this, the communal energy of the crowd chipped in. No one wants to ruin the show, so they laugh along and eventually get into the rhythm of having a good time. It's how people get hypnotised. It's why people lose their minds on *The Ellen Degeneres Show*. Jack noticed that Sam stuttered again near the end of a topical joke, and this time he dropped his shoulder, paused just a millisecond too long. Fiddling with something. *A ring in his pocket.*

Jack leaned in closer, trying to see behind Sam's act. Because this was an important moment. This was the exact moment Sam put his hand on the gun.

Sam covered up this next slip too, but now Jack could see his confidence was faltering. Was he sweating more? His right hand kept drifting under the table as if magnetised. He worked his way through a sketch and some more spoken material, and Jack won-dered if he would have noticed anything was wrong without the benefit of hindsight. But now, re-watching the scene, Sam's discom-fort was obvious.

As the little bar progressed along the bottom of the video, Jack began to feel uneasy. In anticipation of what he was about to see, he thought, but maybe something more. The whole scene felt dif-ferent to how he had been replaying it in his head. It had taken on the perception of this grandiose, front-page story – *Disgraced host*

shoots himself on live TV over child pornography possession! –
in Jack's mind. But the truth on the replay was much sadder. Sam
looked . . . scared.

As the episode progressed Sam became more and more agitated,
though still subtly. He rushed a joke about *Star Wars*, but the cul-
tural reference got a clap anyway. Now was when the warm-up guy
would step forward, off camera, and summon more applause, and
Mr Midnight would read out the names of their guests over the
noise, spinning the enthusiasm into the first ad break. Or, at least, he
was supposed to. Instead, he veered off script.

'Before I throw to a break here, I just wanted to say something.'

In the present, hunched over the screen, no one dared breathe.
Jack resisted the urge to glance at Harry, to see if that mask was
dropping, but, even though recorded and rewatchable, he felt he
couldn't stop watching the video. The moment felt intimate. Like
the energy of this viewing was crucial in some way. By this point,
Sam was ready to die. Could you tell? Jack wondered. Could you
see it, when a spirit leaves the body before the last breath is taken?
Eyes taped shut, you had no way of knowing. But what about when
it's all decided even though you're still breathing? Are you dead
before you die?

'Celia.' Sam said it twice. 'I love you. Forgive me. Change the
channel.'

The events in the video kicked up a notch from there. Everything
started moving. Fast. The gun was up. It was small. Not a chunky
black one, like the police guns Jack was most familiar with. Sam's
gun was smaller: a revolver, silver. Jack only caught a glimpse,
because then it was in Sam's mouth. Someone bumped the camera; the frame shuddered. Sam squeezed his eyes shut. His cheeks
blew out a second before the sound travelled. A sharp pop. One
eye flew open. The horrific death mask that had lingered on Jack's
television screen whisked past in a millisecond. Sam was already

flinging backwards. An arc of blood sputtered from his crown. The plasma behind him caught the bullet in the corner, cutting to black and splintering down one side. Sam's chair, on wheels, slid back with his recoil, before it tipped, and he dropped out of sight behind the desk with a thud. The plasma wobbled and fell after him with another crash.

There was a second of silence. The desk was empty. The only movement was the dripping of blood from the wooden set panelling. Then someone in the audience screamed, and the studio exploded into chaos. There was a thunder of footsteps. People ran past the camera's sight-line indiscriminately. A stagehand practically dove over the desk to get to Sam. Beth had also run onstage, and was talking animatedly into her headset. She looked behind the desk, flinched, and bent over, both hands on her knees, retching.

And then there was someone else, closer in frame, but they were heading neither to the door nor the stage. This person was walking towards the camera, yelling, pointing wildly, down the barrel. Their head was above the frame. A split second before the video ended, the camera tilted upwards and Jack caught a glimpse.

It was Gareth Bowman.

'Turn that fucking camera *off*!'

CHAPTER 10

The footage of the end of Mr Midnight's life lasted eight minutes and twenty seconds. Harry dragged a finger along the bar at the bottom of the video, replaying the fatal shot. Sam was thrown back out of his chair and dropped off screen in less than three of those seconds. Jack turned his gaze. Harry played it again. The sound followed Jack. That tiny pop. The thud of a body. The crash of the television falling after. Harry played it again.

Jack watched Harry's expression; it was focused and intent. His jaw was set. Analytical. His eyes flashed with the movements on the screen, his brother's death reflected in them, as he watched it again and again.

Turn that fucking camera off!

'Is Gareth often in the room for the recordings?' Jack asked Beth, if only because he felt talking might mask that *pop* from the tinny speakers. It seemed strange to him that the CEO would bother with the personal touch on a nightly program.

She thought for a second. 'Up to him. We see him around but he's not a part of the production. Depends if he wants to keep his eye on things.'

'How often?'

'Twice a season. Maybe three.'

'Does it strike you as interesting that he was in the room that night?'

'You're saying he knew something was . . .' Her words ran out of gas midway through her throat. Sam Midford could be heard in the background: 'Change the channel'. She ended up just shaking her head, disbelief and rebuttal all in one.

'I'm not saying anything. I'm asking if you find it interesting,' Jack said.

'I find it unremarkable,' she huffed.

'And he wanted the footage cut,' Harry contributed, looking up. 'Seems like arse-covering to me.'

'Agreed,' Jack said. Seeing Beth about to defend Gareth he added, 'But arse-covering on instinct. Someone's just died and he's broadcast it to a million people. That's his job on the line. And Gareth is a man of self-preservation if anything. He's got to get it off the air, quick. I probably would have done the same.'

Gareth was on autopilot, that much Jack was sure of. In the footage he looked stressed, unsure of what to do and his synapses had landed on one simple action – getting the camera off. It definitely seemed uncalculated. But so did everyone in the video. Beth leaning over and retching. The frantic run for the door by the live audience. The stage manager who lunged over the desk. The only person showing signs of what was coming was Sam.

'If Gareth had some sinister plan, the worst thing he could do is reveal himself on camera,' Beth agreed. The CEO looked mad, but he also looked innocent.

'Once the cameras were off, what else happened?' Jack asked.

'We knew we had to clear the room,' said Beth. 'That seemed like the logical thing. I'd seen him, tipped off his chair, and the blood was just starting to spread, and I wanted to be as far from that as possible, so I started shepherding. It was manic. The shooting had all happened so quickly, of course, so some people saw him do it, but others just heard a gunshot and screams. And if you hear that, these days . . .' She chewed a lip. 'You run. Right?'

It was obvious to Jack she was defending her actions. In the moment, she had taken the same approach as Gareth, grabbing onto anything practical. Later on – maybe when the first policeman had sat her down, maybe when she'd seen the footage replayed – that's when the regret nuzzled up.

Harry, who spelled subtlety with two 't's, either didn't notice or didn't care. 'You didn't try to help him?' he asked. It was calm, not cold, but an accusation all the same.

Beth blinked twice at him.

'You're one of the first up there on the video.' Harry jabbed a finger at the tablet. 'And you chose crowd control?'

'He was missing . . .' She shook her head, pivoted the tablet away from Harry and closed the video. When she spun it back so Jack could see, the video had been replaced with a photo album. In the first picture, Sam was lying on his back, his chair tipped over. The fallen television lay face down behind him. A glistening red puddle flowed from his shoulders, encasing his head like some kind of Aztec headdress. What caught Jack's eye first, though – and there was a lot of mess to catch the eye – was that Sam was wearing shorts. Bright pink boardies with green pineapples on them. He had one thong on his left foot. The other had, assumedly, been flung off.

Jack knew this wasn't unusual in television. TV hosts who had the luxury of sitting behind a desk often dressed formally from the waist up because it only mattered what was on camera. Studio audiences don't mind; they find it quirky and fun. It doesn't matter to the audience at home, because what you can edit out, or edit around, doesn't exist. Sam's body summed up that very discordance: crisp white cufflinks and a pressed blazer; bright pink shorts and bare legs. There was something wrong with the image. A dead man in half a suit.

Jack could also see what Beth had trailed off without saying, why she hadn't dived over the desk to help: Sam was missing the top half of his head. The damage was so bad it looked like it had been bashed in rather than blown out. His jaw hung slack, one side surely dislocated, exposing a mouth full of broken picket-fence teeth. The roof of his mouth was pulverised, a black entrance to a ragged cave. Harry, for once, swallowed his words.

Jack swiped through a few more photos. Most were similar, though time was passing between them. Sam's headdress bloomed. In the photos, everything looked *wet*. Chunks of bone in the blood like the white tufts on Sydney Harbour he'd seen from the boardroom.

In one photo the gun was clear, lying near the desk where Sam must have dropped it before he fell. It was indeed a small silver revolver, the type where you could load the bullets and spin the chamber, which Jack had seen in movies about Russian roulette. It looked like it had a short barrel so Sam could jam it right up the back of his mouth. Looked like it took six bullets.

'Cops take the gun?' Jack asked. Beth nodded.

'They took a whole bunch of stuff. Clothes, all the stuff in his pockets. For evidence, even though it was pretty clear what had happened.' She shrugged at Harry, but more 'sorry-you-have-to-hear-the-truth' rather than 'sorry-I-said-that'. 'But, you know, I assume they were being careful because of the high profile. They gave the rest back pretty quickly, but they kept the gun.'

'The rest of his stuff?'

'We gave it back to Celia, Sam's partner.'

Jack stood, gesturing at Harry and Beth to stay where they were. He needed a moment to think on his own. He looked down at the empty stage and had a strange fluttering in his stomach at the fact that someone had had to mop Sam up. He closed his eyes.

Sam's prone, half-dressed, half-headed corpse overlaid the real stage on his eyelids.

Jack walked around the side of the set and across the backstage area. It was less adorned, of course, than the front, like the inside of a wall – wooden frames and struts, some of it gaffa-taped together. You only film from the front, after all. Just like Sam's shorts. The set had about a two-metre gap between the back wall. Large black road cases with silver cornices sat intermittently on either side of the walkway. Half-a-dozen plush red cinema seats lined one side about halfway down. Propped upright, against one of the cases, was a sleek plasma television. Jack walked over to it. He could see his blurry reflection in the dead screen. A small neat bullet-hole was punched in the top right corner. Concentric fractures radiated out another half an inch, and one long crack reached out and bisected the entire screen. Something in the cracks looked dark. *Wet*. Jack shook the thought.

At least *think* like it's a murder, Jack reminded himself. He didn't have to solve the whole thing; that wasn't what Harry was paying him for, anyway. He just wanted him to believe one thing. Jack just had to latch on to the one thing that made him uncomfortable and solve that. Then do it again with what he'd found from the first answer.

Although, being here, running his finger down the crack in the television screen, Jack felt as if the studio was flooded with sadness, as if Harry really was the ghost of Mr Midnight taking them through his final moments. Because Sam did linger here – not just through Harry's face and style and voice and jokes, but through this broken plasma screen, through the host's chair now upright again, through the sign on the desk that flashed neon with his name. Through the section of floor that was just slightly cleaner than the rest. Bleached. Tragedy normally left marks – bloodstains, ash, tyre-tracks on roads – but sometimes you could see where something awful had happened by absence. This floor is too clean: someone bled here.

And if Jack's previous criteria was that something needed to make him uncomfortable to be worth pursuing, being in this studio haunted by videos and relics of a man he barely knew certainly qualified. Everything on the surface looked like it should be a cut-and-dried, gun-in-mouth suicide. But that's because he was only seeing it from the front. Everything here felt half-suited. Damn it, he thought. Harry was getting to him.

As he was walking up the stepladder for the guest entrance, having finished his backstage lap, Beth was complimenting Harry on his dress sense, saying it had improved. She had one arm on his leather sleeve, saying '. . . even dress like him these days' with a laugh before stopping and looking up. Jack felt like he'd walked in on something private. They were trading memories.

'What else do you film in here?' Jack asked.

'This was a headline program, so just this one. We don't have the manpower to dismantle the set every day.'

'And why's it still up? Surely you have shows clamouring for space?'

'Gareth would tell you it's because he wants to save it for re-creations. A telemovie. I say it's because he's waiting until all this blows over and they find another *man* who looks good in a tie and a suit. Swap the sign out, change the name. Hell, if there's not too much blood on it he can probably wear the same tie.' She meant it as a joke, but there was more than a glimmer of bitterness there. She noticed that Jack noticed. 'Sorry, I've been EP on a lot of these shows. It can feel like a bit of a carousel sometimes. New talent same as the old talent.'

'And we think that the gun was already here *before* this episode?' Jack posed it as a question. Harry and Beth nodded. 'And the security cameras were off, from . . .'

'About a week prior.' Beth sighed, reminded of this fault.

'So it's possible that he could have walked through the set door with a gun on a day when it was open? Hidden it up to a week prior?'

'It's possible.'

'You said he looked nervous because you thought he was going to propose to his partner. But now we know his nerves were caused by the gun under the table,' Jack summarised. Then, the old trick, to help the deductions feel more collaborative, he added, 'Am I getting this right?'

A communal nod.

Jack spun the tablet around, loaded the video and slid to the start, where Sam was smiling and calm. Tracked it forward to where he fluffed the line, drummed his fingers on the desk. One shorter than the other. A nervous tic, Jack had been told repeatedly.

'This moment here seems quite significant?' Jack said. 'Do we think this is when the nerves kick in?'

'He does that every episode,' said Harry.

'Literally,' Beth said.

'Sure. But how often does he stuff up a line?'

'It's TV, so plenty,' Beth said. 'I agree though, there's something off about how he does it here.'

'Who's in his ear?' Jack kept the screen paused, pointed at the little curl of translucent plastic running from Sam's ear down his collar. An earpiece. 'I assume he's got you somewhere?'

'Yeah,' said Beth. 'I've got a headset, I can talk to him if I need to. Mostly I'm on the floor, so I don't use it much, but if we're getting a guest ready backstage, or if we need to pad, I can chime in.'

Jack remembered her headset, a thick fuzzy microphone curled around her jaw. Not the discreet, skin-colour microphones used in theatre, but a proper headset as if she were in a 90s boy band.

'Who else?'

'The director, Wyatt Lloyd. He handles the live edit, so he's normally bunkered down backstage behind a set of screens. He can come in to all of us.'

Jack held two fingers up, counting the number of people in Sam's ear. Raised a third expectantly.

Beth clicked her tongue. 'There are like three other producers. They could come in on walkies. But we're old school. We mainly talk to each other – we trust Sam to keep it going.'

'Is Gareth on the comms?'

She shook her head.

'But anyone could be if they used the right frequency?'

'I gotta be honest with you, I don't really know how they work. So probably. Sure.' She shrugged. 'I don't know how secure it is. But if anyone was on it, we'd all have heard it.'

Jack swapped the video for the photos. 'It's not unusual for Sam to be dressed like this, is it?'

'It's probably the standard here. You should see the news team. He's mainly behind the desk. He'll suit up if he has an episode where he needs to come out from it and we shoot waist down, but he doesn't do that often – he's not Fallon.'

Jack planted a finger on the screen. 'That's our problem.'

It had clicked while he was walking backstage, looking at the backside of the fancy set. The side you don't film. That was what was wrong with the whole scene. The video, the images.

Sam Midford was wearing shorts.

'He's dressed for the broadcast,' Jack explained. 'Because he knows he's going to be sitting behind a desk the whole time. So shorts are fine. But if he's planning not only suicide, but *public* suicide . . .' Jack paused. He could see Beth start to see his point. Harry just stared at him expectantly. 'He's not dressed for it.'

'You'd think he'd wear some pants,' said Beth.

'Exactly!' Jack made a small fist of delight. 'And if we go back to the start of the video, Sam's kicking off the show as normal. It's only at a specific moment' – Jack drummed his fingers to mimic the point in the episode he was talking about – 'that he starts to get nervous.' This was exciting even to Jack now, piecing together the disparate threads into a compelling story. Solving something. After over a year in a prison cell, finally something he was good at. 'But you told us he was nervous first, Beth. Because you thought he was going to propose. But even as we discussed the difference between a gun and a ring in his hand, we forgot to alter your original thought process. Because we stuck to *nervousness*. And he's clearly uneasy, we can see that. And he gets more so as it goes on, but I think we've mis-assigned that as merely nerves.' Jack lowered his voice, put a hand across his chest, putting himself in Sam's shoes. 'I think if I had a ring in my pocket, or a gun waiting for me, I'd be flustered the moment I walked on set. His agitation only kicks in *two minutes* after he sits down.'

'Oh, shit,' Beth said. 'Really?'

'Really,' said Jack. 'And he didn't leave a note.'

'Is that why you wanted to know who was in his ear? Is it even possible to talk someone into . . . ?'

'You're saying—' Harry started.

'This might come as a shock, but I'm starting to believe you.' Jack spoke in a soft exhale, disbelief at what he was saying. 'Your brother was under-prepared, under-dressed, and, from two minutes in, under pressure.' Jack counted off the points on his fingers, both to reinforce his point to Harry, but also to convince himself one more time.

Harry's mouth did a little twitch. Satisfaction? Victory? Relief? Jack couldn't tell.

'That gun sat there for up to an entire week and none of the crew knew it was there. I don't think Sam knew it was there either,' Jack said. 'I don't think he was prepared to die. And even if he was, why not do it in his dressing room? Why not at home? Why here and now and dressed like that? I don't think he had any other choice.'

'Our question isn't whether or not he pulled the trigger,' Beth said.

Believe one thing. Jack finished her thought. 'It's whether he *wanted to.*'

PART 3

REPLAY

Really Important, Help Me Choose
D/L
Instagram poll by Davia Emelia, May 2019

As many as 69 per cent of the teenager's Instagram friends had supported the decision for her to kill herself via a voting poll.
Aidil Bolhassan, Padawan District Police Chief, responding to the death of Davia Emelia, May 2019

CHAPTER 11

PREVIOUSLY

To Sam and Harry Midford, the Wheeler's Cove yearly carnival may as well have been Disneyland.

Every March, because the lucrative summer months were reserved for the more prosperous towns, the flat parkland at the top of the main surf beach played host to a motley collection of amusements, banded together into a carnival by a steel-mesh fence and some jangly music. Nothing fit together. While Disneyland has a carefully constructed route to emotionally manipulate the punters into joy, thrills and snack breaks at the appropriate junctures, the impromptu set-up of Wheeler's Cove's resident fun fair didn't even have a fire evacuation plan. What it did have was a four-and-a-half-metre mini Ferris wheel, a rollercoaster with a bar that sat so high above your knees you had to physically push yourself back into the seat, and dodgem cars with bumpers worn so thin the whiplash would put a rugby player in a neck brace.

Everything was made of metal: the grinds of the mechanics groaned unoiled, and rust came off on hands after every ride.

Salt caked inches thick on the glass displays of the food trucks, and only the youngest or the bravest dared eat from them. The sideshows – and they had all the classics: dart throws, water pistols, baseballs at milk pints and rotating clown heads – didn't even try to disguise the fact that their darts were bent or their targets were glued. They knew they were playing for tourists. For parents too sunburnt, hungover and mosquito-riddled to do anything more than hand their kids twenty bucks and let them run wild.

But it also had flashing coloured lights, raucous music and the hanging smell of butter and fried oil in the air – which, layered on top of sea-salt freshness, truly smelled delicious. In the daylight, the mud-trudged pathways and death-trap rides looked filthy and bare. But at night, something cloaked over the park and there was enough magic in the air to mask all of that. It was rough, it was overpriced and it was dangerous: but it was *fun*. Kids leave Disneyland with fairy floss. At a small-town carnival, they leave with shins full of bruises. And they love it all the same.

The Midnight Twins looked forward to it every year. Harry, the younger twin, had been trying to convince Sam to go for ages. Sam, who had maintained for weeks that he was too old for such *juvenile diversions* (words he spat with the full conviction of a teenager who'd learned a great phrase but didn't fully understand it), had finally relented on the final weekend. Harry assumed it had something to do with his break-up with Lily Connors. They'd split up a few weeks ago, but like all brothers, Harry and Sam didn't really talk about things like that. Harry had known they were fairly serious, though, not least because Sam had yelled at him a few months ago in one of their brotherly spats over something like a TV remote, 'You've never even kissed a girl, you're such a baby!' Harry had pointed out in a huff, not for the first time, that he was only twenty-two minutes younger, and Sam's witty comeback had been a corked thigh.

Perhaps because of the break-up, perhaps because Sam actually did need something to do on a Saturday night, they found themselves trudging across the carpark towards the tornado of joyful screams that seemed to whip out of the middle of the carnival. The carpark itself had been converted into accommodation for the workers; it was packed with caravans and glowing Weber barbecues. The sea hissed in the background. At fifteen, they didn't need their parents to take them anymore, and they'd ridden down on their bikes.

On the front entrance arch, a large cut-out of a surfboard with swirly font listed all of the rides and the individual prices. The Ferris wheel was one of the cheapest, because it was the lamest. Harry tried to add up how many times he could go on the rollercoaster and the whirling spider-arm called the Wizard's Spell. They each had thirty dollars in their pocket, and Sam carried the mobile phone. They had one between them, but Sam had taken ownership when he'd gotten a girlfriend. He was still possessive even though he and Lily had broken up. *I'm the oldest, I'll take care of the phone.* It didn't bother Harry too much; Mum said he could get his own at sixteen, which was edging closer. But over the last few months a lot more kids seemed to have them, so he was starting to feel a bit more left out. He tried not to let it bug him, but Sam was standing next to him sending a text, so he refocused on the sign. He reckoned he could go on four high-octane rides and one slightly lamer one with twenty bucks, and then he'd have enough left over for some food and one sideshow. He'd promised his parents he'd only do one – they said every game was rigged – but he'd been practising the bucket toss.

Despite spending most of the time texting, Sam did seem to enjoy himself. He was happy with Harry's choice of rides (they did the Wizard's Spell twice, in the end, because the line was shorter). They pooled their funds to split chips and a hotdog, and Harry flunked out on the bucket toss while Sam almost won a giant teddy on the rotating clown heads. Harry kind of hoped he wouldn't win, because if he did, he imagined Sam giving the ridiculous bear to Lily and then they'd get back together and he'd be the *baby* again. But it was still exciting when Sam got close.

As the park neared closing, 10 p.m., people had started to trickle out. With the energy of several hundred fewer people, the rickety joints of the place were starting to creep back in. Harry and Sam had four ride tokens left. That was enough for either one of them to go on the rollercoaster or Wizard's Spell, or for both of them to go on the Ferris wheel. Despite the Ferris wheel being the lame option, in a show of brotherly solidarity they decided to do the last ride together.

'Last rider!' called the attendant, waving them through as he clipped the chain across the queue.

Though it was only four-ish metres tall, there was still enough of a view of the park and beach for it to feel cool, and enough vertigo to make it feel a little bit dangerous (not that either twin would ever admit that). Even Sam showed interest, sending a final text and putting his phone away to check the view. Along the beach the waves fizzed onto shore. A bonfire crackled at the far end, under the cliffs (when you got too old for the carnival, you drank beer on the beach, Harry had heard), and shadows of people dancing flicked across the bottom of the rocks like cave paintings come alive. Back inland, the windows of Wheeler's Cove's tiny population were an advent calendar, squares of warm light bridging large gaps. The tops of trees were illuminated occasionally by a passing car. The wheel went around twice and then stopped at the top while a family of four disembarked the lowest carriage.

Sam was kneeling on the seat looking down at the bonfire and the waves. 'Must be Year Twelves,' he said. 'Reckon anyone'll skinny dip?'

Harry crossed the carriage, which wobbled as the weight swapped, and followed Sam's gaze. 'You wouldn't be able to see anything – it's all shadow.'

'Get back on your side.' Sam swivelled around and Harry crossed the floor again, tipping the car back into balance. The wind was kicking up, stronger because they were at the top. He had to raise his voice to be heard. 'Trust me, even shadowed, you'd see me.' He wriggled his eyebrows and they both laughed.

'Hey,' said Harry, after another minute or so. 'Have we stopped moving?'

As he said it, all the lights in the park went out.

Harry would later remember it getting very cold, very quickly. It probably didn't, but now they knew they were stuck up there, it seemed to be the only thing to focus on. The sea wind chilled his neck. Sam blew on his hands.

He knelt on the seat, peered through the bars. The park was dark, each amusement a frozen, jagged shadow. Popcorn boxes blew through the empty lanes. The shopfronts of the sideshows were all buttoned down. It was deserted. The whole scene was bordered by the coloured flags that surrounded the Ferris wheel cabin, like a creepy picture frame.

'Are you serious?' said Sam, who had also hopped up on the opposite seat. 'They closed and left us up here?'

'It's kind of cool,' said Harry, and it *was*, wasn't it? He knew he couldn't act scared, even though he sort of was, because he didn't want Sam to look down on his *baby brother*. Besides, it was every kid's dream to be locked in an amusement park.

That said, it was eerie. Every thirty seconds or so the wind would rock the cabin especially hard and Harry's stomach would go anti-grav for a couple of seconds. 'Just call Mum and Dad. We'll maybe be up here fifteen minutes.'

Sam rubbed his temples and shook his head. 'I can't. The phone's flat.'

'What?'

'It's run out of battery.' Sam shrugged it off like it wasn't a big deal. 'I can't call anyone.'

'Are you kidding me? You wasted all our battery texting your stupid girlfriend?'

'Shut up!' Now Sam was yelling, because that's how brothers fight. Even the one in the wrong has to set the intensity, establish dominance. A brotherly spat is simply a feat of who can yell the loudest and swear the most creatively. 'She's not my girlfriend.'

'Fuck you.' Harry knew the rules of engagement.

'Scared?'

'Fuck you, you fucking . . . fuck.'

'Oh,' Sam said with a snarl, 'stop being such a baby.'

Harry launched himself across the cabin. The whole cage tilted and both of them fell into the bars. Scrabbling across the seat, not quite punching but not holding back either, laying into one another. The cabin swung back and forth, and a horrible screech came from the roof. They stopped and looked up. With both of them on the same side and rocking the whole thing with their violence, the cabin was dangerously tilted. There was a silent agreement that the fight should desist in favour of balance, and each retreated to their own side, glowering venomously but, at least, on steady-ish ground again. A pendulum arbitrator.

There was nothing to do but wait.

'Help!'

'Help!'

'Somebody help us – we're stuck up here!'

Several lights in the carpark were on. They could see people sitting in chairs, drinking. The crazy thing was, they could hear the chink of a bottle occasionally, crystal clear like a chime in a music hall. Or a scratch of laughter. But the wind was rushing in off the sea and spiralling up, so although the sound from below carried near perfectly, their own voices were whisked upwards. Unheard. Occasionally, the familiar beam of light of a passing car on the main road would brush some distant treetops and they'd yell at that too, just in case. They yelled until they were hoarse.

How long until their parents called the police? It wasn't that cold at ground level, but the seaside windchill and the metal cage with its cool plastic seats seemed to exaggerate it.

Sam was shivering. His fingers were blue. He sat on his hands.

'You could climb down.'

'No way.'

'This door's just a latch, not even locked. I reckon if you use the roof of the one below us, and once you get onto that beam there it should be easy enough.'

'You do it then.'

'It's your fault the phone's flat.'

Harry didn't know if he slept. The night blurred past, timeless. Some moments he was counting the seconds, and others he seemed to zone out and when he zoned back . . . was the moon in a different spot? Time must have passed. Sometimes he felt alone, others he remembered Sam shivering across from him. The clink of beers had died down, the lights in the caravans snuffed, the bonfire on the beach down to embers, no dancing shadows left. His stomach lurched every time the wind shook them now. The last car that beamed through the canopy must have been hours ago.

Harry had opened his mouth to yell but his lips felt glued together. They cracked in the corners. All he could summon was a squeak. His nose dripped. Sam had his eyes closed, head to one side. He'd started to cough.

Another flash in time. The moon moved again, bonfire now gone. And, finally, lights snaking across the treetops. Red and blue.

CHAPTER 12

Harry's recount of his night atop the Ferris wheel took most of the drive from Redfern to tell. He'd hopped in with Jack at the train station, because Harry was 'between cars' and Jack had borrowed his father's Golf.

Jack had had an uneasy night's rest. He and his father hadn't spoken much when he'd gotten home. Any dialogue was purely administrative. Peter, still in his red polo, didn't ask him about his day out, the 'new job'. Offered him tea, to reheat some food. Jack said he'd already eaten. They both knew he hadn't.

Jack had retired to his usual confidant, Liam – just speaking aloud to him often helped Jack piece together his thoughts – and fallen asleep in the chair by the window, the soft wheeze of the breathing apparatus lulling him into it. He didn't have a strategy on what to do next. He'd half-hoped running through the day's events with Liam would reveal a path, but he hadn't told Harry that. When they'd left Channel 14, Jack said he'd call in the morning.

He had been woken by a text message at eleven-thirty. Only his second morning out, but now neither in a bed or in a prison, his body was still waking in shock. *Where am I?* His mouth was dry, eyes felt taped. He registered his brother's bed. Sore back from the armchair. Put it together. Picked up his phone.

Lunch, Harry had texted. *Debrief?*

After. Jack texted back. *I have plans.* He didn't like eating in front of people.

Okay. Who's next witness?

Harry's use of formal terms like *witness* still irked Jack. Even if he now believed there may have been some degree of interference involved, the word 'murder' still clicked against his teeth. It was a moot point whether they called it a witness or not: they both knew where they were going next.

In the car, Jack noticed Harry was talking more, perhaps because he felt Jack was on his wavelength. Beth, handing over the iPad as they'd left yesterday, had remained unconvinced. Jack thought he'd use the opportunity of having Harry trapped in the car to fish for a few more details, starting with how Sam had injured his finger.

Harry told the memory lightly, but Jack could tell the experience had left a mark, though not as physical, on him. In particular, the police lights coming through the treetops seemed to upset him, so he truncated the story to the happier parts: the rescue and all that came after. Both brothers had been treated for hypothermia, shock and frostbite. Partly because he'd sat on his hands on the cold metal seat, Sam had been bitten more severely than Harry. Taken a real chomp out of the top of his left ring finger. The doctors hadn't been able to save it. Harry had found the upside of the situation; he now had something his older brother didn't and took great joy in pointing out that, although they were identical, Sam now only comprised 99 per cent of him. Until Harry had his appendix out at seventeen, and then they were even again.

That night was also the beginning of the Midnight Twins. An unofficial nickname at school, because Sam was born fifteen minutes before midnight on 24 March, and Harry was born twenty-two

minutes later at 12.07 on 25 March, it was quirky enough to stick in
the press that covered the carnival incident. The first stories were low
column space: boys rescued, tragedy averted, parents suing the park
for negligence. But soon the press realised there were two identical
teenagers who looked freak-show-good on a front page or a morning TV couch. That might have fizzled out pretty quickly had they
not done an interview on Sam's, but not Harry's, actual birthday and
confused one host so much it morphed into a bizarre routine:

Host: 'Happy birthday.'

Harry: 'It's not my birthday.'

Host: 'Sorry, Sam, someone told me it was your birthday.'

Sam: 'Yes, it's my birthday today.'

Host: 'And you are identical twins?'

Together: 'Yes.'

Host: 'Well, happy birthday, Harry.'

Harry: 'It's not my birthday.'

Host: 'Are you kidding me?'

Together: 'No.'

Host: 'So let me get this straight. Sam, it's your birthday
today . . .'

It had culminated in Harry yelling back at him, 'It's not my fucking birthday, you prick!' That interview had become a viral hit, and
then they were on every talk show in the country. They developed
a script for the interviews. The audience would roar when Harry
accused Sam of being 99 per cent of him. Sam would wriggle his
eyebrows just as he'd done in the cabin, hold up his stumpy finger
and say, 'I'd need to lose a lot more than half an inch to get down
to 99 per cent.' They'd play fight. They'd do the 'Happy birthday'
bit. Their big closer was a game of rock paper scissors – completely
unrehearsed – that would go for dozens of rounds, Sam's stubby
'scissors' on show for the camera to hint at the traumatic backstory.
They took it in completely unrehearsed turns who won.

That had died down, until, at nineteen, they did a reality TV show for semi-celebrities that was pitched to them by a network executive as a 'breast reduction for your career – you'll go from D to B List in no time'. After they did well, placing equal third in a feat of production-meddling and a perfectly timed double eviction, a promoter, who Harry remembered spoke exclusively with a hand on his shoulder, had encouraged them to do live shows. Like stand-up comedy, but sillier, less structured. Instead of being the guests, as they had been on the talk-show circuit, they could invite others on. The promoter had enough pull to get some cult bands and a few TV actors. People came. Then they went to Montreal, one of the largest arts festivals in the world, where TV executives slink in alleys like they've got trench coats full of watches. More hands on more shoulders. Then Gareth Bowman, whose trench coat weighed the most, or so it seemed at the time. And then everything after.

'Left here,' Harry said. Jack changed lanes, squinting through the chalk numbers on his rear-window in the mirror. Price tag.

'Your parents were mad at the fair?' Jack said. 'You mentioned they tried to sue?'

'Half-heartedly. Had to take it out on someone,' Harry said. 'You know how parents aren't allowed to be mad because "thank God you're okay"? My parents were so thankful we were safe, they would have killed the mailman if he put the paper on a wet lawn.' He laughed. 'They were mega-pissed at Sam for flattening the phone battery. Lost the damn thing a day later anyway. Dad hit the roof.'

'How'd the negligence suit go?'

'You ever tried to subpoena a guy who lives in a caravan?'

'No luck?'

'These are the guys that run sideshow alley. Everything's rigged. They always win.' He pointed to the left again. Jack rolled up to the kerb next to a squat brick letterbox with a 17 on it. They were in a wealthy suburb; everything had two storeys and long driveways, the exclusive domain of people who don't put their own bins out. Every lawn was lush, trim and green – no surprise seeing as the sprinklers on either side of the road were in perfect time, fanning between one another in semi-circles without ever touching. The afternoon sun flicked mini-rainbows through the droplets. If you added people in pretty dresses and tap shoes out in the middle of this street, it wouldn't be out of place in a musical. Suburbs like this are all about conformity. Sprinklers keeping time on lawns clean and clipped. All cars black and waxed. Don't park it on the street if it's not washed or a Range Rover. Arses in activewear and almonds activated. Dinner party conversation is politics and allergies. *Oh yes, we're allergic to nuts, paying tax and gluten.*

The house they parked in front of wasn't bucking the trend. Fresh white paint and washed windows, pillars either side of the snaking drive. It didn't look garish, but it didn't look welcoming either. Pulled straight from a catalogue and dropped on an empty plot.

'You okay to see her?' Jack said.

'Sure.' A sprinkler thrummed an arc against Harry's door. He waited until it passed and then levered the handle. A burst of chilled air came through. Sun still up but warmth gone.

'She okay to see you?'

Harry paused. The sprinkler reversed; he pulled the door shut. The water drummed past and Harry opened the door again. Turned back to Jack. 'Why wouldn't she be?'

'I just thought—'

The intermittent spray came back. Harry shut the door. 'I'm not waiting in the car like a dog.' He reopened the door. Put one leg out.

Jack made to reply, but it was a strange argument, punctuated every ten or so seconds by the rotating waterfall, making it difficult to get into a proper fight, or for either of them to leave.

Jack sighed and got out of the car. Harry timed his run to the sprinkler and followed a few steps behind.

At the large double door, Jack pressed the buzzer and said, 'Maybe just let me do the talking here. It's what you're paying me for, after all.'

The real answer was that this could be a delicate interview and Jack didn't need Harry's big mouth rattling the witness. *Witness.* There it was again. Jack had to be careful with those words coming into this house. In particular, he had to keep the word 'murder' off Harry's lips. That was a word they could throw around lightly at the television studio, because they were deliberately trying to be confronting and Gareth reacted to it as a professional accusation: negligence, liability. But make it a personal accusation, and the word became much more volatile.

A clunking from inside the house interrupted Jack's thoughts. Someone was walking towards the door on what could only be a hardwood floor. Of course it was. In this neighbourhood, the reaction to carpet would be at best disdain and at worst anaphylactic.

'God.' Harry's sigh was exaggerated. He took off his brown leather jacket and folded it under his arm. 'Why are you so worried?'

'You're wearing her dead boyfriend's face,' Jack whispered, just before the door opened. 'It would throw me off.'

CHAPTER 13

Sam's almost-fiancée opened the door.

It's a cliché in film and television to present recent widows as brittle, frail. To have the make-up team use pale foundation, ghost-like, and smear dark circles under their eyes. Every time a widow opens a door in a film, they've just finished crying. The message being that, without their husband, they are barely keeping it together. In films, a husband's decline is represented with a different mise en scène: beer bottles and guts, empty pizza boxes, stained singlets and peeling wallpaper. But such decline is reserved for the divorced male, not the widower. *He* might hold a scrunched-up, faded photograph, with tears in his eyes for half a second, before loading up a small army's worth of guns and kicking some *serious arse* on those who dared to take her from him. The message is that, when death is involved, men get on with it while women live with the ghosts. They cry prettily. Fragile as ornaments. *Pretty enough to be ugly*. In reality, Jack had always found women to be more front-footed and practical. They organised the funerals and insurance, and still had the strength to dress the kids and get them to school. It was the men who lived, more often, in the shadow of their past. Asleep in a chair in the corner of their brother's room.

Celia Anderson did not have pale skin or dark eyes. She didn't wipe away a tear as she opened the door. She was barefoot, in jeans and a white t-shirt. Brunette, with her hair tied in a ponytail. Freckles splattered her cheeks: she looked like a child who had just finished baking a chocolate cake and been left alone with the electric beater. She seemed healthy. Well. Jack was reminded of another cliché, that of the widow too pleased and dressed up so they could flit away with a lover or an insurance policy, but he decided that Celia wasn't so blasé. She was just getting on with it. Jack reminded himself that Celia also may well have agreed with the police and media about Sam's death, and may have felt it wasn't worth wasting grief on a recently uncovered paedophile.

The way she quietly examined the two of them was the only sign of tiredness in her, a woman who'd had a lot of knocks on her door lately. Her eyelids fluttered briefly when they passed over Harry. She gave no sign of recognition to Jack.

'Celia,' said Jack, holding out a hand. 'My name's Jack. I'm a friend of Sam's.'

'You're not. But that's okay.' She didn't take his hand. She looked past him. 'You can't come in, Harry.'

'I'm not here to upset you—'

'Nothing personal.' She shook her head. 'But Heather's never even met you. I've just spent the last two weeks explaining things you should never have to explain to your child. That her dad's never coming back. The last thing I need is for her to see him standing in the hall.'

Even Harry couldn't argue with that. Celia hadn't meant it as a barb, but by how quickly Harry moved off the porch and walked back to the car, considering how much he'd wanted to be part of this interview mere minutes prior, Jack thought there was some guilt in his surrender. Harry's words at the studio. *We had a falling out five years ago. Over the show. You record that?*

A falling out so bad that he'd never met his brother's child?

'I've had a lot of people who aren't Sam's friends around. You may as well come in and tell me what you're after,' Celia said, guiding Jack inside. The hallway was indeed hardwood, high ceilings with skylights. Photos lined the hall. Some professional portraits of Heather as a baby, smiling gums in front of a blue velvet backdrop. Others of the whole family smiling on a sepia autumn day, Sam in a baseball jacket with a red stripe down the arm. One of Celia and Sam, sunburnt and happy, holding cocktails on some Greek terrace above deep blue water. One at someone else's wedding, pulling faces in the photobooth. These were happy photos, memories of a man she loved. Celia had kept them up, so she was either choosing to ignore the post-death pornography charges, or she didn't believe them.

She led Jack to a kitchen with a large marble island in the middle of the room. Jack perched on a stool. There was a small girl sitting on a couch in an adjacent room, glued to the television. Children can't watch television and keep their muscles tight – it's a multi-tasking strain on their brain to focus on colours and lights – so she sat with the slack-jawed posture of someone hypnotised. Jack was surprised that she was able to watch TV at all. But maybe she hadn't seen *it*. Maybe she was too young to understand.

Celia plucked the kettle from its stand, but then paused under the tap. 'Is this a tea and coffee conversation?' She tilted her head at the fridge. 'Or do I need a beer?'

'Depends.'

'That means beer.' She plucked two from inside the fridge door. Twist tops. Chinked one down in front of Jack. 'I've had enough of these to know. People have told me a lot of things about Sam the last couple of weeks, and they tend to go one of two ways. Let's just say I've had more beers than coffees.'

'Do you believe them?'

'You know, it sounds strange, but I still don't know. These things happened. They are physically here. He did what he did. I have the death certificate. Those repulsive photos exist. I paid for a coffin, for a man to push him into a furnace. I mean, it's all real. But it's still kind of like it's all made up. You know? Is that why you're here?'

'Sort of. I'm helping Harry. We're trying to look at those things that, as you say, don't feel real enough.' He was careful not to use the 'm' word. 'I thought you might feel the same. The material on his work laptop – can I ask: did you ever see anything like it? At home?'

She shook her head. 'God, no. Never. I mean they wouldn't tell me what it was, so I don't know how bad it was. Not that it, you know, matters. And he loved Heather so much. To think he'd solicit something from someone else's children . . .' She just kept shaking her head. 'Then again, sometimes you don't know. Maybe I'm one of *those* women. Didn't see it. Maybe he played me.'

'I noticed you've still got his family photos on the wall. Part of you believes in him.'

'Maybe I'm trying to decide if it's worth remembering just one side of someone.' She took another swig.

Jack knew the etiquette was to follow along, otherwise people start to notice. He raised his beer and realised it was his first alcoholic drink since he had gone to prison. Not that he had ever drunk much anyway. His soldiers were just like any other battalion, and getting on the sauce made them bawdy. It was a slippery slope. Easier to purge with a sloshing belly. He took a gentle sip, held it in his mouth and felt it fizz.

'So now you tell me. What's your role in this? I can understand Harry wanting to know why, the ins and outs. You can't be a cop, and you don't strike me as a PI either, though I'll admit I've never met one.'

'I'm a podcaster. Used to do cold cases, things cops wouldn't look at.'

That seemed to satisfy her. 'You're in the right place. The police never really seemed to care that he'd died, just the other stuff.'

'That's all they wanted? Do you remember the times you spoke to them?'

'Well, when I saw,' she paused, '*it* happen, at first I was just confused. I tried to call emergency services, but I was frantic and they kept trying to send an ambulance here. After that I called Sam. Then Gareth directly. Even the front desk. No one picked up, of course. In the end, I drove with Heather to the police station. They didn't know what to do with me either. But by then it had really started to hit the media, and so they were sending more people to the scene. They agreed to look after Heather and put me in a car with some of their officers. No one would talk to me when I got there, and I wasn't allowed in. I still remember how I found out he'd actually died. I was asking everybody where Sam was. An ambulance lady, she just put a hand on my arm and said "Oh, he died, honey."' She sniffed for the first time. 'That's how I found out – I don't think she knew who I was. No one knew what to do with me, so eventually they drove me home. Heather and I slept in the same bed. The next day, there seemed to be a more formal process. They came here in the morning, asked me a bunch of questions. Finally they started talking to me, but by then I'd read about it online. Next time they told me about the pictures he had on his work laptop. Asked if they could take the home computer. A week later they brought it back, gave me some of his clothes. I haven't heard from them since.'

'The questions they asked you?'

'Almost all of it was about the pornography. Like the questions you started with. They asked about our family. If he'd ever . . . Oh, God. I asked them if any of it was *her*. I actually asked them that. I hope he doesn't hate me for that.'

Jack didn't need to ask what the answer had been. Family photos were still up in the hall. Mentally, he ticked that question off too. Glad he hadn't had to ask it.

'And he didn't leave a note?'

'Nothing.' She broke this word in two, catching on to Jack's line of questioning.

'Did he know you'd be watching? Did he' – Jack thought back to the ring in the dressing room – 'did he tell you to watch that night? Specifically?'

'He'll normally tell me if it's a good one. But, no, he didn't. Any other show, maybe it's fifty-fifty? If he was a lawyer, would I be expected to watch him preen in every board meeting?'

'He asked you to change the channel, just in case.'

'Like I said, fifty-fifty.'

'When they took the home computer,' Jack said, 'did they find anything?'

'Not a skerrick. You must think what I think then – it's weird that his home computer is completely clean, and yet his *work* computer is filled with it, right?'

'Then what is he asking you to forgive him for?' Jack said. *Forgive me. Change the channel.*

'It doesn't get to me quite so much that he killed himself. I mean, it does. I'm not saying it right.' She licked her teeth. Spoke slower, eyes tilted slightly up in focus, as if she was picturing the words in front of her and plucking them deliberately, one by one, out of the air. 'Let me put it this way. I resent him for making that choice. For leaving us on our own. But we've all had battles. If Sam felt he had only one way out and that was it, I feel sad for him more than anything. And sometimes I hate him for that, but then I feel ashamed. What's that thing where a snake eats its own tail? It's like that. But one thing I can focus on is if someone's protecting themselves by smearing his name after he can no longer defend himself – that doesn't go either way on the snake thing, it just makes me outright mad.'

Jack had been assuming the child pornography was a cover-up, an artificial motive for suicide to draw attention away from the potential murder, but he hadn't yet considered that Sam's death may have happened *first*, and someone, knowing the station would be under scrutiny, had acted on the opportunity to draw attention away from *something else*. He could see now why Celia had invited him in so amiably. She believed there were some unanswered questions too. And while she wasn't yet with Harry in believing that Sam's death was criminal, she still suspected someone was tampering with his legacy.

'Was he having trouble at work?' Jack asked. Whether it was fake evidence for murder or corporate back-stabbing, it also didn't mean it couldn't be both at once. Harry had summed it up best. *Throw a dart.* 'I used to work at Channel 14 too. I know how cutthroat television can be.'

'I don't really know. But everyone liked him.' She eyed Jack. 'Where'd you grow up?'

'Blue Mountains.'

'Thought so. You've got a similar small-town vibe to him. Practical. No bullshit. Sam was always helping out his friends. Writers, directors and, later, producers. Lots of Sam's mates cut their teeth on his show. He was known as a bit of a career starter. If an old school chum had a kid who wanted an internship, Sam would whack them on a camera for a week. Someone makes the big city move and can't find work, Sam'd have a job for them. You ever notice how most actors and actresses come from money, but the talk-show guys don't? *Hosts* work their way up from the bottom. Because they have to be genial, endearing, chat to their guests and make them feel at home. The glitz and the glam is for the A-listers, but the host's job is to make their guests shine. That's why they're all country boys. Hell, Dwyer started out flipping burgers in a shitty seaside town. Same as Mr Midnight. That's how you know someone grew up small. Sam made it to the top, but he took his friends with him.'

'Not his brother.'

'Harry quit.'

'So he says. Was the show stressing Sam at all?'

'No more than usual. By that I mean plenty was usually stressing him. A nightly talk show is always subject to the same pressures. The ratings dip for one week and suddenly the word "rebrand" is on every memo. New hosts get thrown around in the media, which is really just the station itself leaking a list of candidates to see if one clicks with the public. It's how they chose the last Bachelor. Such a scam.'

'How were the ratings?'

'Fine. Genuinely. I know they did the "rumoured host" thing about six months ago, but that was just prior to the series renewal in October for the new year. They were never serious – just trying to scare him into signing a contract on the same money. But the series had been ordered for the whole year. Ratings were fine. No reason to play games.'

Jack googled the hosting rumours Celia was talking about on his phone. It was anchors from other networks. Men in ties and suits with different gradients of silver in their hair. They all looked very similar. *A carousel*. Sam was by far the youngest. Tom Dwyer, whom Gareth Bowman had mentioned hating, was mentioned on one site. All had their own shows on competing stations anyway, so Celia was right: it was artificial pressure.

'None of these guys would be caught dead negotiating with Channel 14,' said Jack, scrolling through the article. Celia nodded in agreement. 'They'd have to sign an agreement before they announced they were leaving, let alone put it in the media. Otherwise they'd risk both contracts going up in smoke.'

Something caught Jack's attention in one of the additional links. A similar list from Channel 12's show *The Round Table*, which listed Sam Midford as a potential host. *Could Sam Midford replace Tom Dwyer as* Round Table *host?*

The Round Table was a guided discussion of the week's news, less scripted than *Midnight Tonight*. Channel 12 promised a 'lively weekly discussion with the nation's best, brightest and funniest minds', where rotating guests debated hot-topic issues. Again, the list was a homogenous blend of white men in monochromatic ties, with one exception. Beth Walters was on there – 'the livewire producer of *Midnight Tonight* could also be a wild card at the end of the season'. While Sam's show had a more satirical bent, not direct competition, threatening to replace him with a rival network's flagship host *and* producer was sure to put the wind up Tom Dwyer, and Channel 12 as a whole.

'Did Sam have an offer from Channel 12?' Jack turned the screen to show her what he was talking about. 'That'd piss Gareth off.'

'Nope. Like I said, it's a scare campaign. Gareth always liked to keep Sam on his toes. "It's my show." That's Gareth's message. Like when Harry quit. Refill?'

Jack put a palm over his bottle. *No thanks*. 'Tell me about that.'

'Harry's told you? Well, they were head-hunted in Montreal, but when they shot the pilot Gareth thought having two hosts was dragging it down. What he didn't say was that twice the talent costs twice the money. Even though they would have happily split the fee. But Gareth is a long-term guy, and he knew if the show did well it would be a pain to renegotiate. Sam was going to walk – he really wasn't coping with the stress of having Harry dropped, until Harry quit on his own. Left it to him.'

'You were together then?'

'We got together soon after. I'm a doctor. We met at the Prince Alfred. I know what you're thinking, and she's his. She's four.

It was a whirlwind. I don't regret it, but we skipped the marrying part.'

'Everyone keeps telling me Harry quit on his own, but he hasn't even met his niece. I'm supposed to believe that's an amicable split?'

'Harry quit soon after I met Sam for the first time, as a patient, not as a romantic partner. I know that much. Sam would have told me more if he was ready, but he wasn't. It's not my place to say otherwise – that's between brothers.'

CHAPTER 14

Jack took another sip of his beer, because he felt he'd started to lose her when he'd declined a second drink, and he wanted to keep up the casual nature of their conversation. She didn't seem to know much about Harry, but she was surprisingly open talking about Sam.

'Beth Walters told me the police returned Sam's clothing to you directly?' he said.

Celia nodded. 'We got everything except his laptop – they kept that. I don't know what use they think I'll have for a bloodstained shirt, but they gave it back anyway. Honestly I thought there'd be some biohazard restrictions. I haven't opened it. I couldn't bear to think of a piece of his brain falling out.' She took a breath. Thought. Plucked the words again. 'Oh, and the gun. Of course, we didn't get the gun.'

'Was it Sam's gun? Did he own one?'

'Didn't think he did.' She shrugged. 'I never saw one, anyway. Learning a lot about him these days though.'

'May I see the clothing?'

She set her beer down. 'Follow me. You right, hun?' Heather, still fixed on the television, looked up as they walked past. She had curly hair. A big mouth, gums primed for her dad's teeth. Didn't seem too interested by the strange man in her house. Celia pointed at Jack. 'This is Jack. He's a friend of Daddy's.'

'I'm not,' said Jack warmly. 'But that's okay.' Celia gifted him a genuine laugh.

Sam's personal items were in a large clear zip-lock bag that Celia kept in the top space of the master bedroom's wardrobe. The bed was made. A pair of children's pyjamas were folded on one pillow. The two of them had been curling up together, Jack surmised. Celia, for all her resolve, couldn't face the empty bed. As she reached up and slid the bag out, Jack noticed the cupboards behind her were bare. Bad memories gone? It seemed too quick. But if she was trying to rid the house of him, why keep his photos up in the hall?

Celia handed him the bag. 'Use the bathroom. It's all dry, but I still don't want it on my covers.'

'You off-loaded all his clothes already?' Jack asked, nodding at the empty cupboard.

Celia shook her head. Looked like a memory had hit her. 'Oh. I forgot about that. Believe it or not, they all disappeared. Honestly, if he hadn't have done what he did, I would have thought he was running away.'

'They were just gone? When?'

'Gotta be honest, I wasn't really focusing on his cupboards that night. You could have stolen my car while I was sitting in it and I wouldn't have noticed.'

'Sorry, of course. You think he was planning on going somewhere then? With all his stuff?'

'Not everything, just the good suits and shirts and jackets. Everything hanging. Like I said, in any other circumstance you'd think he took off. Now, maybe if he planned the whole thing, the only reason I've come up with is if he donated them to Salvos. Get some goodwill before heading upstairs.' She put her hands in the air, sat on the bed with a thump. 'Beats me.'

Jack put that behind another door of unanswered questions. Evidence that Sam was not prepared to die. Why would Sam pack a bag before he killed himself?

Jack took the zip-lock bag into the bathroom and knelt. His stomach rumbled in recognition of the position. False alarm, he chastised, stand down. He upended the bag in the bathtub. He didn't have gloves so he inverted the bag into makeshift protection over his left hand and started to sift through it. There, the pink boardshorts with green pineapples. There, the blood-spattered white shirt, now crinkled and yellowed on the edges. The neatly tailored blazer. Cufflinks rattled in the tub. The coiled cord and earpiece, the radio mic battery pack, which would have sat in Sam's back pocket, were among the items.

Who was in your ear? Jack thought, looking at the earpiece. Beth said it wouldn't have been too difficult to jump on the frequency. And Jack was still of the belief that, maybe, Sam hadn't hidden the gun at all. Even so, what could you possibly say to someone to get them to . . . What else had Beth said? *If anyone was on it, we'd all have heard it.* There was a strange smell of chemicals soaked into each item. Forensic. Jack checked the pockets. A pen. A few dollars in change.

'No ring?' Jack called, as he got to the bottom of the pile.

'Ring?' Celia's footsteps came up behind him. She seemed surprised, then figured out the implication and scoffed, as if another coat of paint had flaked off her memory of Sam. 'Never seen one. If he was proposing, it wasn't to me.'

'His phone?'

'They returned that separately.' Then, ahead of what he was about to ask, 'I checked it too. Only a few numbers I didn't know, telemarketers. He wasn't planning as much as a long weekend, let alone a mistress, or buying a gun on the black market.'

Jack started to rifle through individual items again. He picked up the blazer. The fabric was deep blue, pinstriped, but the collar was black. Like a broken pen had stained it with ink. The 'ink' cracked as he unfolded it. He winced. Celia was standing in the doorway watching. Jack turned the blazer inside out. Sanitary pads were stuck to the armpits. That was a TV trick, to put pads under your armpits to absorb sweating. Again, a man not dressed to die. Half-suited with women's hygiene products under his arms. Jack shook it. Two small white pills clattered into the tub. Jack picked them up. They weren't stamped with any of the main painkiller brands. He held them up. 'He's on meds?' he asked.

'You didn't know that? I thought that was why you're here.'

'What kind?'

'The stuff that doesn't work, obviously.' She crossed to the medicine cabinet and pulled out a transparent plastic bottle. Then a white one. And another. She held up all three. Tossed him one. 'Antidepressants. Take your pick.'

Jack turned the bottle over in his hand. Why wouldn't Harry have mentioned this? He had Jack playing pretend detective when their supposed victim was on medication to help with suicidal intent. Jack wasn't so naive to think that everyone on antidepressants was suicidal, but in that bathroom, the association was pounding him over the head. Besides, Jack had really only started to believe Harry based on his assumption that Sam was a happy-go-lucky flying-high television star. His only even half-decent summation so far had come from the assumption that it was out of character. And now these pills.

Then again, they hadn't spoken in five years. Maybe Harry didn't even know?

Jack's enthusiastic line of questioning slowed. He'd asked one question several times, and the answers he'd gotten had satisfied him that there may be a story here. But he'd only been asking work colleagues and estranged brothers. Maybe he didn't have a conspiracy after all. He should have asked the girlfriend sooner. 'Was he suicidal?' Jack asked.

'He was doing better. I mean, it takes management, a good plan, support.' Celia pointed at the bottle in Jack's hand. 'Those. You take it day by day.'

'So . . .' Jack stared at the bottle. Ran out of words. Tried to find new ones.

'I'd rather you just asked me.' She tapped a foot.

'My brother's sick,' Jack said. 'Well, not sick, but he's dying. Well, he's already . . . Look, it doesn't matter. But if he dies, one day' – Jack clicked the fingers on his bagless hand – 'like that, it would be awful. But it wouldn't be . . . unexpected.'

Celia put a hand to her mouth. Not in shock, but just to touch her own lips. A tic. Jack's honesty had warmed her up again. Her words cracked out of her. 'If I'd come home and he'd been in here . . .' She lowered her hand from her lips to gesture to the bathroom, then started nodding. Blinking. Maybe imagining him on the floor, those bottles empty. Maybe in the bath, water overflowed, tiles stained. 'Maybe. Maybe I would have walked in, and, sure, I would have screamed and cried and done the same things I did, but I'd be lying if a part of me wouldn't have thought: so here it is.'

'And on that night?'

'Didn't feel like that.' Now her head was shaking, that same minute repetitious movement, over and over. 'No. He wouldn't have done it like that. I mean, in front of us? It was so different to what I expected. No. It's hard to find the word. I didn't ever expect it, but if it *happened*. Like you said, if . . .' She clicked her fingers in mimicry. 'I don't know what I'm saying. Like maybe I already did my grieving, while he was still alive. When it was bad, and when I steeled myself on the days when I did expect it. Maybe I got it out of the way. My mum had cancer, same thing. We have to mourn the living sometimes. But not what he did. Not how he did it. God, he was doing so much better.'

'Better?'

'Than the first time.'

'The first time?'

'Five years ago. Sam's first suicide attempt.'

Before Jack could ask any more questions, a young girl's desperate yells – which could only be Heather's – echoed in from the hall. Celia's head snapped up at the sound.

'Mum! Mum!' The voice was desperate, but after the initial rattle of surprise, not terrified. It was the desperate excitement of a child, where the fact they *need* to show you something – a handstand, a cartwheel – causes them physical agony. She was yelling at the top of her lungs. 'Mum! Mummy! Come quick!'

'What is it, honey?'

'Dad's outside.'

'Shit.'

'Harry—'

'Quick! Quick!' A pause. 'They're fighting!'

CHAPTER 15

The fight on the lawn was an all-out scrap. No clean punches, no neat strikes. Harry and another man were in an indiscriminate scruff, rolling over one another while grappling with pieces of clothing or hair. Men like to think when they fight it's impressive, but more often it's just two men spun in a washing machine. Jack personally avoided fights; his calcium deficiency meant his brittle bones broke easily. 'Do you wanna go?' someone had asked him in prison. 'Sure,' Jack had said, 'I'll go,' and left.

As Jack and Celia caught their first glimpse of the spin cycle through the front windows – where Heather was bouncing excitedly on the couch – Harry got on top. His shirt was ripped. A pearl of blood on his lip. His size was working against him: the man underneath was smaller and flailed more. Harry copped a knee in the chest and dropped off briefly before the hurricane of grass stains and ego continued. Jack and Celia rushed out the front, Celia stopping to tell Heather that she needed to stay inside or she would lose iPad privileges.

'Harry!' Jack yelled, rushing over and trying to get his hands on Harry's shoulders.

Harry swatted him away. He almost had the guy pinned, still writhing and kicking. Spit was hanging from his bloodied mouth.

Jack tried again. 'Harry, stop!'

A freezing jet of water doused all three of them. Harry and his combatant scrambled backwards, blinking off their surprise. Jack turned. Celia stood at the corner of a house with a garden hose. Shrugged an apology for hitting Jack. Heather stood in the doorway, technically inside the house but right on the doorline, stopped by the invisible forcefield of fierce parenting.

Harry stood up slowly, panting, wiping his face. He flicked droplets off his left arm. His sleeve, torn at the shoulder, hung low as if dislocated. The other guy was on his knees, facing away, legs shaking like a newborn foal, gearing himself up to stand.

'He was skulking around the porch. He tried the door, but it was locked, so he started going through your bins,' Harry spat, pointing. 'Looking for something!'

'Settle down,' Jack said. Then, 'Who are you?'

Celia stepped forward with the hose as if it were a weapon. An interrogation threat. Don't give it to Harry, Jack thought, not confident Harry would be above waterboarding.

'And why were you going through my bins?' Celia asked.

The guy gave up on finding balance and instead turned by plonking himself on his arse, legs splayed in defeat. At least he wouldn't be running anywhere. He wore grey jeans darkened to black down one leg, just like Sam's cracking blazer, but Jack suspected this was water, not blood. Flannelette shirt, a button missing in the middle. A birds-nest of curly hair, extra ruffled from the fight. He'd come out of it less bloodied than Harry but had grass in one ear, Harry having ground his cheek into the dirt. He was younger too, in his early twenties, maybe only nineteen. He had a public-school sports-field of a beard, unkempt and patchy. If his association to Sam was professional and he worked at the station, he was definitely off-screen talent. Jack rifled through his casting notes, thinking where he'd cast him. Sitcom only, Jack decided. Too shaggy even to be the deadbeat but still charming love interest. Maybe the love interest's bong-friendly best friend.

Jack's internal filing system clicked. He'd made that note before.

'The prison,' Jack said, pointing. 'In the carpark. You lied to me about being a police officer. I thought you were an insurance guy.'

The young man laid both his forearms on his knees in defeat. Nodded.

'Name. A real one. *Officer.*'

'Ryan Connors. These two know about my sister.' He nodded at Harry and Celia. Jack noticed he said 'know about' not 'know'. Harry looked annoyed, a red-smeared scowl. Celia lowered the hose, her eyes soft and focused. Ryan Connors' name had flipped a switch. He interested her.

'And why are you so interested in Sam Midford's death?' Jack asked.

Ryan shuffled, reached for his pocket.

'Slowly,' Jack said, knowing full well he had no recourse in the face of an actual weapon, except a garden hose. Ryan brought up a closed fist to show he was unarmed. He opened his palm and revealed a polaroid, faded with age, of a young girl in a school uniform.

'It's not just *his* death I'm interested in.'

It was a strange party that now gathered around the marble counter-top. Harry and Ryan had been separated and sat diagonally across from one another. Harry had a packet of frozen peas on his left knuckles. Jack and Celia took mediator positions: Jack on Harry's side and Celia on Ryan's. Heather, who'd insisted on joining the gathering, was at the head. Completing the oddity, in the centre of the five, was a resplendent chocolate birthday cake, with white and dark swirls of tempered chocolate standing rigid and tall. 'Forgot I'd ordered it, and of course it showed up yesterday,' Celia had said, plonking it down on the bench in front of them. 'So we'd better eat it. At least it's someone's birthday.' She'd nodded to Harry. Only person so far to get it right, Jack noted. She clattered five plates and served a generous piece each, trying to get rid of it. Jack's sat in front of him like a mountain.

Celia took charge of moderation. 'Before we start, no swearing, no details,' she said. 'We're doing the edited-for-TV version here. We all know what happened but present company dictates our conversation.' Celia nudged her nose at Heather. Although she had gently explained that Harry wasn't Daddy but his twin brother, Heather was still just staring at him, her mouth slowly over-chewing her dessert. Suspicious. 'And no punch-ups. I don't have a hose in here but I do have frying pans.'

All of them nodded.

'That's your sister?' Jack asked, sliding the photo back to Ryan. 'What's she got to do with us?'

Ryan pocketed it. 'These guys already know.' Ryan waved a chocolate-covered spoon at Harry and Celia. 'They haven't told you about her? Lily Connors?'

'Sam's childhood girlfriend?'

Ryan nodded. 'Next-door neighbour too. Hey, Harry. Didn't get to introduce myself before you jumped me.'

'Jack,' Harry interjected, 'I should have told you.'

Celia was silent. She kept a watchful eye on her daughter.

'Told me what?'

'Sam's mental health wasn't . . . He'd tried before.'

'You mean the little fact that he was on antidepressants? That this isn't the first time he's made an attempt? I found the pills in his jacket pocket. Celia told me the rest. Five years ago. Around the time you stopped talking to each other?'

'I don't—' Harry looked at the table. 'I didn't think you'd believe me if I told you about his history.'

'Because then it all fits together?'

'Yes. He'd had brushes before. Pills, drinking while we were on tour. I'd have to spend a night with him curled up in a bathtub, and in the morning it was always "Whoops – did I mix that with that?" When I knew that, sometimes, maybe he was actually trying. Seeing how far he could get. The Prince Alfred was his first time actually admitted to hospital. That's when I quit. Because I could see the toll that having to choose between me and the show was causing him.'

'You gave me a puzzle that was already solved with pieces missing so I'd make a different picture,' Jack huffed. 'That's not important right now. It's your money. I'll earn it.' He turned back to Ryan. 'How is Lily Connors involved?'

'She . . . died.' Ryan drew the last word through his teeth, unsure. Shot a sideways glance at Heather, then at Celia.

'It's okay. She knows about heaven,' Celia said.

'When these guys were fifteen, she was, like, a year and a bit younger,' Ryan said. 'The night they got stuck on the Ferris wheel. Thirteen years ago. I was only seven at the time.' He stopped, unsure how to string these ideas together to answer Jack's question.

'Sam ran our phone flat, remember?' Harry took over. 'When he turned it back on, he had a stack of missed calls. Obviously, a dozen from our parents. But also two missed calls from her. Lily.'

It started to come together in Jack's mind. He could see the childhood trauma affecting Sam through to adulthood. The same way Liam's fall had worked its way into Jack's psyche, always there no matter where he was or what he was doing. Little triggers. Some obvious, like every time he was up somewhere high. 'People aren't scared of heights, bro,' Liam had said, before climbing the rock formation he fell from. 'They're scared of the ground.' Some more subversive, like a slice of cake in a stranger's home.

'Jack, we weren't rescued in the middle of the night. We were rescued in the morning,' Harry confessed. 'The red and blue lights – we were so excited, but they were headed in the wrong direction. Towards home. We didn't know what had happened until they pulled us, shivering and coughing, off the ride at daybreak.' He checked on Heather, sighed, talked around it. 'She did what Sam did. You know. To herself.'

'And he missed her cry for help,' Jack summed it all up.

Ryan, Celia and Harry all nodded together.

'He carried that guilt around for his entire life,' said Celia. 'And it bubbled over two weeks ago.'

'Not necessarily,' said Harry. 'That's why we're here. We're trying to find out if someone made him do it.' Damn it, thought Jack, don't tell her you think it's a murder. 'Jack, I know you think this makes it more far-fetched. That's why I didn't tell you. But think about it. Maybe this makes it more likely? He was more susceptible. Someone taking advantage of his fragile mental health for their own gain.'

'He didn't download those photos,' said Celia. 'I don't care what the police say. Maybe he did everything else, but he didn't do that.' She met Harry's eyes, and in that small gesture Jack noticed that they agreed. Maybe not on murder, but on something.

'Ryan,' Jack said. 'So Lily's on his conscience. That doesn't explain what you're doing here.'

'I'm here because of my dad. Because he never believed Lily did it to herself either. I don't know what you're all saying about "fragile mental states" and that, but Lily was just a normal thirteen-year-old girl. Someone came in and took her from us, and the police couldn't be bothered trying to find out who did it.'

'There was an investigation?'

'No, that's the thing. Wasn't much evidence. Hank never would take it on. But Dad's always been adamant. Back then, everyone assumed he was a crackpot and ignored him. But these days, that kind of stuff is a new normal. Click download. Tell me more. I've listened to your podcasts. You can make everything a conspiracy. Dad would've fit right in.'

You can, thought Jack, I went to jail for it. He thought back to Harry in the prison: 'You've got the head for it,' Harry had said. What he really meant was: you're the only one crazy enough to do this.

Ryan continued. 'Dad's never dealt with it. He's always said it was . . . well, you know' – he glanced to Heather – 'starts with "m".' Took a mouthful of cake. 'He has lots of evidence. I won't do it justice. You should see him, my dad – he'll explain it to you better than I can. But it hurts him, it hurts him real bad. I want him to move on. So when Sam died, it just brought up a lot of memories. I wanted to dig around myself. I was too young when Dad was investigating it. He doesn't know I'm here.'

'Lily didn't ki— do that just because Sam didn't pick up his phone,' Harry jumped to his brother's defence.

'She didn't,' Ryan agreed. He turned from Harry and locked eyes with Jack, as if he was trying to impress the point on him. 'I'm just interested in the links between them.'

'And how's that going?' said Jack.

'Not great.' Ryan scraped a piece of icing smeared on his plate and licked his spoon. 'You gave me the brush-off at the prison, Channel 14 wouldn't let me past the front door, and then Harry punched me in the nose. Don't know if I'm cut out for what you do.'

Jack thought back to his last investigation: sounded like Ryan was nailing his usual process. He was thankful he had gotten through this one without getting beat up so far. 'You have nothing to go on except that they knew each other when they were kids, and now they're both dead?'

'Not quite,' Ryan said. He pointed at Jack. 'I've got you. You're actually the most interesting link.'

'I've never even been to Wheeler's.'

'You haven't. But I've listened to your stuff, dude. You cover . . . well, you know.' He made a *Psycho* stabbing motion. 'People doing themselves in isn't your specialty. So when I saw Harry was talking to *you*, well . . . I started to wonder why you'd be interested in Sam. And from there, if we were even looking for the same thing.' He made the stabbing motion again.

'So now you're telling me it's *two* "m" words?' Jack canvassed the table. Celia shrugged. Ryan nodded. Heather licked her fingers.

Harry spoke first. 'You're saying maybe Sam found out something he shouldn't? About what happened to Lily? It's all one cover-up?'

'Maybe.' Ryan shrugged. 'Think about it. What else connects two . . . thingymajigs . . . thirteen years apart?'

'We're veering into "everything's a conspiracy" territory here,' Celia cautioned. 'Your father and I have actually met, Ryan. He visited us here. We talked about the impact Lily's death had on him, and he told Sam some tips to help him through it. He never mentioned suspecting anything different.'

'Maybe he didn't want to upset you. Talk to my dad, Jack. Please. We still live in Wheeler's.'

Jack didn't really want to travel all the way down to the coast to talk to an old man with what he assumed was a corkboard full of red string webbed between photographs. But a peek into Sam's history was tempting. He looked over at Harry, who was bobbing his head up and down, liking what he was hearing.

'I've got more,' Ryan said, almost begging. 'Lily's case sounds open and shut, I know. She was in a locked room, second storey of our house. No scuffs, no signs of climbing. No broken windows.

But then Lily, you know, H-U-N-G . . .' He looked askance at Heather while he spelled it. 'With a belt.'

'That's enough,' said Celia.

'Sorry. Listen, it's not just my dad who believes Lily was "m"-worded,' Ryan said. 'Sam did too. He wrote us a letter.'

CHAPTER 16

Jack drove Harry home. Celia had boxed them up slices of birthday cake – 'Please, take it. I can't look at it' – and bundled them out of the house. 'All this talk of murder is exciting and all, but I've still got a child to look after.' Ryan, for his part, had been dead set on Jack and Harry meeting his father, Maurice. He'd refused to tell them any more about the letter, said that he couldn't do it justice and that they needed to make the trip to Wheeler's Cove. 'Besides,' he'd said snidely, 'it's my intellectual property and you can't use it in your program unless I say so.' That was a fair point, and whether Jack was making a program or not – he still wasn't sure he had anything to make one out of – he needed to see the letter.

Jack could tell Ryan wanted to get them both down to Wheeler's for a different reason. He was impressed with himself, having stumbled into what might be a real conspiracy. More than that, Jack could see that Ryan possessed the classic younger brother trait of wanting approval from his father. He looked up to him. *He can explain it better than I can.* That must have been harder still, when all the attention was diverted to a sibling who'd died a decade ago.

Ryan had said as much: he had been too young to help at the time. He wanted to solve this for his father.

Harry lived in a less salubrious neighbourhood than his brother, in an apartment block on the side of a busy road in Wolli Creek, a recently popped-up concrete jungle of a suburb next to the airport. The street on which Jack parked was lined with hurricane fencing and corflute construction signage. It was dark; the machines lay dormant. Dust coated the road. The differences between Sam's sprinkler-perfect street and Harry's apartment jigsaw were abundant. Jack wondered just how different the two brothers were. Sure, they dressed pretty much exactly the same. Had the same performer's smile. But behind it all, Jack was starting to see the splits between them. Sam had struggled behind that smile for a long time, and Harry was no amateur at keeping secrets either. Two people, born twenty-two minutes apart, either side of midnight. Two sides of a coin. Did different days make different people?

Harry invited Jack in for a cuppa. Jack went to decline, but Harry looked at him wryly and said, 'Really? On my birthday?' They stepped on sagging plywood up the kerb. Elevator cladded with green canvas drop sheets. The corridor had black marks at hip height along all the walls. A building recently populated. Sloppy movers.

Harry's apartment would have fit a cinematic divorce. There was a sink loaded with dishes, empty takeaway containers on the bench. A washing basket on the couch with clothes half-folded beside it. Jack had thought Harry dressed quite well, but these were tracksuit pants and oversized t-shirts, nothing like the crisp suits he'd been wearing. Harry took off his brown leather jacket and lay it over the back of the couch. He took off his shirt, still torn at the shoulder, and swapped it for a plain blue t-shirt from the couch pile. The room was large, with floor-to-ceiling windows, and there were two bedrooms – Harry's 2 per cent went a fair way. Jack wandered over to check out the view. The city sparkled with night-time lights. Across a small lagoon, airport landing strips blinked red.

'I'll give you the tour,' Harry said, handing him a steaming mug of clear herbal tea. Jack sniffed it. 'Want something harder?'

'No, thanks,' Jack said. Then, 'Nice place.'

'It goes all right,' Harry said.

Jack wondered for a moment if Harry had cared about the huge differences between his life and his brother's. The airport apartment versus the pristine long-driveway McMansion. The single life, complete with half-finished pad thais, against a partner and a child. Anonymity versus fame. Harry had had to pack in his entertainment career to protect his brother's health, and watch Sam's career flourish from the sidelines. A train whined past like a boiled kettle. In the middle of the night, when a plane rattled the windows, did Harry lie alone in his bed and blame his life on Sam?

'How do you know Beth?' Jack asked.

'She was some kind of assistant on one of our early interviews, just getting started in TV. So I met her, but it's not like we hung out. And then when we did the live shows, she popped up again as our tour manager. Sam insisted she was coming on tour with us, and then to Montreal.' Just as Celia had said: Sam made it to the top and he took his friends with him. Harry shrugged. 'So they must have become friends back then. Speaking of back then, are we going to Wheeler's tomorrow?'

'Don't think we have much of a choice,' Jack said. 'If he did leave a note, we need to see it.'

'Why leave a note with the Connors and not with Celia? Or me?'

'I don't know. Ryan said it was a letter, remember – not necessarily a suicide note.' But Jack knew it was a limp deflection.

'You're still on my side. Right?'

Jack blew on his tea. Harry's tongue darted out and tasted the fresh cut on his lip.

'I don't know, Harry.'

'I get it. I didn't bring you up here to argue. I wanted to show you my office.' Harry guided Jack to the second bedroom and opened the door, flicked the light on. It was a room ringed with bookcases. But they weren't filled with books – they were jammed with every type of recording media Jack could think of. One shelf had the black spines of VHS tapes. Another, clear plastic chunky cases for audio cassettes. Translucent-green thin-spined cases for CDs and DVDs. Half-moons of black plastic peeked from cardboard cases: records. Everything had white labels with handwritten black-felt-marker. A desk was built into one of the bookcases. On it sat a radio set with a chunky pair of enamel headphones – no Dr Dre Beats here, these could command submarines – and the type of microphone a TV show's principal has on his desk. The type where you leaned over and pressed down the base with three fingers, where clearing your throat was mandatory. Next to that was a computer with a huge monitor. The hard-drive whirred underneath next to a VHS player, a DVD player and even an 8-track.

On a small table in one corner was a record player. It was the only area without shelving. There hung a framed poster with H-A-R-R-Y spelled out in beautifully painted cursive, a flourish beneath each letter. Four dots under the 'H'. A dot and a dash under the 'A'. Morse code, Jack figured. A small gold plaque had been added beneath this. *Happy 21st, Love Mum and Dad*. Harry saw Jack looking at it.

'That's Morse,' Harry said. 'Dad was a radio guy, professionally, but amateur HAM at home. He got me and Sam these for our twenty-first. He had an office just like this when we were younger; he would go upstairs and put the headphones on and dial in to some of his buddies. Kids think Morse is super-lame, I can attest to that from when he tried to teach us. Neither Sam or I even bothered to learn our names. I realise now he's gone that he was just trying to leave us a piece of him.' Harry looked at the framed poster with affection and memory in his eyes. 'I should learn, one day.'

'Your dad worked in radio?'

'Weatherman. These' – he pointed at the cassettes – 'are most of his broadcasts. Physical media is under-appreciated. There's nothing like the pure crackle of a record scratching on the surface. It's all cloud and digital now. But if we hadn't kept tapes, we'd have nothing left of him.' He slotted one in the tape machine and a crackly AM-style announcer gave the weather for the South Coast. 'Car accident, both of them, maybe six months before Montreal,' Harry said, then pressed stop and picked a record out. 'This is Mum. She was a jazz singer. That's her record player.' He placed the needle in the groove. His mother had a husky voice, beautiful. The sound wasn't as clear as a digital recording, but it felt more earthy, real. She was a crooner, each word pain-and-gin-laden. In a concert hall, songs like these don't fly through the rafters, they sink to the floor. Jack imagined her with a fur shawl, painted fingernails curled around a gleaming silver mic stand. 'Not famous enough to be able to download, can't find her online much, and even if you did, what about in another ten years? So it's the physical stuff that keeps her around. These' – he pointed to a different section of tapes – 'are the homemade ones. Her singing us lullabies. Dad recorded them. Part of his hobby.' He picked up another tape, labelled *Birravale 1987*. 'He was a bit of an audiophile. Sometimes he just would go out, sit by the lake or the waves and record that. Or go to a town and sit in a forest, microphone out. Found this the other day, thought you might like it. Up at those wineries, it's just an hour and a half of birds and breeze. Very relaxing.'

'Birravale is anything but relaxing,' Jack said. 'But you know what I'm going to ask.'

'Of course. Dad passed all this down to me but I've added my own.' He pointed to the stack of DVDs. 'Every episode, opening crawl to end credits, of *Midnight Tonight*. Five seasons, two hundred eps per season, plus specials.'

'You recorded every episode for five years, but you couldn't pick up the phone?'

Harry shrugged. 'Brothers.' As if that explained it. 'This is why I collect on physical. At least there's something left of him now.'

Harry rifled through the discs and picked one, slid it into the DVD player. He sat down in front of the screen. 'Nice to watch the normal ones, sometimes. Seen that other one too many times.' Jack imagined Harry, pallid grey from the flickering glow, scrolling back and forth on his brother's death. He was glad that he had come, to see that Harry wasn't obsessed with the horror of it. He just missed his brother.

'Welcome to *Midnight Tonight*,' Sam was saying. 'Coming up, we've got some very good friends of mine, Coldplay!' He looked happy, enjoying it. His hand, one finger shortened, played that invisible piano. *Tap tap tap tap*. Maybe, Jack thought, his fidgeting was less nerves and more a symptom of the medication Jack now knew he was on. Either way, Sam was smooth and slick and professional. Jack empathised; he wondered if Sam had had the same feeling he'd had at his sickest, of just having to get up, go to work, and get it done. You put the mask on every day. Sam looked like he was as good at it as Jack was.

'Let me show you this one.' Harry paused the episode, ejected the disk, and leaned back, reaching above the screen. He clacked his finger along the spines of the cases. Picked one right at the end, took it out and inserted the disk. The vision that popped up was fuzzy, the image slowly coming into focus as if blinking awake. The set was different, a plain desk with a coloured spotlight and a couch for guests. No entry stairwell, no fancy wooden panelling. The main difference, however, was that there were two hosts. The Midnight

Twins were both standing in the monologue spot in ill-fitting suits. Jack couldn't tell who was who.

'Welcome,' they both said at once and then glared at each other.

'We're the Midnight Twins.' Again overlapping. They swapped another comically exaggerated glare.

'We agreed I would do the welcome,' they said in perfect unison. The audio quality was echoey – you could hear the cavernous sound stage around them. They moved into a routine that had them both talking at the same time throughout the argument:

'No. We agreed I would do the welcome.'

'You said I could do it.'

'You said *I* could do it!'

'Let's settle this!'

This bickering led into their trademark game of rock paper scissors, after which the title card emerged. It was not the flashy neon sign Jack had seen on set, but rather a cartoon font laid directly over the camera image as they both took their seats. *The Midnight Show*. A different title. This was the pilot episode. There was minimal editing, direct-to-video image quality, clunky transitions and missed lines and retakes. No studio audience or laugh track. The production value lay somewhere between an iPhone held in the air at a concert and amateur pornography.

What stood out to Jack first was that the two of them had a natural rapport and unique style on screen. Despite the low quality, there was something there. Second, as they took their seats and started delivering jokes and interviews, was that Sam's hand was resolutely still. Hundreds of episodes later, Sam's nerves would shine through in his damaged hand, but here, recording his first-ever episode to pitch executives, Sam didn't fidget once. Because his brother was by his side, Jack assumed. It had its own sad charm.

'I like this bit,' said Harry, fast-forwarding through. Jack watched with him for a while, but then Harry seemed to forget

Jack was there: he leaned closer to the screen, laughed at something his brother said. He was so absorbed, he didn't notice Jack eventually leave the room. Didn't hear him rummage through drawers for a pen, leave a note saying, *Wheeler's, tomorrow, pick you up,* on the bench next to his empty mug. The room flickered grey and blue through the open door, and the Midnight Twins' mother's voice, husky and sad, filtered through the lounge as Harry watched his brother on screen and listened to his mother sing. Jack left him there. Surrounded by the ghostly voices of his family.

CHAPTER 17

Liam's chest moved up and down. Jack watched it for several minutes, the machine pumping it smoothly. A metronome. Liam was so thin his ribs became a butterfly skeleton threatening flight but never taking off. Up and down. Was Liam so different to Harry's recorded family? It was a dark thought, but Jack couldn't help it flicking through his brain. Harry kept cassettes, while Jack kept the real thing, preserving a living memory. Switch him on and off when he needed to. 'Sometimes we have to mourn the living,' Celia had said, calm and practical. Maybe that was the problem: Jack had never figured out how.

'Hey, buddy,' Jack said, pulling the chair by the window closer to the bed. 'I brought you this.' He put the slice of birthday cake down on the side table. Neither of them would eat it. Jack took the jug he'd brought and poured the nutrient-rich brown sludge into the tube that protruded from Liam's hip. It gurgled as it sucked down. The chest didn't alter in rhythm. Jack wondered if Liam knew when he was fed, some small animal part of him that licked its lips. Jack's soldiers held spears. Were Liam's strewn on a silent battlefield? Was anyone crying for a medic? Part of Jack imagined that the smell of the cake tickled something in Liam's brain, mixed with the sludge he poured into him.

Jack sat down and pulled out the iPad Beth had given him. 'You'll like this. It's starting to get complicated,' Jack said. Waited. Laughed a little. 'Yeah, I know, mate. With me it's always complicated. Mind if I run a few things past you?'

The machine wheezed. The heart-rate monitor kept pace.

'Chronologically speaking, there's a girl, thirteen years ago, who may or may not have killed herself as well. Her brother and her father think it's murder. I know – they're reading from the Harry Midford playbook. Cry murder. Sam agreed, so they say.'

Beep. Wheeze. Beep.

'Good point. Alibi is water-tight. They were both stuck four metres above the ground, it's extremely well documented and they didn't even know she'd died until they got home. Hence the guilt. I mean, I won't know for sure until I see the letter whether Sam believes it's murder too, but at this point, I think it's fair enough to believe it. So, then we track forward to now. Sam's had this girl's death – her name's Lily, did I mention that? – hanging over him for his whole life. He's struggled with depression. Feels he let her down. Yeah, you're right. Survivor's guilt.' Jack didn't dwell on the irony, engrossed in conversation with his silent brother. Both of them were faultless, and yet both to blame. You carry that on your shoulders and it can turn into anything: depression; an eating disorder; a dial tone and a *We Interrupt This Broadcast*. 'Five years ago he made an attempt on his life, was admitted to the Prince Alfred. Let me know if I'm going too quickly for you.' The sludge gurgled. 'And now again, although this time he succeeded. Even with the history, there're too many holes. The biggest one of all is the way the blood drains from his face during the broadcast. He *finds* the gun. He didn't put it there.'

Beep. Wheeze. Beep. Jack could hear his father downstairs, clattering in the kitchen. Out of time with the surgical mini orchestra upstairs.

'So we've got three questions, the way I see it, that will lead us to a suspect. First, where did the gun come from and how did they get it into the studio? Assumedly on this same day they planted the pornography on Sam's laptop. Fair? Yeah, I thought so too. Secondly, how did they get in his ear? And third, what can you possibly say to someone to talk them into killing themselves? Especially to have them make that decision in less than eight minutes, on national TV.'

Wheeze. Beep. That third question was a doozy, as far as Jack was concerned. His business for so long, when he was putting together a podcast or a television show, had been convincing, even tricking, people how to feel. He'd once convinced an entire country that a jailed man was innocent. Jack knew how to make people cry or laugh on cue. But he'd had the whole suite of senses to play with – music, images, words. Could you convince someone to end their life with words alone? And what words would you use?

Words killed people all the time. A parent signs a DNR. A politician in a velvet chair writes a memo that says *Mission approved*. A general yells, 'Fire!' A teenage boy leans across the gearstick, looks at the speedometer, and says to his friend, 'Dare ya.' Hell, Jack could pick up his phone, talk to a doctor on the other side and end a life tomorrow (*it's not killing*).

But that was thinking abstractly. He loaded up and plucked through articles on the iPad. Trying to google cases, see if it was possible. There was more than he was expecting.

In 1816 a convicted larcenist, George Bowen, was charged with 'murder by counselling' after encouraging an inmate in the adjacent cell to hang himself rather than face the gallows. Words, chattered through the bars. His cellmate had used his bedsheets. But with advances in the internet and communication technology, power and reach had changed. In 2014 a young Massachusetts girl was convicted of involuntary manslaughter after convincing her boyfriend to gas himself in his car, going so far as to suggest the parking lot in which he should do so and the details of the carbon monoxide pump he should use. News websites had published the full suite of text messages between them. One chilled Jack: *Just park your car and sit there and it will take, like, 20 minutes. It's not a big deal.* Later, when he'd started to feel woozy, she'd told him, *Get back in.* That was one of many. In 2017 a boy had purchased his girlfriend a rope and filmed her suicide to a live stream, providing a running commentary throughout. In 2019 a teenager had posted an Instagram poll on whether she should live or die. Sixty-nine per cent of people had voted for her to die. She'd thrown herself off a building mere hours later. Back in 2006 a woman had pretended to be a high-school student on MySpace to encourage her daughter's bully to kill themselves, which they did. The law took some time to adapt. In the 2014 case, the charge was involuntary manslaughter. In 2017, as the law caught up with the technology, the charge was child abuse homicide. A long way from 2006, when the woman was merely charged with violating MySpace's terms of use, and even that had been subsequently dropped.

Jack scrolled through more and more cases. 'Yeah,' he said. He absent-mindedly took a spoonful of chocolate cake and ate it. In his mind, he and his silent brother had reached the same conclusion: Sam wasn't the first, and he wouldn't be the last.

Beep. Wheeze. Beep.

'I'd bet that too. So now we just need to know who was talking to him.' The machines hummed. 'No, Liam.' He tapped the iPad. 'You're right. If anyone was in his earpiece the whole team would have heard it. That's a half-a-dozen people. They can't all be in on it. So who else is talking to him?'

Jack tried to remember what it was like on set. He'd never hosted a show, but he'd been on plenty of sets for interviews. He recalled the stimulus. Flesh-coloured tape on your chest. Sanitary pads under your arms (to avoid this, one of his colleagues had gotten botox in his *armpits* so they didn't sweat under lights). Dots under your eyelids from the spotlights when you blinked. Script in your hand. Different coloured highlighter on different sections – here a cut to video, here an ad break. But the coil in your ear, the producer, the director, they're the only ones who talk to the host.

Hang on. *Script in your hand.*

'You're right,' Jack said, giving Liam's leg a little shake. 'Maybe it's not what he was hearing. Maybe it's what he was *looking* at.'

Jack loaded up the video on the iPad. The crowd shots showed the three cameras in their taped positions as Jack had seen in the studio. Sam had a script on the desk. He faltered on the early line, drummed his fingertips with nerves. *Squinted.* Like he was squinting into the barrel of the camera. No. He was re-reading a line. He was squinting at the *teleprompter*.

Jack's heart was hammering. Liam was chattering away in his brain, talking back. Alive in memory. Recorded. Jack zoomed through the footage, hoping for a glimmer of an angle where he could spy any of the words on the prompt. Nothing. A chunky unit that looked like a camera, the teleprompter had side visors to prevent reflections on the text screen, where white text scrolled up a black screen, but unfortunately that blocked any view in audience shots. As always, Sam was on set by himself for the opening monologue. The words were for him and him alone.

Someone was hunched by the unit, in stage blacks and a cap. Sunglasses. As automated as the other production technology became, the autocue remained resolutely antiquated. It still required a manual operator to adjust the speed of the scroll to the presenter's cadence. The video flitted past them so quickly, and they were so bunched up in their coat, that Jack couldn't even tell if it was a man or a woman. Not Beth. She was there in crowd shots, headset mic a black line on her jaw.

Jack reached the end of the video. The gun went off. Sam dropped out of shot. The plasma fell behind him and then it was static. Cut to Gareth yelling at the camera. Why was Gareth at the recording? Beth had told him he sometimes dropped in, but it still struck Jack as odd that he was at this specific recording. Jack checked back. Gareth wasn't in shot when the vision showed the teleprompt operator, so no alibi. But he was wearing different clothes when he demanded the camera be shut off. That ruled him out.

Through the whole recording, there wasn't a glimpse of the tele-prompter screen. A theory Jack couldn't prove. He'd have to talk to Beth about the staff logs tomorrow. Prove it some other way. He squeezed the corners of the iPad in frustration. He wished he could see what Sam was seeing, but his view was only one way. He'd need the camera to literally film a mirror to see back through Sam's eyes. No mirrors on set.

Jack had a memory. Standing backstage, finger on the small perfect circle of the broken plasma television, his foggy self reflected back at him. He scrolled the video. It all happened so quickly, but in the few seconds after the bullet hit, before the screen fell, it had shorted out to pure black.

The perfect surface to reflect white text.

Jack paused the video. Sam was a blur of colour falling out of screen. Behind him, the TV, blank and black, had the fuzziest of text reflected in it.

Jack's *one thing* list was growing.

Did he believe that the pornography was planted? Maybe. Everyone seemed surprised by it, but then, why wouldn't they? He hadn't decided. But there was plenty that he did believe now. He believed that Sam was not prepared to die, based on his behaviour, his clothes and his past. He believed that it was a strange choice to die in public, in front of his partner and child, without leaving a note (more than the one Ryan had suggested, in any case). It was a leap of faith to believe that someone could talk someone else into killing themselves. But the cases he'd researched were reputable sources. It was *possible*. Add that Sam was of fragile mind, on medication . . . And now he knew – not believed, *knew* – one more thing. That someone *had* been talking to him.

Jack zoomed in. The text was mirrored backwards. Jack took a pen and wrote it one letter at a time. Tried not to jump ahead – he wanted to see it all in full. Breathed. Looked at the last words Sam Midford ever saw.

I THOUGHT YOU WANTED THIS.

DON'T BACK OUT ON ME NOW.

Murder by counselling.

Harry was right.

PART 4

RESHOOTS

This is a killing in which the murder weapon was words.
ACLU Massachusetts' legal director, Matthew Segal,
regarding the death of Conrad Roy III, June 2017

CHAPTER 18

On the surface it didn't appear that those eleven words could convince a man to take his life. But Jack didn't know what had come before, or even the context they were in. *I thought you wanted this* hinted that Sam was, in some way, complicit. Jack reminded himself they had no conclusive proof that the pornography was planted (so maybe he *had* owned it). *Don't back out on me now* sounded personal. As if Sam had made some kind of deal. *Forgive me.*

Jack considered ringing Harry. It was late, but he might still be up, in his room of voices. Jack thumbed the dial button on his phone, deciding how much to tell him.

'Jack.' His dad interrupted his thoughts from the doorway. Red polo. Night shift. Name tag still pinned. 'We can't keep avoiding each other.'

'Tricky in this house.' Jack spread his arms. 'No doors.'

'Enough jokes. We need to talk about it,' Peter said. And it was as if they were in Celia's kitchen, talking around *it* for the sake of a child.

No point in subtlety here, Jack figured. 'You want to kill him, I'd rather keep him alive.'

'It's not that simple.'

'It is that simple. We're talking about a switch, aren't we? It's on or it's off.'

Peter walked into the room, placed a hand gently on Liam's ankle. He clocked the cake box, eyes darting back expectantly to Jack. Checked the corner of his lips. Chose his battle and didn't mention it. Ran his thumb over the blankets, tight on Liam's bony limbs as if vacuum-packed.

'It's just . . . maybe it's time.'

'I don't want to talk about this,' said Jack. He changed the topic. 'I need to go down south tomorrow, to the coast. That new job, we've got some leads. Might be a few days. You might not see me.'

'You're poking around murders again, aren't you? This isn't healthy. You've been home *two* days.'

'You know we need the money.'

'Whatever they're paying you, what does that buy? A year? Two? What happens after that?'

'I'll get a new case. Keep going.'

'I don't *want* you to.'

'Well, that's not up to you, is it? *I'm* doing what *I* have to.' Jack slapped his chest on the 'I's.

'And I'm not?' Peter stepped towards him, on the verge of yelling now. 'I've just sat on my hands for two years while you were in prison?' He ripped off his name tag and threw it on the bed. 'I'm sixty-five and I work in a *fucking bottle shop*.'

Jack's father was always softly spoken. After they'd lost the boys' mother at an early age, and then Liam's accident, he and Jack had relied on each other more than most. They didn't have these kinds of blow-ups. Peter never swore. But it was all coming out now.

Jack stood, eye to eye. 'What if this was reversed? Give it twenty, thirty years and you're in a nursing home and you're lying in this bed. Wouldn't you want me to fight for you?' he asked.

'I'd want you to do what's best for me. It's called mercy.'

'Who are we to be merciful?'

'Depends who you're doing it for. Him or you?'

'He's not in pain.'

'He's not anything.'

'He's my brother.'

'He's *my* son!'

The loudest his father had ever yelled stunned them both. Peter took a half-step backwards. His hands were shaking. Liam's chest kept time, unperturbed by the argument. *He's not anything.* A shell. *My* son. *My* brother. Was he either?

'It's your call though, isn't it?' Jack said in a low voice. 'You don't need my okay. Why don't you just do it then?'

'I want you to be involved.'

'No, you don't.'

Peter chewed his lip. 'We should sleep on it,' he said. Anger gone. Surrender.

'No.' Jack wasn't finished. 'Don't thrust this holier-than-thou stance in my face when you won't do it either.'

Those words seemed to pull Peter's spine from him. He crumpled to sit on Liam's bed, hand on his shell-son's thigh. He looked at Liam's face while he spoke to Jack.

'You're right. It is my decision. And I've tried. I had the doctor and the ambulance here four months ago, ready to take him. But I couldn't do that to you. I couldn't have you walk out of prison to an urn on a mantle. What kind of father would that make me? And now you're here, and I've realised the reason I backed out is that I'm not strong enough to decide on my own.' Peter sighed. 'I'm not asking for your permission. I'm asking for your help.'

'It's not fair,' Jack sputtered. Which was such a pointless complaint to the universe, and one Jack didn't often make, even on his knees on tiled toilet floors. But here he had nothing else.

'I shouldn't have to.' He put a hand on his father's shoulder. A bridge between them. Some understanding. Or just to steady himself. The image of his father, standing in this room with paramedics and an ambulance on the lawn, while Jack sat in a prison cell and scratched chalk marks off a wall. It made him feel ill.

'I need you to do this for me. Please.'

'Dad.' Jack's mouth was dry. What Peter was saying finally made sense. Jack had thought for so long that he and Liam had been in separate prisons – Jack's mind, Liam's body – but Liam wasn't a prisoner. He *was* the prison. Jack's. Peter's. His body the bars.

'Don't feel like you're taking anything from him. Maybe it is right. It doesn't seem fair that it's you, but maybe this is the way.' Peter crossed an arm across his chest and laid a hand over Jack's. He said softly, 'You were with him at the start and you'll be there at the end.'

Jack jerked his hand away. *There at the start.* Up the top, before Liam fell. Jack had been there too. He'd kept it a secret until, at last, he'd told his father before he went to prison. *There at the end.*

'I didn't mean it like that,' Peter stammered as he saw Jack's reaction. 'You know I don't think . . .'

'You did.' Jack backed away.

'I said it wrong.'

'You're saying that I put him there, and now you're asking me to finish him off.'

'That's not what I meant.'

'It's not what you meant,' spat Jack, 'but it is what you said.'

If there was a door he would have slammed it.

Down the stairs. Keys from the bowl. Out to the car. Engine on. His father didn't chase him outside. Jack pulled the car in a circle back onto the road. Headlights scanned a silhouette in the doorway. Ground the gearstick. Tears in his eyes. He was short of breath. Stomach sick. Shoulders seized tight. He was so mad and insulted and upset it was like he'd gone a few rounds in the ring. He'd never had an argument like that with his father. His hands were shaking and he couldn't stop them. Their barbs were only words and yet he still felt physically bruised. As he drove away, one thought kept circling through his head.

Words kill people all the time.

CHAPTER 19

Jack tore through suburbs at fifteen kilometres over the speed limit. Part of him planned on going to the television studio, part of him didn't care where he was going. He just needed to be out of that house.

He ground his teeth, another symptom of his illness. Sometimes he felt like grains of sand were stuck to his tongue. Couldn't spit them out. He cut his mouth often, his teeth were tongue-sharpened shivs. His mouth was sweet, sticky. The windscreen was blurred; he flicked the wipers. No change. No rain. Tears in his eyes. Gritted his teeth harder.

When he'd told his father that he'd been with Liam when he fell, Peter had responded with warmth and forgiveness. He'd told him that he'd never blame a freak accident on a twelve-year-old boy. That it wasn't his fault. Hearing that had been monumental for Jack's condition, a real turning point in him being able to regain some control. He knew where he'd be without that support – mouth dripping, gums worn. He now saw more clearly through Mr Midnight's eyes. It wasn't Sam's fault that Lily had killed herself, but he had missed her call for help. It wasn't *not* his fault either.

At least that's how it felt. Jack understood Sam more now than he ever had. Because Peter's words had physically hurt Jack, hampered his breathing, tightened his neck, soldiers at the armoury, bile automatic in his throat. *We went up together. Liam slipped.* Whether Peter meant it or not, he had inadvertently unveiled Jack's biggest fear: that his father didn't believe him.

The road hummed underneath him as the needle climbed. The view through the windscreen blurred with tears or rain, or both. Lights whipped past. All it would take was to turn the wheel slightly, a few degrees to the left . . .

It's not killing.

Depends who you're doing it for.

He glanced in the rear-view mirror, but didn't recognise the man staring back. His brow was furrowed and his eyes shone viciously. His forearms were stretched out in front, disappearing from view beneath the mirror's frame. Jack knew it was because he was grasping the steering wheel, but he couldn't help thinking that the man in the mirror had his arms outstretched because he was throttling the life out of someone.

Channel 14 was the only building on the block with lights on. The glass atrium exuded a fuzzy glow, the type that made your nose twitch and eyes water. Jack didn't really know why he'd come. The autocue discovery was exciting, but there wouldn't be anyone to interview until morning, the studio likely locked. Was he going to go in and re-watch Sam on a loop, over and over, until daybreak? He'd seen him die enough times. But the building had many positives. It was open. He had a security pass. It wasn't the 24-hour KFC across the road. Overall, it seemed like the healthiest option. Lots of boxes ticked.

Jack turned the car off and got out. His nose told him it was cold but, for once, his circulation was pumping hard and he was blooded and warm. He walked to the entrance and stood outside the glass. Inside, the security guard had his feet up, reading a book. He'd be easy to sneak a pistol past, Jack thought, except for the bloody metal detectors. The television screen was still cycling through those idiotic promos. Big block letters thundered onto the screen. WHO. Then the flash of several faces, turning to the camera in slow motion. WILL. The cinema on fire from the longer promo. DIE? A close up of a gun firing. Then a date and time. It was an ad for the soap opera the security cameras had been turned off for. An *event*. Jack thought it was tactless. Surely Channel 14 was sick of deadly *events*.

He got out his pass and was just about to press it to the sensor when he heard a voice.

'Yes, I know. I'm here now.'

Beth Walters' voice was clear and strong in the night. She was coming around the corner from the staff carpark. Jack ducked off the path and into the dark, squatted behind the hedge. He looked back at the entrance. Beth wore a knee-length overcoat and was on the phone. She had her back to him, hand against the door. It slid open. She stood in front of it for a moment, her free hand clenching the air in frustration.

'You promised,' she said. There was a pause. The next thing she said was muffled – she was lowering her voice in anger – but Jack caught the end of it. It sounded like she said, 'If I have to deal with another bloody skeleton . . .' Then a sigh. 'All right. All right.'

Then she was inside. The door slid closed behind her and Jack watched the mime play out behind the glass. The security guard spun in his chair, recognised Beth and nodded her through. She ended the call, tossed the phone and a handful of junk into the plastic bucket, and walked through the metal detector. Then she took her stuff and disappeared onto the news floor. The guard returned to his book.

Jack stood and followed Beth's path into the foyer. The security guard looked surprised to see him, but Jack had the right credentials so the guard waved him through. Jack collected his tray of items and walked across the news floor. Almost all the booths were empty. One scruffy head was hunched over next to a pyramid of bright-green cans. There was an industrial vacuum cleaner sitting in the walkway. The questions in his mind were piling up. Why was Beth here in the dead of night? And whose skeletons was she hiding? Jack was, like any good producer, prone to hyperbole, but he had the common sense to know she wasn't talking about actual skeletons. It was shorthand for those in someone else's closet. Those of whoever she was talking to. Whoever's secrets she was tired of covering up.

There was light to his right – shadows on the walls, movement, more than one person – in the direction of Stage Three. As Jack got closer he could see the hydraulic door was open a person-sized crack and the studio lights were on inside. Jack's heart quickened. He walked to the opening.

And felt a hand clasp his shoulder.

'Not another step,' Beth Walters said from behind him.

CHAPTER 20

Beth had removed the overcoat, revealing a svelte black jacket, frilly blouse underneath. Her hair was styled in waves, lipstick on. Very well dressed for such a late-night excursion.

'Not tonight, Jack,' she said. She sounded flustered, like she didn't have time for bullshit. 'What the hell are you doing here?'

'Could ask you the same thing,' Jack said.

'No, you couldn't. *I* work here.'

'Surprised to see you pulling overtime.' He nodded towards *Midnight Tonight*'s studio and took a half-step towards it.

Beth stepped quickly around him, blocking his way. Stopped short of putting a hand on his chest. 'I'm serious, Jack. I don't have time for this.'

'What are you doing in there?'

'What part of *piss off* don't you understand?' she hissed, glancing around as if someone might spy them talking.

'And what do you think my job is?' Jack took another step. Beth didn't give any ground. His chin was at her forehead; her breath feathered his collar. Jack wasn't the type of man to push her out of the way just to satisfy his curiosity, and she knew that.

'Jack—' Now her eyes were pleading, looking up at him. 'Just go.'

Jack tried to figure out if she was scared – of someone else? – or if she was nervous.

'It's the teleprompter,' Jack said. It took Beth a moment to figure out what he was talking about. 'Sam wouldn't have done it on his own. Someone convinced him to do it. I don't know how, but they did it through his autocue.'

The revelation didn't crawl across Beth's features with the slow dawn of shock, but rather with the surprise of a torch flashed on and off. Her jaw clenched, neck tense, and then it was gone.

'Away from the door,' she said softly.

She led Jack into the *Breakfasters* studio. It was eerily empty. Jack had always found empty film sets disconcerting. Everything so plastic and cheerless. *The Breakfasters* was a permanent fixture, so the cameras were set in position. So too was an autocue: a television screen, bulbous glass like it was from the 80s, inside a four-walled cone. It was a big unit, almost like another camera.

'This' – she patted it – 'killed Sam?'

Jack nodded. 'I think he was influenced, yes. I know you won't believe me.'

'Have you heard of *13 Reasons Why*?' Beth asked, which was so off topic it surprised Jack. He thought she'd be more doubtful. He shook his head. 'It was a popular young adult drama, targeted at, like, teens and up, I suppose. The whole concept of that show is centred around this high-school girl's suicide. And the finale, well – they went there.' She shrugged. 'Showed it all on screen. Graphic stuff. In the bath with a razor blade. Ballsy broadcast move. We wouldn't have done it, but, hey, we're a commercial network.'

'They got complaints?'

'Fuck-tonne.' Beth nodded vigorously. 'Schools, parents. People said it gave their kids ideas.'

Jack had received the same complaints when he was making his show. Accusations that he was 'putting ideas in people's heads' and 'glorifying violence'. It was nothing new to filmmakers who kept up with current events – people complain because they don't like seeing the real world thrown back at them. They want the sanitised, Hollywood version. Jack knew if he showed people the grim reality, the Lily Connors of the world, they'd complain that they may as well be watching the news.

'Thing is,' Beth continued, 'they might have been right. Researchers are now saying there was a spike in youth suicide the month that show aired. A significant one. They are saying there's a correlation. It's just a study or two, but it's got broadcasters on notice. Duty of care, and all that.'

Jack thought about this. His research had led him to believe that people could be influenced by text messages, phone calls, online messaging. Cult leaders used to have the market cornered on brainwashing, but now it could be anyone with a voice, a phone or a book. Why not a television show? And it wasn't as ludicrous as *brainwashing* but it was just as vicious. 'That's why Gareth's so keen to shut this down?'

She nodded. 'If there's something to be found, he wants you to find it first. Because it's our fault. We put that to air. I've had nightmares – how many ideas have we put in people's heads?' She swallowed. There was guilt there. Jack could see she held it on her shoulders. She'd seen Sam's bloodied mess of a head. 'It's like people who shoot up a school because they play *Grand Theft Auto*.'

'More than that,' said Jack. 'I've read about kids who've done it because they were told to.'

'I've seen those on the news. But these stories are about teenagers, Jack. Their emotions are a warzone. You're telling me someone can do the same to a grown man?'

She was right. All of his research had been younger people (except for the case in 1816, but that man had been on death row in the first place). It didn't make Sam's death impossible, it just made him unique.

'He had history. Medication. Previous attempts,' Jack said.

Her silence said enough. She hadn't known.

'Even if—' She hesitated. Trying to build the scenario. She couldn't. 'I mean . . . What words would you use?'

Jack handed her the slip of paper that he'd transcribed the lethal words on. She read it aloud, slowly, unconvinced. Jack told her it was just the end of the script, what he'd managed to grab from the reflection in the broken plasma screen. The killer could have said anything in the eight minutes preceding. She was nodding as he explained, but her eyes were staring at those eleven words as if they had the power to set the paper alight.

'I need the autocue script,' Jack said. 'For the rest of it.'

She looked up, frowning. 'We don't have scripts.' She swivelled the autocue so Jack could see it. 'These are made of glass and mirrors and screens. It's just a reflective unit – there's no computer inside it. No memory or storage. Scripts are run off a USB stick or an iPad. We tend to prefer iPads.'

'Okay, so I need the iPad.'

She shook her head. 'We delete prompt scripts. There's no need for them, because it's supposed to be the same as the normal script. That I can give you, no problem. But I checked before I gave it to you, just in case there was sensitive company information on there, and, honestly, there was nothing like this.' She took a breath. 'It gets worse.'

'Of course it does.'

'I've had that day stuck in my head for weeks. I go over the details. Our operator . . . it was a different person to usual. Maybe he was sick, swapped a shift? Sometimes we have interns.

I don't know. When I showed up there was someone in his spot, ready to go. It's a frantic job putting a live TV show to air. I just assumed someone had sorted it, ticked it off my list and got on with my job.'

'Did you talk? Remember anything at all about them?'

'They were wearing a cap. Big coat indoors. I thought it was unprofessional but I didn't talk to them. I only saw them from the back. Got a thumbs up before we rolled camera. After, God, it was just chaos. It's not like we did a headcount. I'm sorry, Jack. You know how producing a show works – if something's not broken, I'm not dashing around trying to fix it. At some point you trust everyone is where they're supposed to be and doing what they're supposed to do.'

And the security cameras were off, Jack almost sniped but held his tongue. All of this left him with only the screenshot of the footage. A fuzzy, hunched-over spectre in a blink-and-you'll-miss-it crowd shot.

Beth's phone buzzed. She pulled it out, checked it. 'I really do have to go, and I really do have to ask you to leave.'

Jack ignored her. 'This mystery operator. They talked their way in. They know how to use the tech. They managed to secrete a gun under the desk. This seems like someone who knows what they're doing.'

'By "someone who knows what they're doing", I assume you mean someone who works here?' Beth cocked an elbow, hand on her hip.

Jack was suddenly aware that she'd taken him away from anyone who might see something happen. There was a long silence. Jack could see Beth weighing up whether to take the accusation personally. It was strange: in the empty *Breakfasters* studio, it felt as if they'd cut to a commercial break.

All or nothing, Jack figured. 'Whose skeletons are you hiding?'

Beth's forehead crinkled; she pursed her lips. It was either a look of concern or she didn't understand the question.

'I heard you,' Jack said. 'Outside, on the phone. Why are you here so late, and why are you so keen to see the back of me?'

Beth's look of concern changed slowly, the tide coming in on a wry smile.

'Skeleton *crew*,' she almost shouted.

Jack immediately felt foolish. A skeleton crew was the bare minimum number of people required for production. She was here in stage make-up, dressed for work, not sabotage.

Beth continued just to rub it in. 'I don't have enough of a team to make what they want me to make, so I was telling Gareth I was sick of working with a skeleton crew. Damn it, Jack, why don't you just accuse me outright? I'm on the video, I'm not operating the prompter. You've got my alibi. Jesus. I'm here at fucking' – she checked her watch – '*one* in the morning because I'm getting spanked over putting his death to broadcast, and working grave-yards is my penance, okay? And I've worked too hard. I'm not letting my career sink because of what he did. So I'll take the slops and smile, and say it's delicious and *still* ask for more. Because that's what you do here if you ever want one of those.' She waved an arm towards the four vacant panel chairs nearby.

'Do you want to sit in that chair?'

She looked at her phone again. 'I have work to do. Do I need to get security?'

'I'm allowed to be here.'

'Not tonight.'

'Did Channel 12 offer you a job?'

'What?' She grimaced like she was allergic to the question.

'Channel 12. Tom Dwyer. *The Round Table* – were they head-hunting you? I saw the list of new host options in the tabloids.'

'Come on, Jack.' She kept checking over her shoulder. 'You know how these things work. You've gotta make sure the stars don't feel too comfortable, otherwise you get a dictatorship. Tom Dwyer was on our list, and Sam was on theirs. I read about these things at the same time as the rest of the public. Full credit to Channel 12 for actually spicing up their demos, though I don't know whether to take it as an insult. 'Cause they use that as a threat. 'Watch out' – her fists exploded into little fireworks of mock-surprise either side of her head – 'We might replace you with a *woman*.' She wriggled her fingers as if saying something scary.

'So what are you hiding here?'

Seeing Jack wasn't going to drop it, she checked over her shoulder, then whispered, 'It's a finale, okay? We've flown back three people from the jungle and we're choosing a winner. Filming three endings. Because someone always spoils a reality winner these days so you need to throw in a few fake-outs. Terrorist security comes second to television these days. No one is supposed to know. By all reports, they're still in the jungle. That's why I'm working with a small crew. And then you blunder into the middle of it? I can't have this set exposed to *anyone*, let alone someone who walks around with their own recording equipment. And if I stuff up again . . .' She spoke quickly and with a harsh edge. *I'm telling you because I have to, but I'm not happy about it.* Her eyes flitted over Jack's face as she spoke, looking for signs she'd convinced him. Her voice softened for a final plea: 'I'll ask around about the autocue tomorrow. Let's swap numbers – I'll call you, I promise. But tonight, will you do me a favour and just go?'

Jack walked back to his car. Sat in it, engine and lights off. He believed her, but he still had too many questions. He wanted to see if anything else happened. Besides, he had nowhere else to go. The 24-hour KFC had a bright fluorescent-white sign glowing across the road. Jack focused on Channel 14.

Beth was in the building a while, two hours or so. Jack had forgotten to check the time when she'd gone in. Amateur. He reclined his seat, eyeline level with the window. It was a fairly futile effort. A bright red VW Golf with a *For sale* sign is not the best stake-out vehicle. Not only was he underprepared, but he was also out of practice. He almost missed her coming back out. He was rubbing his eyes and then she was standing in front of the entrance, having a cigarette. She ground it out with her toe, then knocked on the glass and waved her arms at the security guard. Shrugged animatedly. That was a familiar dance: *forgot my pass.*

This time she was inside less than twenty minutes – Jack remembered to clock it – and then she was going for good. She blew a misty breath and tied her coat, walking off the path and around the side of the building. Two minutes later her car pulled out of the staff carpark. Jack lay back in his seat as she turned, her lights scything in a semi-circle above his head. When he sat up, she was merely brake lights.

Jack couldn't face home just yet. He briefly considered the absurdity of asking for refuge on Harry's doorstep, but decided against that too. He levered the seat down all the way and shut his eyes.

Jack had slept in cars before. His illness sometimes ran him on rails, like sleepwalking, where he wouldn't remember pulling himself out of bed and, fridge already raided, driving down to the all-night supermarket. Waking up with the seat back, head tilted as if at a barber, with no recollection of how he got there, gathering evidence on his body's autopilot afterwards. Searching the car for his own clues. Crumb-laden, foul-mouthed: it wasn't hard to figure out what he'd done. Multiple receipts would show he'd been in three, even four, times. Some nights he slept until morning and drove home. Other nights he'd be woken, possum-eyed in the glare of an officer's torch clacking on the window.

Even with all his experience, he slept badly. The bright white light from the KFC sluiced through the car and made the back of his eyelids glow red. He was fitful. The dashboard clock either crawled minute-by-minute or jumped forward in miniature increments. Ten-minute brackets were small victories. Eventually, the skips became larger.

When he woke next, he'd lost an hour. The white light was brighter. Closer.

CHAPTER 21

Whoever penned the phrase 'All roads lead to Rome' hadn't been to an Australian coastal town, where all roads lead, instead, to the fish 'n' chip shop.

Wheeler's Cove's fish 'n' chip shop was no different. It was called Gone Fishin' and had pale blue walls with a vinyl cut-out of a breaking wave framing the awning. It was full to bursting behind the plate-glass windows. Line out the front like a nightclub. Red and white umbrellas were staked through circular tables, most of which were taken up by silver-haired retirees in billowy white linen shirts. Teenagers, wetsuits peeled to hips, stood in circles or sat on the gutter and spread their newspaper-bound chips on the footpath. Surfboards were stood upright in the bike racks or piled three-deep against any available wall, including the window of the newsagent next door. Inside, people pushed and yelled their orders, cash in raised fists, as if placing a flutter on the dogs. Of course, it was cash only. The menu was chalk, hand-scrawled. Two asterisks marked menu footnotes:

*Tomato sauce: 50c extra.

Vegetarian options: Get fked.

It was early afternoon by the time Jack and Harry got into town. Jack had a crick in the neck from his night in the car. On the way he'd handed the iPad, on which he'd screenshotted the final frame, to Harry. Harry had read the words aloud just like Beth had. Slow, like he was learning how to read. Jack asked if the words had any special significance, or if Harry recognised them at all, and Harry simply shook his head. He was overcome with emotion. Eyes shining with welled tears, a big smile. Jack had never seen anyone so happy to be proved correct.

The highway out of Sydney went south for about an hour, before bending left into a densely forested hillside. From there was a steep descent marked with signs asking drivers to *Limit compression braking*. The opposite side of the road was dotted with cars that had pulled out of the climb early. The bush was overgrown, rainforest-like because of the water pooled and running down the hill. Glimpses of blue ocean were rare but popped up between the bends. SUVs, back windows blocked with baggage, drove past with children's faces pressed against the windows. The road levelled out at the same time as the trees thinned, ears popped and brackish air replaced the tang of brake pads on the tongue. Fifteen more minutes to Wheeler's.

The population was listed on the *Welcome* sign as two thousand, but Jack suspected the sign might have generously included pets. The entire town was propped on either side of the main road, which followed the cove in its concave bite of the coast. There were no side streets or turns. On the right, with the water, the houses were squat, timber-slatted buildings with salt-rotted fenceposts. On the left, dense foliage led up the hillside, the occasional gouged-gravel dip in the kerb or rusted letterbox the only clue of a long-winding driveway heading into the bush. To Jack's eye, it seemed there was no school, no hospital and no police station. There was one petrol station so ancient the pumps would have coughed dust, and which, Jack thought, if this was a horror film, was almost guaranteed to have an attendant spit tobacco and offer you a 'shortcut'.

Even with a bright, clear sky, Wheeler's Cove wouldn't have qualified for a tourism brochure. The beach was pebbled and grey – no famous soft yellow Aussie sand – and the ocean itself was metallic and choppy. Waves didn't glide into shore; they smacked into one another with the force and crack of duelling antlers. Surfers, no more than wetsuit-clad black dots at this distance, bobbed up and down in the middle of it. A small bridge split the town in half, and underneath the water flowed through to form a small lagoon. That was closer to making the brochure, with sandy banks, sunbathing and children splashing around. Green and silver tents rippled on the side of the lagoon: a small caravan park. Further along was a lone pub.

The carnival was seaside – Harry had told him it would probably still be there for late March – and Jack had caught his first glimpse of the Ferris wheel that had trapped the Midnight Twins and taken Sam's fingertip. It slowly spun, as if turned by the breeze. The carriages were colourfully painted and rainbow lightbulbs lined the spokes, but the lights weren't on and in the daylight all the paint was faded. Jack pulled into the parking lot alongside the makeshift caravan village.

Ryan Connors had suggested they meet at Gone Fishin' because it was easy to spot. As Jack and Harry walked through the parking lot, Jack peered into the row of caravans. A family, ranging in age from a toothless elderly man, to a beer-bellied guy in a black singlet about Jack's age, all the way down to a baby cradled on its mother's stomach, sat around a portable Weber barbecue in a semi-circle of canvas camping chairs. The man in the singlet was standing, drinking from a brown glass stubby. He took a swig, then dumped a healthy pour on the meat.

Jack and Harry walked past the carnival entranceway, which had a hessian-covered fence pulled closed and a sign that read,

Opens 4pm. Jack craned his neck upwards. The Ferris wheel was petite, only a few metres at the peak. Despite what had happened to Liam, Jack wasn't scared of heights – he just respected them – and he caught himself wondering if he would have had the guts to try to climb down. Even with the sun at its peak, the wind was blowing inland now, crisp off the water. A long night up there would have been horrible.

'Yeah,' Harry said, reading Jack's thoughts. He shrugged. 'Doesn't look so scary to me now either.'

At the fish 'n' chip shop, Harry braved ordering while Jack hung out the front to scout a table. It was an everything-cooked-in-the-same-fryer establishment. One where, if you were stupid enough to come at a peak time – lunchtime, or a warm night with a late sun – they didn't call out the orders, just threw the butcher's paper packages on the counter and, if you'd waited your fair amount of time and the parcel looked about suitable for the size of your crew, you just grabbed it and were happy with what you got. This was a no-complaints establishment. Not enough salt? Shake a dread-locked surfer on it. Too much salt? Grow a pair. Harry's TV charisma served him well, as did the informal preferential system of being 'from around here', and he came back quickly with a medium chips. He held the parcel upright, where he'd torn the top off, and gripped it like a bouquet. He offered it, and Jack – who wasn't afraid of hot chips, he was just respectful of them – took a couple. Chewed slowly.

'I'm sorry to bring this up,' Jack said. 'But the money landed. You only paid me ten thousand dollars.'

'Transfer limits,' said Harry. 'Gotta do it in pieces per day. I got you, mate.'

Ryan Connors showed before a space opened up at an umbrella-ed table. He was wearing thongs he was too cold for, boardshorts he was too dry for, and a t-shirt with a joke slogan he was too old for.

His hair was, if possible, even curlier and scruffier than it had been after fighting: salt-styled. He had a small scab on one ear, and a purple and black storm cloud brewed above the horizon of his eyebrow. Ryan wriggled a chip out of Harry's parcel, jerked his head in the universal sign for *follow me* and they walked up the hill.

'Be glad you didn't get a seat,' Ryan said. 'Kids don't sit on the kerb out of politeness. Gary and Michelle' – he snaffled another chip – 'the owners, don't pack up the benches at night. And this is on the walk home from the pub. So they've all been pissed on.' He breathed through his nose like he was powering up. 'Fuck, they make good chips, though.'

Harry took the hint and handed him the whole package, which Ryan took with delight, tearing down the sides as they walked, licking his fingers. His thongs slapped against his heels. He was walking quickly, excited. Really burning thong rubber.

The Connors' house was on the left, opposite the water, with a steep leaf-strewn driveway. Four steps into the drive, it was noticeably colder. The trees stretched out with fat green leaves that blocked the sun, the air damp. Down from the canopy, there were hundreds of hip-height ferns. Harry, pointing into the foliage, said his childhood home was a five-hundred-metre bush-bash through. Jack imagined Sam questing through the shrub, he and Lily meeting up in the dappled sun, lying in the dry leaves. Or at night. It was easy to think here, quieter, calm and secluded. Soft croaking frogs replaced the fizz of the ocean. A perfect place for a teenage rendezvous, Jack thought as they approached the house. It was the same white-painted weatherboard-slatted build as those along the beach, but while those were wind-whipped and paint-peeled, this was moss-streaked and water-stained. Two-storey, with brown wooden roof-tiles nailed down like scales. Rope swing out the front, a red plastic kayak on the lawn. It wasn't luxury, but it was peaceful. In TV land, this was the type of place that a high-powered advertising executive inherits from her dead father – Jack could see her walking up the drive, flicking her heels at every wet leaf that papier-mâchéd itself to her feet – and decides to fix up, learning about small-town friendships and love along the way.

Except for the ambulance in the driveway, Jack's script would have been perfect. Had something happened?

Ryan didn't seem put off by the ambulance. He caught Jack looking at it and said, 'Oh good, he's home. Don't freak, we're not gonna see, like, a dead body or anything. Dad's an ambo.'

'They let him just take it home?' This seemed surprising to Jack, but he didn't know any paramedics. Maybe things were more relaxed down the coast.

'Man's gotta eat,' Ryan said. 'He does the whole stretch for the hospital in Arlington, like thirty minutes away. This is in the middle of the route. Parked at the fish 'n' chip shop, parked here – does it matter? Better to keep the thing on the road than at the hospital, if something happens.'

'It takes thirty minutes to get to a hospital?' Jack said.

'Ah, sick. I see what you're doing. Right into the investigation. Depends. The night Lily died, he did it in fifteen.'

'Coming or going?' asked Harry.

'That time, he came from the hospital,' Ryan answered cheerfully, clearly not enough of an aspiring investigator to note the real question: *where was your father the night your sister died?*

Jack was impressed. Harry had astutely established an important fact. Maurice Connors wasn't home when his daughter died. The two of them were starting to think alike.

'Maybe that's why he keeps it close,' Harry said, looking at the ambulance. They hopped onto the porch. The floor was pocked with holes, gaps in the planks, not large enough to roll an ankle in, but they would swallow up dropped keys. 'He doesn't want it to happen again.'

Ryan chewed slowly while he nodded. 'Or he likes Mum's cooking.'

'Your dad's home for lunch?' Harry asked. 'Does he know we're coming?'

Ryan's eyes flashed. The black cloud on his forehead jumped and he smirked as he opened the door. 'It's a surprise.'

Maurice Connors' face moved so little, Jack suspected his son's animation compensated for it. He and a woman Jack assumed was his wife looked up at the sound of footsteps. His expression didn't change as, mid-bite of a ham and cheese sandwich, he took the two men in, and said flatly, 'What's he done?'

Jack liked him immediately. 'Can we sit down?' Jack asked.

'Don't know you yet.' At this, Maurice put the sandwich down, dusted his fingers. Thick blue veins ran ridges on his hands. 'No point sitting if you'll be leaving soon. I recognise you.' The last was to Harry. Maurice just rattled off his thoughts like he was reading a shopping list.

'Harry Midford. I used to live next door.' Maurice didn't react, so Harry continued. 'Sam's brother – he's on TV a bit.'

'Yes, I know.'

'And this is Jack Quick,' Ryan said. 'He's a documentary maker. Solves *murders*.'

'Ryan,' the woman admonished, her platinum blonde curls jiggling as she shook her head. 'He doesn't need this.'

'But Mum—'

'It's fine, Sue.'

'Blood pressure, love.'

'Well, if I pass out,' Maurice said, standing, 'zap me with the thing in the driveway.'

'We're not here to cause a scene,' Jack said. 'Ryan told us about

Lily. He said you might know something that perhaps wasn't listened to properly thirteen years ago. About her death.'

'Dad, he solves *murders*,' Ryan repeated. 'Ones no one believes. Like hers.'

Jack shook his head. 'I'm not going to tell you I'm here to solve her murder. But I am here to listen.'

'What's he told you?' Maurice asked.

'I told them about the letter, Dad,' Ryan said. Maurice sighed.

'Ry,' said Sue. 'Your father's worked really hard to put this behind him.'

Ryan looked crestfallen. Jack knew he had built up their visit as a big event in his mind, figuring they'd kick the door down and blast the case wide open. To him, Sam's death had connected with the mysterious letter his father had received and, if linked, brought a new opportunity to discover the truth. Maurice had believed for a long time that Lily had been a victim. His still-living son had to share the attention with his sister, and now was Ryan's chance to not only impress his father, but, if he could put it to bed at last, perhaps get his real attention back too.

Sue's worry over reopening Maurice's amateur investigation seemed genuine. Jack wouldn't admit it to himself, but he knew Sue had one more reason to be concerned. If Sam was killed because he knew something, they might be putting Maurice in danger too.

'It's okay,' Maurice said, and gave his son a squeeze on the shoulder. But it was one of resignation, not pleasure. Ryan looked at the floor. 'If you've already told them as much. They've come all this way. Wait here.'

Maurice led Jack and Harry upstairs and to the left. Lily's old bedroom had been rejigged as an office. A desk, neatly organised, sat by the window. The remnants of the girl that used to live here were a child's single bed with a metal frame and a pink doona, and a framed collage of photos hanging by the door. Lily looked like any teenage girl. Her collection was as Jack would have expected: schoolyard snaps of a group of friends; a netball team; one major hair-remodel, jet black with a blue streak. She also had a habit of chucking up two fingers – it alternated between *peace* and *up yours* – in photos.

'Sam bought her that.' Harry tapped the corkboard. Jack noticed she had a green-gemmed ring that was clearly a favourite.

'Sorry about Ryan,' Maurice said. 'He gets his hopes up. There's not much to see. If you're looking for fingerprints or hair or anything, you probably missed the boat.'

'Tell us about the night she died.'

He swallowed. 'I was at work in Arlington. Hadn't even got the call from the police yet, but the emergency doc pulled me aside and gave me a heads up that they were bringing someone in. Maybe just in a cop car, he thought. Said the address was mine. I got back here as fast as I could. Ambulances can really move.'

'And when you got here?'

'There were cops everywhere. I just kind of ran in. I was in uniform, so everyone just assumed I was the paramedic – they would have kept me out if they'd known I was her father. I still didn't know what exactly had happened, otherwise maybe I would have kept myself out. Maybe not. I remember feeling like my heart was in my knees when I saw everyone gathered in here. She was . . .' He looked at the closet, blinked a few times and sat on the bed. 'She was in there.'

'Can I?' Jack asked, hand on the closet door. Maurice nodded. Jack opened the walk-in and looked inside, Maurice peering in after him. It was empty. A silver bar ran across the top of the space. Otherwise, it was unremarkable. Harry just stood in the doorway, watching Jack's examination. 'You don't have to tell me what you saw, but it might help.'

'She was hanging. Hung herself? Been hung? I'm not sure what phrase my therapist wants me to use. He says when I say it a certain way there's an implication . . . I don't know. It was a belt, leather, men's style with a big square silver buckle. I remember the buckle because we had to put a chunky necklace on her for the funeral, it had cut into her so badly.'

'She took one of yours?'

Maurice shook his head. 'Not mine. I asked around. But a lot of shops sell belts – it's not like she was buying a gun. No one remembered selling her one.'

'What happened when you found her?'

'The police in the room realised who I was pretty quickly, I guess when I started screaming. I had bruises down my arms from them dragging me out. They locked us in the kitchen. You know something bad's happened when a stranger makes you tea with your own kettle.'

'And Ryan?'

'Ryan was only seven. We did our best to keep him occupied. He was interested in why all the people were in the house, but he was happy enough to be staying up late and watching television.'

'Why does he say you think it's a murder?'

Maurice stood up and peered into the closet. 'For a long time, I did,' he said. 'There's no point lying to you because everyone in town knows it. Someone else will tell you if I don't. For years, I tried to find something more behind it. There was blood on the carpet, you know that? People think it's less messy, hanging, but the back of her heels were all cut up from scraping against the carpet. It was so *violent*. She was missing a fingernail. Every time I saw someone with a facial scar, I wondered if she'd scratched them.'

'Did you have any hard evidence?'

'I couldn't see my beautiful girl doing this. It felt so wrong. The police refused to take it further, to look deeper. No one else could have got in or out. The window was locked and only locks from the inside. So does the door – I know it's not great parenting, but *you* try arguing with a teenage girl who wants a lock on her door. And locked it was. Until Sue went to say goodnight and said she heard noises on the other side. Thuds, a struggle. By the time she got through, well . . . Point is – that's a closed room. No one in. Or out.'

'She asked for the lock?' Jack said, levering the door. He was surprised that the lock was on the inside. A slide bolt. Pretty durable for a teenager's bedroom.

'Couldn't talk her out of it. Brought it home one day from the hardware store herself. Said she wanted privacy,' Maurice said. 'Puberty, I guess.'

'I get it,' Harry said from the doorway. 'You decided it had to be a murder because that's the only way it made sense.' Harry said it like he knew it was true, because it was exactly what he'd done with Sam, Jack thought. Harry proceeded into the room and started fiddling with the locks on the window. Checking them, Jack realised. The windows were easily big enough for someone to slip through, but that couldn't have happened if they were found locked from within.

'Sue found it tough, me hunting ghosts and rumours. We'd fight. It got worse. And at school I knew Ryan was known as the kid with the crazy dad trying to play detective. No one believed me. I was angry all the time. I know things about hanging no parent – no person – should know. How long it takes blood to stop getting to the brain. The colour cheeks go. It's not blue – everyone thinks it's blue, but it's a greeny-grey kind of thing. There's a map of new red freckles and thin lines across your cheeks, in your eyes – a constellation of ruptured blood vessels.' He took a deep breath and blinked back a memory. 'There I go again,' he said. 'I'm grateful Sue got me into therapy. The guy I'm seeing – he made me realise that I had to choose between the family I'd lost and the family I still had.' He rubbed a hand over the blanket. 'A family is a bucket with a hole in it. You fill it up with a wife and kids, and sometimes it's so full it sloshes over the sides. It's magic. But from the moment you have kids, they're leaving. From the moment you say "until death", you're dying. It's a slow leak, but it's a leak. Mine had a bigger hole than most. I realised I had to plug it up.'

'What changed?'

'I did what I had to. What I didn't want to. I found a way to let Lily go. It was the hardest thing I ever did.'

Jack knew already he didn't have the same strength for Liam. His dad had shown him that. His voice cracked as he tried to keep the interview moving, to distract himself. 'That's why Sue doesn't want us here. We're a leak.'

Maurice nodded. 'She's worried you'll excite me. Set me back in therapy. I don't want to think about Lily's death like that anymore either. But it's okay, I've moved on.'

'No one believed you?'

'No one. Except' – he pointed at Harry – 'your brother.'

'Ryan told us about a letter from Sam,' Jack prompted.

'Of course he did. I was just giving you context before I showed you.' Maurice stood and walked to the desk. He opened the drawer and flicked through a few documents, removing a plastic sleeve with a single piece of paper inside it. He walked over to Jack; didn't hand it to him, but held it out for him to read. The light shone off the plastic and Jack had to tilt his head to read certain sections. Harry peered over his shoulder. The letter was short, typed and undated. It was noticeably old, a few years even, with faded ink. Scarred from refolding. This was no suicide note.

Dear Maurice,

It's funny how everything important people have to say to each other seems to come in three-word packages. Every important moment. If you love someone, that's the obvious one. If you hate someone, too. And there are the three words that I owe you, that I think you haven't heard enough in the years since Lily died: I believe you.

You've always been right. It was staring me in the face the whole time and I didn't see it. So I'm sorry for not believing you. No one did. I know this now, and I'm sorry it took me so long to figure it out. But figure it out I have. There are three more words for you now that I finally understand: Lily was murdered.

Sam

There was a silence in the room as they absorbed the words. Harry shut his eyes and chewed his lip, eventually speaking first. 'Did he tell you anything else?'

'He never mentioned it again.'

'You talked? Celia said you visited them?'

'A few months ago, yeah. That was probably the only time I saw him since getting the letter. Celia let me know he was struggling. Depression. She was hoping I could help him move on as I had. Let him know it wasn't his fault.'

'He apologises twice in the letter.' Jack pointed to the repetition of the word *sorry*. 'When did he write this?'

'A while ago. Before he was on TV, I'd say.'

'Five years. Jesus. He never forgave himself for that stupid flat phone,' Harry said.

'What phone?' There was a warble in Maurice's voice as he struggled to keep his disaffected tone. *New evidence?* He still wanted to know who had murdered his daughter. Sure, he had a great speech about how he'd moved on, but deep down he never could. Not really. No one ever did. Jack had his brother in a bed. Harry had a room full of voices.

'Missing her calls that night . . . This letter was his apology for that,' Harry explained.

'The missed calls, yes. I saw her outgoing log. She reached out to him.' Maurice squeezed the letter. He knew about those. No new information. 'That was why Celia invited me to talk to him, because he was holding on to that guilt. I think we all sit and wonder what we could have done after something like this. Those little ripples. You know I swapped a shift with a mate so he could go to the football? If I hadn't, and I'd been with her, would we be here? Or would she have done it another time? I don't blame him for not picking up the phone. I told him that.'

'He blamed himself well enough,' Jack said. 'I haven't said it out loud yet, but I assume you watch at least some television?'

'I didn't see it happen, but I know what you're talking about.' Maurice grimaced.

'Then,' Jack said, 'not to reopen old wounds, but if I tell you we have suspicions that Sam's death wasn't suicide either – or at least it wasn't without coercion – I'm assuming you'll arrive at the same place I have?'

Maurice stuck his tongue between his teeth and reread the letter. 'I'm happy,' he said, looking up at Jack. 'I really am. It took me a long time to get here. And don't tell Sue, but I promised I wouldn't lie to you. And part of me does want you to know. Hell, you make podcasts – maybe the world *should* know. Maybe it will help someone else.'

'He found something,' Harry whispered.

'I think that sounds plausible.'

'But this letter was written ages ago, wasn't it?' Harry asked.

'Maybe when he wrote this he'd figured out *how*, but didn't know *who*. He's accepting that it was a murder, but he doesn't say any more than that. And if he only found that out recently, and was about to drop it on someone, maybe they took their chance to cover it up,' Jack said.

'Yeah, that sounds right.' Maurice seemed to be struggling with whether to reopen those doors, unplug that bucket, restart the leak. He swallowed. 'Then I'd say the person who murdered my daughter is the same person who killed your brother.'

CHAPTER 22

The carnival was in full swing when Jack and Harry walked back down the hill from the Connors'. The sounds filtered up to them: the whole thing clanked like an old ship coming to port.

'I know Dad was actually stoked to see you there,' Ryan said. Salt air and sunlight had recharged him somewhat. 'Just had to play it cool in front of Mum, you know?'

'Your dad's been through a lot, Ryan,' said Jack. 'But therapy's for him as much as it is your mum.'

'He still believes it though, doesn't he? You can tell when someone's lying or not? Done enough of these interviews?'

'Sometimes.'

'Tell me he doesn't believe it.'

'Yeah,' Jack said, watching the kaleidoscope of the carnival lights below. 'He still believes it.'

'Is the letter all he had?' Harry asked.

'Well, yeah, but, like, her fingernail and stuff. What if she scratched someone? Where did the belt come from? The thuds from her room. And now Sam's dead too because he found out who the killer is.' His mouth dropped into an O. 'Oh. My. God. We're not looking for a murderer – we're looking for a *serial killer*. Record that. Perfect cut to ads, right? I'll say it again if you want to record it.' He put on a slightly deeper voice, aiming for gravitas. 'We're not looking for a murderer—'

'Serial killers don't have motives, they have methods,' Jack interrupted. 'And I'm not recording, I'm just canvassing at this stage. *If* this is true, and that's a mighty big if, and the second killing came from the first – the motives are the same. It's all about covering up the same thing. That's your garden variety murderer.'

'You think I'm stupid,' Ryan huffed. 'I'm not stupid. I know it hurts Dad to bring all this up, but that's the point. Sure, he goes to therapy now but he barely talks and he pads around the house like he's on rails. He hasn't changed his mind – he's just saying what they want him to. I used to do the same thing at school, after Lily died. They kept asking me how I felt, and if I ever said "sad" they'd bring in the cavalry. Until—'

'Until you just learned to stop saying you were sad,' Jack finished. He'd done the same thing with his own mental health plan, when form after form was placed in front of him and he was trying to avoid the high-security wing in the hospital. He didn't get better. He just lied better.

Ryan nodded. 'Doesn't matter what he says. It's still there.'

'Maurice said he was angry. You think he still is?'

'He didn't hit us, don't get the wrong idea. Angry at her, maybe. At himself more though. I was fifteen-ish at the worst of it and I remember he didn't sleep. Didn't do discipline, either – I could get away with anything. He had a big shaggy beard.' He exploded both hands in front of his chin to complete the picture. 'They gave him a warning for hanging around the police station. Got suspended from work for stealing pills. Getting into scrapes. Other parents at school didn't like it.'

Harry nodded his agreement. 'Big blow-up at our parents once. I remember.'

'He was a tin-foil hat away from Mum leaving him,' Ryan said. 'That's when he cleaned up.'

They'd reached, through natural inertia or attraction to lights and sounds, the carnival. The grass turned from green to brown, trampled underfoot. Paper cups and chip packets formed in windy eddies between the fence posts. The sun was near setting, hanging over the ocean, and the colours and lights on the rides were starting to pulse into the navy sky. Families were trickling in, heads tilted up, neon reflecting in their eyes – it was like townsfolk drawn out to a field to watch a spaceship land.

Jack glanced at the others, pointing at the entrance. 'May as well,' he said.

Harry nodded.

'I have to go pull beers. Work,' Ryan said. Jack did his best 'what-a-shame' face, but didn't quite pull it off. Harry put one of his giant hands on Ryan's shoulder and gave him a squeeze. Ryan said, 'You'll keep me in the loop, yeah?'

They both nodded disingenuously.

Harry, impatient as usual, powered off towards the entryway. Jack turned to follow, but felt a hand on his elbow.

'Jack.' Ryan was staring at him with an intensity he hadn't shown before. He pressed a piece of paper into Jack's hand. 'I bet he didn't show you the photos, did he? His files?' Ryan's eyes flitted at Harry's back, still walking away from them. He spoke in an urgent whisper. 'Dad had a suspect.'

Jack unfolded the paper. It was a pencil sketch of the Ferris wheel. But it was more like a schematic: the height was marked out with a long vertical bar, 4.5 metres. There were calculations using the radius and the speed on the side. Numbers of distance and time. 'I don't understand.'

'Why do you think I waited for you at the prison? I was following *him*, not you. When I saw him visit Long Bay I knew something was up. Then I saw you were getting out. Why the hell is he talking to someone who investigates *murders*?'

Jack thought back to the day he'd left prison. He had assumed the questions Ryan was asking – 'Did he seem weird? Like, his mental state?' – were about Sam. *I'm just interested in the links between them.* The only real link left was Harry.

'He? You mean Harry? Your dad told you his suspicions?'

'No, I found this in his files.'

'I don't know what this means.' Jack gave the paper back to him. 'Harry's got a pretty solid alibi.'

'On the surface, sure. But now the only person who spent the night up there with him is dead. Look at those calculations: Dad was onto it. Why do you think he had a blow-out with Harry's folks? Unless he was, you know, accusing their boys of something.' Ryan tried to push the paper back, but Harry had realised Jack wasn't beside him and had stopped walking, started to turn. Ryan scrunched the sketch into his pocket. 'Before he gave up, he was trying to figure out how someone would not only get down, but *get back up again.*'

On the way to the entrance, Harry pulled a piece of paper out of his pocket and squashed it into Jack's hand. Jack unfolded it. It was the photo of Lily, jet-black hair with a blue streak, from her corkboard. That was why Harry, who Jack thought would have been more interested in her room, had hung by the door.

'We have to give this back,' said Jack. 'This is all they have.'

'You can give it back.' Harry put both hands in the air, signalling he wasn't involved. 'Means you'll have to admit to stealing it.'

As if summoned by the conversation they were having, they walked past a police car. Jack swerved, stashed the photo, and rapped on the driver's window. It slid down with a whir.

Jack celebrated a silent victory as he saw the age of the cop inside. Old enough to be useful, and then a few more decades. For trees, you count rings; on a cop, you count the blood vessels in their nose. The further from the city you go, add in the scalpel marks to their cheeks and neck where skin cancers had been removed, stitched, scabbed and scarred over. Stale smoke wafted out the window. This guy had been on the beat a long time. Definitely thirteen years.

'Hi,' said Jack. 'My name's Jack Quick. I'm a reporter. Of sorts.'

'Which sort?'

'The sort that looks into cold cases.'

'Oh, yeah? Not many of those around here.'

'I'm honoured to be in the presence of the world's best detective.'

'Don't be a fuckwit, son. There's not much that goes unsolved here because everyone knows everyone. Someone goes missing – pretty good idea who done it. Got a hit and run – if anyone catches a glimpse they'll know whose car it is. Anything more serious . . . well, it's a small place. They get nervous. Smell it on them. Police work here is waiting.'

'Murders?'

'Only a couple of those here in my entire life – two's a couple, yeah? – and both of them, *both of them*, handed themselves in. What's your piece on again?'

'Lily Connors.'

'Thought you said you wanted mur—' He paused, drummed his fingers on the dash. Then recognised Harry. 'You spoke to Maurice.'

'We have.'

The cop scratched a hand through his wispy hair. Let out a great hacking cough. Jack could tell he knew the case, if only by the exasperation Maurice must have seen a thousand times, and tried to imagine him thirteen years ago. Jack assumed, even back then, his doctor would have been begging him to quit smoking. People only remember medical marvels for what they overcome: terminal patients with five months to live who fight on for years; coma patients who sit bolt upright in bed, ask what year it is. But there were other medical miracles too, like a man who, after decades of smoking himself in his car like brisket, kicks on.

'I know you probably think you're helping them. They've lost a lot, sure, but they almost lost more.'

'Ryan?'

The cop shook his head. 'Apparently it happens to paramedics a lot. Their job is to save people, you know, and when they don't . . .' He pulled a cigarette from his pocket and hooked it into his top lip. 'I guess it's hard to live with.'

'Maurice?' Harry spoke up.

'Planning to OD. Prescription stuff – luckily someone noticed some bottles were missing before he tried.' He cupped his hand around his lighter. Spoke in a small echo. 'Easily enough to lay him out. Want a dart?'

'Ryan told us his dad was suspended for stealing drugs from the hospital,' Harry said.

'Yeah, well, he's not going to tell you his old man tried to kill himself, is he?'

It made sense to Jack now. Ryan wasn't only hoping to impress his father by finally solving his sister's death. He was scared he'd lose him too if he didn't.

Jack thought back to his brother's room, sifting through the stories of people who, seed planted, had been led to suicide. Of Sam, who had potentially been convinced to do the same. Because suicide, as an idea, is not something talked about. Train delays because someone's painted the front windshield go unreported. Celebrity deaths get ruled as 'non-suspicious'. Articles with even a passing mention of the topic list helplines and mental health links. Because it's a topic so dark and so unspoken, a seed growing in shadow until – perhaps with the wrong words in the wrong ear – it blooms. Like the spike in suicides after the teen drama TV show Beth had told him about. An idea that fed on silence, on being tucked away. 'Didn't realise you'd thought about it,' that juvenile guard had said, and Jack, who up to that point hadn't been thinking about it, was suddenly thinking back over all the times he'd actually wanted to. And a trigger was one thing. Maurice had *seen* it. His daughter. The blood-vessel roadmap on her cheeks. The black slug of a tongue. That wasn't a seed in the corner of his mind – that was a tattoo on the inside of his eyelids.

The cop took Jack's silence as understanding. 'Now you see why I want you to leave them alone?'

Jack nodded. 'Just tell me, do you believe him?' he asked.

'I believe that *he* believes it, I guess.' The old man's cigarette flared as he drew breath. 'But from a police perspective, it's case closed. Without a doubt. There's a room with a locked door, no evidence of anyone in or out that I saw, no disturbance at the property. The world's changing, sometimes too quickly for someone like me, and police work, our law, the way we do things, is changing too. Maybe if it happened now . . .' Another cough. Then he shook his head. 'I'm putting ideas in your head. We barely have the fancy stuff down here now, forensics and all that, let alone a decade and a half ago. I'll tell you what I told him. How does a murderer get out of a locked room? They don't. Simple as that – no one's there to pull the trigger, it can't be murder. Word of the law.'

Can't it? thought Jack, but he didn't interrupt.

'I was in that room, and I'm telling you what I told Maurice for eight whole years. Move on.'

'She might have scratched someone,' Harry said. 'We were told she was missing a fingernail.'

'I burn my fingers and this chat's finished.' The cop gestured to the nub of the cigarette still in his fingertips, shrinking with the time they had left. 'Drop it. I don't know how else to say it. Hell, I'll tell you as a copper if it helps make it feel compulsory.' He pointed to the badge on his shoulder. 'Drop it.'

'Is that a threat?' said Jack. 'We're not doing anything illegal.'

'I don't need to threaten you. This is a small place – I tell anyone some skinny not-from-here bloke is here looking funny at little girls at the fair, and small-town justice will sort you out better than I can. You're hard to miss, you two: big one, little one. Timon and Pumbaa. Oh, look.' He flicked the cigarette butt out the window, where it bounced off Jack's shirt with a spark, and raised his eyebrows in mock surprise. 'Burned my fingers.'

The window buzzed up, halfway. The cop paused it. Considered a moment.

'I'll tell you this just so you don't bother the Connors with it. You're pissing on the wrong tree. I was in the room. I've seen it before, and it's always the same. That's the hardest thing to see, really, because you kind of see it through their eyes, at the end. I guess you're right about one thing. She died fighting.'

'The struggle Sue heard? Her fingernail?'

'Not self-defence.' He shook his head, grim with the memory of it. 'She changed her mind. They all do.'

CHAPTER 23

The park was free to enter but you had to buy little perforated tickets to go on the rides. Tails of pink hung from kids' fists and pockets. You had to buy in multiples of ten, but the rides cost three tokens each, ensuring you either left with one in your pocket or headed back to buy more. Harry bought ten. It was almost like a strange date. They walked around looking at the attractions. Harry bought a Coke and a deep-fried hotdog. Jack bypassed the food truck. For all his experience in vomiting, he drew the line at salmonella. Everything, including the rides, was on wheels: the food in a retro-fitted RV, coffee in a kombi with the side cut out, sideshows packed into horse-float-like stands. Adding the caravans in the carpark, it was a moveable city. Easy to disappear into.

Harry stopped at one of the sideshows and handed Jack his coat. Jack noticed it had a familiar red stripe on the arm, filing the information for later. Harry handed over three tickets and tossed three rubber balls perfectly into angled red buckets.

'Keep it,' Harry said, when the woman tried to hand him an oversized panda. Perhaps a novelty plush was one irony too far on this faux-date. He turned to Jack as they walked away. 'Spent a lot of time here as a kid. Lily used to work here and she taught Sam, and Sam taught me. It's all backspin – roll it down the inside edge. Watch this.' They stopped and watched the stand from a distance. The woman was explaining how the game worked to a family. She threw a ball into the furthest bucket and it settled. Seemed easy enough. Then she got the rest of the balls from the bucket and handed them over. The targets were close enough to be unmissable, but all three bounced out. The woman shrugged animatedly. *Bad luck*. 'If the answer's impossible, the question's wrong. It's not a level playing field. When she threw hers there were already two balls in there,' Harry pointed out. He was right. She was showing a new kid now. Demonstrated with one ball, landed it, and took three out to hand to the next punter. 'Deadens the bounce.'

It was an unspoken agreement where they were headed. Eventually they completed their circuit and stood beneath the Ferris wheel. Harry gave the attendant their three tickets each (they'd leave with one left, just as they were supposed to) and waited beside a steel step until a carriage came around. The same guy who had swished beer on his barbecue opened the gate for them. Black Singlet. He'd swapped the black singlet for a flannelette shirt and the stubby for a can of energy drink with a lightning bolt on it, but it was the same guy, with a bristly chin that could scrub toilets. His breath was foul as he growled at them to each stay on their own side of the cabin for balance. 'Goes round three times,' he said, and then, 'No funny business.' Jack couldn't tell if he was presumptively homophobic or if he was genuinely concerned about structural integrity. Based on the man's scowl and the maintenance history of the ride, Jack figured it was both.

The plastic seat was cold, with a right-angle. The whole thing jolted as it started to move. Harry, who was heavier than Jack by at least one metric unit of Traumatic Childhood, maybe two, immediately tipped the carriage his way. He was looking through the bars at the park. The lights on the Ferris wheel's frame changed the colour of his face every few seconds.

'How'd you find the Connors?' Jack said, still turning over what Ryan had told him.

'Hurting,' Harry said. The wheel moved quickly. They were near the top now. The door was only held shut by a small metal hook like a bathroom stall. Easy to get out of. Jack watched the headlights from the main road light the treetops. He thought about Sam and Harry, up here together, watching the red and blue lights go through the trees, in the wrong direction, and not knowing what they were for. He wondered if his father had had a similar experience when Liam had been injured, if the orange SES helicopter had rattled his walls and rippled the treetops and if he'd thought, *My boys are out there*, or that it was someone else's trouble.

Harry continued. 'That room was sealed tight. No crawl space in the closet. Inside lock on the window, just like Maurice said. If it was all locked up tight, it's difficult to see how anyone could get in and then back out without disturbing anything in that room.'

'Maurice thought the police didn't take it seriously enough. If they weren't treating it as a murder scene, they might have missed something because they weren't looking for it. Sue broke the lock, right? It can't have been Ryan – he was only seven – and Maurice wasn't home. Once she sees her daughter, she's not going to be searching the room.'

Jack thought of something Celia had said: 'You could have stolen my car while I was sitting in it.' And even if Sue hadn't been overly distracted, she would have had to phone the police, look after Ryan. At some point, once she got the door open, she would have had to leave the room. It was haunting, but in that situation, seeing what she would have seen, did you do something so simple as look under the bed?

Harry nodded. 'The ball's already in the bucket.'

Their carriage stopped at the apex. Jack looked down. It was a compact ride, but he was impressed by the height. The tops of people's heads moved through the alleys and arenas below like blood cells in a vein. It was busier now, the crowd thicker. He wondered if someone would look up if he shouted. In the carpark, Jack saw the police cruiser, lights off. Surfboards stacked upright tiled the fence like dragon's scales. Further away, white froth slapped the rocks and the sea reflected the stars like puncture marks. Like a constellation of broken capillaries.

'Pretty high up,' Jack said. He peered over the edge. 'It'd be dangerous but it wouldn't be impossible.'

'Sam and I argued over that. Neither of us wanted to do it.'

'Door opens pretty easy. Not locked.'

'You checking my alibi?' Harry smiled.

'Just saying.'

'Sam lost a finger. It was in the paper. He didn't kill her, if that's what you're thinking.'

'Yeah,' Jack agreed. His tone was petulant, but he actually did think Harry was right. Sam's alibi was watertight. There was no denying he felt guilt over that night. Whether it was something as simple as missing her calls or not being there for her was up for debate, but he certainly hadn't killed her. For one thing, it would be quite a feat of athleticism to get down there. And not only get down, but get back up. Secondly, why would he have written a letter saying he'd figured out Lily's murder? Even if Jack disregarded the implausibility of those two events, there would be a witness. Someone who watched his brother climb down, ostensibly to get help, but who instead came back empty-handed and even climbed back up to sit with him the rest of the night. And why would Harry hire Jack when he already knew the answer?

No. Sam hadn't killed her. But if it had been *Harry* who climbed down . . . Well, then the only witness had died two weeks ago. Perhaps a brotherly pact had been backed out of.

Ryan suspected something like that. But then why would Harry get Jack involved? To see if anyone was onto him, to make sure he'd get away with it?

About a quarter of the way through their second turn, on the way up but not quite at the top, the cabin jolted and Jack instinctively whipped a hand out, grabbed cold metal. He was still looking down. This was only a short stop while one of the families in a lower carriage exited, but Jack still found himself wondering if, depending on how cold and long the night was, he would have tried to Tarzan his way down.

'I know what you're thinking,' said Harry slowly.

Jack suddenly felt like the carriage was too small. Too high. Too jerky in the breeze, hanging by a single hook in the middle of the roof and tilted, always, towards Harry, because Jack was far too light. It all suddenly felt too close. Four metres in the air with nowhere to go. 'Very funny,' Jack said. 'You set this up?'

'You're thinking it's not that hard to climb down.' Harry followed Jack's gaze at the spokes of the wheel. 'Just a big jungle gym.'

'Yeah.' Jack smiled weakly. 'That's what I was thinking.'

The stop seemed longer than it should have been. Jack was just beginning to wonder if Harry really had set this up, and wishing he could be on firm ground away from him – *Dad had a suspect* – when he looked down and saw Black Singlet walking away from the ride. Someone else hopped in the booth. An innocent delay: a shift change. But something about this movement made him pay attention.

'In my defence' – Harry brought him out of it, laughing it off as the wheel jolted into action again – 'it was heaps windier.'

*

Jack spent the rest of the wheel's loop watching Black Singlet thread through the crowd. He was easy to keep in sight because he strode deliberately, without the ambling, sightseeing pace of the punters around him. Jack's thought on watching Black Singlet leave had expanded. When the ride had stopped for the shift change, he'd tried to put himself in the Midnight Twins' shoes. Sure, two teenage boys, the last ride of the day, and a slack operator keen to blow the top off one, added up to negligence. But Lily had called Sam *twice*. Sam's guilt stemmed from the fact that he could have saved her if he had been there. But, as fate would have it, he wasn't.

But what if fate had nothing to do with it? If Sam was the only one who could have intervened in Lily's death, it was pretty damn unlucky that he had been stuck four and a half metres in the air and out of the picture. Unless he'd been left there on purpose.

Which was why Jack had decided to pay a lot more attention to the ride operator sliding through the crowd. Because it was an interesting coincidence that Black Singlet had chosen to leave the moment after Jack and Harry had boarded. Rides in these fairs were owned, each family unit laying claim to their space in the wagon-train from town to town. The lifestyle stuck. It was a safe assumption that the operator had been around a while.

Maybe he'd recognised Harry. That was worth keeping an eye on.

Black Singlet slipped through a gap between sideshows, towards the circle of residential caravans. But the ride had dipped by then, and Jack could no longer see over the tops of the stalls.

'Goes round three times, but we can get off now if you've seen enough?' Harry said.

Jack shook his head, and their carriage glided through the entry–exit platform and rose again. Jack craned his neck to catch a glimpse of Black Singlet, but he'd lost track. The makeshift campsite and the carpark beyond were dark enough that nothing at a distance was identifiable. He could only see what lights shone across. A glowing cigarette. A blue wash of someone looking at their mobile. A soft yellow light flicking on in one of the caravans. A pair of headlights rotating through the carpark revealed the white sheen of the police car Jack had approached before.

Jack could see a blurry shadow in the caravan window, which was veiled with a thin curtain. The shadow inside was waving its arms. 'Harry,' Jack whispered, pointing.

Harry turned and followed his gaze. The shadow was now moving its arms a lot. Talking animatedly? On the phone? Then the shadow bent down, disappeared from view under the window frame. Harry, thinking Jack was pointing out an unimpressive firework that had just snaked up from behind the caravans and popped, shrugged.

'You recognise the guy that let us on?' Jack asked.

'Yeah,' Harry said indifferently. 'David, Dennis . . . something.'

'Did he work here back when Lily did?'

'Yeah, probably. Hers was just a summer job. He's a lifer. Oh . . . you think?'

In the carpark, a wash of oscillating red and blue now splashed the side of the caravans. For some reason, the police car had turned its lights on. No siren. An interior car light spilled onto the bitumen as a door opened, then was gone as it closed. Replaced by a tiny pinprick of light – a torch. The small circular glow started to float its way from the police cruiser towards the residential caravans.

'It just strikes me that he saw you and scurried off. And now' – Jack nodded at the torchlight bobbing through the parking lot – 'it seems the police want to talk to him too.'

In the caravan, the silhouette was back. One of the arms looked longer now. Like it had a second elbow, pointed rigidly at the roof. Then the arm extension bent at a right angle. But backwards.

Double-jointed. Something chunky at the end of it, light shining through a small loop.

Jack turned back to the policeman's flashlight, firefly in the dark, getting closer. Then he realised what it was in the window.

The person in the caravan was loading a shotgun.

CHAPTER 24

'Hey!' Jack started to yell. 'Hey!' He had his phone to his ear immediately, having dialled triple zero. People on the ground nearby looked up, but his voice wasn't carrying across the park. And then the loop of the wheel dipped them back below the sightline, and he lost all view of the lights and shadows.

The last thing he glimpsed was the silhouette of the gun, and the flashlight – the lone cop – moving inexorably towards it.

'Calm down, mate,' someone in the carriage above yelled.

'What's going on?' said Harry, who'd clearly missed the shadows.

Jack pointed through the bars and was about to continue when the emergency operator picked up. He told them where he was. Told them there was an officer about to find themselves in serious shit. 'At the carnival,' he said again. 'In Wheeler's Cove. You need to call them immediately.'

'All right.' There was typing on the other end of the phone. 'We can send an officer to you.'

'You're not listening,' said Jack. 'They're already here.'

The lady asked him to clarify, but Jack's attention was diverted. They were at the bottom of the ride now, not yet docked. He had the gate already unlocked and, despite the protests of the new attendant, jumped the last half metre, landing in a sprint and bolting off the platform. Harry was yelling behind him, slowed by having to extricate his larger frame from the carriage, but Jack didn't turn or wait. He knew where he was going. And he knew what would happen if he didn't get there fast enough.

He was yelling the whole way, for police, for help, for anything. But people in groups don't respond well to panicked alerts. Groups either parted or stepped forward to slow him down, ask him what was wrong. He weaved under consoling arms and good-intentioned blockades. Half the people didn't even notice him, unless he slopped their beer on the way through. He knew Harry would be somewhere behind him, but had no time to check. He realised it might look like he was being chased. He jostled and pushed. Copped an elbow to the nose. That confused him, and suddenly he felt pressed in and disorientated. It seemed like there were more people with each step. And noise. The murmured hum of a crowd having a good time sounded instead like the footsteps of Roman soldiers.

And then space.

It was like leaving the atmosphere. That moment in films where the rattle of the spaceship ceases and the director pulls back to the wide shot, watching the spaceship go from rocket launch to serene glide. The air was suddenly less pressed and the sound less obfuscating. Jack was at the edge of the crowd, next to a small alley between two sideshows. He dashed into the gap. Only twenty metres or so until the caravans. So close.

It didn't matter.

Over the hum of the fair behind him, Jack heard the *crump* that could only be a shotgun firing. Someone screamed, confirming it.

Jack burst out the other side. The light in the caravan was off. The first thing Jack saw was a long finger of light, splayed across the ground. A dropped torch? Or a torch in a fallen hand, the cop lying behind it, gurgling his last breaths?

A yell from inside the caravan dispelled that theory. 'Police!'

The window became a flickering reel. Three bright flashes. A heartbeat after, the sound hit. Not a thunderous *bang*, but a small series of bursts. *Pop pop pop.*

There was a blur of motion as, across the park, people started to realise what was happening. Other caravan lights came on, shadows flitting past in all directions. In the carpark, engines started.

Jack walked steadily towards the now dark and silent caravan. As he got closer, the light inside flicked on again. The door was speckled with a constellation of glowing spots. A shrapnel blast. The shotgun had fired through it.

Jack made the gamble that because the shotgun blast had come first, and the pistol shots second, the cop had come out on top. He yelled, 'Civilian, unarmed!' and pushed the door open.

The park was quickly evacuated, which was a beautiful migration to watch, the floating cells bleeding out into the street. It hadn't been panicked. People clearly knew something was wrong, but very few knew the scale of the gunfight – or that there'd even been a gunfight – just over the fence, so it was only when they saw the ambulance out front that they formed a pack, pushing against a row of men in fluoro yellow vests with glowing red batons, camera phones held in the air. The police had set up a floodlight in the carpark that lit the whole scene. Another half-dozen cars had arrived. People bustled back and forth. Those dressed in hairnets and shoe-coverings were going in and out of the caravan. Camera bulbs flashed. It looked like a film set.

Jack had, unsurprisingly, had the caravan door slammed in his face. But not before he'd glimpsed inside. The caravan was pretty standard: one large room with a bed under the window, then a small living area with a table, padded bench and kitchenette. Black Singlet was slumped against the bottom of the fridge, not moving, a large red smear behind him on the white door (like the way a fancy restaurant put sauce on dessert plates, Jack thought morbidly). Blood pulsed rhythmically from his neck, and a pool under his legs was steadily growing too. Shot at least twice. There was a shotgun, threatless, on the floor beside him. Cracked at the middle, mid-reload. The cop had been standing in front of the table, pistol still in hand. On hearing the door open, he'd spun around and jabbed the nose of his gun in Jack's face before realising he wasn't a threat and lowering it.

'This is a crime scene. Bugger off,' he said, slamming the door. Opened it again a second later. 'Carpark. Don't go anywhere.'

It had taken until the crowd thinned in the carpark to find Harry. He had been inside the park, still trying to push through the crowds. He said he hadn't heard the gunshots, but that a commotion had been obvious, with a couple of the carnies running through the park and herd mentality taking over the rest of the crowd. Inside, the police had arrived and were shutting down the rides. Harry told Jack that since his and Sam's misadventure, all the emergency services had keys to the equipment. He'd tried to ask an officer what happened, but they'd been too busy shepherding people to answer.

Jack told Harry as much as he could. From what he had pieced together, it seemed Black Singlet had fired the shotgun through the door, missed, and in response the cop had unloaded back at him. Jack tried to remember the sounds. Three or four pops, he thought. An ambulance was there, but it hadn't moved since it pulled up. That meant that those shot had no need for an ambulance. Jack looked for an officer on their own to ask, but everyone in even a semi-official-looking vest was swamped with similar questions. It was a small force spread thin.

Jack felt a hand on his shoulder.

'Jack,' someone said. Familiar smell of smoke. Voice like cellophane being scrunched. The old policeman, who'd asked him to stay.

'I didn't give you my name before,' Jack said, surprised the crinkle-cut officer knew it.

'I'm not saying you're on a list—'

'What happened?' Jack cut him off, uninterested in what the local cops thought of him.

'Can't say.'

'Anyone hurt?'

'Can't say.' He scratched a scab on his weather-hardened neck. Though he knew what Jack had seen. 'You know David Winter?'

Winter was the detective who'd handled the murder case Jack had interfered with eighteen months ago. He was more of a PR specialist than a detective and tended to work cases with a high level of media interest because he was calm under pressure and didn't cave to tabloids. Jack found it curious that not only were the Sydney police involved in *something* down here, but they'd also sent their high-profile spokesman. The NSW police investigating Sam's death as a murder would be laughable. So what were they doing here? Winter was also as straight-laced as a Sherrin, and he didn't like Jack at all. In fact, Winter had seen to it that, even though Jack had eventually solved the crime, he had gone to prison for his vigilantism.

Jack's grimace must have conveyed their history, because the cop continued. 'Right. Well. Message from him. Wants to speak to you tomorrow, so don't go anywhere.'

'Why's a Sydney detective plucking around Wheeler's Cove?' Jack asked.

'Can't say.'

'My car's in the lot. Can I get it out at least?'

'Tough.'

His threat turned out to be empty. The police realised pretty quickly that keeping over a hundred people's cars overnight wasn't as practical as they wanted it to be, especially with families and children wanting to get home, and they didn't have the manpower to shuttle everyone. Eventually, deciding that the real crime scene was not in the main lot, they relented. People queued up to be individually escorted to their cars. They had to walk around the circumference and enter from the far side – under the floodlight, moth tornado in the beam – and be guided out by an officer so as not to interfere with anything. It was nearly midnight when Jack and Harry finally got back to the car. Jack tried to spy any black bags on trolleys as they were walked through, but screens, like they used for shot horses, had been erected.

Jack's phone buzzed as he started the car. A text from his father. *Home tonight?*

The hi-vis guy in front of the bonnet had one arm out, sweeping the other across his body like an air traffic controller. Jack put the phone in his lap, rolled through the lot, following directions. His leg vibrated. Jack stopped at the entrance to the highway, picked up the phone. Another message.

Maybe it's easier like this. Look, I meant it when I said I wasn't strong enough to choose. But maybe it's hard to talk about. I know your life is all scripts and words and big speeches but I'm not so great at it. Sometimes I use the wrong ones. So it's simple. If you tell me yes or no, that'll be what we do. Together. I won't bring it up again.

There was a pause, the three dots that meant someone was typing on the other end. Then gone. As if there was something more to come but Peter had deleted it, or didn't have the words for it. The space in between words almost as powerful as the words themselves. The phone vibrated again. *Love, Dad.*

Harry, mistaking Jack's hesitation as not knowing which way to turn, suggested a motel he knew in Arlington. Jack exhaled in silent relief. His momentary fear of Harry had been overtaken by his fear of having to go home. His family was just like the Connors, a bucket with a hole in it. Liam a pebble at the bottom, Jack and his father pouring out around him.

I had to choose between the family I'd lost and the family I still had.

Maurice grieved like Jack, like Harry too: with rebellion and non-acceptance. It must be a murder. It's not killing. The lies they told themselves to keep the truth at bay. Such masculine bravado: all masks.

Found a way to let Lily go.

Yes or no.

Words kill people all the time. Jack's father was giving him an out. He could extinguish a life with a text message. The chance to be faceless. Jack couldn't do it, not tonight. He pulled the car onto the road, tossing his phone on the backseat.

They rolled into the brick archway alongside the reception of the Catch of the Day motel. The sign had a Tom Sawyer-esque caricature of a small boy in overalls fishing. The tagline was: *Mo-Money Mo-Tel.*

'This counts as expenses,' Jack said.

Harry got out and buzzed the after-hours intercom. The owner, a full-cheeked woman with a smile that made her eyes disappear, came out and they had a short discussion. Jack could hear it, muffled through the window.

'Is that . . . Sam? Sammy Midford? All grown up?'

'Depends. Do you watch TV?'

'Not much.'

'In that case' – Harry stuck out his hand – 'Sam Midford.'

The owner went inside, then came out a couple of minutes later, handing over a key and something larger and handled delicately – a cup? – to Harry. Harry came over to the car, slapped the keyring against the window so Jack could see a large number 4 written in texta, and then walked towards the rooms. Jack parked in the spot spray-painted with a yellow four and got out. In front of the room was a small glass table with an overflowing ashtray and two green plastic chairs. Also on the table was a mug with cling-wrap over the top. Milk, Jack assumed. This was the kind of place that gave out individual portions on check-in.

'Bad news,' said Harry, key in the door. 'Apparently, we've picked a bad weekend. There's a triathlon here tomorrow. This is all they have.' He opened the door and flicked on the light. A shared room, twin beds. Their strange date continued. The beds were thin, short and each had one fawn blanket tucked so tight as to tear. Harry tossed the key on the bed closest to the entrance and held the door open for Jack.

'Should have got you the fucken panda.'

CHAPTER 25

'You think I killed my brother?'

Harry's words floated from the dark. Jack was lying fully clothed on top of his blankets. He'd been awake for what felt like hours. Harry had turned the TV on initially, and Jack had listened with his eyes shut, the end of a movie with lots of yelling and cars revving. Harry must have fallen asleep, because the credits music faded out and was replaced by some inane late-night gameshow with simple but impossible to win puzzles. 'Call now if you can tell us the secret word!' A voice familiar in the way that all late-night TV hosts sound, because they need that generic accent that makes an audience feel like they've met them before. Like a radio co-host, giggly and familiar. Jack got sick of the drone, staggered over to the bright TV, hand shielding his eyes, and flicked it off. Lay back down. His movement must have woken Harry, because that's when he spoke.

The two beds were parallel, a metre and a half between them. There was a light directly outside the window, a fluorescent tube that buzzed softly and burned at either end. The curtains were threadbare, sun-worn, and the light cast the room in a dappled, underwater filter. That was a good thing. Harry's bed was under the window. Jack would see his shadow if he moved.

'I've considered it,' Jack said.

'And?'

'Be pretty stupid to hire me if you did.'

The bedsprings creaked. 'Are you scared of me?'

'No.' Jack didn't know if he was lying.

'Good.'

The wall rumbled as the room next door flushed their toilet: it sounded like they'd shat nails as the pipes rattled. They were quiet for a few minutes. Harry groaned, slapped the bedside table with a searching hand, then rolled back, phone in his hand, blue glow on his face.

'Is it in the news yet?' Jack asked.

'They're saying there was an incident at the carnival.'

'Choice of words.'

'You think someone died?'

'Didn't look good when I saw him. Besides, you don't pitch tents otherwise.'

'You think that means the cops believe us?'

'If Lily's dad couldn't get an investigation after more than a decade of trying, I very much doubt I'm the one who's changed their minds,' Jack said. 'There's something they're after, but I don't know what it could be. Let's say we're on our own until we know we aren't.' He changed topics. 'Was Lily depressed? Bullied? Everyone's told me she killed herself, but not why she would. Let's pretend it's not a murder, for a second.'

'Ryan, Sam, and Maurice all believe it is. Sam said in his letter.'

'I know. But that word's powerful. Too powerful. Maybe we need to stop throwing it around. Just to help us think. You knew her, right?'

'A little. As in, I knew her a little, not that she was a little depressed.' Harry clicked the phone and the glow disappeared.

'She and Sam broke up?'

'Yeah.'

'Was she upset about that?'

'Don't know.'

'She wore his ring. They must have been semi-serious. I'd be surprised if she wasn't upset. Why'd they break up?'

'You and your brother ever talk about girls?' Harry said. Jack was silent. 'Exactly.'

'You're wearing his clothes.' Jack dropped the accusation into the dark. He'd noticed when Harry had handed him his jacket at the carnival. The coat was the same one Sam had been wearing in the photos on his family's walls. A sports coat with a red stripe up the sleeve. Jack closed his eyes, remembering how Harry had taken the brown leather jacket off before they'd gone up to Celia's door: she would have recognised it. After, he'd been dusted up in mud and grass stains. Celia wouldn't have noticed the regular clothes – the shirt, the pants – behind the damage.

Jack listened to Harry breathe, waiting for the creak of bedsprings. Harry didn't get up.

'Even though we weren't talking, I still watched every episode,' Harry said. 'You've seen my archive – I recorded them. So of course I was watching when he did it. At first I thought it was a stunt, but Twitter picked it up pretty quickly. I drove to his house, to check if he was okay, I guess. I wasn't going to say anything, but I just wanted to see him get home. Then Celia comes rushing out, just like she said she did, with Heather in her arms. Hammers that four-wheel drive down the street, and, would you believe, leaves the front door flapping. By then the news was firming up. They were all saying he was dead. And I don't really know why I did it, but I just walked in. Just wanted to see how he lived. Twenty-two minutes, Jack.' Harry sighed. 'He's twenty-two minutes older than me and our lives are completely different. Sometimes I wonder if I was born on the twenty-fourth and he was born on the twenty-fifth, would we be different people? Would we become each other? It's stupid, but I put on that stupid fucking brown leather coat and looked in his gleaming fucking white bathroom and I wanted to be him. I guess I'd always looked up to him – he was the older, better version of me. And every news outlet in the country was now saying he was dead. So I took them. I grabbed an armful of everything hanging in his closet and I walked out to my car and I drove home. I dumped them on my couch, and watched and watched and watched *all* of my old episodes and it was like watching the life I missed out on, and I *wished* I could be him. So the next morning, I put his face on, like I do every morning, but this time I'm talking about the way he smiles, the way his eyes crease like he's pleased to hear whatever you're telling him, the way he's always thanking his guests by grabbing their shoulder, the way he talks . . . God . . . Sam had a way with words. He was always the clever one. He wrote all our jokes. He'd just whack a script down and it would be magic.'

Jack remembered all the times he'd thought Harry's mask was dropping, that snarl that lay under the smile when they were at Channel 14. That bravado, that confidence, the neatly pressed clothes and the tailored coats, those gleaming white teeth, those big meaty hands always reaching out.

Harry said, 'When I met you in the prison, I felt like I was wearing this different skin. I was so in control.' He paused. 'I tried my brother on. And I liked it. Twenty-two minutes. Could have been me.'

'You're not on two per cent either, are you?'

'I'll pay.'

'Jesus.'

'I said I'll pay. I scraped ten grand together.'

'You said you were between cars, but you sold your car for that, didn't you?' Jack thought of the chalk price on his own windshield, how selling it was his family's own rock bottom.

'I'll pay.'

'You're killing me.' *Not just me*, Jack didn't say. That money was time for Liam. Now he did actually have to find something to make a show about, something to sell to Gareth Bowman. He was back where he started. Before that, even. The rooms in prison were smaller than in this motel, but the blankets itched less.

'Are you going to stop?'

'Depends. Which version of you am I supposed to believe when you tell me you didn't kill your brother.'

Harry's voice was so quiet it limped across the gap in the beds.

'Well, that's the thing . . .'

'We'd been on tour a long time,' Harry started to talk, at the ceiling in the dark. Jack realised why Harry was more comfortable talking in darkness, the same as at the station: it was because he wasn't wearing his brother's face. 'And he was struggling. He never really got a hold on Lily's death, didn't process it, but you already know that. What you don't know is how bad it was. I told you there was drinking, that there were pills, mixed together as if he were trying to write himself off. But it was literally every night. He'd be standing in the wings, sold-out theatre, fucking swaying on the spot. Yet every time he walked out into the spotlight it was the same smile, the same eyes. You wouldn't know. And then after, in our hotels, he'd just keep going. Now, we were young and on tour and I loved a drink too, but this wasn't a bit of fun gone too far. Sometimes it seemed like he was doing it deliberately, to see how far he could push me with it.'

And just how far did he push you? Jack thought, but didn't say.

Harry kept talking. 'Then we got back from Montreal. And we had this pilot, and Channel 14 said they loved it, but they thought I was dead weight and wanted Sam on his own. I told Gareth that

Sam on his own was a ticking time bomb, but he wouldn't listen. And it wasn't that Sam refused to drop me, it was that I refused to go. I told you that Sam stood up for me because I wanted you to think he was a good guy, so you'd look at his computer and stuff. Truth is, I wanted to stay. Sam looked good in the spotlight, but I *wanted* it. And then one night I got a phone call from the hospital. I'd had these calls before, whether from nightclubs or restaurants or promoters or girlfriends, but this was the first time it was a hospital. I raced down there, like I always did, because that's what younger brothers do – we're on call – and they told me that this was a suicide attempt. I knew he had a problem, but I always maintained that he just wanted to numb something. Just got a bit wild, didn't know when to stop. But now I know maybe he was trying to drink himself to death. Celia was his doctor that night – that's how they met. She told me that, with what he took, there was only one conclusion. They pumped his stomach. They had to keep him there until it was deemed safe enough to let him out again. He was adamant that it was an accident. Wrong pills. Wrong beer. And . . .'

Harry lost his train of thought. 'Fuck, Jack. He was sitting in the bed smiling at me with his fucking TV-host grin. They said he'd be okay – because he always lands on his feet, always gets up again, and it's me that actually has to put the work in. He just puts that smile on and says something clever and it's all okay again. And maybe now I realise he had a mask on just the same as I do. But back then I was still going to these fucking meetings at Channel 14, who kept asking where my brother was, and I had to lie to them and say "It's just me today", and I could see them ruling a line through our pilot then and there in that fucking boardroom. And all the while he's lying in this private hospital pretending like he didn't try to kill himself, and I'm – you've gotta understand this, I was so *angry* with him, and I'm trying to fix his television show that they don't even want me on. And I can't even remember what he said. I can't.

But I knocked this vase of flowers over. There was glass on the floor, big fucking shards of it.'

Harry was breathing quickly now. Throes of memory.

'And all I could think about was picking one of them up. I wanted to hurt him. I wanted to hurt him so badly. And then I'm staring at these shards of glass and he says something snarky like "Settle down, cowboy" and I just . . . I just . . . snapped.' Harry's voice calmed, almost as if he stepped away from the memory and was recounting as an observer. 'I picked up a piece of glass. I put it on the bedside table. Slowly. Deliberately. So it made a big dramatic clink. And I said to him, nice and clear – and I remember exactly what I said because how could you forget destroying your brother like that? I said, "Quit putting on a show. Do us all a favour and do it properly next time."'

Harry sniffed. A truck's headlights scanned through the curtain. Jack could feel Harry's pain: something spat out that could never be taken back. Words so hurtful they scar. Jack was never a man who used his fists, but he knew the violence of words. They had put him in prison. And he protected himself from them often. His medical condition was the 'b' word. They had sat around Celia's kitchen table, discussing the 'm' word in front of her daughter. 'It's not what you meant,' Jack had said to his father, 'but it is what you said.' Words kill people all the time. Slowly, quickly – *yes or no* – but they do.

'I quit the next day,' Harry said.

'I'm sorry, Harry. You can't feel respon—'

'Someone talked my brother into killing himself. We've got that far. I'd pay anything to know it wasn't me that put the idea there. That it wasn't me that did it.'

'That was five years ago. You're paying an awful lot of money to imagine forgiveness from a brother you weren't even talking to.'

'How much are you spending to keep your silent brother alive?' Harry sighed. 'Look, I'm sorry. That probably overstepped it.

The money's nothing, right? Sam's got insurance, but it doesn't pay on suicide. I'll get a cut of that if we find this bastard. That's what I was planning to pay you with.'

'And if we don't?'

'Then that would prove that what I said *was* his turning point. And I deserve nothing anyway.' Jack could hear the bedsprings now. Harry was standing, his shoulders square in the frame of light. 'Forgot to lock the door,' he explained.

Jack thought, out of the blue, of Lily Connors. A girl who had bought herself a bolt lock for her bedroom door. *Puberty, I guess.*

What was she afraid of?

'Don't bother with the door. If I'm supposed to believe what you and the Connors are telling me,' Jack said, 'this killer won't even open it.'

CHAPTER 26

Jack slept little. His mind was a blur of questions.

First, he needed to find out what it was that Lily had been trying to protect herself from – why she'd begged her parents for a lock on her door. And that was just Lily – he hadn't even started to dissect last night. Clearly Black Singlet had something to hide at the carnival. Enough to shoot at a cop over. Enough to die for. It was all too much of a coincidence to be unrelated.

But it seemed from the letter that Sam had figured it out.

Jack needed to know what steps Sam had taken that had led him to the killer. The problem was, Jack knew nothing about Lily. Harry didn't either. The only person who really knew her in the lead-up to her death was Sam, and it was proving quite difficult to ask him questions. Her death hadn't even been reported online, though little from the area really was – not even the two other murders the policeman had mentioned last night. A girl had done quite well in a reality singing competition – that rated a mention – and otherwise it was entries from Lonely Planet guidebooks or travel blogs promising 'Australia's Best Hidden Beaches' that captured the news cycle of the area.

It looked like most kids from Wheeler's Cove went to school in Arlington, where there was a single school for grades one to twelve. Unlike schools now, with honour rolls and sports teams plastered on their websites, thirteen years ago Arlington High School was standing on the doorstep of the digital age, uninvited. He couldn't find any record of Lily Connors, not even a photo of a sports team or from a school dance. Sam and Harry Midford were mentioned alongside the school, but it was in articles either to do with the Ferris wheel incident or their burgeoning entertainment careers. To complicate things, Lily had died back when not everyone had social media – young people like her were just starting to get mobile phones or, in Sam and Harry's case, sharing one – and it wasn't so easy to just log on and snatch someone's location or phone history from a tower. Not that Jack could do that anyway – he wasn't a cop. He had to see through Lily's eyes a different way.

But maybe it wasn't Lily's eyes he needed to see through. Sam had solved it. Had he lain here, in some milk-in-a-cup motel, and asked the same questions as Jack? And, if so, had the answers he'd come up with led him to a killer? Maybe Jack needed to look through two pairs of eyes: through Sam's watching through Lily's. That was his job after all, to watch and to listen. Back when he'd been in league with the police, when officers thought he could make them famous rather than their current suspicion that he would drag their name through mud, what would he have asked for? Forensics. Phone records. Emails. He couldn't ask for that now.

Jack considered leaving. Harry was sleeping soundly – Jack could get out the door without him knowing. He was already dressed. He didn't owe Harry anything. The ten thousand dollars he'd paid so far would give Jack another month of three-hundred-and-fifty-seven-dollar days to find more income. But only a month. He didn't believe Sam's insurance would pay out on some wild coercive-murder theory anyway. Jack was pouring the water into his brother's bucket and it was still coming out. He'd told Harry he'd take his money and not feel a thing, but now he knew him, now he knew what he was trying to do, walking away was more difficult. Besides, he had to keep going, to find something valuable enough that Gareth Bowman would pay handsomely for it. Or, hell, he'd swindle him and sell it to Tom Dwyer if it kept his brother alive. And to top it all off, what else was he going to do? Go home?

The sun was just up. He refocused. Forensics; email; phone records. Jack called Celia. He figured he could trust her. If she'd killed Sam for money, for the life insurance, then suicide wasn't the way to go about it.

'Jack,' Celia said brightly, without a hint of the early morning in her voice. 'How's it going?'

Jack, who wasn't expecting small-talk, skipped straight to 'I found Sam's clothes.'

'Oh?'

'Harry's wearing them.'

'Poor Harry,' she said, then gave a light-hearted huff. 'Tell him it's okay. I wasn't using them.'

Jack remembered her saying that she hadn't known why the brothers had fallen out, that Sam had never told her he'd been trying to drink himself to death and pushed it too far, but her intuition had clearly filled in a few blanks.

'I'm down in Wheeler's Cove,' Jack said. Their conversation woke Harry, so Jack stood and walked outside, taking a seat in the garden furniture by the door. His lungs constricted in the cold air. The ring of parking spaces was wet with dew, dotted with dry grey rectangles from those who had got an early start. A shirtless man was having a cigarette and drinking from a black can across the lot. The iron mesh of the chair grilled a pattern on Jack's back. He wriggled until it hurt less.

'Remember what Ryan told us? He was telling the truth. Sam did write the Connors a letter. I've seen it. It wasn't a suicide note, though. It was from five years ago. He says he figured out someone killed Lily Connors.'

'Oh, shit. She was really murdered? And he solved it?'

'He said he'd figured it out. But he didn't say who. Maybe he found that out recently. Down here, she seems to have a cloud around her. Her family is convinced it's murder, but no one seems to want to talk about it. Especially not the police. I'm trying to fill in the gaps. Did he talk to you about her at all?'

'I mean, I knew she died. About the missed calls, how he lost the top of his finger. I suppose he told me what he couldn't avoid, the scars I could see. The phone thing was one of his triggers, I guess. If I called him and he missed it, I'd send him a text straight after. Just to explain why I'd called. Otherwise he got anxious. Heather's primary school for next year has a mobile phone policy. Can you imagine? God. He was *not* a fan of that. No phones until she's eighteen, he reckoned. I told him he was welcome to parent a phone-less thirteen-year-old if he wanted, but he'd have to clean the blood out of the carpet himself.' There was a clatter, and the refrain common to any parent of 'Put that down.' 'Sorry. Heather,' she offered by way of explanation.

'Did he tell you about when they were kids? About why they broke up?'

'You mean why she might have . . . No.' She thought a minute. 'But, I mean, they were teenagers. It's all very dramatic. You're in love until you aren't.'

'Was he talking about her more in the last few weeks?'

'I don't . . . This is sad, Jack. You think I'd cherish every memory, that those last few weeks would be all technicolour replay in my mind. Maybe I'd see him playing with Heather and smiling, giving me a kiss on the cheek as he left for work. That's how memory is supposed to go.' Jack understood: if he was making a show, he'd put a hazy glow around the borders of the screen to show that a character was having affectionate recall. Breakfast worked well, usually: a man in a half-done tie whisking through a kitchen, taking a slurp of coffee or a bite of toast without having time to sit down because he has to 'rush off for a meeting', kissing his wife with his mouth full. It was a scene from every movie.

Celia was still talking. 'Maybe it's because I didn't know it was coming, maybe it's because I'm a bad person, I don't know, but I didn't catalogue those last few weeks in that way. Everything blurs together as our normal lives, just going on. Is that bad? That I remember *him*, but also can't find anything particularly memorable?'

'Not at all,' said Jack. 'I'm asking for specific details. I don't expect you to remember all of them. But I'm trying to follow his footprints. You said you checked his phone? Emails?'

'Well, yeah. It's not like I keep tabs on him. But I wanted to check for *those* things. The things they said he had.'

Jack already knew she hadn't found anything. 'Did he mention Lily at all?'

'As far back as I read, no. I'm sorry, I have to get Heather ready for child care. I wish I could tell you more, I really do. And I know *everyone's a suspect* or whatever.' Jack could almost hear her air quotes. He noticed a grey sedan that was too well-waxed glide into the motel, stop in front of an adjacent room and idle. 'But I'm not covering anything up. You say he was investigating a murder for five years, and that's a surprise to me, because it was business as usual. Normal, everyday life. As everyday as it gets when he was depressed or kind of disconnected, but he took his meds and we talked and he seemed okay. Genuinely, I didn't notice a thing.'

'You're alive until you aren't,' Jack reflected.

'Something like that,' Celia said. 'Thanks for what you're doing, Jack.'

Harry opened the door as Jack hung up. His hair was spiky, showered. T-shirt and jeans, his own clothes, no shoulder pads or neat creases. The gleaming teeth were hidden. He hadn't shaved in a couple of days and it was starting to forest his jawline. He still looked like his brother, but it was no longer uncanny. Midnight split them. Without the slickness and the photoshop. An apartment by the airport instead of a house in the 'burbs. Twenty-two minutes. Same same but different. Harry had said he wished he could be his brother. Jack wondered momentarily if that jealousy applied to his high-school girlfriend.

'Still here,' Harry said, taking a seat next to Jack.

'Still here.'

That summed everything up pretty well. You, me, Liam, Sam, Lily. Jack thought of everyone still strung up in memory, not let go. We're all still here.

Detective David Winter got out of the sedan. Jack recognised him by his walk, stiff-limbed like he'd been set in clay and hadn't quite cracked it off his joints. He'd lost hair since they'd last met in court. What was left was as silver as a polished coin, each strand like fishing wire. He had a firm, sweatless handshake.

'Let's go for a drive, Jack,' he said. Clipped voice, perfect diction. Years of dealing with the media meant carefully chosen words so as not to be misquoted. 'And you can tell me why every time we zip a bag up, you happen to be there.'

CHAPTER 27

Detective Winter drove Jack to the Arlington police station, which was a squat brick building across the road from the hospital and flush with the fire station. Jack figured if he got set on fire and needed extinguishing, justice for his arsonist *and* medical treatment, Arlington had him sorted with a one-stop-shop. Jack had tried to get Winter chatting, but he was as tight-lipped as a brace-face in school photos. Winter's repeated line was that he wanted everything on the record and best to do it at the station. Jack expected nothing less.

The station didn't have a sign out the front, just peeling laminate letters on the sliding door that said *lice*. Whether that was deliberate graffiti or lack of maintenance, Jack wasn't sure. Inside, there was one room, no reception and four desks. Three of them had chunky iMac computers so old they may as well have been a slate and chisel. The fourth had a laptop heavy enough to lobotomise someone with a good whack.

Jack was also willing to bet the room was witnessing more activity than any local officer had seen in a long time – perhaps ever. There were at least three people to a desk, propped on foldout chairs or flipped milk crates. The few electricity outlets were pulling over-time. Power boards were everywhere, hanging vertically against the walls, every socket with a double adapter. Black cords snaked the room, running up the walls like vines. Two printers were on a table by the wall, both whirring busily. It looked as though one had been freshly purchased. Like the shiny new coffee pod machine, moun-tain of capsules beside it. People were hurrying from desk to desk with arms full of paper, sloshing coffee mugs. The speed setting was dialled to ground floor, Channel 14.

The back wall had two doors with square plastic windows, one open and one closed. Holding cells. Not for serious offenders; they didn't have beds. Just wooden slatted benches like gym chang-ing rooms. Easy to hose down. A single steel toilet in each. Winter walked Jack through to the cell with the door closed, stuck a key in.

'Seen enough of these,' said Jack, hanging back.

'There's no interview room,' said Winter. 'Or an office. We're making do. I promise you, just a chat. Don't worry.'

'Wasn't worried. Haven't done anything.'

'We'll get to that.'

Winter opened the door. In the centre of the room was a sin-gle chair, pointed towards the bench. On the bench, the box for the new printer served as a mount for the detective's laptop. He shoved the box to the side and moved his chair back as far as it would allow. Jack sat on the bench, their knees almost touching. Winter leaned over and swung the door closed. Looking at Jack, he propped the latch on the inside of the door rather than click-ing it shut. *Just a chat*, he was saying. A peace offering. Jack took his recorder out, put it on the bench and splayed his hands: *not recording*.

'I'm going to ask you the same question you're going to ask me, so we may as well get started,' said Jack. 'What the hell happened last night?'

'There was a planned police operation that resulted in loss of life.'

'Don't give me the press release – I can read that in the paper. You want to talk, let's actually *talk*. Loosen up.'

'I'm interviewing you.'

'No. I have agreed to provide you an interview. Different thing.'

'Right,' Winter said. His eyes darted to the recorder as if making sure it was off. 'I will get to the details, loosen up as you say, once I've asked a couple of questions. An interview with police is voluntary because you're not under arrest, but you know that. But providing false evidence or otherwise perverting the course of an investigation *is* illegal, but you know that too, from experience.' He paused to let the insult dig in, then rubbed both of his hands down his thighs to his knees. 'But,' he said, his voice softening, 'I have no interest in holding or charging you. It would be difficult, dare I say impossible, for you to be connected to this. But you like sticking your big nose in things and, if I'm honest, I'm interested in how you beat us to it.'

'Was that a compliment?'

'I don't do compliments, Jack. I said you had a big nose.'

Jack almost laughed, but Winter had said it with such sincerity Jack wasn't sure if he knew it was a joke. He nodded instead. Winter took out a pen and a Moleskine notebook.

'You know Sam Midford?' Jack asked. 'His brother has hired me to look into his . . .' Jack almost said the 'm' word, but pulled back. He didn't want to lie. But he also didn't want Winter to see him as a fool. He still didn't know the details of last night's 'operation that resulted in loss of life' so he figured it was best to play it coy. 'Into the reasons behind his death.'

'He committed suicide,' Winter said. 'That's me loosening up. I'll tell you, the forensics are undeniable there. Case closed.'

'He's paying me for denial, then,' Jack said, which he now knew was truer than anything he'd said so far.

'When did you come to Wheeler's Cove?'

'Yesterday. It was supposed to be a day trip, but you asked us to stay. So here I am. Cooperating.'

'And what did you hope to find here?'

'The Midnight Twins had a significant life event – I would say a traumatic one – thirteen years ago at this carnival. I'm building a history, so I thought it was important to have a look.' Jack scratched at the wooden bench. He wondered if this really was the only place they could talk, or if Winter thought locking him in a cell again would somehow compel him to spill his guts. It wasn't working. 'You're a bad date, having me do all the talking. Your turn.'

Winter looked at his notes for a second. 'Last night, an officer approached a residence. He was fired on, and returned fire. The assailant was killed.'

'If that's as loose as you get, this is going to be a short conversation.'

'I had an interest in keeping tabs on you, Jack, once you got out of prison.' *I'm not saying you're on a list . . .* 'And I know you're poking around with Harry Midford. But like I said, that's a sensationalist case, and it's a suicide. Seems to suit some flashy TV show or whatever. Doesn't bother me. What does bother me, and why I asked them to keep you here until I could get down here, is this.' Winter sucked air through his teeth, then leaned forward and picked up one of the manila folders. He opened it between his legs and rifled through, landing on a photo. Mugshot. He was portly, had a rugby player's square head; they could have rotated the height gridlines and it would have been more useful. *That's the one, officer, I remember he had a four-foot-two forehead.* Even upside down, Jack recognised him. Black Singlet. He looked younger. Less dead.

Winter spun it on his lap. 'Recognise him?' he asked.

'I saw him at the carnival. Ran the wheel. I also saw him later, shot to bits. Don't know his name, if that's what you're asking.'

'Dennis Slater,' Winter muttered as he flipped through the next few pieces of paper. The name didn't mean anything to Jack except that Harry had got it right. 'You know your problem, Jack? You think you're a bit of a hero, that *you* have to be the centre of whatever's going down. But you forget among your hypothesising, your questions, your little recorder and your shit-eating grin that I can smell from Sydney, that there are dozens of people working their arses off to put the bad guys away *the right way*. You don't have the evidence. You don't have the tact.' The tendons in his neck were tight as guy ropes. 'There's been a crime here, and you are *getting in the way*.'

Jack found it surprising that, of all people, Winter had been investigating Sam Midford's death just the same as he had. He was as by-the-book as they came. Jack felt elated that he, too, had been sniffing for something fishy.

But the feeling of camaraderie quickly faded. How could Jack be in the way? Winter had said he believed – no, he knew – that Sam's death was a suicide. Jack was working off what Harry was telling him and what they were chasing was a whisper, a word in a man's ear, a death in the past. What crime was Winter talking about?

It dawned on Jack. 'You're here because of Sam's computer?'

'You think we're not interested in child pornography on a celebrity's computer? You think we're not interested in a guy who kills himself on national television? I swear to God, if you're in possession of any illegal material—'

'Oh.' Jack stood up. Winter rose too, blocking the exit. Chest-to-chest. 'So that's why I'm here. I haven't seen any of the photos. I told you, I'm here building a history.'

'I have an officer who almost died.'

'And that's my fault how?'

'Suspect got nervy. Because you were asking questions about something you shouldn't have.'

'Was he a suspect before you lot shot him?'

'I'll ask the questions.'

'Don't hang this on me. Who's the cop?'

'Senior Sergeant Waldren.'

'Tell him he's a fucking idiot for starting a shoot-out at a family carnival.'

'It might not have been a shoot-out,' Winter bristled, 'if you hadn't been snooping around asking questions.'

'I didn't say anything to Dennis Slater. He sold me a ticket to the Ferris wheel. That's it. And I'm sure I'm the easy fall guy,' Jack continued. 'You've got my history. You don't even need me here to hang me out to dry. So the police got someone shot and I'm your front page. But I wasn't even near it when it happened. You want to talk about making a suspect nervy, maybe don't splash the parking lot with red and blue lights next time. Quite frankly, I think we've got better things to talk about than you trying to lock that door on me again.' Jack pointed to the cell door. He shook his head. 'If I'm honest, I'm here on a long shot. I'm as surprised to see you as you are to see me.'

'The images on Sam's computer, they were—' Winter cleared his throat, rubbed his cheek. His eyes were red-rimmed, black sand coves underneath. 'Pretty bad. You know what I'm saying? But we can't get an ID on the girl, which is a problem. On something like this, it's important for us to try to find out where it's coming from. Especially when it involves people of profile, like this, there's always a fear that there may be . . .' He was hesitating, Jack knew, on the word 'ring'. His eyes darted to Jack's recorder, making sure it was off. 'More.'

'Like drugs,' Jack said. His mind was processing Winter's words. *The girl.* Just one. Jack had always assumed it was a bounty of pornographic content. But now, just *the girl.* 'Sometimes it's better not to take the little guy off the streets. You find the source instead.'

Winter nodded. 'So you tell me how I've been working on these images for weeks, and you blunder into it before we do? I advise you stop lying to me, Jack. There's no *possible*' – he drew the word out like chewing gum, accusing – 'way you could be aware of the connection between Dennis Slater and Sam Midford without being in possession of something you're not supposed to have.'

'Connection?' Jack finally figured out why Winter was here. 'Oh my God. They had the same photos. Sam and Dennis.' He pointed at Winter. 'But you can't have known that. Otherwise you wouldn't be so pissed that I beat you to it.' Winter's forehead crumpled like it had sat down. 'So the cops must have found them after Dennis died. In the caravan? The same ones that were on Sam's computer. That's why they called you in. Add me into the mix, and you couldn't get here fast enough. That's why there are so many of you. It's not just this one police shooting, you're trying to crack a pornography ring.'

'I didn't say any of that,' Winter said, but Jack could tell by his retreating tone he'd got it mostly right. 'I brought you in here to ask you to stop snooping around before any more of my officers get shot at.'

'If you didn't know Dennis had pornography, why did Waldren approach the caravan?'

'It was exploratory. The suspect fired first.' That was Winter's media training kicking in. Short declarative sentences. No room for misinterpretation.

'Exploratory? What was Waldren looking for if you didn't know the photos were the same until *after* Slater died?'

'A police officer makes a thousand decisions a day, Jack. He was following a tip. Let's call it intuition and leave it at that,' Winter deflected. But Jack could tell it irked him.

'A tip?'

'You called emergency, they radioed him. He was checking it out.'

'I called emergency *after* I saw him approaching the caravan.'

Winter paused. Thought about it, and wrote something down.

'Who'd your senior sergeant talk to?' Jack continued. 'Can you be sure that call ever happened? Ask dispatch.'

'Coastal town, Jack. There is no dispatch. You'd better make damn sure you've got nothing to do with this before you start throwing accusations around,' he muttered.

'It's not my fault an officer got shot at.'

'It's not. But if you knew something dangerous was going on down here, why didn't you tell anybody?'

'I genuinely don't know anything about the photos. I've been working under the assumption that Sam's were planted. I did call triple zero at the fair. I tried to warn them.'

'Why would you think they were planted?'

'What did Waldren tell you about Lily Connors?'

Winter flicked back through his notepad and read from it. 'Suicide. Decade old. Her dad has a bugbear about it, always believed it was murder. We've been watching this case from Sydney. Waldren hasn't been involved. Only heard about it when I got here.' Winter shrugged. 'Seems like your bag.'

'And if I told you that I think Lily *was* murdered, and Sam Midford found out who did it, so he was murdered as well and the photos were planted to cover it up, what would you say to that?'

'That *is* a long shot.' Winter rubbed his jaw and exhaled through his nose in defeat. 'But . . . it does sound more like you.' He stepped back from the door.

Jack idled in the sunshine out the front of the station. Winter had asked him to wait while he made a few calls, just in case he had any more questions, and Jack said he didn't mind provided he didn't have to wait in a cell. It was only fifteen minutes before Winter emerged.

'I'm not playing the murder game with you, Jack, but if you find anything more about the pornography it would be in your interest, legally, to pass it on to me,' Winter said, then did something he'd never done before. He extended his wax-paper hand. 'I spoke to the emergency operator you called,' he said. 'And I do owe you thanks. You did call us. You were trying to help.'

Jack shook his hand. 'Tell me. Was Lily Connors in any of the photos?'

'You think Dennis Slater killed Lily Connors thirteen years ago because he'd been taking photos of her? And when Sam figured it out, Dennis covered his tracks by killing him as well? Am I close?' Winter raised his eyebrows in disbelief.

'More or less.' Jack shrugged. 'Except I don't believe you've stumbled into it, or that it ends there. I think this is just tying up loose ends.'

'I don't have the forensics on a girl who died thirteen years ago. And Lily Connors' suicide is not part of my, or anyone's, remit. If you get me a photo, I can have a look.'

'Hang on.' Jack pulled the stolen photo out of his pocket. He didn't let Winter see it, just in case he asked where it came from. 'Black hair, blue streak in it?' He raised his eyebrows at Winter, who returned his look stoically, unimpressed. 'Not always though. Um . . . freckles. Like a birthmark kind of thing on her neck. Ah . . . Pierced ears? Like, a silver ring with a green, ah, jewel I guess, in it?'

'Can I have that?' Winter put out his hand.

Jack held it out. *The girl.* Didn't let go. 'Ask Waldren. Is it her?'

Winter snatched the photo. Looked at it and thought for a second. 'You know that even if I could tell you that, I wouldn't.'

Winter went back inside. Through the glass panels, Jack saw him stride to the senior sergeant's door and rap on it. Hard. Winter had been robbed of the opportunity to give Jack a spray. He was still loaded, needed a new target. Jack had given him enough ammo to ask some questions of his own team.

Looking around, it was surprising how industrial Arlington was compared to the almost pop-up nature of Wheeler's Cove. Buildings were low, flat and had sheet metal roofing. Even the hospital was only three storeys high. The ground was concrete, and the entire block Jack was on, and, he suspected, the entire town, was dead flat. No hint of the ocean on the horizon. A row of fast-food restaurants sat opposite. Despite the flurry inside the station, the emergency sector was relatively quiet. Jack walked down the steps and considered whether it was too far to walk back to the motel. Winter hadn't offered him a lift. Though Jack figured he was technically owed one, he didn't fancy being cooped up any longer with the man who'd put him in jail a year and a half ago. He closed his eyes, let the sunlight warm his eyelids.

His phone rang. He answered it. Beth.

'I asked around,' she said. She was eating something, sending wet slaps through the phone. 'No one really noticed the swap in the cue operator. Most people stopped paying attention to when Brad – that's the usual guy – was off. Those who did apparently thought the same as I did, that there was someone there, ready to go, and so it was problem already sorted. Everyone kind of trusts that Sam knows what he's doing, so it's not like we're often focused on the prompter.'

'What did Gareth say?'

'Gareth?'

'He was at the recording, remember?'

She chewed. 'Well, I didn't really ask Gareth. Just the crew. But, Jack, he wouldn't recognise half the guys who work on his shows. He's not the type of CEO who remembers everyone's birthday, goes around back-slapping – not sure if you've noticed. He's not going to have a clue if the autocue's got a different person on it.'

'Hmmm.' Jack gave a disappointed grunt.

'Don't worry, I have something. Like I said, people have stopped caring when Brad takes a sickie. He's known for it. I've worked on all kinds of shows and, look, if the stagehands want to smoke a bit of weed, I'm not going to crucify them. If they're still getting the job done, that is. But Brad likes the harder stuff. Not too sure what, but let's just say that he's known for writing himself off. Bit too much of this, bit too much of that. Said he had gastro, spent the day on the bathroom floor, you know, with both taps running. Everyone knows what that means.'

'When did he find out about Sam?'

'Next morning at work. It would have been quite a shock, but I don't think he knew how relevant he was to it. He just scrolls the autocue. Only someone as insane as you can turn that into a murder investigation. Seems to me like he chalks it up as one of those coincidences. You know? Skip the cinema and miss the pile-up on the highway? Counts himself lucky not to have been there.'

'Thanks, Beth,' said Jack.

'No dramas,' she said. 'No more late-night visits, hey? It's nice talking in the daytime.'

All this information was useful, but it still wasn't fitting together. Jack's mental picture had pieces missing. It bugged him. The simple answer was that it must have been Dennis who Lily had feared, hiding behind a locked door. She would have known him, too, if they'd both worked at the fair together. For some reason, he'd had to silence her. And if Sam had eventually realised it was a murder, and then thirteen years on finally uncovered who the killer was, it also seemed plausible that Dennis would come after him. He clearly had no qualms about killing, having fired through a closed door at a police officer. He had no reason to do that unless the police lights scared him. But something wasn't adding up for Jack. First, it did require the belief, which remained unconfirmed, that Lily Connors was in the photos. More discordantly, a man whose immediate response to seeing an approaching policeman was to unload a shotgun in public was unlikely to have the subtlety to stage not one, but two, complex suicides. It didn't fit. But it was similarly unconvincing that this was not related at all. So it had to be somewhere in the middle.

Jack had learned to trust his gut. And he had a feeling about two things.

That Lily Connors *was* the girl on Sam's computer.

And that the senior sergeant was lying about the radio call.

CHAPTER 28

Maurice Connors was sitting on the floor of his ambulance, both doors swung open on their hinges, under the awning of the hospital, drinking from a takeaway coffee cup. Plastic red letters spelled *EMERGENCY* overhead. Jack spotted him and walked over. Maurice patted the space beside him, and Jack hopped up into the square cabin. The base was metal, cold; his legs swung just above the ground.

'Slow day?' Jack said.

'Slower than yesterday. You come to ask me about who got shot last night?' Maurice asked.

Jack shook his head. 'I have the name. Is the officer okay?'

'Hank's fine.'

'Hank?'

'Waldren. Crinkly old bastard, vacuum-packed around a skeleton. If you've met him, you've smelled him.'

'I've whiffed. The dead guy – know him?'

'As well as anyone around here knows the carnival folk,' said Maurice. 'Can't say we had family barbecues.'

'There's a suggestion that he was involved in—'

'Yeah. I read the news this morning.'

'It seems odd. Too convenient that Waldren was there, that the guy fired through a door, but not when his life depended on it.'

'Hank's not involved, just unlucky. You ever heard of suicide by cop?' Maurice shrugged. 'Maybe he fired through the door because he *wanted* the police to come in and shoot him. Because of, you know, all that stuff. It's an ugly business, taking one's life. I told you, I've read too much about it since Lily's death. There are a lot of ways to do it you wouldn't even think of. Dennis wanted Waldren to unload on him – so maybe he is your guy and the loop's closed. That's what I reckon.'

'Do you think Lily was in the—'

'Jack.' Maurice put a hand on his shoulder. 'I appreciate what you're doing. I really do. A couple of years ago, I would have been right with you, kicking down doors. But I don't want to think about that anymore.'

'Even if—'

'Even if,' Maurice said. 'If they got him, they got him. If they didn't, what changes?'

'I know people didn't believe you for a long time. I'm telling you that Harry and I – we do. We have proof now. There're murders that don't look like murders. And if we can link these two deaths together – if there's a bigger fish – we might still get your daughter justice. And if it is cut and dried, and Dennis is all there is, then closure. Knowing for sure. Isn't that worth it?'

Maurice popped the plastic lid off the top of his coffee, set both the lid and the drink down beside him. He took a small bottle of pills from his jacket and dropped two into his palm.

'Don't worry,' he said, looking up at Jack with a smile. 'They told you I got busted stealing pills? Tried to kill myself?' He nodded at the tablets in his hand. 'Everyone always watches me funny when I get a bottle out. But you know what the solution to taking too many pills is? More pills.' He tipped them into his coffee, tapped the cup twice on the floor of the ambulance and swirled it in his hand. He tilted the coffee at Jack. 'Not these ones. These are just sugar pills. I used to flog these from the nurse's station so I could take them in front of my family. When I was still hurting and I felt like the real thing made me go dull and numb, and it wasn't fair to have the pain just go like that. I felt like it was cheating not to suffer for her. I felt like that was supposed to be my punishment. And now' – he took a sip – 'I'm a good boy who takes all of his medication. But I got hooked on these things. Not too sweet. They make a damn good cuppa.'

'You're changing the subject.' Jack waved away Maurice's tilted cup.

'I told you about the pills for a reason, Jack. I can't go back to that.'

'It's different now. Because it's not just you anymore.'

'You're kidding, right? Harry's as obsessed as I was,' Maurice said. 'And you're an ally bought and paid for.' He almost laughed, then closed his eyes for a second. 'I'll tell you something, but don't you dare tell my wife.'

Jack nodded compliance.

'I watched the *Midnight Tonight* video online,' Maurice confessed. 'I shouldn't have. But I did. Because you're romping around getting my hopes up. Honestly, seems a pretty clear-cut suicide to me. You have proof otherwise? Not theories – I live in the real world now – actual proof?'

'I still don't know how Dennis, if it's him, got out of Lily's room. I'll admit that.' Jack drummed his fingers on the metal floor. He knew he needed to tell Maurice something tangible to get him on side. This man was finished with guesswork, he wanted things he could feel. Hard evidence. 'But her death, as you suspect, would have been a classic staging. The murder takes place before, and then you fill the props in, set the scene. So whoever's first on the scene buys the narrative.'

'Which everyone did,' Maurice said, nodding. That wasn't enough for him. 'So what makes Sam any different?'

'Thirteen years of practice. They've evolved. Whoever this was, they didn't just cover up a murder, they got Sam to do it for them. Maybe the same for Dennis, if he was baiting the police into a shoot-out. They can do that. They talked Sam into it, threatened him through the autocue.' Jack remembered he'd seen the silhouette waving its arms, as if talking animatedly. On the phone perhaps. Being persuaded.

Maurice shuffled and did a small hop out of the cab. The suspension lifted under Jack as the weight dropped. Maurice stretched his back, paced in front of Jack, thinking. Stopped and leaned against the door.

'I'm sure you'll forgive me, but you're telling me a grown man got *cyberbullied* to death? As this town's resident conspiracy theorist: you're total batshit.'

'Whoever this is,' Jack said, 'to be able to stage that, they're clever. I have more evidence – the images on Sam's computer were also found in Dennis's caravan. Too much of a coincidence. If Lily was in the pornography, or even knew about it, old mate Ferris Wheel would have had motive to kill her, sure. But if they were killing Sam to protect themselves, why leave their own product on Sam's computer? That's too many breadcrumbs. Unless it was part of Sam's *investigation*, and it's been blown up because of how conveniently awful it is.' Jack thought through the theory as he said it, and it made sense. Gareth had used the pornography to move the spotlight away from criticism of the network. Maybe Sam had it for a different reason.

'It sounds like you're telling me that it's already solved,' Maurice said. 'Sam had the photos on his computer as part of his own investigation. Maybe that was how he solved it, tracked down Dennis. Dennis is dead now anyway, so even if Sam didn't get him, it's all tied up.'

'It's too neat,' Jack said. 'That's my point. We're buying the narrative. Whoever did this was smarter than Slater – has to be.'

'I can't believe I'm saying this, Jack, because God knows I've heard it enough myself. But if no one's there to pull the trigger, it can't be murder.'

Maurice seemed to take a small note of satisfaction in using an argument that had certainly put him in his place in the past. Jack had heard it before too, from Hank Waldren, in fact, in the carnival carpark. *Simple as that – no one's there to pull the trigger, it can't be murder.*

'Sam says "forgive me" on that tape.' Jack continued. 'If not for the photos, then what for?'

'There's only so much I can talk about her like this,' said Maurice, closing off the conversation. 'I'm afraid I've reached my limit.'

Jack knew that all it would take was the right evidence to crack Maurice wide open again. Jack refused to believe he could just stop believing it; maybe he stopped *wanting* to believe it. But Maurice did believe it, somewhere hidden under layers of Valium and therapy. And whatever Jack had clearly wasn't enough to excite him, to break down the wall he'd built himself in his mind. Jack suddenly realised, after watching Maurice pace and think and talk about his daughter and his past, that there was one question he hadn't asked yet. And it was one he desperately needed an answer to.

'Can I ask you one more thing?' Jack said. He saw Maurice baulk. 'About my daughter?'

'It's about her but it's not really about her. It's about my brother,' Jack said. Maurice nodded warily for him to continue. 'He's, um, he's been sick. A long time. Comatose. That's still sick, isn't it?'

'I'm sorry.' Maurice had stopped pacing and was standing still. Jack scraped the back of his calf against the steel step, if only so the feeling would take his mind off the words he was trying to find.

'We might have to . . . well.' He cleared his throat. 'It might be time for him to move on. Dad's ready to let him go. I'm not.' He fumbled out his phone, handed it to Maurice, who read Peter's text message with a stern focus.

'Your father is a brave man.' Maurice handed the phone back. 'He's letting you say no, but he's giving you an easy way out too. Where you can make the decision but he'll do the hard stuff. That's why you haven't replied? Maybe you want it done but don't want to admit it. Your father's giving you that option. Then again, maybe you don't want that, because I felt the same way. Because you need to suffer through it or you're cheating. Is that your question?'

Maurice had Jack pegged in more ways than one. Jack's eating disorder had, in part, manifested from watching his brother gurgle down food through a tube. Likewise, the ability to simply walk away from Liam's death, to unplug the machines and have the house cleaned and bank balances grow and return to a semi-normal life, instead of being mired in his brother's illness, felt similarly undeserved.

It wasn't that it was too sad to watch Liam die. It was that it was *too easy*.

'How did you let her go?' Jack said.

'I didn't,' Maurice said simply. 'She's still around. She'll pop up every now and then. In my dreams. Or I'll just be driving along and she'll say something. But – and here's the real thing – I get to remember her differently. Before, because I mixed her up with what I wanted – like closure, pain – the memories I had of her were blood on the carpet, missing fingernails. She was angry and sad and scream-ing, and every thought I had was not actually about *her*, it was only about what happened *to* her. And now—' He sighed, smiled, and Jack could tell just how hard he'd worked to get where he was. 'I'm allowed to just miss her. And that seems much more fair.'

Jack understood. All he had for memories of Liam was a wheezing machine. A metronome heartbeat. A fight with his father. Chalk marks on a wall. Did he even remember, properly, before the accident?

'Sometimes it's not about letting them go,' Maurice said. 'It's about getting them back.'

Jack considered this. Maurice walked out of sight around the side of the cab. Banged the metal. It thrummed like Jack was inside a drum.

'Come on. I'll give you a lift to your motel,' Maurice called from outside. 'It'll be fun. I'll put the siren on.'

CHAPTER 29

By the time Jack dropped Harry home in Sydney, another half day, the sun was weighted and the news of the coastal shooting had gone nationwide. Harry had read various news articles out to Jack on the drive: *Pornography Ring Exposed at Family Carnival*; *One Dead, Police Officer Hero*. A chubby-cheeked Indian boy had gone viral with an eyewitness account featuring finger guns and *pew-pew* noises. Jack thought the accuracy of his account varied. Especially when the helicopters and explosions came in.

That was why Winter had been candid instead of tight-lipped, Jack realised. Jack wasn't being fed confidential police information. He was getting the story they wanted out there. The arrogance to have thought he was getting the scoop. Winter wanted Jack, an inevitable leak, to do just that. A shoot-out in public is tricky to put a positive spin on, but the emotional justification of taking down some real monsters is a fine tonic. It was the same rub that Gareth had used to turn Sam from a victim into Good Riddance. Jack was impressed by Winter. A man who was bad in a fight, but could punch up a press release.

Jack accepted Harry's invitation for a drink. He'd already

decided, after mulling on Maurice's advice, that he'd go home tonight. Probably. But he wasn't in any hurry. And he wasn't much of a drinker, so one beer would soften his nerves.

Harry's apartment made more sense on a second visit. The mess through his kitchen, the pile of cheap clothes – his real clothes – and mismatched furniture: this was the difference between him and his brother. And sure, Harry had played dress-up, but he'd only been able to cover up the surface. The recordings he kept, they made sense too. He'd never mended things with Sam, and so had instead created these one-way conversations as substitutes. It was easier to pretend your brother was talking to you than to actually talk to him, Jack knew. Jack decided that Harry's apartment was like the inside of Maurice's brain. Shelves of tributes, memories.

Jack feared the library inside him would be an empty room, only a bed and a silent machine. He didn't have hundreds of hours of ready-made memories. And in his mind he stepped into the room, curtains closed for taped eyes, and there was dull moonlight across the bed, an island in the centre that seemed further away than possible, and then the mattress that only had wrinkled divots in the shape of limbs, shadowed as if filled with dark water. Maurice had managed to open the curtains, fill his room up again. Jack didn't know how just yet.

Harry handed Jack a beer. Chinked it, wandered into his office. Jack took a sip and followed. The bookshelves were still in ordered chaos. Harry's whole family was in this room – their voices and their objects. His father's twenty-first present on the wall, Harry's name spelled large. His mother's record player. His brother's face, frowning with concentration, fossicking on the *Midnight Tonight* shelf, choosing an episode.

'Do you have favourites?' Jack asked.

Harry didn't turn around. 'I have least favourites.'

'Put on the pilot. I want to see you together.'

Harry walked his fingers along the spines and pulled one out. In silence they watched the last time the two brothers had been on screen together. Now that Jack knew what had happened between them it had a special resonance. The last time Sam's hand was still and confident.

'How long before Sam's first attempt was this?'

'Days,' said Harry. He squinted at the screen. Sam was doing a piece to camera. 'Can't tell, even now.'

Jack didn't know Sam well enough to agree, but he couldn't find anything dark in his performance, in his smile. This was a man thinking of ending it all, trying to drink and drug himself to oblivion, and at the same time solving his childhood sweetheart's murder. At the time of this taping, he'd either already written the letter, or was about to, according to Ryan's timeline. *Before he was on TV.*

Harry ejected the disk, swapping it for the final episode. Sam had better make-up, a nicer suit, and the lighting was refined, but otherwise not much had changed.

'Five years later and I couldn't tell either. I used to imagine he was talking to me. That's why I recorded everything. But now he's dead, and I can't force him back to life just because I want him to speak to me. You know?' Jack nodded; he knew better than he'd admit. 'And no matter how many times I watch this, he still dies at the end.' Harry scrolled through the video as he spoke. Sam's mouth was opening and closing, hand jumping up and down with nerves. 'And every time, I'm hoping for something different. Nup. Exactly the same.'

Jack watched the screen. He'd seen this video more times than he could count, and yet, right in this moment, it felt like there was something more there. Something Harry had said? Jack had always thought it odd that Sam was more nervous five years into his hosting career than when he was pitching to the networks. Yet he'd put that down to Sam having had his brother by his side to calm him.

But now Jack knew that Sam was struggling even back then, and had made his first attempt soon after. So why was he so calm and collected in the pilot? Jack was talking himself in circles. He'd watched this a hundred times, and it was the same as the last time he'd seen it, and the same as the time before that.

'Stop,' Jack said.

'Huh?'

'Seriously. Stop. Rewind it. Back to the start of this, when he clears his throat.'

Harry rewound it and they watched again from where Sam stuttered at the autocue – where they had assumed his killer had started talking to him. It was as they'd seen before. He stumbled on the word. Took a breath. A nervous tic of his left hand, drumming.

'Nothing,' said Harry.

'Go back a season.'

'Which episode?'

'Doesn't matter. Any.'

Harry picked one, swapped discs, and started to fast-forward through it. Jack stopped him when he saw Sam's left hand move. They watched it.

'Back to the last one.' Jack said.

'What are we looking for?'

'Look closely,' Jack said, as Sam did his double take on the autocue, started to become anxious. Harry leaned forward, still couldn't see it.

'What?' he said, eyes up close to the screen.

'It's not nerves. It looks like a random drumming of the fingers, but the first three seconds is always identical. See?' He pointed. 'First, he puts his index finger down four times.'

Harry flitted back through the episodes. His forehead crinkled as he tried to figure out what Jack was telling him, saw that he was right. Sam was very deliberately plunging his left index finger down four times in quick succession. *Tap tap tap tap*. It was like he was playing the same opening bar of the same song on an invisible piano, and then he scattered into random jazz.

Harry shook his head. 'I don't get it. Isn't that what a nervous tic is? What's significant about that?'

'We've spent the last week looking for someone who kills with words, and you two stubborn brothers have managed to forgive each other without saying a single one,' Jack said. Brothers refusing to talk to each other was nothing new, and now he knew the shard of glass in the hospital room was the slice between them. But he hadn't realised the significance of Harry's recording at the time. 'You recorded every single episode, Harry. Don't tell me you hate him.'

'I don't, but—'

'That's the thing. This collection, all of this – he *knew* you'd record it. Just like you did for your mum, for your dad. He knew, or hoped. Or both.' Jack's heart was hammering. He'd looked around the room and knew he was right. He and his father were doing the same thing, unable to talk, looking for a faceless answer, hoping the other would find it without having to admit that either was wrong, or right, or anything at all. A silent, masculine family. Jack and Harry were hunting a killer who wielded words as weapons, but sometimes the gap between words screams loudest.

'What are you talking about?'

'You said your dad tried to teach you. It looks like Sam learned. And if he was expecting you to record this, then maybe one day he was hoping you would learn too. You're waiting for him to forgive you? There's too much pride between brothers for either of you to admit that you were wrong, that you were sorry, so you're saying it in different ways. You're doing it now, after he died, sure, but he did it too. But he didn't *want* to talk to you either. So he thought of something else. Maybe he would have told you eventually, but five years was just not enough. It's like writing you letters and putting them in a shoebox instead of sending them. He's talking to you, Harry. He's been talking to you for the last five years.'

That invisible piano riff was not a series of musical notes but a series of deliberate taps of the fingers. Some slow and some fast. And there was a poster on the wall that matched Sam's finger movements perfectly. One that Harry had gotten from his father, a radio guy, for his twenty-first birthday.

His name, with Morse code underneath.

The first four taps of Sam's left index finger matched the four dots under the letter H. Then middle. Ring. Little. Thumb. Sam swapped fingers each letter.

Every episode for the last five years, Sam had been sending messages starting with the same word.

H-A-R-R-Y.

CHAPTER 30

HARRY.

LILY'S HERE. SHE GAVE ME A GUN.

Harry set the pen down, having transcribed Sam's final message. They'd searched for a Morse code template online and worked letter by letter. They had to pause it often and replay. Sam was quick, fingers darting on the desk. Able to read the autocue and tap at the same time. Five years of practice.

LILY'S HERE.

Solutions rushed through Jack's mind. The killer on the autocue knew about Lily. That was how they'd done it. Sam, who Celia had said was sometimes depressed or disconnected, might have believed it *was* Lily, talking to him from the grave. His fragile mental state was able to be pulled into that delusion. Is that how you drew the guilt out of someone? The final message on the autocue was in first person. *I thought you wanted this. Don't back out on me now.* Like they were a team. The meaning behind it was clearer now: *Join me.* And Sam Midford, wrapping his hand under the desk, feeling like it was what he deserved, replying *Yes*.

If Lily was in the photos, and they weren't planted, Sam had had them to help his investigation. And if he was looking at her like that, dipping into the past, how traumatic it must have been to see her words on the autocue.

SHE GAVE ME A GUN.

Winter's theory that Dennis Slater had been spooked by Jack asking questions about Lily Connors had never held water with Jack. It was a sensible solution, an easy one. It had all the bad guys dead at the end. And Dennis, in possession of images that – Jack was now confident – included Lily, was certainly a 'bad guy'. But Jack hadn't even properly met Dennis, let alone pointed the finger. Sure, Dennis may have been spooked by recognising Harry, but his reaction seemed quite rash. Add to that Jack's doubts about Dennis's ability to even execute the two crimes, and it felt like there was someone else in the picture. What had Winter said? 'Especially when it involves people of profile, like this, there's always a fear that there may be . . . more.' If someone had been feeling the heat from Sam's suspicions and decided they were ready to pack it in, killing Sam and leaving breadcrumbs back to their associates seemed a fair way of tying up loose ends.

The only person in town he'd actually asked about it was Hank Waldren, sitting in his patrol car, who had all but demanded Jack stop digging around. And then proceeded to do exactly that. Three gunshots seemed a lot. And the fabricated story of the radio summons. The shotgun was cracked to load shells. Or unload. Maybe, when he saw a familiar face, Slater was putting his gun down?

Suicide by cop, Maurice had called it. 'Whoever's first on the scene buys the narrative,' Jack had said himself. And he knew that for whoever was behind Lily's death, then Sam's, and now maybe even Dennis's – constructing a narrative was this killer's skill. Their MO.

And then there was Lily's impossible murder. Maurice had spent years presenting theories and evidence to the local senior sergeant only to be told by him that his evidence wasn't good enough. *No one's there to pull the trigger, it can't be murder.* Even if Maurice had found something explosive, Hank wouldn't have admitted it if he was involved. It would have been easy to gaslight Maurice, make him look obsessive or insane.

And if Hank Waldren had known that Sam Midford was the person Lily would call in distress . . . If he was working with Dennis Slater, who ran the damn ride, it made sense that once they saw the Midford Twins get on, opportunity had called and they'd been left up on the Ferris wheel that night *on purpose*.

'He thought Lily was talking to him.' Harry rubbed his temple. Thinking. Coming to the same conclusions Jack had. 'Would he believe that if he wasn't taking his medication?'

'He had the pills in his pocket,' Jack argued, but then remembered what Maurice had said about the sugar pills. 'But you're right. Maybe it was for show. Taking them out of the bottle for Celia to see, but pocketing them. It's plausible. Harry, Waldren was in Lily's room. He told us. That puts him first on scene in two deaths.'

'Seems a stretch, Jack. Even for you.'

'If Waldren was the first responder, he might have got there fast enough to lock the window he'd used to get in and out. Sue Connors kicked the door in, but if she was cradling her daughter, would she see him flick a window lock? If he says nothing was disturbed, there's no one to dispute him. By the time Maurice got up the stairs, he said the room was full of people.' Even as he was saying it, Jack knew he was clutching at straws. He couldn't shake the feeling that there was something dodgy behind the carnival shoot-out, but the locked-room solution seemed pretty risky for a murder. It would have been ballsy of Hank Waldren to stride right on in, to bank on Sue not checking any part of the room. Lily's death had too many holes.

It was late, they were tired, and Jack realised he was doing what he'd promised he wouldn't: trying to fit the evidence to a narrative rather than the other way around. If anyone was going to accuse a police officer, *especially* Jack, they needed something bulletproof.

And while Jack's theory kind of fit Hank Waldren, it needed the waistband taken in, the hem brought up.

'I hear you. And I agree he's been around a lot of bodies. But let me ask you this: what if Sam had been asking Waldren questions? What if us asking those same questions made him piece it together, realise what Dennis Slater had done?' Harry's gaze lingered on his brother, paused on screen, on his final two words.

'You're saying that he *did* go to the caravan with intent, but not with self-preservation on his mind? Looking for justice?'

'Maybe. Maybe not. But maybe Sam told him his theory. And he's just one guy. Where was Ryan during the shoot-out? Matter of fact, where was he during the taping? Are you discounting the whole of Channel 14? There's no link between Hank Waldren and the station. Twelve hours ago you accused *me*.'

'If the answer's impossible, the question's wrong,' said Jack, mimicking Harry at the carnival. There were two impossibilities in Lily's death having been a murder: that Lily's door was locked, and that the killer got out. Was the ball in or out of the bucket? What question were they asking? And Harry was right: Waldren wouldn't have been able to get into the television studio. Even if he was involved, it wasn't enough. Winter had said, 'There's always a fear there may be more.' Celebrities fall like dominos in these kind of scandals. It's an elite circle. Who else in such a circle had a connection to that shitty little seaside town?

'We need more,' Harry said. He swapped the discs, an episode back. They waited for the finger taps and slowly dissected the rhythm of the words. Jack peered at Harry's notepad.

HARRY. HEATHER'S STARTING DANCE NEXT WEEK. I'M PROUD OF HER.

Harry swapped it for another episode, randomly chosen from the pile. Sam looked younger, trying on stubble. A couple of years ago. His finger tapped out the intro. Harry scrawled the rest.

HARRY. YOU SEE THE NEW BOND MOVIE? YOU'D LIKE IT.

Without asking, Harry went back to the first broadcast episode. Sam's hands moved more slowly. Less confident with a new skill. Bung notes. Typos.

HARRY. HOPE YYOU LIKE THIS. SEE YOU UN THE OTHET SIDE.

Jack had half-expected this episode to carry a resonance, an apology or acknowledgement of what they'd been through. But there were no confessions here. This was the mundane, the everyday. The family group message, the social email. Anyone else would pick up the phone. But not stubborn, hurt brothers. This was the only way Sam was brave enough to say anything. Not ready for Harry to listen yet – he knew Harry wouldn't have learned Morse code – but not willing to waste the years either. He hadn't forgiven him, but he hadn't forsaken him either.

Harry's eyes were reflecting the screen. Wet. He was smiling. He reached for the next disc: Season One, Episode Two.

'See you tomorrow, Jack,' he said, as he swapped discs. 'Waldren'll keep. There may be other clues. My brother and I have got some catching up to do.'

My brother and I have got some catching up to do. The words resonated in Jack's head as he finally drove towards home. He was exhausted after barely any sleep the night before, staring at the motel ceiling wondering if Harry would strangle him in the dark. While he was curious about the contents of Sam's messages, he knew they were for Harry first, on his own. Harry would be up all night transcribing. Jack would read them in the morning.

SHE GAVE ME A GUN. Those five words were especially chilling. Jack had asked himself many times what words could talk someone into killing themselves. He'd asked other people. Maurice had called him batshit. 'A grown man got cyberbullied to death?' he'd asked doubtfully. People seemed to insert the phrase 'grown man' into insults to imply someone is not worthy, that their fallibility, their flaws, would be better attributed to a woman or a child. Jack was familiar with it – hated it. He'd heard it a lot, from uncles or cousins talking about his vomiting, to the new guard in the prison. Maybe that's why he approached the fact that a grown man had succumbed with less incredulity than most. Yes, online harassment was dangerous to teenagers; it was clear they were more susceptible to influence based on the articles he was reading. But pretending that any problem could be isolated to one group of people was to put your head in the sand. A grown man can have anything.

'This grown man has bulimia,' Jack said aloud in the car, finishing his thought. He realised he'd used the word in full. First time in years.

What words could you use? SHE GAVE ME A GUN. Would the ghost of a dead girl do the trick, if someone got close enough to manipulate him like that? Waldren was around a lot of deaths down in Wheeler's, but of course he was. He was the only cop for half an hour's drive. Who was also able to get into the television studio? Operate the autocue? Who?

Jack almost forgot he was driving. Two glints in the road ahead gave him slight warning of an animal, but not enough. He felt the suspension hop before he'd even feathered the brakes.

He pulled over and got out of the car. The moon was bright overhead. He was next to a well-maintained park with a small playground. It was late enough that the steel on the equipment glistened wet. The jolt hadn't felt overly dramatic, and for a second he thought he may have missed it, but the black smudge in the middle of the road was undeniable.

He walked over to it. A fox. Just enough of the moon to see it as this section of the street was between streetlights. His car seemed to steam behind him. Hissed and settled. Jack didn't expect the fox to have survived. The tyre had crushed it through the middle. The fox's lips were curled back over its top fangs, and a trickle of blood leaked from its tongue onto the blacktop. Its ribs shuddered with gargling breath. Up and down. Wheezing, like a machine. It let out a long slow moan.

Jack wanted to cry, but couldn't summon any tears. He was tired, no emotions left. The fox growled again. It was low and strangled, blood gurgling in the animal's throat.

Jack walked back to the car and opened the boot. His skin, pallid in the day, looked mouldy in the dull tail-lights. He dug around for a blanket or an old towel to wrap the animal in. He dislodged a toolbox and scattered it. Banged his thumb with a large, cast iron wrench. Couldn't find a towel.

Behind him, the growls had gotten quieter. Rasping.

It's not killing.

Who are we to be merciful?

He walked back over to the animal, the wrench heavy in his hand.

Peter was sitting on the stairs when Jack opened the front door.

'Jack . . .' Peter said, not looking up.

'I killed a fox,' Jack said. He didn't mean to, it just blurted out.

'How?'

'I hit it—

with a wrench

—with my car.'

'Is it damaged?'

'It's dead.'

'The car.'

'Oh, I'm not sure,' Jack said, and sat down on the step below. He put a hand on his father's knee.

'I don't blame you, you know,' Peter tried again.

'I know,' Jack said. 'Sometimes that makes me mad too. I feel like it happened and I got to live on and he didn't, and I feel someone – anyone, you – should hate me for it.' He knew exactly how to sum up that self-punishment now. The same way Harry had let the rift between him and Sam simmer without forgiveness – Harry liked it; he felt it was deserved. Maurice's words had been so accurate, Jack reused them. 'I felt like it was cheating not to suffer for him.'

'I don't hate you.'

'What did I *just* say?' Jack laughed, though the chuckle came out in bursts between the words, an old car starting.

His father glanced upstairs. 'You talk to him more than you talk to me, you know that?'

Jack went to retaliate, then realised it was an invitation. Not an accusation. 'What do you want to talk about?'

'Tell me about your case.' Peter squeezed Jack's shoulder. Didn't linger. No surveillance. 'There's blood on your hands.'

Another calm observation. Jack looked down. Flecks of blood had flown up onto his hands, and he rubbed them together, but the blood was stained onto his palms like freckles. Cancerous little spots.

The blood had dried hard. Jack went to lick his thumb to rub them away, recalled dragging the fox off the road without gloves, and refrained. Peter stood and went to the kitchen. He came back with a tea towel damp with warm water. He knelt at the base of the stairs and gently wiped Jack's hands with it.

'You read about Mr Midnight?' Jack asked. Peter nodded. 'He didn't kill himself. Well, he did. But someone made him do it. He was sick, and someone used that against him. Made him think he had to. I think it's also related to a murder thirteen years ago. I don't know, I haven't figured that out yet.'

'You will.'

That was the difference between Peter and Liam: Peter talked back.

'His brother – twin brother actually – hired me.' The towel was soft and warm on Jack's scars. 'He's paying me.'

'I figured. It's a good thing you're doing for your brother. It really is. Selfless. Must be good to have your old job back too, though, I reckon. Give you something to do.'

'It's just for the money.' What little there would be of it now, anyway.

'Sure. But don't tell me Liam did this.' Peter reached behind him and picked something up. It was the cake box, empty but not clean. A dark chocolate smear across it.

Jack remembered taking a single bite while running through the case with Liam. He didn't remember eating the whole slice. Normally, he'd feel that inside himself, a physical lump in his gut that would stay until he got it back out the only way he knew how. He was angry, hurt and upset, but he hadn't reverted to purging. Instead his soldiers were sleeping, fed. Jack remembered his mouth tasting sweet, sticky, in the car. The grains of sand, crumbs on his tongue. The KFC light had gotten closer in one of his sleeping time blinks, but he knew that while he'd moved the car, he hadn't gone in. His teeth hadn't tasted sour enough. When was the last time he vomited?

Peter continued. 'It's okay to like doing something you're good at.'

Jack cracked a smile. 'You've been sitting on the stairs for two days and that was the best psychobabble you could come up with?'

'Oh, come on. I thought it was all right. I brought a prop.' Peter waved the cake box.

'It was pretty good.' Jack's laugh sputtered and misfired again. It's hard to laugh and cry at the same time. You flood the engine. 'I'm sorry I yelled at you.'

'It's okay.'

'It's not.' He paused, hung his head and spoke softly. 'It's selfish. I just don't want to lose him.'

Peter lifted Jack's chin with his index finger. 'Neither did I,' he said.

They were speaking in different tenses. But there was understanding there now. Peter thought Liam was already gone. *Sometimes we have to mourn the living. It's not about letting them go, it's about getting them back.* Jack would catch up, they both knew that.

'So,' Peter said. 'Mr Midnight?' The tone of his voice was trying to be casual, but Jack could tell he was really trying. And suddenly it was just as easy as talking to Liam.

'I think he figured out this girl – her name's Lily, did I mention that? – was murdered. Like five years ago, but I don't think he knew whodunnit until recently. Problem is, she was in a locked room. One window, one door. The window had a latch on the inside and the door had a slide bolt, also on the inside. No one in or out, or at least that's how they wanted it to look. But there's an answer, because Sam Midford figured it out. And I think that's what got him killed. Someone's covering their tracks. But I've got a problem with his death too, because it's *also* a locked room. Not literally – there were hundreds of people around, and Sam pulled the trigger himself – but it's the same problem. Someone got a gun past a metal detector. Someone was in the room, pretending to be the autocue operator. Same thing as the girl. Like they were never there at all.'

'You know there was someone there? For certain?'

Jack nodded. 'They're on camera in the crowd shots. But they're well covered, big coat and cap, and they would have known it's only shot from specific angles.'

'So get them walking in and out of the building.'

'Security cameras were all turned off – some bloody soap opera was filming something secret. A character dying, some school shooting or something. Trying to be edgy.'

'Shopping centre,' Peter said.

'What?'

'In the soap. It's called *Many Summers*. They've been building it up. It's not a school shooting, it's at a shopping centre. They like to draw from things in the news. So this girl, Holly – her ex is this lone wolf kind of guy. And her new boyfriend's an actor, and he's got a film premiere. Bryan works at the cinema, but he's always been in love with Hol . . . What?' Peter must have seen the look on Jack's face. 'I work nights, I had one son in a coma and the other in prison. I've become quite the expert.'

'No, Dad. You watch what you want.' Then, jovially: 'Is it that big a deal?'

'Would be. If *Moon River* hadn't got there first. They had a school shooting last week, pulled the steam out of *Summers* a little bit, I guess.' Jack remembered hearing something similar at the studio.

'*Moon River*?'

'Yeah, that's the one on Channel 12.'

A door slammed shut in Jack's mind. One of his soldiers drew their sword. But, for once, it wasn't pointed at Jack's throat. *Who do you want me to kill, boss?* the soldier seemed to say. And Jack thought, for the first time, he might know. Jack stood, walked to the lounge. Turned on the TV. Watched a minute of the television program he knew would be on. Came back to the hall in almost a stupor.

'Shit.'

'What?'

'You're better at this than Liam is.'

'Did I solve it?'

'Maybe. Look.' Jack's mind was whirring. He was struggling to find the words. Peter filled the gap by taking Jack's hand back to continue towelling. Jack was still processing what he'd seen on the television. 'I have to go again. But it's not because I'm running away. I understand what you've been trying to tell me, I do. It's just that I'm not ready.' Jack swallowed, then added, 'Yet.'

'You do what you have to. When you are, I'll be here.'

Peter wiped the last of the blood from Jack's hand. Drew the towel slowly over his scars.

'It was just a fox,' Jack said.

'Yeah.' Peter slung the towel on his shoulder, then leaned forward and kissed Jack on the forehead. 'Just a fox. Turn the light off when you go.'

CHAPTER 31

Channel 14 at midnight was becoming a familiar sight. Except this time Jack wasn't drawn here through vagrant magnetism with nowhere else to go. This time he knew exactly what he was looking for.

He parked on the road, end of the hedge rows – fuck the traffic – and rushed to the main doors, swiped his pass and blew past the security guard. Through the metal detector with his keys and phone held up in his hand – the light went red and there was a *brrrrr*. The guard stood. Jack did his best *I know, but I'm doing it anyway* grimace. A unique facial contortion – crushed brow, half-smile – the type made when cutting someone off in traffic: a perfect mix of *sorry* and *fuck you, buddy*.

Jack ran through the news floor. Televisions were hanging from the roof, still flashing the ratings package. That's what had clicked for Jack, talking to his father. He recalled those ads, spruiking the mass shooting. People running from a cinema. A zoomed-in gun firing. Sound effects and thumping bass dialled to eleven. A major character death, so secretive it required the security cameras to be turned off for filming. And what had Jack seen backstage at *Midnight Tonight*? A row of plush red cinema seats, lining the walkway. Props.

They'd filmed the death in the *Midnight Tonight* studio.

That was how the killer had got the gun in. How do you sneak a loaded gun through a metal detector? *You don't.* The problem was the question he'd been asking. No one had had to sneak anything in. They could have carried it in, high and proud. Even though it was just a few gunshots, perhaps a routine day on high-octane crime shows, for a network soap opera it would have been a significant stunt. Multiple takes. They would have had trained weapon handlers on site, guns and ammunition. Sure, they'd all be blanks, but they'd look real. A lot of unfamiliar people had access to Sam's studio that day. How hard would it have been to walk straight through and say 'I'm with them,' holding up the gun as a prop? The ball already in the bucket.

That all seemed clever enough for the killer. If they could talk people into suicide, surely they could talk their way through a security guard nose-deep in a Tom Clancy novel. But the whole plan would have hinged on one thing: confidential knowledge of Channel 14's most deep-cover script. Without that information, they wouldn't have known when or where to be. They wouldn't have been able to plan the whole thing.

And that information would have been extra hard to come by, seeing as Channel 14 was on lockdown for all things sensitive – reality TV show endings, confidential midnight filming – because Channel 12 kept pipping them to the post, and it was pissing Gareth Bowman off.

Jack had confirmed his suspicion at home, turning on the TV. He'd seen the exact program that, in his mind, proved it. Now, the sliver of light behind Stage Three's hydraulic door beckoned him. He thought he knew what was inside. But he needed to see it for himself.

Someone was leaking scripts to Channel 12.

The reason why was simple: Harry had said so, right back at the start. *Half the people here would kill to sit in that chair.*

Someone sick of the carousel of men hosting the same programs in the same suits and the same ties.

I've been EP on a lot of these shows . . . New talent same as the old talent.

Someone who sought to curry favour by jumping ship, only to be burned the same way by Channel 12, finding that their potential new career was nothing more than a scare campaign in a newspaper. That they were just a pawn, used to put pressure on lowering the value of a host's new contract.

Watch out . . . we might replace you with a woman.

Someone who snapped, perhaps, and finally realised that if they ever wanted to get a seat at the table – or the host's desk – they had to play it just as cutthroat as everyone else.

Because that's what you do here if you ever want one of those.

Jack walked into the studio. The heat of the stage lights hit him, studio active, everything up and running. Just like it had been the last time he was here. There was a clatter of movement. More than one person inside. One voice, much clearer over the top of it. A voice, late night in a motel in Arlington, that Jack had thought had the generic radio co-host familiarity needed for this kind of gig. But his senses hadn't been at their best. Late night, low-volume television, Harry breathing, blurred light in his eyes as he flicked it off. He hadn't realised the voice actually *was* familiar.

He walked around the bay of audience seats and it was almost like Mr Midnight was alive again, though the desk had been moved to one side out of shot. There was only one cameraman, centre position. One sound technician. Skeleton crew. The two remaining plasma screens flashed a game of Hangman with several letters missing. The words 'car brand' flashed.

Beth was in the middle of explaining the game's rules when she saw him. She faltered. Looked just like Sam Midford had when he realised he was going to have to die.

CHAPTER 32

To her credit, Beth smiled her way through another hour and a half of inane gameshow material – 'Call now . . . I have to give this money away tonight . . . my boss upstairs is telling me that my job's on the line if I don't give it away . . . you know what, I've got another five hundred dollars . . . trust me, you'd be doing me a favour if you won this money' – before finally wrapping the show at two in the morning.

Jack had taken a seat and watched. So much made sense. *Call and Win* aired live from midnight to 2 a.m. That was why she'd been in such a hurry to get rid of him the last time. Why she was wearing lipstick and nice clothes. There hadn't been some jungle reality finale. She'd just had to be on stage. Afterwards, she'd stepped out for a post-show cigarette before going back in to pack up.

When they called cut, Beth didn't run. Instead, she walked over, flipped a chair beside Jack and sat down. The two crew members were rolling cables, which helped Jack feel safer. She wouldn't try to kill him in front of them. Then again, she'd as good as killed Sam Midford in front of a million.

'I didn't want you to see me like this,' she said.

'Channel 12 buttered you up, didn't they?'

'They used me,' she said, looking at her knees. Jack couldn't tell if she was embarrassed, or if she was annoyed that her ambition was so obvious. She'd brushed away the question when Jack asked if Channel 12 had offered her a job previously. But there was bitterness there. *So I'll take the slops and smile, and say it's delicious and still ask for more.* 'I don't know why I thought it would be any different to here, but somehow I did. They said if I slipped them a few things – winners, plotlines – those kinds of things, that they'd sort me out over there.' She looked mournfully at the empty set. One of the spotlights went off with an industrial clang. 'You've gotta understand. I anchor Sam's whole fucking show, I write the damn thing. Those are my words. My words getting laughs, applause breaks. Mine.'

'That's why Sam took you to Montreal.' It wasn't a question. Things Harry had told him sparked in his head. In his airport apartment: *She popped up again . . . Sam insisted she was coming on tour with us.* In the motel: *He'd just whack a script down and it would be magic.* 'You were writing all their scripts. From the beginning.'

Beth nodded. 'That's all TV is,' she said, 'women making men look good. I was a production assistant on the clip of them that went viral at the start. Sam was so nervous. I gave him a couple of witty lines to return fire on some questions I knew our host was going to ask – because I wrote that interview too – and when that went well, he wanted me to stick around. How fucking naive of me to think all I had to do was wait my turn. The only thing Gareth would give me was to be giggly and jiggly past midnight. Kept saying I needed more screen time. So I thought, fuck the lot of them. And Channel 12, yeah, they made me feel like it might actually happen. They ran that article.' Jack recalled Beth's name on the list of possible replacement hosts for *The Round Table*. 'And that buttered me up, so when they started asking for things, I guess I wasn't so hard to convince. I thought that if I just kept giving them the things they were asking for, my time would come. And when they started crushing us in the ratings . . . Gareth was fuming, upgrading the security on all our shows, locking down scripts. Guess it helps that he sees through me sometimes, hey?' She blinked away tears. 'And I fucking *bought* it. But when they could have offered me a contract, they didn't.'

'Was that when you decided you had to get rid of Sam yourself?'

'Wait—'

'Who helped you? Dennis Slater?' That was an important question, because Beth's alibi was sound. She was on camera *not* touching the autocue. Which meant she had an accomplice. Perhaps Sam was nothing more than a mutual enemy – that tie between the city and the sea – but what had brought them together?

'No one helped me. It was over email. Hang on, I thought—' She was interrupted by a wave from the crew. She waved back.

Jack stood. 'Let's walk,' he said. 'You in front.'

'You're scared of me?' She didn't stand.

'You killed Sam. We haven't even got to Lily Connors.'

'Wait.' Beth sounded genuinely shocked. 'I didn't know anyone would *kill* him. How do you kill someone with a script? That's all he asked for. God, you're going to think I'm so fucking stupid. Until you told me about the prompter I hadn't even thought about the correlation. I've been giving Tom our scripts for months.'

'Tom Dwyer?' Jack asked. 'Host of *The Round Table*?'

'He contacted me directly. I'd just seen that article come out, and Tom talks a really nice talk. And I thought I had a chance to get out of these stupid gameshow graveyard shifts. He said I had talent – he was the only one who said that. God, I believed him. He was smooth. And he's a small-town guy, I told you, and he knows what it's like to work your way up. And then he asked for a few things, a little insider gossip at first. And then it was reality TV winners. And then it was shooting scripts for *Many Summers*. I think I knew he was using me, near the end, but it's like, I've given him enough that if I don't keep giving him more, well, what was it all for? Chasing your sunk costs, you know? And then he asked for the *Midnight Tonight* scripts, and it seemed so small fry compared to the other stuff. And I thought it might be a writing test, or maybe they'd just make Sam look like a hack. Either way, I thought that meant I was finally going to leave him in the dust. Without me, Sam had no show. He was supposed to go down, sure, but he wasn't supposed to *die*.'

She made to stand. Jack put a hand out. Like he'd be able to stop her if she ran through him. But she stopped midway, sat back down.

Jack stared at her. 'You're accusing Tom Dwyer of murder? He has no motive. He got the scripts he wanted. The murder's on you.'

'Legally?' Beth scoffed. 'Will that hold up?'

'Manslaughter will,' Jack spat, recalling the news he'd read. The young man who had gassed himself on his girlfriend's instruction: that was ruled manslaughter. Involuntary, if Jack remembered the judgement correctly, but there was precedent. The laws were changing. Murder wasn't off the cards, if the law progressed. Either way, there was a crime to be answered for.

'No.' She was either shaking her head or shivering, Jack couldn't really tell. 'No. No. Why do you think I've been trying so hard to help you? I told you about the prompter. I gave you all the footage. I interviewed our operator for you. All the truth. I'm on your side.' She pleaded. She was crying in hitches, her chest bumping up and down. 'It is my fault, I know that. I *saw him*, on the ground. And that's why I wanted you to figure it out without seeing my involvement. Because I put that to air, and it's like that *13 Reasons* thing – I told you about it because I've been having nightmares about it, can't stop reading about that shit because I want it not to be true. If even one person acted on seeing it, God. Fuck. That's duty of care. The civil suits . . . My life is over.'

Her breathing settled. She sucked in air through her nose and exhaled, for a full minute. Looked around the studio, barren and cast-less, camera dead. A room that used to be bustling with laughter and a sweaty warm-up guy and a smiling host. Now empty.

'I'm scared,' she choked out.

'You should be,' Jack said.

CHAPTER 33

If Gareth Bowman was surprised when he walked into the board-room at nine-fifteen, he didn't show it. He set his KeepCup down and scanned the room. Jack could see him trying to figure it out. Three people he knew, one he didn't. He didn't shake hands or intro-duce himself to the fourth. Instead he sat down, squeaked back in the chair. He still had a red ring around his eyes from his morning squash game.

'Right,' he said, very matter-of-factly. 'Who's suing who?'

It had been a tense wait for Gareth to show. Jack had seated Harry and Beth on opposite sides of the table to stop them throttling each other. Jack had waited until dawn to explain to Harry over the phone what he'd learned from Beth, because he thought Harry would stomp into the studio straight after. And he had, but at least the sun was up. When Jack had convinced him that they would all wait for everyone to be in the boardroom, Harry had immobilised himself into his chair like a car on bricks. 'I'm not letting the schem-ing bitch out of my sight,' he'd said. Beth, for her part, had slept a little with her head on the table, comfortably warmed, assumedly, by Harry's withering glare.

Harry had brought a scrawled notepad of Sam's Morse code messages, so Jack had busied himself reading them. It was a catalogue of Sam's life, everything he was proud of and wanted to tell his brother about. Films, his daughter, footy scores, holidays. It felt like reading a Facebook page of status updates. But underneath, it was a sad transcript of a missed connection, a catalogue of things unsaid. In the last few weeks, there were four or five obscure references to Lily. SOMETIMES I THINK IT'S HER WHO CALLS. A snapshot into Sam's delusions as they went further. I THINK SHE'S BEEN HERE. SHE GAVE IT BACK. Someone was taunting him. Jack had no idea what 'it' was. But there were no pointed fingers or accusations. Crucially, there were no names.

The fourth invitee, Detective David Winter, had been convinced, at length, by Jack that he'd learn something new about the pornography on Sam's computer. It wasn't a huge lie – there was, after all, still a potentially high-profile distribution ring operating – but Jack still felt thick-tongued telling it. 'There are people I get up early for, Jack,' Winter had said on arrival, pulling up a seat at the end, sequestered from the others like an adjudicator. 'You're not one of them.'

'Did you bring a gun?' Jack had asked. Winter, fully suited as if he were an accountant, no sign of a weapon bulge in his coat, waved him away without comment.

Completing the party was a three-pronged speaker phone in the centre of the table, with Hank Waldren dialled in. Jack pictured him chain-smoking. Beth must have had a link to the coast, an accomplice, and Jack needed Hank to be part of the conversation for Winter, but he hadn't told Waldren any of that. They'd dialled him at nine, and he'd sat silently other than checking in every five minutes with 'Still here.' Jack would reply the same, and the room would keep on waiting.

Everyone was already on edge, and Gareth's attitude on arrival hadn't helped. Harry was agitated. Beth was watching intently through tired, cried-raw eyes. Jack knew he had to choose his first words carefully. As if on cue, his phone rang. His father. *Shit.* It hadn't even occurred to Jack he'd been gone all night. He knew he couldn't take the call, in case he came back and someone had been thrown out the window. But he was equally disappointed because he'd felt they were finally getting somewhere. He didn't want his dad to think he wasn't trying.

'No one's suing anyone,' said Jack. 'But we need to talk about the night Sam died.'

'You got a show for me?'

'Not yet.'

'Yeah,' said Harry gruffly. 'We've got a fucken show.'

'No suit today?' Gareth taunted Harry. 'Realised you don't live up to him after all? Just an imitation.'

Harry went to stand. Jack put a hand on his shoulder.

'Gareth,' Jack said, 'we know someone here was leaking information to Channel 12.'

'I wish I was surprised,' Gareth said. 'Why do you think I was at the recording? Something stunk. Seemed like it was coming from *Midnight.*'

At this invitation, Beth straightened, challenged Gareth with a stare. He clicked his jaw as he processed the implication. Winter shifted too. Minutely, but Jack noticed.

'All I wanted—' Beth started.

'You deceitful little—'

'There's a lot we don't yet know,' Jack said.

'Fraud. What more do you need to know? Fraud, that's what this is. *Fraud.*' He chewed his lip as he whisked himself madder with that word. 'Was it Tom Dwyer? Were you fucking him? I will spin his jaw. Shit. Fraud!'

'What about murder?' Beth shot back. 'Huh?'

'Beth, I don't think—' Jack said.

'I was worried that people might start to catch on to what I was doing. So I had a back-up plan,' she said. Her voice was darker now, throaty. She looked up at Jack, then across to Gareth. 'I knew if you found out what I was doing, you'd react just as you are now. So I needed a scapegoat. Just a few breadcrumbs that might get the rumour mill going. Make it look like Sam was doing it, not me. That's why you were in Studio Three. My little breadcrumbs, they *worked*.'

'What are you accusing me of?' Gareth asked.

'Jack.' She turned to him, pleading. 'You've got to believe I wouldn't kill him. But we both know who would have been really pissed off. Someone who thought they'd just found out their prime-time star was leaking their biggest shows.'

'What? Is that why I'm here?' Gareth turned on Jack. 'Are you fucking kidding me with this? I don't have time for you, Jack. Fuck your story. You and Harry, in five minutes your presence here is trespassing. You.' His finger cut a jagged heartbeat in the air, pointing unsteadily at Beth. 'You too. I don't even want to see you clear your desk. Don't even bother explaining. Next time we talk, it'll be in court. You signed an NDA, if I recall.' He laughed. 'You are so fucked.' He stood, headed for the door.

'No one's leaving yet,' said Winter from the back.

'Who are you?' said Gareth.

'Police,' Winter said.

'Well, arrest one of these lunatics then.'

'Lunatics will be arrested when I'm good and ready.' Winter folded his arms.

Jack grimaced as his phone buzzed again. Gareth took a seat like a petulant child. Muttered something about fraud under his breath.

'Jack,' said Winter, 'I'm interested in the pornography. Not this horsing around.'

'Pornography? I fuck actual women, if you must know,' Gareth huffed. 'I don't need porn.'

'I meant the stuff on Sam's laptop.'

'I'm still not sure if someone put it there or if Sam uncovered it in his own investigation,' Jack said. 'Gareth, I'm not accusing you of anything. Beth, once you decided to get rid of Sam, I think you found out about Lily Connors.'

'If you had the photos, that's possession.' Harry sneered at Beth. 'If we can't prove manslaughter, we'll get you on that.'

'Waldren.' Jack spoke up, redirecting the conversation to the speaker phone. 'Dennis Slater had the same photos that were also found on Sam's computer. Let's assume he's responsible for making them. If someone knew enough about Lily Connors to scare Sam into doing what they wanted, I figure they'd know a little about Wheeler's Cove. We know how Sam died. Now I want you to help us find out how Lily did.'

'Not this again,' Waldren crackled through the phone for the first time.

'You're accusing me of *two* murders now?' Gareth wasn't mad anymore. He was nearly delirious. 'Why would I give you access to the station if I was a serial killer? I don't know who Lily Connors *even is*. Sam couldn't live with himself, sick bastard, so he killed himself.'

'That's the narrative you *want* us to see,' Beth replied.

'What did I just say?' Gareth made a beak with his hand and snapped it shut. His hand quivered as he did so. 'Is this a courtroom?'

'Jesus.' The phone crackled again.

'Are you accusing a police officer?' Winter leaned forward on his elbows, spoke over Gareth to Jack.

'Hank, the way I see it, it's one of three people. There are two people in this station with motive, but I can't pin either of them to Lily Connors. Beth, here, wanted Sam's job. Gareth, the CEO, may have thought his hotshot anchor was leaking valuable scripts. Either way, that person found themselves working with Dennis

Slater. Because Lily was the way to break Sam. And *you* approached his caravan, unannounced and with no probable cause. I don't believe you were radioed by emergency. Maybe you knew enough already – you were Maurice Connors' sounding board, after all, and Sam figured it out. Maybe you solved it too. Maybe when I walked in asking questions, you realised it would just keep going. Taking care of Dennis Slater was your way of putting an end to it.'

Jack paused. There was nothing but silence from the speaker. Winter didn't interrupt. 'I'm not interested in you. He had a shot-gun. Your story holds up, and that's how I'll tell it. But Sam is dead. And Winter would have cut me off by now if he wasn't interested. Tell us if you knew who Slater was working with here. Tell us why you lied about the radio.'

'Hank, mate,' Winter finally spoke up. 'I believe you. But I asked around. No officer said they asked you to flick your lights on and check out the caravans. Let's put this to bed.'

There was a long pause. Gareth rocked back in his chair, resigned to the farce. Beth was still crumpled across the desk. Jack was leaning in tightly to the phone so he didn't miss a whisper. Then Waldren crackled through.

'I don't know what to tell you except the truth.' There was a collective exhale as Waldren spoke. 'I took the call just like I said I did.'

Jack couldn't say it was a lie without directly accusing the officer. He looked around for support, but everyone was waiting for his next move. Winter had lent his faith but now lost it. Harry was scratching circles in the table varnish.

'This is a waste of time,' Winter said.

'Thank you!' Gareth exclaimed, validated.

'Hank.' Jack leaned into the phone, 'They're clever enough to get an autocue. Maybe they could get on your frequency. Did Sam come to you for help? Did he solve this?' He spoke deliberately. 'Do you know what happened to Lily?'

'I do know what happened to her,' Hank crackled. 'She killed herself. Her family learned to live with that. So should the rest of you.' He clicked off.

'Jack.' Winter's voice was gentle. It reminded Jack of how the doctors used to talk, back when he was a patient. 'When was the last time you slept? Ate?'

Jack's mind was spinning. He was struggling to breathe. He had no answers. He felt weak. Light. Not in control. And his phone just kept on fucking buzzing. When had he eaten? This was supposed to all click together neatly. Instead his soldiers were stamping in time, egging on the fight that left Jack battered and bruised in the dirt in a circle of shields and spears, and chanting for someone to come in for the kill. Baying for blood.

'Who *the fuck* is Lily? Is anyone going to tell me who I'm supposed to have murdered' – Gareth aimed this cockily at Winter – 'or can I go now?'

'A friend of Sam's growing up,' Winter said. 'She killed herself over a decade ago. And as far as I'm concerned, you – and everyone else for that matter – are innocent of that.'

'Sounds like there are only two people linking this station and what happened to this Lily chick. One of them's dead, and the other one's sitting' – Gareth pointed at Harry – 'right fucking there.'

Jack was furious. He couldn't think. Those fucking soldiers. He'd been beating them, he had. And he wasn't a fool; he knew he would break again, and he'd purge and regret it and reset the calendar and count from day one again. Of course he would. A ten-years-clean smoker still itches for a cigarette. Jack would always run his teeth along his gums. And he *would* fail. But not today.

Not today.

Internally, he yelled at his soldiers and they stepped back in a rustle of steel. Space to think. He had been so focused on the deaths being linked. He *knew* Sam had been forced to kill himself. He had physical evidence, on video. Gareth on camera at the filming. Beth admitting to giving information to Tom Dwyer. That was motive. Gareth could have thrown off a coat and disappeared into a crowd simply by being himself. Beth could have had an accomplice. But neither were linked to Lily Connors, whose death was still a suicide, even after all this digging. Maurice believed differently. So had Sam. So did Ryan. They all thought it was murder. And it just had a feeling about it, of something not adding up. It had made so much sense there in Lily's bedroom: *the person who murdered my daughter is the same person who killed your brother.* What was he missing?

Gareth was standing by the door. Was Jack really going to let him walk out before he solved this? *Back!* he yelled at his soldiers. *Think!*

'Buy a new suit for court,' Gareth said to Beth, then turned to Jack. 'You make a podcast out of this, you better use some real careful wording or I'll have you for defamation too.'

Then the CEO walked straight out of the room. Winter rose, followed, gave Jack a consolatory squeeze on the shoulder as he passed and said, 'He's right, Jack. Take it easy throwing around words like murder. They mean more than you think they do.' Harry just looked shell-shocked.

As annoying as it was, Gareth had a point: the only link between the two deaths was the Midford brothers. And that both murders were impossible. That didn't help much.

Unless . . .

What if *that* was the link? What if the link between them was that both murders were *impossible.*

What if these two deaths weren't connected by their killers? What if they were connected by their *method*?

How does a killer get out of a locked room? They can't. It's impossible. *If the answer's impossible, the question's wrong.* It struck Jack. *Don't bother with the door . . . this killer won't even open it.*

What if the killer never sets foot in the room in the first place?

The world's changing, sometimes too quickly for someone like me, and police work, our law, the way we do things, is changing too. Maybe if it happened now . . . Waldren had lamented in the carpark, before changing the topic.

Lily had died back when MySpace's only legal recourse was 'breach of terms of service'. But these days the same thing had been ruled manslaughter. In some cases, murder. Waldren knew that.

He wasn't ruing the fact that they lacked the forensic tech to catch a killer, as Jack had thought. He was ruing the fact that he couldn't *arrest* one. Because the law hadn't caught up. And he couldn't tell Jack that now, because you can't sully someone's innocence with that accusation. Any evidence would only point towards something that wasn't even a crime at the time. Maurice had spent a decade telling Waldren there was a murder, and Waldren hadn't been telling Maurice he was wrong, he'd been telling him there was *nothing he could do about it.* These days, people were aware of the dangers of online bullying. Sam himself hadn't wanted his daughter to have a phone until she was eighteen. *Of course he hadn't.* Especially if he had known how dangerous they could be.

'Sam was with you the whole night,' Jack whispered.

There was such a long pause he thought Harry hadn't heard him. Then: 'This again?'

'I can—'

'You think he climbed down, killed her, and then came back? And I covered it up? I'm really not in the mood to be called a liar, Jack.' Harry was seething.

But being four metres in the air wasn't much of an alibi when you had a weapon in your pocket. Harry had told Jack that Sam had been nose down in his phone the whole night, and then 'lost the damn thing a day later'. Because he didn't want anyone to find out what was on it. Were two missed calls really enough for all that guilt

Sam carried? Maybe not. But they didn't know what Sam had said to her before he didn't answer her calls. Jack would put money on a few phrases: DON'T BACK OUT ON ME NOW.

Gareth had sagely advised Jack to be careful with words, to choose them carefully. Winter had told him words like 'murder' meant more than he thought they did. In an investigation where words were wielded as swords and spilled blood, Jack hadn't been careful enough with them. He hadn't been paying enough attention. Harry had called it a *murder* from the start. So had Sam's letter, and he'd just kept using it. What had Sam's letter said?

I'm sorry for not believing you . . . I'm sorry it took me so long to figure it out. But figure it out I have . . . I finally understand.

'Understand' had always seemed such a specific word to choose. So personal. And what had he said on television?

Forgive me.

His letter was an apology.

Sam hadn't solved a murder. He'd confessed to one.

'Lily Connors *did* kill herself,' Jack said. 'But Sam Midford told her to.'

CHAPTER 34

Harry groaned like he'd been shot. It was long, guttural and pained. A half-dead fox on a highway. He stood up and left the table. Paced outside the boardroom, shaking his head. Jack watched him, his mind still shutting those final doors.

Maurice Connors had been right all along. He had known his daughter had been as good as murdered. He must have seen the texts on his daughter's phone after she died.

I THOUGHT YOU WANTED THIS.

DON'T BACK OUT ON ME NOW.

But how did Tom Dwyer play into it? The information Beth was feeding him had been crucial to the killer's plan, because it told them when and where to go. So if she wasn't an accessory, Mr Midnight's television rival sure was. He'd grown up down the coast . . . Unless . . . Jack looked at Beth, guilt-racked and slumped on the red oak, and realised he believed what she'd told him. She wasn't complicit. She just hadn't known she was opening doors for a killer to walk through.

'Beth,' Jack said. She groaned, head still buried in her elbows. 'This is important. Did you ever meet Tom Dwyer?'

She coaxed her head up from her arms and gave him a limp stare. Her eyes were bloodshot, wet. Nose tip pink. She looked the way Jack had seen himself sometimes: in a mirror, braced over a sink, gums fizzing, tired. *I have nothing left.* Her head gave a little shake. *No.*

'And it probably made sense to you that he didn't use an official email considering what you were doing. Like a Gmail or something?'

She nodded. Jack could see her making the same connection he had. It hadn't been the real Tom Dwyer asking her to leak information. She slumped back on the table.

It was all so close to fitting together. Jack took a breath. Try to think of it like a television series, he told himself. Where is the starting point? Episode One.

Episode One. Five years ago, Sam writes a confession. Perhaps as part of his therapy, to deal with his guilt by owning up to his past. That's the moment a killer was inspired, Jack was sure.

That's their starting point. Now, Episode Two—

Hang on.

Five years ago, before Sam's first suicide attempt. *He was adamant that it was an accident. Wrong pills. Wrong beer.* Jack believed Harry when he said Sam had been trying to drink himself to death. But, maybe, that time it wasn't an accident after all. Did that work? Jack's phone rang again. This time he answered it.

'Dad,' Jack said. His father was crying. Hard. Jack felt a shard of guilt, tight in his shoulders. 'I'm sorry I didn't pick up. I was caught at the station.'

'Thank you.' His father was talking more clearly now. 'Thank you.'

What was he thanking him for? Jack was struggling to keep up with the conversation, memory still whizzing through him.

The person who murdered my daughter is the same person who killed your brother.

Those words were deliberate. Jack should have known the definition of 'killing' better than anyone. Suicide was not murder and murder was not killing. And yet they were. The word 'murder' was evolving. The person who killed Sam Midford *was* Sam Midford. The same person who had 'murdered' Lily Connors.

Five years ago, around the same time Maurice had been suspended for stealing drugs from the hospital. 'Easily enough to lay him out,' Waldren had told them, fearing that Maurice had stolen the pills to try to kill himself. *Wrong pills.* Not himself.

I found a way to let Lily go. It was the hardest thing I ever did.

'Dad, I'm sorry. I'm in the middle of . . . I don't understand.'

Jack was trying to figure out how quickly he could get to Wheeler's Cove. Then he heard his brother's name – *Liam* – in between the muck of his father's emotion, and snapped to attention.

'Liam? Dad, what about Liam?'

'I'm proud of you,' Peter said, still talking in snapshots. 'Must have been so hard.'

Panic was rising now. These were the wrong words if Liam had taken an emergency turn. *Proud. Hard.*

'Dad,' Jack said slowly, 'where's Liam?'

'Well.' Peter was confused, didn't understand the question. 'They came and got him.'

No. Oh God. Oh fuck. No.

'Who took him?'

'Guy in an ambulance. Picked him up an hour ago.'

PART 5

REVENGE

You gotta buy a lock. In case
someone walks in. You know,
like Ry or someone.

Yeah, good idea.

. . .

You got everything? Belt's a
good idea. Can't snap as easily.

You there?

Don't tell me you did it
already :P

I'm nervous.

Why are you nervous? We talked
about it. The way you've chosen
will be easy and you won't even
know until it's over.

I love you so much and I just want this because you want it. You'll be so much happier, and that's all I want.

I thought you wanted this.

I mean, I do want it. I'm just being silly.

You're right. Of course you are.

Thanks for always being there for me babe.

Don't back out on me now.

Text messages between Sam Midford and Lily Connors, 2007

CHAPTER 35

Harry wasn't on the landing, maybe walking off his anger instead of beating the pulp out of Jack. But Jack didn't have time to look for him. To tell him everyone here was innocent, but the crimes were just as connected as they'd thought.

It wasn't the lack of knowledge that plagued Maurice, it was the frustration that he did know, that Sam had texted his daughter encouragement, and there was nothing he could do about it. That was why he'd gotten into scrapes with Harry's parents. He was pointing the finger, and rightly so, but he didn't have any legal backing for it. *What phone?* Maurice's eyes had sparked when they'd discussed it. Jack thought it was the electricity of new evidence, but no: Maurice had thought someone else finally agreed with him, but now that was dangerous. Because the messages on Lily's phone were motive. Motive to kill Sam.

He sprinted down the six flights of stairs and through the foyer. He didn't have Maurice Connors' phone number. He tried Ryan. It rung out. *Fuck.* On the street, his illegally parked VW was being levered onto a tow truck. *Seriously?* He tried calling Ryan again as he ran up to the truck.

A flash in the corner of his eye. Lights, red and blue. Same colour lights as a police car. Enough to spook Slater, thinking it was Maurice's ambulance outside his van. Winter had mentioned that the call specifically asked Waldren to turn his lights on. Jack would have bet that ambos had the same frequency as police too. Waldren had been telling the truth. He just didn't know who had called it in, that it was an ambulance hopping onto his frequency.

The lights were in the fast food carpark, across the road. Just a quick wink. *Come here.*

He ignored the VW and ran across the road. The carpark was sparse; no one wants fried chicken at ten in the morning. Ambulance in the far corner. Reverse parked, no one in the cab. One of the back doors flapped open. Jack slowed his approach. He didn't have a weapon. He didn't care. Liam didn't have time. Jack got to the bonnet, around the driver's side. Up on tiptoes to see through the window. Empty. Around the side. He heard familiar beeping, wheezing, soft in the air. Clenched his fists. Emerged around the side, ready for a fight.

No one.

Jack whirled around. Was this a threat then? A message? A trap? There was no one there. He looked into the rear. His brother was strapped to a gurney. Jack breathed deeply in relief, in time with the wheeze of the breathing machine. All still plugged in.

Jack went to step into the cab when he felt a rough hand on his shoulder. Something plastic covered his nose and mouth. Then he was dizzy.

By the time he realised it was a gas mask, he was already falling.

The first thing Jack noticed when he came to was that he was upright. On his knees in the dirt. His wrists chafed, tied behind his back with coarse rope. He blinked away the sunlight, tried to look around. Felt a scratch like he'd shaved rough. Rope on his neck.

The ambulance was in front of him, doors open. Jack could see the blue sheets on the bed. Looked like a person on them. Maurice was sitting on the floor, legs dangling, just as he had been when they'd shared a cup of tea. The ground under Jack's knees was packed clay-dirt that had been trampled by hundreds of feet. All the grass dead. Long shadows splayed across the ground from looming tall structures all around. Not trees; these shadows were jagged. For a second, Jack thought he was in a shipyard. Then the glare softened as he turned his head, and he realised that the structures were all stationary carnival rides. Salt on his tongue. Wheeler's Cove. The park was deserted, not reopened since the shooting. A severed piece of blue and white checked tape fluttered from the entrance gate, keeping people away. Broken, assumedly, by Maurice driving through it.

Jack tried to stand but his legs wobbled and he pitched forwards. Forgetting they were bound behind him, he tried to put his hands out. His fall stopped anyway, the rope on his throat tight. He gagged. One of his knees was still on the ground, but it was pivoting him like a spinning top. His eyes stung. Plumes of dust rose up as he tried to stand again.

He felt hands around his ribs, lifting him into a standing position. Jack's legs threatened to give out again, but he forced his knees to lock and stayed upright.

'Can't have you go like that,' said Maurice, stepping away from Jack.

'Let him go,' Jack rasped.

'I've got no problem with your brother. He can't talk. You, on the other hand, you shouldn't have told me you'd figured out the autocue. No. You talk way too much. About your brother. About your dad.' He put a hand on his heart. 'Your beautiful father. Letting you be a coward. Poor old man – all I had to say was you sent me. So easy. I have the costume already.' He gestured to his paramedic's uniform.

'You're a murderer. What you did to Sam—' Jack was working the hands behind his back.

'Apparently not!' Maurice yelled. 'Because according to the law he *didn't* murder Lily, did he? So how could I have murdered him? Huh? That's some double standard you've got there, Jack. Don't call me that disgusting word.'

'What he did was unforgivable,' Jack said. 'And yes, it was murder, manslaughter, *something*. I believe that too. But that doesn't make what you did to him okay. No one knew things like this could happen when suddenly, overnight, everyone had phones, the internet. But we've learned more now. What people can do to each other these days. They were just kids. How many times do they comment on a video, or a Facebook post: *go kill yourself; fuck off and die.* They don't know the power that has until it's too late. He was just a kid.'

'He knew. The things he said. He *wanted* her to—'

'I'm not defending him, he did what he did. It was awful. But his intent, and yours now, those are very different things. Sometimes the world moves faster than we're ready for. You think you're the only one who suffered that learning curve?'

'I'm the only one who had to look at his fucking face on television every night, knowing what I knew.' His eyes were bulging. He walked over to Jack, calmly spoke in his ear. 'The things he wrote to her: *You gotta buy a lock. In case someone walks in. You know, like Ry or someone.*'

Jack was too busy looking for an escape that he didn't fully understand what Maurice was saying. He considered kicking out at Maurice, but he didn't want to fall again. What was he tied to? He looked up. A collection of fibreglass domes, like looking at the hulls of a dozen boats. The Ferris wheel.

'*Belt's a good idea. Can't snap as easily.*'

Maurice was in his other ear now.

'I love you so much and I just want this because you want it. You'll be so much happier, and that's all I want.'

Maurice was counting out on his fingers.

'Don't back out on me now.'

Jack realised he was reciting Sam's final text messages to Lily. He knew them by heart.

Maurice spread his hands. 'Sound like a stupid teenager to you?'

He had come too close. Dropped his guard. Jack made to head-butt him, but Maurice stepped back half a step and swept Jack's legs out with a kick. Jack fell again, the rope hitting him like a punch to the throat. Jack spun on the rope, sideways now. Felt hands on him again. Upright. Dusting his shoulders.

'He knew what he was doing, but he didn't understand it,' Jack croaked. 'But you do. You tried to kill him five years ago.'

'That was inelegant,' Maurice said. 'I hadn't planned it well enough. He was trying his best to do it himself, anyway, and just needed that little extra nudge. But I almost got caught. And you're right, that would have been distasteful. Luckily, everyone thinks I'm unbalanced enough that I was going to use the drugs on myself.'

'That's why you calmed down. Everyone thought you were better, that you had finally dealt with your grief and moved on. You hadn't. You were just planning something else.'

'I'm actually glad I didn't kill him the first time. It would have been too easy for him. It was missing that crucial element: I wanted him to feel what she felt. And, oh, I know *everything* there is to know about what she felt. What's about to happen to you – that's almost what I had in store for him. I had this planned out too. I know Ryan showed you my sketches. Because Lily died on her own, in her room, and no one noticed. So I wanted everyone to *see* this. I want people, fifty years from now, to google Sam Midford and see the awful thing he did and the man he was. A quiet death from pills, that would be too much of a rockstar death.

I wanted people to hate him for what he did. So, something public. Something awful. Like I said, I had this thing all planned.' He gestured at the park. 'But I don't sleep well, you see, and I recognised the lady from that awful late-night gambling show in one of those rising star articles. And, well, shit – turns out she's Sam's producer. It was a leap of faith that no one hosting those shows is where they want to be in life, but a good one.'

'You pretended to be Tom Dwyer.'

Maurice was almost delighted by the deception. 'I had this idea that if I could get to him at the studio, I could do something there. But Beth was a sieve, and once I saw the opportunity . . . I couldn't shake it. It felt right. Like justice. And then all I had to do was get her to send me scripts. I kept tipping off Channel 12 anonymously so she'd see results, feel like it was getting through. She wanted to be in Sam's chair so much, she was only too happy to help. I had shooting schedules, episodes, staff contacts.'

'The autocue operator?'

'If drugs can make people better, they can make people sick.' He shrugged. 'I know a guy on opiates when I see one – I've treated enough of them. An ambo's a junkie's best friend, so he took kindly to me. No trouble giving him something to take him off the board when the time came. Then I just had to learn the cueing app. Even an old man like me can scroll an iPad.'

What had Beth told him about the operator? *Bit too much of this, bit too much of that.* Similar to how Harry had spoken about Sam: *Wrong Pills. Wrong beer.* Both drugged. 'And Dennis Slater?' Jack probed.

'He's a pig,' Maurice said. 'He worked here at the carnival with Lily. That was why she and Sam broke up. Because she went off with Dennis. They say "hooked up". And, oh man, you don't date a carnie kid here. That's bad press, doesn't matter who you are. She was bullied at school for it. Sam was the worst, the things he said to her in those messages. The things Sam shared with his classmates – things she *sent* him.' Maurice fought back tears. Hatred or sadness, Jack couldn't tell. 'She was only thirteen, Jack. Boys, what they wanted from her. By the time I got a hold of the photos it was too late to take them to the police. They all thought I was tin-foil-hat certified.'

'That's why you had to get rid of Dennis. If the police identified Lily, you were worried they might find their way down here to ask questions, and Dennis was someone who could connect the dots?'

'He deserved it. She was a notch on his belt. He pulled the pin out of the grenade, tossed it to Sam, and walked away.'

'You always planned to kill him? He didn't do anything. Sam shared the photos. Did the damage. That seems . . . *inelegant*.' Jack used Maurice's own word back at him. He recalled something else Maurice had said, in Lily's bedroom: *And part of me does want you to know. Hell, you make podcasts – maybe the world should know. Maybe it will help someone else.* 'You said you wanted to make a statement by doing this on television, and maybe that was the plan at first. The photos were triggers for Sam – it was your way of haunting him, right? But they were also part of the story. Until they started getting looked at too closely, and then you had to make something tidy. And yet, you do all this, you make this statement, and now you hide? You even realised you were telling us too much. You told us to look for someone with a facial scar, even though you knew why her fingernail had come off. You used her photos to incriminate an innocent man. You're not doing this for your daughter.'

'He deserved it. If they hadn't . . . If he wasn't . . .' Maurice set his jaw. 'Everything I've done is for her.'

'You're working pretty hard to cover your tracks for someone who doesn't mind getting caught. Dennis was a chance to close the loop. I'm another one. He wasn't important enough to die, but you've fabricated a reason so you can make peace with what you needed to do *for you*. If this was really about her, if this was about Sam paying for the awful things he did, Dennis Slater wouldn't be dead, and I wouldn't be strung up.' Jack thought he felt some small give in the rope on his wrist. Thin wrists were good for something. Maybe he imagined it. He kept working his hands around the rope. 'You can let me go.'

'You're right,' Maurice said, after a few seconds of calmly watching Jack twitch against the rope. Jack hoped he was taking stock of the situation, seeing what he'd *really* done, and that maybe he'd find mercy. But his tone was measured, calm. Not regretful, but accepting of where he was and what he was doing. 'I wasn't expecting to walk out of that TV studio – all I had was a stupid coat and hat on – but I was ready to pay that price to share her story. To make it right. But then it was chaos, and no one stopped me leaving. And the photos – I needed to probe his memories. I wanted him face to face with the worst of what he'd done. And then afterwards, they spun against Sam in a way I couldn't have predicted. I wasn't expecting to come home, but I did. And my family – it felt whole. I meant what I told you about living with the best pieces of her, and I like where I am now. But then Ryan had to go and get you involved. More attention down here, which I wasn't happy with. So I saw the chance to wrap things up cleanly with Slater.'

'We all bought it, too. The same sets of photos in both murders—'

'Don't use that word,' Maurice said flatly. 'If Lily doesn't deserve it, they don't either.'

'Both crime scenes, then. They read like you wanted them to: that Dennis had made the images, sold them to Sam. A closed loop. You radioed Waldren. But only after you'd threatened Dennis, told him you were coming for him, to get him agitated enough to arm himself. If I've learned one thing, it's that you're very convincing. He sees the red and blue lights, and thinks it's your shadow in the parking lot. Signs his own fate by firing through the door. Suicide by cop.'

'I gave him fair warning.' Maurice smiled. 'Cowards like him will always try and shoot you in the back, I figured, and I figured correctly. I also figured carnies are packing, but, shit, I didn't know he had a *shotgun*. A bit of luck. Waldren saw what I wanted him to see and took care of it for me. I told you, Jack, I've spent thirteen years researching all kinds of suicides. I hated using her photos like that, but that was supposed to be the last time, enough to send you home.'

'Tell me how you coerced Sam. I need to know what words you used. You pretended to be Lily? For Sam to believe that, you must have been pushing him a long time.'

'Sam's conscience did all the work for me.'

'Not really,' Jack said, remembering how Celia described Sam's pills: *the stuff that doesn't work, obviously.* 'When you visited Sam, to pretend you were forgiving him, I suppose – Celia told me about the visit – you swapped his medication. Those sugar pills you have. You wanted to be sure he'd be susceptible.'

Maurice gave a smile at that. 'Okay, sure. I did. You know, Sam invited me there. He was doing some awful twelve-steps thing. And this one must have been confessing to those you've hurt or some bullshit. Same reason he wrote that letter, I reckon. And you know what he said? He said that he'd been mad at Lily for seeing someone else. That's it! Mad. And he said that when they were messaging, and she was upset, and he was mad – that damn word again – he felt like she would do anything for him. So he asked her to. You know what he said? "Just to see if I could."' His face had turned into a snarl. 'I was already planning to kill him, but that pushed it over the line for me. Lily was a teenage girl. He's a grown man. The meds were to even the playing field. I know Sam's medical history – prone to psychosis, depression, mood swings. So I swapped the pills when I used the bathroom.'

'And you kept reminding him, didn't you? Putting Lily in his thoughts. A few telephone calls.' Celia: *Only a few numbers I didn't know, telemarketers.* On the prompter: SOMETIMES I THINK IT'S HER WHO CALLS. 'And you left Lily's ring in the dressing room, right?' Someone had seen it, which was why the whole set was buzzing about the proposal that day. But it wasn't an engagement ring, it was Lily's. The ring Sam had given her as a lovestruck teenager. I THINK SHE'S BEEN HERE. SHE GAVE IT BACK. '*That's* what the photos were for. You were in his head all right. But putting the gun in his mouth is another level. I've been thinking about what words you'd use to kill someone. To have them make that decision, and on national television. How could he do that to his family? There's only one way I figure he would have done it for you, like that, in public. And that's if he didn't have a choice. If he didn't do it *to* his family, but he was doing it *for* them.'

'Harry's getting his money's worth,' Maurice said slowly. Sniffed. 'Okay. I had to be sure he'd do it. The decision had to happen in the forty-two minutes he was on. So he needed some more pressure.'

'You threatened them.' Jack had already surmised. 'His family.'

'I told him it was him or them. Or, Lily told him, to be exact.'

'That's not a choice.' Jack said. 'You wanted to prove you could talk someone into killing themselves, but you didn't give him a choice. That's like putting a gun to someone's head and having them shoot someone else. You're not pulling the trigger, but you haven't proved *shit*. You cheated. That's what makes you a murderer.'

'I asked you not to call me that.' Maurice gritted his teeth. Then he relaxed, looking up at the wheel. It seemed to calm him. 'Well, what I'm about to do to you changes that, I suppose. But this is only because I have to, understand?' He didn't lower his gaze as he spoke, head still tilted skywards. 'You know, in the old days they used to hang people differently. It was only later they invented the more humane drop-execution. They used to tie people to a horse, slap it, and let it run, dragging them until they strangled to death. None of this quick neck-breaking stuff you see in the movies. Like I said, I've had a lot of time to do my research. Lily's neck didn't break. Yours won't either.'

And then he was walking. Past Jack, who swivelled with the balance of the rope. Managed to turn. Stretching his back, there was less pressure on his neck and he took a few unrestricted breaths. Meanwhile, Maurice was unclipping a hip-height rope, letting himself into the operator booth. Jack recalled Harry telling him all the local emergency service workers kept keys to the rides since the incident.

'You saw the sketches – my measurements.' Jack remembered the hand-drawn diagrams of the Ferris wheel Ryan had shown him. Ryan had thought it was his dad's research. Instead, Maurice had been designing a torture device. 'This is what I first planned for Sam. Lily lost a fingernail, begging for relief, and I wanted him to feel that. To feel that fake victory of squeezing another breath, when really it's already over. Until I found something better. But I'd always wanted to use it. You're the guy who gets people killed for ratings, so I think it's fitting. That's your narrative: you come out here and kill your own brother, before sending yourself off like the attention-grabber you are. So everyone sees you.'

'Stop, please.'

'Set to top speed, this wheel takes one minute forty to go around. That's probably a minute, minute twenty in the air, and the rest on the ground. Three minutes without oxygen is enough to give you brain damage. You'll probably pass out well before that. You'll want to stay awake if you can, because you'll need to hit the ground with your feet in order to get your breath back. Either way, you won't last nearly as long the second time because there'll be less oxygen in your blood. If you make it round a third time, you'll have even less. And that's if you don't fall. But you will. And once you miss that chance to get your breath back, then you're in the air for nearly two minutes before you get a chance to take another one. I'll leave it on until it drags your lifeless body through the dirt.'

There was a burst of jangly music, masking the long slow groan of a machine waking up. Jack sucked in as large a breath as possible as the slack disappeared.

Maurice was yelling over the noise. 'Try to keep up.'

CHAPTER 36

Jack's hope that he would be gently lifted into the air was quickly dispelled as the first jolt felt like it would tear his head clean off.

He let out a tiny gasp of breath in surprise. Immediately clamped it off. That was a precious resource, he chastised, not to be wasted.

Then he was in the air, the ground moving away, and it wasn't like he was being lifted, lofty and high, it was like he was being *pulled*. As if strapped to the back of a horse. His feet paddled the air. Knock that off, Jack thought. He didn't want to waste energy – and therefore air – struggling. He had to make it back around to the ground, and then he could reset, figure things out. The natural inertia of his suspension meant he started swinging. The rope bit in, sawed his neck – back and forth, getting wetter.

He had no idea how long he'd been in the air. He'd had a vague idea to count seconds, but that had gone out the window the instant his feet lifted off the ground. He couldn't look down, chin locked skywards; all he saw was blue.

Something smacked him in the back. Cold, metallic. That must mean he was at least a third of the way around. If he was hanging straight down – he must have been tied to the bars of a carriage, and not underneath, if Maurice wanted him to complete the circle – then for him to hit the spokes, the cabin must have been above halfway, moving back towards the centre so Jack would swing back in and bounce against the frame. Was halfway too much to hope for? He couldn't tell if he was going up or down, rope tight with gravity.

He gagged, felt vomit dribble down his chin. Then the metal on his back was gone with a shirt-tearing scrape. This meant he'd swung back out. Two-thirds, Jack willed. Stars were bursting in his eyes, which felt as if they were ballooned with water. The sides of his vision were closing in, like looking through a tunnel.

His left foot hit the ground first. A jarring surprise that drove his shin up into his kneecap, which slid uncomfortably. Something wrong there. Didn't matter. Eyes open. Ambulance further away now. Police tape flapping. Maurice was standing in the control booth, watching on gleefully.

'One!' he yelled, holding up a finger.

CHAPTER 37

Jack felt the rope tickle his neck as it went limp on his shoulders. He gulped in huge sucks of air and risked a look at the carriages. His rope was trailing towards a bright pink one, which was still going down. Soon it would be at his level. And then it would go sideways, and then up. Jack briefly considered that if he could grab on to a carriage he might be able to complete a lap with less pressure on his neck. But his hands were tied. He couldn't grab a carriage. What if he got on one?

The thought was interrupted as the rope thrummed tight. Jack winced as he limped after it. It wasn't going quickly, but it was constant, which meant that even if Jack could outrun the rope, every time he stumbled it pegged back any ground he'd made. He got ahead of it. Stood under the rising carriages. Took a breath, braced himself.

Lift off.

By halfway up the second time, he was losing consciousness. His neck was chafed, slick with blood. He was blinking in huge black spots. His tongue felt foreign, blown up and shoved back in his mouth. The black spots were getting longer now. Maybe it'd be easiest to just slip into this sleep?

Then the ground punched both of his feet again.

He wasn't ready for it. Spilled onto his front, scrambled to his knees. Used a few precious seconds to catch his breath as the cabin descended. He heard Maurice yell 'Two!' When he got his senses back, the cabin was in front of him. Moving away. The rope started to lift off the dirt.

Get on it.

He rushed on all fours. Tried to stand, but the millisecond he sacrificed doing so meant the rope went taut and knocked him back down. This time it spun him on his back. His heels skittered in the dirt, peddling against the movement. Lost a shoe. The rope pressed on his throat but didn't choke just yet.

Keep up.

Jack's brain screamed. And then the rope started to go up. Gently tilting his head up, like his father's finger levering his chin. Jack grappled it. Felt it pull, dragging him the last metre, and then his body hoisted, dust-covered and skinned. His feet lifted off the ground again.

And then he realised the worst of it.

He hadn't taken a breath.

Now Jack was panicking.

He knew he wouldn't make another rotation. The next time he hit the ground, he'd be unconscious, dragged like a ragdoll through the dust. He tried to keep his eyes open, take in one last image. The ground, about two metres below him now. The sky, vibrant and bright, and getting darker. One last glance at his brother, but the doors to the ambulance were closed. Lack of oxygen to the brain. Three minutes. That was all it had taken with Liam.

Jack wondered, perversely, how far around he'd get before he passed out. Was there a blackboard with neat ruled lines showing

names and records like at a fishing tournament, somewhere? Jack
at the top. *Two and a half laps.* Well, not quite two and a half. He
hadn't felt the scrape of metal on his back, which he now knew was
when he'd passed the apex and started to swing back down.

In fact, had he stopped moving?

There was yelling. The rev of an engine. Jack, still only two or
so metres up, was able to tilt his head down. Someone was running
across the park. Maurice. The ambulance had its lights on. Why
were the back doors closed? Then there was a roar of an engine, and
the ambulance spun its wheels, started reversing.

Maurice was still running towards it. He was almost at it. But
the ambulance was reversing and picking up speed. Maurice saw
it wasn't stopping and stepped out of the way. But the ambulance swung into a broadside skid, the flank whipping round, and
Maurice was there one second, gone the next, replaced by a smear
on the side panel.

That was the last thing Jack saw. The tunnel in his vision slowly
closed. Vision gone, his other senses still there but dulled. The rope,
still trying to saw through his neck. His left eye felt like it might
burst. The garish music from the wheel. The throttle pumping.
The squeal of brakes. Something collided with his legs, pulverising
one ankle, bones floating in the skin-sack of his foot. It didn't hurt.
Nothing hurt anymore.

And then the strangest feeling under his toes. The ball of his
good, shoeless, foot.

Cold metal.

The roof of the ambulance parked underneath.

PART 6

WE NOW RETURN YOU TO YOUR REGULAR PROGRAMMING

Yeah, exactly, so stop doing that.
There is more success than there
are failures.

Are you kidding me?

You have to look at it that way
and people only fail because they
have the same mindset as you.
Thinking they'll fail.

I really want to believe you.

Why don't you.

You can't think about it. You just
have to do it. You said you were
going to do it. Like I don't get
why you aren't.

I don't get it either. I don't
know.

So I guess you aren't going to do
it then. All that for nothing. I'm
just confused. Like you were so
ready and determined.

I am gonna eventually. I really don't know what I'm waiting for but I have everything lined up.

. . .

Don't do it in the driveway. You will be easily found . . . . Find a spot.

I don't know. I'm thinking a public place. If I go somewhere private they may call cops.

Well, then someone will notice you.

Do you think you will get caught? I mean, it only takes 30 minutes; right?

Just park your car and sit there and it will take, like, 20 minutes. It's not a big deal.

. . .

*Oh, okay. Well I would do the CO.
That honestly is the best way and
I know it's hard to find a tank
so if you could use another car
or something, then do that. But
next I'd try the bag or hanging.
Hanging is painless and takes like
a second if you do it right.*

. . .

Are you going to do it today?

Yes.

Like in the day time?

Should I?

*Yeah, it's less suspicious. You
won't think about it as much and
you'll get it over with instead of
wait until the night.*

Yeah then I will. Like where?
Like I could go in any enclosed
area.

*Go in your truck and drive in a
parking lot somewhere, to a park
or something. Do it like early.
Do it now, like early.*

. . .

Okay. I'm gonna do it today.

                             You promise?

I promise, babe. I have to now.

                             Like right now?

Where do I go?

                             And you can't break a promise.
                             And just go in a quiet parking
                             lot or something.

Actual text messages between Michelle Carter and Conrad Roy III, 2014

EPILOGUE

Jack opened his eyes – thankfully not taped shut – to bleached white and a symphony of beeps and wheezes. Was this what Liam felt like?

In a mild panic, he wriggled his finger. *Please move* . . . It moved. He went about investigating the rest of him. Everything hurt. His tongue was dry and biscuit-rough. There was a sharp throbbing in his left knee, and he could feel nothing below his right. His throat felt trodden on. Neck itched. He reached up a hand to scratch it and all he felt was gauze. He pried a finger underneath it, which came away sticky. Held it up: bright red.

Harry was sitting under the window, flicking through a magazine. He saw Jack move and walked over. Harry flashed him that TV smile, but it finally felt like his own. He was wearing a crisp pressed shirt, cuffs rolled up to the elbows, tucked into pinstripe trousers. Nice clothes, for Harry. Not his brother's.

'Apparently I broke both of your legs,' Harry said. 'Sorry about that.'

Jack went to speak, but nothing came out. The crackle of an untuned radio.

'Only just missed you. After I stormed off – I think it was because I knew you were right – you weren't there when I got back. I saw you from the window powering across the road to the KFC. Figured, I don't know, that maybe I should hear you out. So I followed you. By the time I got there, I saw someone barrelling you into the back of an ambulance and blasting off down the street. I tried to follow in a cab. Man, he was punching it. Sirens on, the lot. I lost him pretty quick, but not before I knew he was on the highway south. Ambulance. South. I'm slow, but I pieced it together.'

Jack rolled his tongue around. Took a cue from Ivan Fraye: one word at a time. Fishing hook down the throat, drag a word up, scraping along the way. Eventually one crumbled out of his lips. 'Liam?'

Harry put a hand on Jack's arm. 'He's all right, mate. Across the hall. With your dad, who's taking turns between rooms. Much nicer bloke than you are, don't know how you came from him.'

A chuckle made Jack feel like his head would split in half. 'Mau . . . rice?'

Harry shook his head. 'Got in the way.'

Jack nodded. The smear on the side panel. Closed his eyes.

'I'm going to pay you the rest,' said Harry. 'Beth's emails are a pretty big paper trail. Cops are interested now so they can do all the computer stuff. They've got the script for the autocue. He tells him to, all right. He says he has Heather's life in his hands, gives him a time limit. So much for talking him into it. There's no ambiguity in that, no choice.'

'Hmmm.'

'So it's not manslaughter, it's outright murder. Sam's insurance pays out. I'll pay.'

Jack shook his head. Fell back to sleep.

*

He awoke briefly to chatter. Daylight. Celia was sitting now, Heather in her lap. Harry was standing, reading a book to his niece. No one saw Jack open his eyes. He couldn't keep them open for long. Just words, as he drifted back.

'Come for dinner some time.' That was Celia. 'She should see more of you.'

'Okay.'

'Will you do me a favour? It might be weird. I just miss him.'

'Okay.'

'Will you stay a bit? Just sit here? Put the jacket on? And don't say anything. Just sit?'

The next time Jack woke, Peter was asleep beside him, LiquorMania shirt on. Name tag clipped to it. His chest moving up and down softly. But it fluttered and settled and paused and jumped like he was real. The opposite of Liam's metronomic pulse.

Jack could see Peter's phone was beside him on the arm rest. He forced himself to sit up, looked around the room. Beside him, there was a small table with a motley collection of his things. Keys, his phone, his audio recorder. Maybe there was a show in there somewhere. A small mirror. His eyes looked jet black. Blood-filled from the broken blood vessels.

Sitting up, he could just reach his father. He leaned over. His fingers felt unused and they struggled with the clasp. Got it. He looked at Peter's nameplate in the moonlight. Tossed it in the bin.

He picked up his phone. Infinity missed calls. Swiped past the notifications, messages.

Words kill people all the time.

Jack knew that now. He believed it. And there was only one more left to use.

YES OR NO.

Jack typed a word. Deleted it.

Typed a different one. Just to see what it would look like. How it felt in his hand. Deleted that too.

He gritted his teeth. Made up his mind. Typed.

And pressed send.

This novel contains themes of suicide and mental health. If you or someone you know needs help, you can contact the following organisations:

Lifeline: 13 11 14
Beyond Blue: 1300 22 46 36

ACKNOWLEDGEMENTS

I would like to mention that every coercion case referred to in this book that does not interact directly with the characters in the novel is a real event. Quotes used are from publicly released court transcripts or news articles. In a book about the power of words, it is a pleasure to reserve the final few to thank the many people who helped bring this book to life.

Thank you to Beverley Cousins, my publisher. Your guidance, your vision for what this book could be and your willingness to let me take risks (try calling your publisher and saying the words: 'Right, so it's about – get this – *scary words*') and push me on the hard questions were invaluable in shaping this novel. Though this is my second novel, this is the first book we've run the entire race together, and I am looking forward to many more. Amanda Martin, my editor, thank you for solving the endlessly labyrinthine problems that my renegade plotting throws up, and keeping everything in line. I am grateful for your patience, attention to detail and tenacity through a thoughtful and incisive edit. Thank you for always providing 'gentle nudges' instead of 'Hey moron, have you forgotten this was due two weeks ago?' Thank you to Nikki Lusk for proofreading the novel. Thank you to Adam Laszczuk for the amazing and haunting cover, and Midland Typesetters for the internals. Emily Cook, my publicist, thank you for championing my work at every turn: the confidence and energy you bring to talking about my books astounds me. Thank you to Nerrilee Weir and Jordan Meek, who work tirelessly in selling and administering rights. Justin Ractliffe and Julie Burland have gone out of their way to make me feel at home at Penguin Random House. More than those I know personally, there is a behemoth of a team in sales, marketing, design, production and more who gets a book off the ground. To everyone behind every desk/laptop/notepad/iPad/wheel/printer at Penguin Random House Australia, thank you.

Thank you to Pippa Masson, my agent, for who this was also our first full book together. A literary agent is the dartboard of an author's petulance, and I am indebted to your absorption of my darts. Thank you for your assistance, diligence, temperament and, most of all, patience. Pippa is ably assisted by Caitlan Cooper-Trent – thank you, Caitlan, for the fantastic catalogues and pitches of my novels. The support of everyone at Curtis Brown has been extraordinary. Thank you all for helping me chase dreams.

I'd also like to thank Karen Yates and Liz Alexander for producing the audio editions of my works so wonderfully. Grace Heifetz and Kimberley Atkins got me started on this train years ago, and I owe them thanks.

My family – Peter, Judy, Emily and James – thank you for supporting my books and writing. My early readers and fellow authors Helen Scheuerer and Tom Gibson provided insightful feedback. And to Aleesha Paz, rather than list your virtues: thank you for everything.

I am writing these acknowledgements from self-isolation in April 2020. The world has changed a lot in the last few months, and it may well change a lot more before this book is released.

Authors, bookshops, festivals, theatres and more are facing uncertainty over what's to come. To every artist, author, bookseller and distributor: we are vital. To every single reader: you help make us so with every book you read. I am grateful you've chosen to spend your time with mine, and I hope you enjoyed it.

GREENLIGHT
Benjamin Stevenson

Shortlisted for the Ned Kelly Award for Best Debut

Four years ago, in the small town of Birravale, Eliza Dacey was murdered. Within hours, her killer was caught. Wasn't he?

So read the opening titles of Jack Quick's new true-crime documentary. A skilled producer, Jack knows that the bigger the conspiracy, the higher the ratings – and he claims Curtis Wade was convicted on flimsy evidence and shoddy police work. Millions of viewers agree.

Just before the final episode, Jack uncovers a minor detail that may prove Wade guilty after all. Convinced it will ruin his show, Jack disposes of the evidence and delivers the finale unedited, leading to Wade's eventual release.

Then a new victim is found bearing horrifying similarities to the original murder. Has Jack just helped a killer walk free?

Determined to set things right, Jack returns to Birravale looking for answers. But with his own secrets lurking just beneath the surface, Jack knows more than anyone what a fine line it is between fact and fiction. Between life and death.

Now there's only one option left. The truth.

EVERYONE IN MY FAMILY HAS KILLED SOMEONE
Benjamin Stevenson

Soon to be adapted into a major HBO series

Agatha Christie and Arthur Conan Doyle meet *Knives Out* and *The Thursday Murder Club* in this fiendishly clever blend of classic and modern murder mystery.

I was dreading the Cunningham family reunion even before the first murder.

Before the storm stranded us at the mountain resort, snow and bodies piling up.

The thing is, us Cunninghams don't really get along. We've only got one thing in common: we've all killed someone.

My brother
My step-sister
My wife
My father
My mother
My sister-in-law (former)
My uncle
My stepfather
My aunt
Me

Discover a
new favourite